PRETTY POLICEMAN

BY FIFER ROSE

"Love is a fire. But whether it is going to warm your hearth or burn down your house, you can never tell."

-Joan Crawford

TABLE OF CONTENTS

Content Warnings

Please be aware that this book contains crude language, instances of graphic violence, and features at least one character who touts homophobic garbage, using religion as an excuse to do so. Don't worry, he'll be swiftly delt with, and any hurt suffered by our main character will be followed up with a heaping helping of comfort.

Oh, this book also contains (extremely) detailed sex. But do we really need a warning for that?

CHAPTER ONE

"Quit staring."

"I'm not."

"Oh, you are, honey, and I don't blame you. Those shoulders go on for dayzzz."

"I feel like you said that with a 'z'. Possibly multiple of them."

"Oh, I did, sweet pea. And that ass. I have one word for it: yum."

"You literally *sound* like you're drooling. Are you sure you're not the one who's been staring, Tessa?"

"Of course, I have been!" She didn't sound the least bit ashamed about it either. "Look at that gorgeous specimen of a man. If he's not the offspring of some Greek god's bastard, I will chop off my right tit."

He wrinkled his nose. "Gross."

Even as he pretended to gag over his partner's declaration, however, Micah found his gaze – and attention – drifting back to the man they were discussing: the supposed descendent of a Greek god.

He was tall, at least a couple of inches past six feet, and the suit jacket he was wearing clung to the expanse of his impressively broad shoulders. Said shoulders tapered off to form a trim waist, under which matching pinstripe pants gripped onto thick thighs – which Micah hadn't known he had a thing for until now.

Seriously, even from a distance, Micah knew those things had to be ripped. The man's entire body looked rock-solid. Micah couldn't quite make out any facial features, but if there was any justice in the world, the man must have had the epitome of a butter-face.

Still, Micah could probably look past it, considering, as Tessa had so eloquently put it: "that ass".

"Micah," Tessa hissed into his earpiece. (Speak of the devil.) "I said to quit. You're not even trying to hide your ogling now."

"You also said to look," he couldn't help but point out, but he obediently dropped his gaze to the ground, anyway. He was wearing a pair of shabby red Converse. There were holes on the top of the right one where his toes threatened to peek out, and the left had a loose outsole that liked to flap when he walked.

Not exactly his usual style, but it wasn't like Micah had picked them out himself. In fact, he hadn't picked out any part of his current ensemble.

"I meant metaphorically. You're in the middle of an undercover operation. You can't let yourself be distracted by every hottie that walks by; you need to keep your wits about you."

Okay, first of all, that wasn't just any hottie. Secondly-

"You're my handler," he pointed out. "*You* need to keep your wits about you."

"Oh, you don't worry about my wits, honey. I'm not the one that's thirsting after some babelicious stranger, completely ignoring the potential john coming in at three o'clock."

Micah tensed, subtly peeking in the direction she'd indicated.

Tessa was right.

A man dressed in a cheap suit was quickly approaching, the graying hair near his temples and the deep-set wrinkles of his brow indicating he was probably in his late forties or early fifties. His uneven gait and the stumble in his step meant he was probably drunk.

Micah tried not to grimace as the man got closer and he spotted the wedding band on his finger. The guy didn't really fit the profile they'd come up with for their perp – he was too old and looked to be married to boot.

Most likely, he was just another asshole going through a midlife crisis – not the serial killer going around killing male prostitutes they were searching for.

Micah voiced his thoughts aloud, muttering lowly into the mic hidden in his shirt – if the obscene, canary yellow crop top he was wearing *could* even be considered a shirt. "I doubt he's our guy, Tess. Too sloppy."

7

"Probably not," the woman agreed, "but you never know. You of all people should know that looks can be deceiving. Let him pick you up. If nothing else, you'll be able to arrest him for solicitation."

Resigning himself to do as she suggested, Micah let himself sink into the brick wall he was lounging against near the mouth of an alley. He winced as the brick scratched against his exposed lower back where his shirt didn't quite cover the skin, but he forced himself to school his expression as the man moved closer.

Honestly, he hadn't expected to be picked up within the first fifteen minutes of his shift.

"How much?"

Apparently, Mr. Midlife Crisis wasn't one for small talk. Which was unfortunate because Micah needed him to actually say the words. "How much for what?" he asked.

"Don't be coy, you little tart." Micah fought the urge to wrinkle his nose when the man took another step forward and the stench of alcohol hit him straight in the face.

He wasn't intimidated – or, at least, that was what he told himself when arms braced themselves on either side of his head, effectively trapping Micah against the brick wall. Sure, he didn't have his Glock, but Tessa was watching out for him. Not to mention the fact that he was well-versed in hand-to-hand if worse came to worst.

"$100," Micah said, knowing he was highballing the man even before his bloodshot eyes widened in disbelief.

"$100?" he repeated, scoffing. "For a loose hole like yours? I'll give you $50 if you can even make me bust my nut."

This. douchebag.

Micah had planned on just wrangling the man's hands behind his back and arresting him as soon as he'd said enough to incriminate himself, but now he was pissed.

"Oh, I'm sorry, I thought you were asking after my mouth," he retorted. "If you want a piece of the filet mignon, the going rate's 300 bucks."

He heard Tessa sigh into his earpiece, and judging by the dull *thud* that followed, could perfectly picture her banging her head against the steering wheel of the undercover van she was parked in across the street.

"300 bucks?" Mr. Midlife Crisis sneered. "Who do you think you are? Sluts like you are hardly worth the time it takes for you to get me off."

"You're the one who approached me, buddy," Micah reminded him. "Must be worth something."

Admittedly, he wasn't expecting for the guy to take him by the hair, backpedal him into the alley, and smash his head against the wall. The hit wasn't hard enough to make his ears ring, but Micah's eyes watered involuntarily when the man's grip on his hair tightened, and he leaned his face into his personal space. "How about this, you little bitch? Since your ass is apparently off limits, why don't you get on your knees so I can show you how you *ought* to be treating your customers with that smart mouth? Consider it a free lesson. If you manage to bring me to finish, I'll even think about leaving a tip."

Alright, play time was over.

This guy was more than just your typical drunkard looking to pick up a hooker – he clearly didn't give a rat's ass whether Micah was willing to blow him or not, he was going to *make* him. The fact that there were *real* people out there working the streets and being treated this way – probably pretty regularly – made anger burn hot in Micah's gut. He was about to elbow the asshole in the throat and force him to *his* knees so he could slap the zip ties he had hidden on his person for just this reason around his wrists when Mr. Midlife Crisis was abruptly pulled off of him-

"Get your fucking hands off him!"

-and punched in the face by the man he and Tessa had been ogling but five minutes earlier.

Micah watched, taken aback, as the Greek god lookalike pulled back his fist and pummeled the man again. And *again*. His assaulter fell back onto his ass after the third hit. He scrambled backward awkwardly, attempting to shield his bloody face from more attacks while simultaneously doing the crab walk.

Micah may have laughed if he weren't so stunned.

As things stood, the guy shouldn't have bothered hiding his face. His rescuer (unneeded though the assist may have been) had no problems targeting the man's mid-section with his foot instead. The man let out a pained yelp when a kick connected sharply with his ribs.

"Micah," Tessa hissed in his ear.

It was enough to break him out of the surprised stupor he'd fallen into.

"Stop him before we have to make *two* arrests."

She had a good point. It would hardly be kosher to have to drag his knight in shining armor (more like shining Armani, but the point still stood) in for assault right after he'd saved Micah from the human garbage currently yodeling on the ground.

Micah lurched forward. "Stop!" he yelled, all but flinging himself at the man. "Stop! He's not worth it," he insisted, grabbing his rescuer by the arm.

The man startled at the contact, turning to face Micah. The scowl he was sporting did absolutely *nothing* to take away from his attractiveness.

A jawline that was both sharp enough to cut glass and yet covered in enough stubble that you knew it'd leave a pleasant burn behind when it rubbed up against your skin? *Check.*

Absolutely ridiculous cheekbones? *Check.*

The bluest pair of eyes Micah had ever seen peering down at him under thick, expressive eyebrows? *Check.*

Micah was honestly shocked he hadn't spontaneously combusted the second the man had turned his head – he was *that* attractive.

For a long second, the man just stared at him. And then-

"What are you doing?" he asked gruffly, pointedly eyeing the hands Micah had wrapped around his bicep (and what a nice bicep it was) like they had personally offended him. "This guy was hurting you."

Micah cleared his throat, horrified to realize saliva had begun forming in his mouth at some point while he'd been gawking at the Adonis before him. "Uh… stopping you from committing murder?"

It came out as more of a question than he'd intended.

"I'm not going to kill him," the man replied, sounding offended. "I'm just making sure *this* is what springs to mind the next time he even *considers* touching someone against their will." The man punctuated his point by delivering another swift kick to the man on the ground – this time to the meat of his thigh.

The guy howled, and Micah knew there'd be a baseball sized bruise there the next morning.

"That way, he'll never be able to get his dick up again – that is, if I let him keep it."

A man threatening to castrate another man – even if it was in some weird defense of his honor – should *not* have been a turn on.

Apparently, the prospect of losing his bits was enough to finally get the man on the ground scrambling to his feet. Shoulders hunched and one arm curled protectively around his stomach, he booked it out of the alley as fast as he could hobble, hurrying back onto the street it was connected to.

Mr. Dreamboat took a threatening step forward, clearly intending to give chase, but Micah tightened the grip he had on the man's arm. "Hey, *no*! What are you doing? Stop! Just let him go!"

The man could have probably shaken Micah off of him if he really wanted to, but he didn't. Instead, he just glared. "He was hurting you," he repeated himself, like Micah hadn't heard him the first time – like he was crazy for not wanting retribution.

"I'm fine," he hastily assured the man. "Just a bump on the head is all."

After all, it wasn't like Micah could tell him that Tessa already had a cruiser en route to pick the guy up and arrest him for solicitation and assault.

The man eyed him like he didn't believe he was "fine" at all, which (unfortunately) prompted Micah to keep talking. "I'm good, honestly. Completely unblemished. Peachy keen. Hunky-dory."

Hunky-dory? What the hell was wrong with him? He sounded like some wannabe cowboy from those western dramas his father used to make him watch as a kid. This was New York City, for Christ's sake.

Thankfully, the man didn't address his odd choice of phrase. Although he *did* keep staring. On the plus side, his expression had lost most of the anger it'd contained when Micah had first grabbed him. (Though the bicep he was holding was as tense as ever.)

Abruptly realizing he was still touching the man, Micah hastily released his arm. He cleared his throat. "Sorry about that."

The man's brow screwed in consternation as his eyes continued to drink Micah in. "*You're* sorry?"

Micah didn't know how to respond to that. "Um..." he floundered.

Luckily, it didn't seem like the man actually expected an answer. "What are you wearing?"

Micah blinked at the sudden change of subject, glancing down at his current ensemble. The tight leather pants and revealing crop top were essentially a costume, and Micah hadn't been particularly bashful when it had come to putting them on – it was his job, after all. But, somehow, under this man's critical gaze, he found his face heating up in embarrassment. "Uh... c-clothes?" he eventually managed to stutter out.

The wrinkle in the man's brow told Micah what he thought of *that* answer. "Where's your coat?" he demanded.

Micah felt his jaw loosen of its own accord. Was this guy serious? "Well..."

(He was *so* eloquent this evening.)

"It's November," the man interrupted sharply – before Micah was even able to begin mustering up an explanation. "It's supposed to get to below freezing tonight." Almost as if in agreement, the wind decided to gust through the dingy alley they were standing in, goosebumps immediately erupting over Micah's bare arms.

Regardless, he couldn't help but be a bit annoyed.

After all, there was no way the man in front of him didn't *know* he was a prostitute. (A pretend one in this case, but the point still stood.) Feeling suddenly defensive, Micah crossed his arms over his chest. "Yeah, well, I can't exactly show off the goods under a puffy winter coat, can I?" he bit out sarcastically.

The strange man didn't seem to have a response to that – he just continued to stare. It was unnerving. And maybe a little bit sexy.

Micah immediately did his best to block out that thought.

Another blast of cold air making its way down the alley did the trick. An involuntary shiver took hold of him, and Micah immediately tucked his hands up under his armpits in an effort to keep them warm.

"What?" Micah barked defensively when the man's frown grew.

That word seemed to spur him into action. Abruptly, the man began unbuttoning his suit jacket. "Come here," he commanded.

"Why?" Micah asked, half-horrified he was being propositioned by the guy who had just saved his ass, and half-hard in his pants because, well… it was cold, and the silk dress shirt the man was wearing under his suit did little to hide his pebbling nipples, *alright?*

Don't judge him.

Micah was transfixed by the sight in front of him and had to fight back a yelp when the man suddenly took him by the arm and dragged him into his space. He immediately attempted to yank his limb free, but the man held fast. "What are you doing?"

The man's actions were answer enough when he forced Micah's arms through the sleeves of his jacket and tucked it around him. It was about two sizes too big and not nearly as toasty as the fur-lined parka he usually wore on nights like tonight, but Micah found his insides warming regardless.

He swallowed. "You don't have to-"

"You hungry?" the man asked before Micah could tell him he didn't need his jacket. After all, he wasn't a *real* street walker.

Micah blinked. "Um, well-"

Once again, he did not give Micah the option to answer. "El Taco Rosa has the best tacos in Queens."

Micah had no choice but to stumble along as the man pulled him out of the alley and manhandled him down the block.

"You okay?" Tessa whispered in his earpiece. Honestly, he'd forgotten that she was listening in. Realizing his friend was waiting for some kind of response, he hurriedly worked a hand through his hair – their predetermined signal that he had the situation under control.

Still, he knew she wouldn't be happy if he allowed himself to be dragged away from the area they'd specifically chosen for their operation. She'd freak if he didn't stay in her line of sight. (The alley had been bad enough.)

The reminder that he was still on the job made Micah plant his feet and abruptly yank his arm from the man's grip.

He looked surprised.

"Look," Micah said, making sure to sound appropriately scornful, "I don't need your charity."

The man frowned. "I'd hardly call a couple of tacos charity."

A second later he was pulling Micah into the establishment he'd inadvertently stopped them in front of. It was official – Tessa was going to kill him. (The cursing in his ear was proof enough of that.)

But Micah forced himself to put his friend and handler out of his mind when the man dragged him to one of the many booths lining the front of the restaurant. The good news was there were plenty of windows. "Sit," the man demanded, and Micah complied – if only because he was fairly certain Tessa would be able to see him from the booth he'd chosen.

He must have been right because the "f-bombs" going off in his ear were greatly reduced once he sat.

Still, he might not have agreed to sit if he had realized the man was going to slide into the same side of the booth as him, effectively trapping him against the wall. He reached over Micah to grab a laminated menu and Micah caught a whiff of his cologne. Or maybe it was just him. Either way, Micah was pretty sure it was illegal for someone to go around smelling so good – like Christmas trees and cedar wood, and something spicier – something distinctly *man* – wrapped up in a six-foot, three-inch, musclebound package.

"I know I said that their tacos are the best, but order whatever you want," the man instructed as he set down the menu in front of Micah.

Micah pursed his lips. "I'm fine," he insisted.

The guy glowered. "I didn't ask if you were fine. I asked you to open the menu and pick out something to eat."

Micah gritted his teeth together, not sure if he was more concerned by the man's bossiness or how his body was reacting to said bossiness. He squirmed in his seat, resisting the urge to adjust himself in his pants. "Look, I don't accept food for my... services," he decided on finally. "It's a cash only deal so-"

"Jesus!" the man exclaimed, and Micah couldn't help the pang of satisfaction that shot through him when he caught sight of the sudden red tinge on the man's cheeks. "I'm not trying to purchase your- your services. You're what? Sixteen? I'm just trying to buy you dinner. You're skin and bones."

Sixteen? *Really?* Micah knew he'd been chosen for this job because of his "sweet baby face" as Tessa liked to put it, but... sixteen? He supposed it explained the man's extreme reaction to him being accosted outside. Ignoring the relief (there wasn't an ounce of disappointment in him, really) that the guy wasn't trying to purchase his "services", Micah settled into his seat and reluctantly picked up the menu, pretending to look it over. "I'm twenty-three," Micah pointed out grumpily, telling the truth. "And I have plenty of muscle on these bones. I could even kick *your* ass if I wanted to."

He side-eyed the man next to him. You know, *maybe.*

The man snorted. "Yeah, and I'm a god."

"Ah-ha! So you admit it!"

The guy scrunched his nose in confusion. (It was stupidly adorable.) "What?"

Micah willed away a blush. "I... nothing." He took a deep breath, slapping back down the menu. "Look, thanks for all this, really. But you don't have to worry about me. And to be honest, I have things to do so if you just want to scooch over..." He lifted his hands, making the universal sign for him to scoot.

The man only raised his eyebrows. "Yeah, *illegal* things."

Pretend illegal things, Micah corrected mentally, but he didn't have time to ruminate on that when the man kept talking.

"Look, the way I see it, you have two options," he said sternly, turning so he was practically looming over Micah. "The first is you sit back and enjoy the meal I'm about to buy you. The second is you go back out on the streets." He took a breath. "But know this, if you choose option two, I'm going to follow you. And I'm going to chase off every potential john that even sniffs in your direction."

Micah knew his eyes were blown wide by the time the man had finished his tirade. "You can't do that!" he protested. *So much for catching their perp.* "Why would you-?!"

The man folded his arms over his chest. "I'm sorry. Did you miss it when that guy out there tried to *rape* you?"

It sent a shock of ice through Micah's veins the way he put it so plainly. He pressed his lips together. "I had it under control," he muttered.

The man's incredulous expression made it clear what he thought of *that.* "Maybe we should just skip all the way to option three instead and I call the cops – tell them I found a minor soliciting outside of my restaurant."

Too late for that, Micah thought, perhaps a tad hysterically. Also-

"This is *your* restaurant?" he demanded incredulously. The man couldn't have been much older than thirty. How could he *own* a restaurant?

He waved a hand. "I'm an investor," he said, like it was no big deal. "Regardless, the point stands. So, what's it going to be?"

Micah supposed there were worse things than eating supper with an absolute bombshell of a man. Maybe if he tried hard enough he could even pretend this was a real date and not a pity meal from a stranger who thought he was an underaged prostitute.

"Don't you dare," Tessa hissed in his ear, but Micah had no idea what she was forbidding him to do. He figured the best plan of action would be to sit with the guy, let him order him something to eat, and then duck out of there as soon as the opportunity presented itself.

The man must have been able to see the resignation on Micah's face because he released what sounded like a relieved sigh before calling a waitress over. A pretty Hispanic woman with dark brown hair and equally dark eyes began making her way over to them. Her eyes widened, however, when they took in the man currently holding him hostage.

"Usted!" she exclaimed before rushing the rest of the way over. She threw her arms around the man, all but smashing his face into her breasts as she squeezed him. *"Ha pasado demasiado tiempo desde la última vez que vi tu cara!"*

Apparently, they knew each other.

"Adella, *cómo estás?"*

And… apparently, his savior in shining Armani knew Spanish.

Micah was not impressed or turned on in the slightest. The guy was bilingual. So what? The gravel in his voice as his mouth wrapped around each accented word didn't cause his dick to twitch in his too-tight pants. No way, José.

See, he could speak Spanish too.

Sort of.

Enough that he caught the gist of what they were saying to each other as the two slipped into a conversation in front of him. The woman – Adella – was apparently quite upset that she hadn't seen the man in so long. She seemed happy enough to see him now, however.

She had finally released the guy from her death grip when her eyes drifted to meet Micah's. She appeared startled to realize the man she was accosting had company. Micah offered her a brief, aborted wave, and a pleased grin slowly formed on her face. "And who is this?" she asked, abruptly switching to English.

"I'm-"

Before Micah could answer, however, she turned to the man sitting beside him and launched into another spiel – speaking Spanish once more. He was mortified to catch the words *"encantador"* (charming) and *"guapo"* (handsome) as she gestured emphatically at him.

Micah wasn't sure if he was relieved or annoyed when the man shifted tactically and blocked him from her sight with his body. "Enough, Adella. Can't you see you're scaring him?"

Scaring him? Okay, he was definitely annoyed.

"Please, if you haven't frightened him off by now, I don't have a chance in *el infierno* of doing so." She blatantly peered around the man's shoulder. "I'm Adella, by the way, it's nice to meet you, *precioso*."

Had she just called him "precious"?

"Adella," the man warned before Micah could manage a response, something menacing in his voice that hadn't been there before.

The woman pursed her lips at the tone, but it must have done the trick because she sighed before taking a step backward. "I see taking on more work hasn't made you any more bearable over the past few months," she snapped before turning her attention back to Micah, her expression and tone softening as she pulled out a small notepad from the pocket of her apron. "What can I get you to drink, *precioso?*"

The man beside him twitched.

Micah couldn't help but be amused by the woman's antics. Before he could open his mouth to answer her, however, his abductor was speaking. "He'll have a glass of milk – whole if you have it."

Micah blinked in disbelief.

Milk? What was he, a kindergartener?

He forced himself to hold his tongue as the man followed up that proclamation by ordering his own drink – whiskey on ice, since, you know, he was an *adult*. Unlike what he obviously thought of Micah.

Micah waited for Adella to leave before making his opinion of that particular fact known. "Milk, *really?* I told you. I'm twenty-three, not five."

The man raised his eyebrows. "You got ID to prove that?"

He did as a matter of fact.

The precinct had been thorough in prepping him for his current role. They'd provided him with a driver's license to go along with his fake identity – not that he imagined many johns would ask to see proof of age before soliciting him for sex. Still, he couldn't help but feel smug as he pulled the license out of his pocket and slid it over for the man to inspect.

He wasn't expecting for a ghost of a grin to pull at the corner of the guy's mouth. "Peregrine?"

Micah refused to be embarrassed by a name that wasn't even his. He didn't feel any heat creep up his neck at all as he quickly swiped the license back from the man, shoving it back into his pocket. "My parents were hippies, okay?" *More like his co-workers were cruel bastards.* "Anyway, what'd you get saddled with?" he demanded in retaliation.

The man frowned. "What?"

"Your name," Micah clarified. "I can't keep calling you my knight in shining Armani, or alternately, my *kidnapper*," – he made sure to stress that word – "in my head."

The man frowned. "Oh. It's Damon."

"Damon," Micah repeated slowly, letting it sit heavy on his tongue. It was a perfectly respectable name – strong and masculine. It suited the man.

A muscle in Damon's jaw spasmed at the sound of it spoken in Micah's soft tenor, his eyes drifting to his mouth.

Embarrassed, and sure the man thought he was a complete freak in addition to the whole prostitute thing, Micah grasped for a conversation starter, rolling with the first thing that popped into his head. "So, you and the waitress clearly know each other."

The man – Damon – tore his gaze away from Micah's mouth, offering a nod. "That's Adella. She's not actually a waitress here. She co-owns this place with her wife, who's also the head chef."

Micah frowned in confusion. "I thought you said this was *your* restaurant," he pointed out.

"I said I was an investor," Damon corrected, waving away the technicality. "We also grew up together. Adella was the only daughter of our maid."

A maid. So Damon had been born rich. Micah supposed that explained how he could afford to finance a restaurant at such a young age.

"Is she the one that taught you how to speak Spanish?" Micah asked. "It's pretty flawless."

His grasp on the language. Not the man himself, obviously.

"No, that was mostly her mother, Mrs. Cortez. Although Adella did teach me an unsavory phrase or two."

Micah couldn't help but snort. "I bet. Did she get you into a lot of trouble when you were kids?"

"Ha! This guy?" Adella interrupted loudly, suddenly back with their drinks, setting a short glass of amber liquor down in front of Damon and an alarmingly full glass of white milk down in front of Micah. "Yeah, right. You're sitting next to the biggest stick-in-the-mud to ever grace the planet. When I was a girl, I was half-convinced he was a robot. This cold bastard has been wrapped up in his work for as long as I can remember, and I've known him since he was in Pull-Ups." She shook her head in mock sorrow. "It's quite sad, really. I keep waiting for something to give, for him to find a reason to let himself loosen up a little – actually *enjoy* life." Adella shot Micah a particular look. "Though maybe he finally has."

The implication was more than a little ridiculous.

Micah and Damon didn't even *know* each other, and despite Adella's assumptions, they weren't on a date. Even if Micah wasn't literally dressed like a prostitute at the moment, the guy sitting next to him was eons out of his league.

"Gee, Adella," Damon snapped, yanking Micah from his self-depreciating thoughts, "thanks for the glowing review."

She ignored Damon's obvious ire, only shrugging. "His sister, on the other hand, now she knows how to party."

Micah raised his eyebrows, turning to Damon. "You have a sister?"

The man grimaced, taking a sip of his whiskey. "Three of them, actually."

Micah could only imagine the suffocating cloud of estrogen surrounding the poor guy growing up. He probably should have been pitying, but honestly, Micah couldn't help but feel a little bit jealous.

He had always dreamed of having a big family as a kid.

"Joelle and I used to do up Damon here in dresses when he was a boy. He looked fantastic in pink – still does, I imagine."

"Are you planning on chatting our heads off the rest of the night," Damon interrupted sharply, back to glaring at Adella, "or are you actually going to take our order sometime in the next hour?"

Adella huffed, Damon's barbed words rolling off her shoulders like she was used to his gruffness – which, by the sounds of it, she probably was. "I'm all ears," she assured, once again pulling out her notepad.

"Good. I'll take the shredded pork and refried bean tamales with a side of rice."

"And you, *precioso?*"

Micah supposed he could grow to enjoy the silly nickname if it caused Damon to look *this* annoyed every time Adella uttered it. Besides it could be worse – "Peregrine" for example.

Micah quickly scanned the menu, instinctually eyeing the cheapest item he could find – which looked to be a platter of nachos with queso dip. Glancing at Damon, however, Micah had a feeling he wouldn't be impressed with the meager order. "Uh, I'll have the trio of tacos, please," he decided after a minute.

Damon *had* said they were the best in Queens, after all.

"Good choice," Adella promised. "I'll be back with those in a second."

Micah wasn't sure whether the woman meant that as an assurance or a threat. Either way, she shot one last piercing look Damon's way before turning and disappearing back in the direction Micah assumed was the kitchen.

"So," Damon said, breaking the silence they'd descended into with Adella's departure. Micah couldn't help but notice how much softer he sounded with her gone. "What about you?"

"What about me?" Micah asked, twirling the paper straw in the glass of milk Adella had left for him. He supposed the striped things were good for environment, but he imagined he didn't have long before it got soggy.

"You have any siblings? Surely, you can't have more meddling women in your life than I do. Maybe a brother?"

Micah shook his head. "I'm an only child," he admitted easily enough.

Damon frowned. "And your parents?" he pushed.

The man's attempt to wheedle answers out of Micah was hardly subtle – especially to someone trained in interrogation techniques. Still, Micah found himself reluctantly impressed with how Damon managed to keep the conversation focused on Micah instead of himself.

He decided to indulge him. After all, it wasn't like he was *really* a prostitute named Peregrine Davis. Damon would never be able to connect any of the information he gave him back to Micah Hart – first year criminal detective of New York City's 105th precinct.

"My mom died when I was young," he revealed, words practically tripping over each other in their haste to escape his mouth. "Brain aneurysm." He'd discovered quickly after her untimely death that the faster he said it, the less painful the memories that assaulted him were. Sort of like pulling off a Band-Aid. "One day she was here, and the next, she was gone."

Micah braced himself for the onslaught of awkward apologies he usually received after revealing this particular tidbit about himself, but he was pleasantly surprised when the man only tensed, and then after a handful of seconds, offered a "that's terrible" in a deep, rumbly voice.

Micah cleared his throat, oddly appreciative. "Yeah," he agreed. "Anyway, my grandparents died before I was born, so it's just my dad and me."

Damon nodded, opening his mouth before abruptly closing it and pausing, almost like he was gearing himself up to say something, or debating whether he should say it at all. "And... does your dad know?"

Micah stiffened. "Does he know what?" he asked loftily, playing dumb, though he suspected he knew exactly what Damon meant by the question.

Damon sighed. "Does your dad know what you do for money?"

"What, you mean, that I sell myself on the side of the street like a cheap pretzel?" he sniped.

"No," the man snapped right back, "that his only child is putting himself in direct danger from the dregs of society who would like nothing more than to hurt him."

"Do *you* want to hurt me?" Micah pushed back.

Damon jerked backward, like Micah had physically retaliated against him. "What? I- of course not!"

"Then *why* are you doing this? You think I buy this Good Samaritan act? *No one* is this nice."

"Like I said, I'm just trying to help you."

"And how do I know you're not going to demand compensation for your so-called generosity? I mean, you didn't give me much choice but to accept it, dragging me in here, trapping me in this booth, and forcing your company on me." It was a low blow, but Micah wasn't finished. "Does it make your cock hard?" he demanded. "Making people feel indebted to you? Forcing them to be at your mercy?"

Damon didn't visibly react to the lurid accusation. In fact, for a long moment, he just stared. "I don't know what sort of lowlifes you've spent time with before," he finally said, words slow and sure, "but I would *never* force myself on you – or anyone for that matter. I'm not trying to scare you. I just want to help."

It was irritating how genuine he sounded. And Micah had a feeling that if he really had been a prostitute, he would have grabbed the lifeline the man was trying to throw him with both hands and not let go for the world.

But he wasn't a prostitute.

He was an undercover cop. And he had to leave before Damon figured that out. So instead of melting at the words, Micah jutted out his chin in that stubborn way he was told he sometimes did and crossed his arms over his chest. "And if I told you the best way to help me was by moving out of the way so I could get back to work?" he challenged.

Damon swallowed. "Then I stand by what I said before. I'd let you go, but I'd follow you right back out onto the streets and chase away all of your potential... work."

Outrageous.

No one should have fretted over a stranger this much. But, somehow, Micah believed him. He *cared*. And by caring, Damon was *this close* to impeding on an investigation into a serial killer.

Micah couldn't let that happen. He felt as stuck as he first had when Damon had all but frog-marched him into El Taco Rosa. Unless...

An idea suddenly occurred to him. "And what if I asked you to move because I'm a handful of seconds away from pissing myself?"

Damon blinked, thrown by the sudden change of topic. "What?"

"I have to pee," Micah deadpanned.

Damon frowned, a little wrinkle forming in his brow. "Then I suppose I'd tell you the bathroom is to the left of the kitchen," he said, even as he began shifting out of the way, "but I'd also warn you that I'll be waiting right here for you to return."

"Of course," Micah muttered, acting annoyed, but secretly elated. As long as there was a window in the bathroom, it wouldn't matter if Damon was standing guard at the front of the restaurant.

Micah hurried in the direction Damon had indicated, refusing to glance backward at the man, even as he could feel his gaze practically burning a hole through the back of his jacket – well, Damon's jacket. He ducked into the men's room.

"Jackpot," Micah muttered, immediately spotting the tiny window on the far wall, right between the pair of sinks and the single stall and urinal. Better yet, he was alone.

"You're not really going to squeeze out of a window, are you?"

Micah jumped. He had nearly forgotten that Tessa was listening in. She knew him well. "Uh, yes, I most certainly am."

"But it was just getting good," she whined into his ear. "If there was a microwave in here, I'd be heating up popcorn."

"Fuck you, Tessa." He hauled himself up onto the counter of sinks, unlatching the window. No screen. Perfect. "You didn't even want me sitting with him."

"That was before I realized how adorable he was. Honestly, he's positively smitten with you."

"Adorable?" Micah hissed, ignoring the rest of her psychotic babble. "More like an overbearing asshole. Can you believe he thinks he can tell me what to do?"

"Yeah, well, he also thinks you're a prostitute – and he's *worried* about you. I'm seriously melting here. I mean, the window you were sat in front of was pretty blurry, but even from across the street, I could see him making heart eyes at you. He's going to be devastated when you don't come back."

"More like relieved his moral compass doesn't have to figure out what to do with an underaged prostitute anymore." Even Micah didn't believe his own words. For whatever reason, the guy was genuinely concerned. "Besides, how else am I going to get out of this?"

"You could always tell him the truth. You know, that you're undercover," she offered.

Micah scoffed, even as he started contorting himself to fit his upper half through the window. "Yeah. Youngest criminal detective on the force, blowing his cover on the very first day of the biggest case he's ever been assigned to. How does that look?"

Micah could picture the woman wincing in his mind's eye. "Not great, admittedly, but probably worth it if you got laid by *that* out of the deal."

Micah glowered at nothing. "You are the worst."

"No, I'm just married – and living vicariously through you. There's a difference."

"You love Jasper," Micah protested.

Tessa sighed, like she was disappointed to agree with him. "That I do. But I'm betting even he would understand if he saw the guy."

"Exactly! And let me tell you, that stubbled jaw is even more absurd up close. There's no way he's actually attracted to me – he just pities me. Probably thinks of me as his next rich-guy community service project, helping the poor, little hooker he found being assaulted in the alley."

Tessa hummed. "Yeah, well, I'd do him even if it *was* a pity lay."

Micah snorted, choking on his spit, and as a result, nearly fell off the dumpster located conveniently on the other side of the bathroom window. He hopped down, hustling through the alley. "I'm nearly back to the front of El Taco Rosa. Do you have eyes on Damon? Is he still in the booth?"

"Affirmative, but I can tell he's getting agitated."

That was Micah's signal to speed walk *away* from the building, in the opposite direction he'd originally been loitering at a block away from the restaurant. "Pick me up at the next crosswalk?"

Tessa sighed. "Sure, but I think we're going to have to call it. We've only cleared one spot for tonight, and I have a feeling tall, dark, and handsome might come looking if we go back to it."

Tessa was right, unfortunately. Disappointment churned in Micah's gut.

By the time he and Tessa returned to the precinct, he'd managed to convince himself that the disconcerting feeling had everything to do with being unable to complete his job for the night, and nothing at all to do with the fact Micah would probably never see the guy – his knight in shining Armani, Damon – ever again.

CHAPTER TWO

Ever since he was a kid, Micah had wanted nothing so fervently than to become a decorated police officer. He'd spent entire Statistics and Anthropology classes in high school daydreaming about saving innocent civilians from hardened criminals, chasing down "bad guys" and solving case after case as an ace detective.

Somehow, he never quite imagined… this.

He was working the streets again, loitering on a corner near a cheap motel – no more than a handful of blocks away from where he'd been assaulted on Saturday. Assaulted and saved by an unreasonably attractive man hellbent on filling his belly with authentic Mexican food and dressing him in layers to protect him from the cold.

Not that Micah had given the man another thought since he'd squeezed himself out of that tiny bathroom window a few nights ago.

He definitely didn't daydream about broad shoulders during his morning showers or reminisce about thick thighs at night while he lay in bed trying to sleep.

That'd be weird. Not to mention inappropriate.

And even if his thoughts *did* sometimes stray into the morally questionable area of wondering how dark the man's blue eyes turned in the grips of arousal or how thick and purple his cock got before the brink of release… there was simply no way Micah was going to be able to get it up in this weather.

It was at least ten degrees colder than the last time he'd gone undercover, and the wind made it seem closer to twenty. It was only November, but there was no doubt winter was quickly approaching.

Of course, it didn't help matters that he was in a skirt.

It clashed horribly with the too-tight red shirt and bomber jacket he was wearing – not to mention the same torn-up sneakers he'd donned last time, but Tessa had assured him multiple times that he looked effortlessly sexy – you know, in a grungy, New York City prostitute sort of way.

As for Micah, he stood by his assertion that there was absolutely *nothing* effortless about a man wearing a pleaded, schoolgirl-style skirt. On the corner of a mostly deserted street. Mid-November.

Unlike his last attempt at pretend prostituting, there were no drunk johns to keep his mind occupied. No shot of adrenaline rushing through his veins to keep him warm. No ridiculously handsome Good Samaritans coming to his unnecessary rescue.

Not that Micah *wanted* to see the guy again or anything.

He was just bored. And cold. His testicles felt one stiff breeze away from retreating back into his body permanently.

Micah didn't know if it was just the difference between a Saturday and a Tuesday, but he'd seen absolutely zero action since he'd started loitering on the corner shortly after six. He'd been standing there for hours, and while he'd endured plenty of leers – one ballsy frat boy had even attempted to stick his smart phone up under his skirt and get a picture – the most suspicious thing to have happened all night was an elongated Rolls-Royce slowly rolling past where Micah had situated himself against the brick wall of an out-of-business barber shop.

For a handful of tense seconds, Micah had honestly thought it was going to stop, that some rich asshole was going to roll down the back window, beckon him over, and proposition him for a blowjob. But the black, sleek vehicle eventually turned the corner and disappeared into the night.

It had stood out in the bleak, decrepit neighborhood of Queens Micah found himself in, if only for how obviously expensive it was, and sadly – the most exciting thing to have happened his entire shift.

Huddling as deep as he could into the collar of his jacket, Micah watched idly as the dust and pollution unique to the city danced under the streetlights shining above him. Unable to stifle a yawn, he rubbed tiredly at his eyes.

"Micah," Tessa scolded in his earpiece, "quit it. You're smearing your eyeliner."

"Sorry," he muttered sheepishly. He honestly didn't know how girls managed to go days at a time without ruining their makeup. It was only about the fifth time he'd rubbed at his eyes tonight. He probably looked like a strung out raccoon by now – not that he thought it'd be a deal breaker for any potential john set on approaching him – or their perp for that matter.

The serial killer the press had "creatively" dubbed the Hooker Hunter was still on the loose.

So far, the NYPD had attributed seven murders to the man, but there could have easily been more victims out there. Prostitutes were one of the most underreported missing people in the country, after all.

All seven victims had been young men, and they all had all been known to exchange sexual favors for money – hence the nickname. The victims had ranged in age from eighteen to twenty-five, which was why Micah had been chosen to go undercover over more experienced detectives.

Of course, it wasn't only the itch to prove himself that motivated Micah to catch the guy. The Hooker Hunter seemed to strike at least once a month, and it'd been over three weeks since the last body had been discovered. Micah wanted to nail the bastard before he hurt anyone else, force him to face justice for his crimes, and give the families of the victims some closure.

Unfortunately, based on the action he'd seen thus far, Micah didn't think that would be tonight.

He glanced around. While a random pedestrian hurried by every now and then, there were only two other people stupid (desperate) enough to be out loitering in this weather. Two women were huddled on the other side of the nearby motel, wearing even less clothing than he was, and it didn't take a genius to know they were probably prostitutes – real ones.

Micah pressed his lips together. "Maybe we should call it a night," he muttered into his hidden mic. "Should I ask those two over there if they need help? Offer to hook them up with some beds at one of the local women's shelters?"

Tessa sighed. "You know what they'll say." A pause. "Give it another hour or so. You can approach them if they're still out then. I hear the real degenerates don't come out until after ten, anyway."

Micah frowned. Real degenerates. *Yay.*

"Easy for you to say. You aren't the one freezing your balls off."

"Well, then maybe you should be wearing a warmer coat."

Micah jumped. Stuck between internally cussing out himself or Tessa for not noticing someone approaching (though judging by the muffled cackling in his earpiece, she *had* noticed), Micah whipped around to face the person who'd managed to sneak up on him.

Though he'd known who it was as soon as he'd heard that smooth baritone.

"I- sorry. You scared me."

"I guess that makes us even then."

Micah blinked at the man's – at *Damon's* – flat tone. He sounded entirely unimpressed. "Um... what?" (He really needed to work on his eloquence when confronted with a pretty face. After all, not all criminals were as ugly as their crimes.)

"Don't you think that you scared me – when you disappeared the other day?" Damon elaborated. A muscle in his jaw ticked. "Honestly, I didn't know whether to be impressed or concerned that you could fit through such a small window."

Micah frowned. "I thought you'd be relieved to have me off your hands," he fibbed. "Or, I don't know, maybe mad that I tricked you."

Damon crossed his arms in front of his chest. He was wearing a fitted suit – just like the first time Micah had seen him – and he couldn't help but notice how the fabric strained against his bulging biceps.

(Micah may have to take back that assertion about his dick being unable to react to anything in this cold. Damon, it seemed, was the exception to every rule in the universe.)

"Oh no, I was mad," Damon assured. "Mainly at myself for not seeing it coming. Mostly, though, I was just worried. And confused. Is my company really so abhorrent that you'd rather turn into an icicle out here than sit inside a nice, warm restaurant with me and enjoy a meal?"

Wow. Damon was really good at this guilt-tripping thing. So good, Micah actually found himself feeling bad – and *apologizing* – despite the fact that the man had strong-armed him into El Taco Rosa in the first place. "Sorry," he muttered, eyes flittering to the ground as he toed a crack in the sidewalk with one of his dirty Converse. "It's just... I had places to be."

"Places like this?" Damon sounded about as impressed as Micah's captain had when he and Tessa had returned to the precinct hours early on Saturday, having to report that the location they'd spent all day scouting out had been compromised.

And just like that, Micah didn't feel bad anymore. "What's it to you?" he demanded hotly, eyes flying back to the man's ridiculously handsome face. He was forced to tug his bomber jacket more tightly around himself when an impressive gust of wind breezed by, but his temper wasn't cooled in the least as he added irately, "You *know* what I do for a living."

Damon frowned, not immediately answering. "Where's the jacket I gave you?" he asked after a moment, apparently deciding on ignoring Micah's question all together.

Micah fought the urge to shuffle awkwardly. It hadn't occurred to him to leave behind the man's suit jacket in El Taco Rosa's men's room, so it'd ended up at his apartment. He'd felt pretty guilty about it considering it was probably worth more than his monthly paycheck. Not guilty enough that he hadn't pressed it to his face a time or two to get a whiff of its owner's uniquely masculine scent, however. (It's not like he masturbated as he did it, or anything, okay? He wasn't a complete pervert.)

"It's... at home," he decided on eventually. "I'll get it back to you, I swear!" he added quickly after. "I'm not some thief."

The opposite of one, actually. His job often involved *returning* stolen merchandise to its proper owner.

Damon looked constipated at Micah's impassioned defense of himself. "I don't want it back."

Micah frowned. "Why?" Then he felt his shoulders tense as the probable reason occurred to him. "Afraid I ruined it with my filthiness? That I let some john ejaculate all over-"

"No," Damon snapped, looking ruffled for possibly the first time he'd met him, and Micah couldn't help but feel a bit of satisfaction at that. "I just wanted to know why you weren't wearing it. Or a hat for that matter. It's cold out here – colder than it was the last time I saw you."

Honestly, what was it going to take to get this guy to stop *caring* so damn much? It was making some very uncomfortable feelings stir in Micah's chest. (And groin.)

Still, it was Micah's job to chase him off, so he rolled his eyes before glancing down and gesturing at his skirt-clad legs. "Yeah, sort of hard to showcase the merchandise in a boxy suit jacket."

Damon's eyes followed, and Micah had the pleasure of watching him freeze – like he somehow hadn't noticed Micah was decked out in a school's girl skirt until just now. The man's Adam's apple bobbed. But just as suddenly as he'd fallen into his stupor, he broke out of it, abruptly taking Micah by the elbow and dragging him forward. "That's it. You're coming with me."

Micah was alarmed (and only a little aroused) by the declaration. Also, he was hit with a strange sense of déjà vu. "What? *Hey!* You can't just force people to-"

"You said yourself that you're freezing," Damon interrupted, sounding unreasonably... well, reasonable, as he pulled Micah away from where he was supposed to be *again*. "You need to get out of the cold, get something warm in your stomach."

"*What* is your obsession with feeding me?"

"If you fed yourself, it would be a non-issue," Damon sniped back.

"And what exactly do you think I'm trying to do here?" Micah shouted, finally finding the wherewithal to tug his elbow out of the man's grip.

Damon had turned to face him when Micah yanked his arm away, but he froze when his words reached his ears. His stern gaze wavered, before eventually dropping. Like Damon suddenly found the ground interesting – like Micah had somehow *hurt* his feelings, which was stupid. Micah wasn't about to apologize for pointing out the realities of his (pretend) profession.

Even if some deeply buried part of himself hated disappointing Damon for whatever reason.

Luckily, he didn't have to say anything. Damon squared his shoulders before lifting his gaze from the ground, drilling Micah with his blue gaze. "I'm sorry." He sounded painstakingly sincere. "I know next to nothing about you and your life, and you know even less about mine. I'm not trying to judge you or make you uncomfortable." He ran an agitated hand through his hair. "I know this is weird – you probably think I'm crazy – but for reasons I can't explain, I feel… drawn to you. I haven't stopped thinking about you since Saturday. I *need* to help you. I know it doesn't make any sense, but I can't help but feel validated since the universe has seen fit to throw us together again."

Micah snorted, even as his heart fluttered at the man's proclamation that he'd been on his mind since their last meeting. "The universe? How do I know you're not just some depraved stalker?"

Damon frowned, and Micah knew he wasn't imagining the hurt on his face now. Guilt made his stomach churn. "Sorry," he muttered, knowing what he'd said had been uncalled for. "I know you're not a stalker. Just some weirdo who gets his rocks off helping charity cases like me."

Damon's frown didn't lessen, but after a moment, he sighed. "Will you come with me then? Just to get out of the cold and eat something, at least? No strings attached, obviously."

Micah's answer should have been an immediate "no". Instead, he hesitated like the goddamn fool that he was.

Misreading the reason for his wavering, Damon immediately tacked on, "We don't have to go to my place or anything. I have a standing reservation at a nearby hotel if you're more comfortable with that."

"Say no, you idiot," Tessa hissed in his ear, and Micah opened his mouth to do just that when-

"*Please.*"

It wasn't fair, the way that word rolled off his tongue, and Micah really couldn't be blamed for what happened next. He dared anyone to deny this man anything he asked for when he pleaded like that. "Okay."

An "f-bomb" went off in his ear, but Micah steadfastly ignored it.

"I- really?" Damon seemed surprised, like he'd been gearing himself up to have to convince Micah further. "You'll come with me?" he sought to clarify.

Micah shuffled from foot to foot. "Well, it *is* cold," he allowed.

The grin that lit up Damon's face was bright enough to power the solar panels of all of the city's skyscrapers, and Micah felt vaguely dazed. "I've got to go get my car. Promise me you're not going to go anywhere," he ordered.

Like he was going to back out now. "Promise."

Damon looked like he wasn't sure if he believed him – and who could blame the man after Micah's last disappearing act? Regardless, he allowed his eyes to rove over Micah one last time before turning on his heel and jogging down the sidewalk.

As soon as he was around the corner, Tessa was spitting fire in his ear. "What the hell do you think you're doing?"

"I don't know," Micah admitted – it was nothing but the truth, after all. "But I dare you to withstand the power of his *please*."

"…You're as soft for this guy as he is for you, aren't you?"

"What? No!" A pause. "And he's *not* soft for me. He feels bad for me because he thinks I'm a prostitute."

"And you realize you're not *actually* a prostitute, right? This is not some fucked up version of Pretty Woman. You're a *cop*."

"I know that!"

"Then tell me why you're humoring this guy."

"You heard what he said. He's hellbent on helping me, for whatever reason. I figure if I let him get it out of his system – buy me some McDonalds and a room at a cheap hotel, or whatever he's thinking – he'll move on. We won't have to worry about him butting into any more of our operations."

There was a sigh in his ear, a little exasperated, but mostly amused. "I take it I can't talk you out of this?"

"I thought you liked Damon," Micah pointed out. "You were all but pouting when I ditched him in El Taco Rosa on Saturday."

"Yeah, well, I had eyes on you then. You weren't getting into some unknown vehicle with him, going God knows where. I wasn't *worried* for your safety."

Micah winced. "I can take care of myself, you know that," he scolded gently. "Besides, I've got the department's mic and earpiece on me. It's not like you can't track my location."

"I guess. You know I'm not going to be able to sleep all night, though, right?" A pause. "If I'm going to be wide awake anyway, and you're going to have the mic on you, you might as well keep it on-"

The little snoop wanted to eavesdrop on him. "Not a chance," he said, cutting her off.

"But Micah-!"

Micah only felt a little bad about pulling out his earpiece and shutting it off while Tessa was mid-sentence. He quickly hid it in his sock, where his disabled mic immediately followed.

Just in the nick of time, too, because moments later, what could only be Damon's vehicle pulled around the corner. Micah shouldn't have been surprised, but he could feel his jaw loosen regardless.

Of fucking course. The Rolls-Royce. He could only watch in a silent sort of awe as the back door opened, and Damon stepped out.

"That was *you* who drove by earlier?"

"Not me – my chauffeur, Geoffrey. I told him to slow down when I recognized you. I didn't want to intimidate you, though, so I had him park around the back."

Micah blinked, not sure how to respond to any of that. "Oh."

Luckily, Damon didn't seem to expect a response. "Come on," he said, gesturing at the open door, "get in."

Taking a deep breath, and amassing his courage, Micah stepped off the sidewalk and crouched into the vehicle. He scooted carefully across flawless leather seats. It was as immaculate on the inside as it was on the outside, and afraid to touch anything, Micah put his seatbelt on before carefully folding his hands in his lap.

It was more spacious than the back of any four-door vehicle had the right to be, but Micah still felt crowded when Damon slid in after him, shutting the door behind himself. There was a divider between them and the driver, giving them a sense of privacy.

"So," Micah chattered nervously as the vehicle start moving – the engine ran so smoothly, he wouldn't have noticed if it weren't for the passing buildings outside the tinted windows, "you own a restaurant, and apparently make enough money to employ a chauffeur." (Not the mention the fucking Rolls-Royce.) "What is it that you do, exactly?"

Damon shrugged, seemingly blasé about the amount of money he made. "I work in finances," he said vaguely.

Micah raised his eyebrows. "What, is that code for money laundering or something?"

He didn't mean it offensively – it came out without thought, honestly – but Damon stiffened. "I'm good at what I do," he said after a moment, choosing his words carefully.

Micah snorted. "Yeah, me too."

Damon stared. (Yeah, Micah couldn't believe that had just come out of his mouth either, considering the man thought he was a hooker. Thank God Tessa *wasn't* listening in, or he would never live it down.) He cleared his throat. "Uh, anyway… how far away is this hotel exactly?"

"Traffic's light. It shouldn't take more than thirty minutes to get there."

Thirty minutes. Micah could handle that without somehow embarrassing himself further. Probably. It's just… he greatly underestimated the effect of being trapped in a small space with a man that looked like he descended from a god would have on him. His cologne, or whatever Damon had on, didn't help matters either. It was a mix of cedar, Christmas trees, and pure sex.

Micah blamed the flush he could feel creeping up his neck on the fact the heat was blasting, and on absolutely nothing else.

"Are you okay?" Damon asked.

"Great," Micah assured tightly, trying his best not to breathe too deeply. He felt like Edward frickin' Cullen meeting Bella Swan for the first time, except instead of wanting to drink his blood, he wanted to slurp Damon's cum from his cock.

Jesus Christ, it was like the longer he sat there, the more brain cells he lost.

"Do you want a drink?" Damon asked, casually opening a latch to reveal a built-in cooler. Like it was no big deal whatsoever.

Micah laughed nervously. "I don't suppose you have any beer in there?" Anything to ease his nerves.

A wrinkle formed in Damon's brow, and Micah fought the urge to groan in annoyance. "I told you; I'm twenty-three. If you can't trust me, how am I supposed to trust you?"

It took a beat, but after a moment, Damon's frown lessened, and he sighed as if conceding Micah's point. "I don't have any beer, but there's champagne."

"Sounds great."

Pulling two glasses out of another hidden compartment (because why not?), Damon poured Micah a glass first and then one for himself.

Micah forced his brain to power off as he sipped on the bubbly drink. It tingled going down, and left his throat pleasantly warm, and Micah felt the tension in his shoulders slowly ease.

The silence that filled the car was slightly more comfortable with a drink in his hand, and Micah tried to relax as Damon fiddled with his phone beside him.

True to Damon's word, it wasn't more than half an hour later that the vehicle came to a stop, and the divider was rolling down. The huge, musclebound man behind the wheel, with his shaved head and impressive array of colorful tattoos crawling up his neck, was not exactly what Micah had pictured when Damon had told him he had a chauffeur named Geoffrey.

For some reason, he'd imagined a weathered, old man with a huge gray mustache and a top hat.

"We've arrived, boss."

Geoffrey didn't so much as glance at Micah, but he wasn't offended. He was too busy gaping at the high-rise the man had parked in front of.

"You have a standing reservation at The *fucking* Mark?"

Damon opened his door. "Is that a problem?"

If Micah didn't know better, he would say the man sounded amused.

Micah tried his best to compose himself. "Nope," he muttered to himself. "No problem at all." He downed what remained of his champagne before hurrying out of his own door, ignoring the fact that Damon was holding his open for him.

Micah did his best not to gawk at his surroundings as he followed Damon inside the hotel lobby. He was worried the pair of security officers at the front doors would approach – Micah felt more than a little out of place wearing a skirt in The Mark, for Christ's sake – but Damon must have been well-known there because neither of them glanced their way twice once they caught sight of him.

The pretty blonde behind the front desk perked up as soon as she spotted Damon. "Mr. Romano, sir!" she greeted brightly. Micah spotted a plated nametag attached to her blouse – "Jennifer" it read. "We weren't expecting you."

"Is that a problem?" he asked coolly.

"Of course not," she rushed to assure him, "you know we're always happy to serve you. Anything you want, I'll *personally* make sure you get it."

Micah couldn't help but notice how she smooshed her breasts together at that last part, accentuating how perky they were. He was struck by the thought that she made a more convincing prostitute than he did, and an amused snort escaped without his permission.

The noise attracted the girl's attention, and she finally seemed to notice Micah. Her mouth parted in surprise for a moment before a tiny frown formed. "I see you've brought a guest. All of our suites are booked, but I'm sure I can find him an open room somewhere."

"There's no need. He'll be staying with me."

The girl blinked. "I- are you sure?"

Damon didn't verbally respond, and Micah was standing behind him so he couldn't see the face he made, but it must have conveyed his irritation well enough because the poor girl flushed before handing him a key card. "Here you are. Please, don't hesitate to let us know if you need anything at all."

"I'll be ringing room service shortly," Damon informed her tersely before taking Micah by the elbow and dragging him towards what must have only been the elevators.

"You're… you're really rich, aren't you?" Micah asked as he examined the man's reflection staring back at him from the ridiculously shiny doors.

Damon didn't respond beyond an amused quirk of the lips, but Micah supposed he didn't have to. The fact that he had a standing reservation at The Mark spoke for itself.

The elevator released a pleasant chime before the doors opened.

The ride up to Damon's suite was uneventful, and in only a few minutes, Damon was swiping his key card to let them in.

Micah literally tripped over his own feet when he saw the room. "Woah."

He knew Damon was watching him to gauge his reaction, and that his eyes were probably bulging out of his head like a cartoon character as he stared, but he couldn't help it.

The living room part of the suite alone was bigger than *two* of Micah's apartments put together, and the vaulted ceiling and huge windows lining the back wall only made the room seem larger. It was obvious that it had been furnished with luxury in mind. An opulent white rug covered dark hardwood floors and was surrounded by a cream leather couch and two matching oversized chairs. Off to the right, Micah spotted a kitchenette with granite countertops that was filled to the brim with stainless steel appliances.

So this was how the other half lived.

Micah was broken out of his stupor when Damon continued on into the suite. Toeing off his shoes (he wasn't about to ruin the white rug), he quickly followed.

"The bathroom's down this way," Damon said, leading Micah to one of two doors on the left side of the suite. The other must have been the bedroom. "Why don't you clean yourself up? I'll order dinner in the meanwhile."

On one hand, Micah could choose to be offended that the man thought he was in need of a shower. On the other hand, he wasn't about to turn down the chance to check out whatever kind of bathroom a place like this came equipped with.

"Okay," he agreed easily enough, locking the door behind himself before examining his surroundings. Like the living area of the suite, the bathroom was decorated in monochrome. Light fixtures hung from the ceiling and fanciful sinks sat suspended atop the double vanity.

Micah wasted no time checking out the shower. The showerhead had *sixteen* settings! He was tempted to check each and every one out. In the end, though, he couldn't ignore the jacuzzi tub in the corner.

After turning on the water as hot as he could stand, he stripped off his clothes and sunk into the tub. The groan he let out when the jets shot scorching hot water at his stiff muscles was practically obscene.

Good thing there was no one around to hear it.

Micah allowed himself to become fully immersed in the experience, letting conscious thoughts taper off (for once) as the water massaged him.

He wasn't sure how long he was in the tub, but his fingertips were practically prunes when a knock on the door brought him back to reality. "Everything alright in there?"

"Fine!" Micah called. "I'll be out in a minute!"

Damon was about the only thing that could pull him away from this tub.

Pulling the plug, Micah made himself stand as the water drained, grabbing one of the fluffy towels on display on a metal rack near the tub. After drying himself off, he used the same towel to wipe the condensation off the mirror that had built up from the steam.

He was confronted with his reflection.

Cheeks pink from the heat and dirty blond hair damp from his impromptu bath, he looked a mess. Objectively, Micah knew he was attractive enough, with a smattering of freckles across his nose and wide eyes that weren't quite green and weren't quite hazel either. A particularly memorable one-night stand had once called them a "kaleidoscope of mesmerizing color".

Still, his boyish charm didn't quite match up to the magnetism of the man on the other side of the door. Not that it mattered. This wasn't some lurid rendezvous.

So what was he doing, examining himself in the mirror like some nervous virgin?

Annoyed with himself, Micah turned away from his reflection. There was a fluffy-looking robe hanging near the door, but it'd probably be weird to wear it, so he sighed before forcing himself to pull back on his own clothes – well, clothes the department had picked for him, anyway. The skirt was even harder to put on when his legs were still wet, but somehow, he managed.

He glanced once more in the mirror to make sure everything was in place before finally exiting the bathroom. He immediately spotted Damon in the kitchenette. Every inch of the countertop had been covered in various food containers. There was also a charcuterie board filled with meats and cheeses, a bottle of unopened wine, and particularly eye-catching: an entire tray of chocolate-covered strawberries.

Micah blinked, hesitantly making his way over to the man and frankly ludicrous amount of food. "What? Did you buy the entire menu?"

Damon frowned, but Micah didn't think he was imagining the hint of red to his cheeks when he answered, "I wasn't sure what you liked."

"I'm not picky," Micah assured, code for: "I'm poor and I'll eat anything."

Damon handed him a plate. "Fill it up and sit."

Micah didn't need to be told twice. Examining the contents of the containers, he confirmed his suspicions: Damon really *had* ordered a little bit of everything. There was orange chicken on a bed of rice, some sort of pasta with colorful vegetables, spring rolls, even pizza.

Micah took a little of it all – he'd been standing on that sidewalk for hours before Damon had shown up, okay? – and topped it off with a generous helping of chocolate-covered strawberries.

Pulling out one of the upholstered stools surrounding the kitchen island, Micah dug in. He started with the orange chicken and quickly had to swallow down a moan of satisfaction. It was the perfect mix of sweet and savory, with a little kick of spice at the end. "This is amazing," Micah praised, forking another piece of chicken into his mouth before following that up with a spring roll. He couldn't ignore the strawberries any longer after that, picking up the largest one and popping it into his mouth. Sweetness burst on his tongue, pairing perfectly with the bitter chocolate. Juice threatened to dribble down his chin, and he quickly licked his lips.

When he finally managed to tear his gaze away from his food, Micah saw that Damon was openly staring and was promptly mortified. "Sorry. I'm being a slob."

"Don't be sorry," Damon rebuffed throatily, and Micah couldn't help but notice that his eyes seemed to be stuck on his sticky lips. "I bought it for you."

Micah willed away a blush. "Well, you have to eat something, too," he insisted. "I'll feel weird otherwise."

Damon frowned, but obliged. Micah watched as the man took a plate and filled it with some pasta and various meats and cheeses before pulling out a stool by Micah.

Micah waited until he had forked a bite of pasta into his mouth before asking, "So… finances, huh?"

Damon didn't choke or show the same momentary unease he had in the car when Micah had inquired about his job. "I dabble in shipping operations, but work in real estate mostly," he explained plainly instead. "I own hundreds of buildings in New York, mostly in Queens and Manhattan – some commercial and some residential."

"*Hundreds* of buildings?" Micah repeated incredulously. "As in *plural*?" Forget real estate mogul, this guy was a tycoon.

Damon waved a hand. "It's not nearly as impressive when you consider the fact I inherited most of them when my parents died."

And just like that, Micah felt bad for prying. He winced. "Oh, wow. That... that sucks," Micah said honestly. He would know. Not about inheriting hundreds of millions worth of property, obviously, but losing a parent... *that* he could relate to.

"It does," Damon agreed solemnly, before clearing his throat. "Anyway, as you can imagine, conducting business takes up the majority of my time. Adella wasn't kidding when she told you it doesn't leave time in my life for much else." He paused. "What about you?" he asked. "I mean, besides..." he hurriedly attempted to backtrack.

It was nice to know Micah wasn't the only one who could stick his foot in his mouth on occasion. "It's not the Lord's work, I know, but old men seem to enjoy my talents well enough, so..." Micah shrugged.

"I didn't mean-" Damon tried again sounding flustered – or maybe frustrated – and Micah felt a bit bad for teasing him.

"I know, it's okay," Micah assured, throwing the man a bone. "Honestly, when I was a kid... I wanted to be a cop."

It was a bit too close to the truth, and maybe Micah shouldn't have said it, but it was out before he could second-guess himself.

Damon raised his eyebrows, a complicated expression overtaking his face.

"What's that look for?" Micah demanded, slightly offended. He *was* on the force, after all – a criminal detective, as a matter of fact. "Not *all* cops are power-hungry assholes, you know. Sure, it's a position of authority, so maybe the profession attracts more jackasses than most, but overall, it's just like any other job. There's bound to be pricks in any population. In my experience, most people on the force just want to help."

Damon shook his head, seemingly in disbelief. "I can't imagine many people in your profession share the same sentiments."

Micah rolled his eyes. "Know many hookers, do you?" He pouted. "And here I thought I was your first."

Damon snorted, a touch of a grin pulling at his mouth. "I don't know," he teased, "even if you're right, and not all cops are pigs, Officer Peregrine isn't exactly intimidating."

Micah choked on a bit of rice he'd scooped into his mouth; he'd honestly forgotten he'd given Damon a fake name. "Okay, confession time," he said after he managed to swallow his food. "Peregrine Davis isn't my real name. It's just an alias – a stage name, if you will – for when I'm working."

Judging by the man's soft smile, he wasn't exactly surprised. Micah had a feeling that not many people had the honor of seeing such a gentle expression on Damon's face. "I figured it might be," the man admitted quietly.

Micah's insides were *not* swooping like a preteen girl's whose grade school crush had just smiled at her for the first time. "Well, aren't you going to ask me my real name?" Micah pressed.

"What's your real name?" Damon asked, somehow sounding like he was humoring Micah and was desperate to know the answer at the same time. It must have been the mix of his sultry tone with the intense gleam in his eye.

Should Micah tell him? Just his first name?

It was unlikely Damon could connect it back to his real life, but it seemed like a stupid risk regardless. Still, for some reason, Micah *really* wanted Damon to know. (It had nothing at all to do with wanting to hear what it sounded like rolling off his tongue in that smooth baritone.)

Micah toyed with his bottom lip, undecided. "Well, I can't just go around giving my name out for free," he said, taking the coy route in an effort to avoid having to make a decision.

A frown was suddenly marring Damon's handsome face, and he leaned backward. (Micah hadn't even noticed how close the other man had gotten to him until just then.) "How much?" he asked crisply, pulling out a leather wallet from his back pocket.

To Micah's credit, he was only baffled for about a second before recovering. "What?" he squawked. (*Sort of* recovering.) "No, you pompous asshat. I mean, you have to share something about yourself first. You know, like, an information swap."

Damon blinked, clearly taken off guard. (Exactly how much money had he been willing to pay for Micah's name?) After a moment, however, he cautiously put his wallet away. Then… "My favorite color is black."

Micah laughed. It quickly faded away, however, when Damon didn't join in. "Wait. You're serious?"

Damon's frown deepened. "What's wrong with black?" he demanded.

"Nothing, but that's not what I meant. You have to be real and tell me something no one else knows about you. Not something so basic as your favorite color."

Damon's stare was intense, and it was no easy task keeping eye contact. After a few tense moments, the man's brow furrowed in consternation, but to Micah's surprise, he didn't back down. "I wanted to be a baker when I was a kid," he finally said, words somewhat stilted. "Before all of this fell into my lap."

It was probably a stupid question, but… "Can't you just quit? If you still want that, I mean."

Damon shook his head. "It's not that simple. I enjoy what I do for the most part, and like I told you, I'm good at it. And more importantly," he paused, hesitating for a moment before continuing more softly, "more importantly, my sisters and what remains of my family – *this* is what they need me to be."

It was painstakingly honest, and Micah couldn't help but gravitate towards it – towards Damon himself. Almost without his permission, one of his hands reached across the countertop and placed itself on top of Damon's. "My name's Micah."

"Micah." His name rolled off Damon's tongue like it belonged there, and the sound of it went straight to his cock. Overcome with the sudden (sudden? *ha!*) desire to kiss him, and refusing to second-guess the urge, Micah leaned in and pressed his mouth to Damon's.

He was only able to enjoy the sensation of a warm mouth mashed against his for a handful of seconds, however, before he realized the other man had stiffened under his ministrations.

In alarm? Disgust? Had Micah totally misread the situation? Was Damon even attracted to other men?

Fuck.

Convinced he'd screwed up royally, Micah jerked backward. "I'm so sorry-"

He needn't have bothered attempting to apologize, though, because the word "sorry" hadn't even fully left his lips before large hands were gripping his face and Damon was lunging forward, his mouth crashing back onto his.

Much like his personality, Damon's tongue was a force of nature, and Micah had no choice but to *take it* as the man pushed in and lapped at the roof of his mouth and sucked on his tongue like he wanted nothing more than to devour him.

Not that Micah was complaining.

Damon tasted a bit like the creamy pasta he'd been eating and a bit like mint, but under that was the uniquely salty flavor of *man*, and Micah couldn't get enough of it. He gave as good as he got, attempting to battle Damon for control of the kiss even knowing full well he didn't have a shot in hell of succeeding.

A little thrill shot through him when he took Damon's bottom lip between his teeth and the man moaned aloud.

He didn't have much time to bask in victory, however, before Damon was suddenly clearing the countertop with one wild swipe of his arm, plastic containers and shiny metal platters clattering to the floor with a loud *crash*. The next second, he was gripping Micah under his bare thighs and lifting him out of the stool he still half-sat atop of and depositing him on the kitchen counter.

Damon invaded Micah's space, one hand reaching up to hold the back of his neck in place as he absolutely destroyed Micah's mouth with his tongue, the other clenching so tightly at his right hip that Micah *knew* there would be bruises come morning.

He could feel the outline of a hard dick pressed up against his own, and *holy fuck*, Micah was going to come in his pants like an inexperienced teenager.

Fuck if he wasn't going to bring the other man right along with him though.

At some point, he'd wound up clutching at the collar of Damon's dress shirt, and desperate to get his hands on the man's hot cock – to see if he could fit his fingers all the way around him or not, to swipe his thumb across the slit of a mushroom head – Micah began tugging sloppily at the man's belt.

The entire while, Damon never stopped *mouthing* at him, lips moving on from Micah's mouth to suck at his jawline, slowly making his way to his ear, harsh stubble rubbing against Micah's neck.

Micah might have been embarrassed by the needy noises he was making in the back of his throat if he could bring himself to care.

But all he cared about was getting to Damon's cock.

He managed to unbuckle the man's belt and unzip his fly, but it wasn't until Micah was blatantly shoving his hand down the man's pants that he realized something was wrong.

"Wait."

Lost in a haze of lust, Micah didn't immediately hear Damon. In fact, the words didn't register at all until his fingers were brushing against satin boxers and an ironclad hand was suddenly wrapped around his wrist that Micah realized the man was talking. "Micah, stop!"

Damon's harsh tone brought him careening back to reality. "What... what is it?" Micah asked, breathless and confused.

Damon swallowed hard. "I... we can't do this."

Micah nearly laughed. The man had just attempted to *swallow* his tongue, he'd been practically *chewing* on his face. Surely he wasn't serious.

There's no way Micah could have misinterpreted the situation so horribly.

But Damon looked deathly serious – and worse, regretful.

Micah buried his face in his hands. "Oh God." He was a fucking idiot.

"I shouldn't have-"

Not giving Damon a chance to finish his sentence, Micah pushed the man backward out of his space and jumped down from the counter. "You shouldn't have what?" he snapped. "Got intimately acquainted with the taste of my mouth? Pressed your huge cock up against my crotch without expecting a whore like me to actually want a piece of it?"

Made me think someone like you could possibly want someone like me?

"I'm sorry."

"Save it," Micah bit out, not sure if he was more irritated with the man for leading him on or at himself for daring to believe it. "Just... stop talking." He shouldered past Damon, stinging with rejection yet impossibly hard in the fucking skirt he was still wearing.

Jesus Christ.

He needed to get the fuck out of there before he somehow managed to embarrass himself further.

"What are you doing?" Damon asked, but he didn't follow Micah as he marched across the room, obviously sensing he needed space.

"I'm leaving," he announced plainly, jamming his feet into his shoes.

That got the man moving. "What? *No.* Hey, wait-!"

And that was Micah's cue to dart out the door. He booked it down the hallway. There was a bellhop by the elevator who hadn't been there when he and Damon had arrived, and the college-aged kid watched with wide eyes as Micah smashed the elevator's "down" button over and over again.

Thank whatever deity was watching over him, the elevator was already on their floor and opened pretty much immediately.

"Hold the elevator!" he heard Damon shout somewhere down the hall, but the doors were already closing, and the last glimpse Micah got before they shut completely was a frazzled-looking bellboy, looking like he wanted nothing more than to join Micah in the elevator.

(Micah hardly blamed him. Damon sounded *pissed.*)

He was sure it took longer to descend than it had to take the elevator up to Damon's suite. When it finally stopped at the lobby, the elevator released a pleasant chime as the doors opened, and

Micah had to fight the urge to make a scene by sprinting across the grandiose room.

He settled for speed-walking towards the glass doors that signaled freedom from the fucked situation he found himself in. He noticed one of the security guards pressing a hand against his earpiece, like he was listening intently to instructions, before his eyes swiveled and suddenly met Micah's. They widened. "Hey, you-!" he started, attempting to reach for him.

Micah elbowed him hard in the gut and bobbed under his arm before darting outside. He heard the man's partner yell after him, but Micah ignored him, hotfooting it down as many blocks as he dared – bulldozing past a few unlucky people still roaming New York City's sidewalks at ass o'clock at night – before finally daring to duck into an alleyway.

At some point, he'd lost a shoe.

It was a long while before his heart stopped pounding and he had the wherewithal to hail a cab.

He called Tessa as soon as he got home to his studio apartment (which looked especially pathetic after spending time at The Mark) and told her everything.

She was quiet for a long while. "Are you seriously telling me that you somehow lost your shoe during this dramatic escape?"

Micah fought the urge to groan. "*That's* what you took from that?"

"Sorry, it's just that for a while, I was convinced we were immersed in some weird, gay-as-fuck version of Pretty Woman. Now, I'm leaning towards Cinderella, except instead of a prince, you've managed to entangle yourself with some hot billionaire who would rather feed your little string bean body than fuck you."

Micah sighed. "You're the worst, you know that, right?" But he couldn't deny that a smile was pulling at the corner of his mouth for the first time since disaster had struck at Damon's suite.

"Would I take pleasure in your pain?"

"Yes, yes you would," Micah accused.

"Well, on the bright side, you know his full name now. If you decide you want to look him up after our investigation is over, well…"

Micah snorted. "I think Damon made it pretty clear he's not interested in any sort of relationship with me that's not motivated by pity."

He'd *humiliated* Micah.

Which begged the question… why couldn't he squelch the tiny bit of hope buried deep in his gut that he'd run into the man again during his next stakeout?

CHAPTER THREE

"Suck that succulent, little lip back into your mouth and stop pouting."

Micah shot Tessa an unimpressed look from where she hovered over his shoulder, frizzy wisps of red hair escaping the ponytail she'd forced it into despite her efforts to tame her wild mane. "I'm not pouting," he protested before allowing his gaze to drift back to the computer screen he was sat in front of.

"Oh good. Because that would be pretty ridiculous… you know, considering our department was just credited with catching the Hooker Hunter, the serial killer who's been terrorizing New York City prostitutes for the past six months."

A guest of a rundown motel in Queens had called 9-1-1 in the early hours of Thursday morning, when she'd heard screams and what sounded like a struggle in the room next to hers. When police had arrived to investigate, they'd discovered a man assaulting a young, male prostitute, who'd been stripped and bound naked to a chair.

"Yeah, but *we* didn't do anything. Jensen's the one who got a confession from this Jacob Normandy guy – who I'm still not convinced is our perp, by the way."

Normandy's victim had been a prostitute, yes, and he'd been tied up – a criteria they'd been using to identify victims of the Hooker Hunter since they'd all been discovered with rope burn around their wrists and ankles.

But only the hands of Normandy's victim had been bound. And he'd been raped.

Whilst the bodies of the other victims had all been found naked, none had shown signs of sexual assault – though Micah conceded that kind of evidence wasn't always obvious.

But the man – Jacob Normandy, a thirty-six-year-old construction worker from Brooklyn with a receding hairline and squinty blue eyes – had readily confessed that he'd been responsible for all seven of the slayings they'd publicly accredited to the Hooker Hunter.

"I mean, you saw the tape. Normandy was a little *too* happy confessing all those murders to Jensen, don't you think?" He'd taken sick enjoyment in relaying how he'd kept his victims alive for days, tied up and gagged as he tortured them, before finally strangling them to death.

"You've always been good at behavioral analysis, but you know some killers just *like* the spotlight; they enjoy taking credit for their gross crimes."

Micah frowned. "I guess. Though I still don't understand why Jensen got to be the one to interview him. We've worked just as hard as him on this case. It's not like *he* had to go out and wear a skirt in subzero temperatures."

Yusuf Jensen had been a detective only half a decade longer than Micah, but somehow he had a foot in the door of every department of the precinct. He was charismatic, and not entirely unfortunate-looking, but Micah didn't understand his popularity with the higher-ups. The man thought he knew everything, and that his way of looking at a case was the only way. He never listened to anyone else's ideas, let alone Micah's, who he tended to boss around like he thought he was some sort of secretary instead of an equal.

Although, *technically*, Jensen was considered a first-grade detective, while Micah, as the newest *and* youngest member of their department, was merely a third-grade detective.

Regardless, Micah despised him.

At least they didn't have to work together closely that often.

Jensen always assigned himself the interesting cases. Micah, on the other hand, was often given the safe, boring ones – petty crime, mostly. He floated between property damage claims, narcotics cases, and the occasional burglary. Going undercover in a bid to lure out the Hooker Hunter was the most excitement he'd seen since officially joining the force earlier in the year.

Tessa frowned. "Is that what's had you so grumpy the past few days?" she demanded. "Come on, Micah, you know what's important is that-"

"-is that the perp's been caught and will face justice for the crimes he's committed, and the families of the victims will get some closure. Yes, I know. I would never imply otherwise."

Even if Jensen *was* an asshole whose oversized ego hardly needed any more stroking. Even if it meant his brief stint working an actually *interesting* case was over. Even if it meant he never got to go undercover again and thus had no reason to run into-"

"Then what's got your panties in such a twist? You've been frowny since yesterday when the news broke. I thought you'd be happy you didn't have to squeeze into another skimpy outfit. I mean, it's supposed to *snow* tonight and... wait."

Micah glanced up from the computer, just in time to see a grin slowly form on Tessa's freckled face.

Oh. *Oh no.* Micah's stomach clenched.

"It's because you don't have an excuse to see Damon again, isn't it?"

A beat of silence.

"What? No!"

Judging by the fact that Tessa's grin only grew wilier at his response, Micah didn't think he'd been overly convincing. (For fuck's sake, if he ever wanted to get another undercover gig again, he'd really have to work on his lying.)

Unable to contain her laughter when Micah groaned and buried his head in his hands, Tessa cackled freely. "Shut up," he hissed, glancing around surreptitiously and hoping none of their co-workers were paying them any attention.

"Sorry, sorry," she apologized, but she didn't look it at all as she wiped tears of mirth from her eyes. "Though I hardly understand your angst. I mean, you know his name, Micah, and you're on the police force. You have a whole database of information available to you. It's easy enough to find out where he lives if you really want another chance at getting in his pants."

"Not only would that be a *highly* illegal use of police resources – not to mention, creepy as hell – you're forgetting one teensy, tiny problem, Tessa."

"Oh, yeah? And what nonexistent problem has your imagination managed to conjure?"

Micah glowered. "How about the fact that he made it *extremely* clear he's not interested?"

Tessa snorted. "Yeah, that's why he attempted to debauch you on top of his kitchen counter."

"He was caught up in the moment, but trust me, he snapped out of it quickly enough when he remembered I suck cock for money. Then he couldn't get away from me fast enough." Micah's face didn't redden at all when he spit the word "cock" out at his friend. Nope. Not one bit.

"Okay, first of all, you balls-to-the-walls ran away from him, not the other way around, and secondly, you don't *actually* suck cock for money – just for your own pleasure," she pointed out reasonably.

Micah winced. It sounded even worse coming from her mouth. "Can we stop saying the word 'cock' in the workplace?"

"You said it first."

Micah glared. "My point is, why would I want to get involved with someone who plays fast and loose with people's emotions like that? I mean, if I truly was a prostitute, he would have really hurt my feelings."

Who was Micah kidding? Damon *had* hurt his feelings.

"Have you considered the reason for his cold feet might *not* have been because he was disgusted with you? Like you said, he thinks you're a prostitute. Maybe he was worried he was pressuring you, or concerned you thought of him as just another customer or something."

Micah frowned. "Even if that *was* true – which I highly doubt – what am I supposed to do? Randomly show up at his place – which, probably some ludicrous mansion, by the way – and tell him I'm not actually a prostitute, just an undercover detective pretending to be one? And by the way, do you maybe want to bang? Or at least take me out on a date? I mean, it sounds ridiculous."

"Sounds like a kickass meet cute, actually. I mean, Jasper and I met at a Starbucks. Totally boring."

"Tell that to Jasper's testicles, pretty sure you nearly burned the skin right off them when you dumped your coffee on his crotch if his rendition of your first meeting is to be believed."

"It was an accident!" Tessa protested. "And besides," she said, gesturing at her protruding belly, "clearly there was no lasting damage."

Micah snorted. Clearly not – considering the woman was over seven months pregnant, *with twins*, nonetheless. She'd been pregnant for nearly as long as Micah had been a member of the precinct, one of the reasons he and she were often partnered together on the same boring cases. Micah couldn't deny that he loved working with her, though. (Just loved *her*, actually.)

Even if he couldn't help but wonder what it said about his social life that his best friend was his thirty-year-old pregnant co-worker.

Tessa pressed her lips together. "Well, even if you're not going to pursue this guy – which, by the way, I think is a mistake – there's no reason you can't find someone else to fill the void. You know, nearly everyone is heading to Club Trinity tonight after work – to celebrate the high-profile arrest. You should come too."

Micah frowned. "Why are *you* going to a club?" he asked, pointedly eyeing her distended stomach.

Tessa rolled her eyes. "I'm pregnant, not handicapped," she said. "Besides, I've heard good things about this place. Apparently they serve huge-ass pickles with their bloody marys." *Of course, the pregnant lady was focused on the size of the place's pickles.* "Plus, it's not nearly as expensive to get into as it's fancier counterparts since it's still new. I heard whoever is responsible for the place *also* owns The Seven Deadly Sins, so you know it'll be an experience."

The Seven Deadly Sins were possibly the seven most exclusive clubs in New York. Scattered across the five boroughs, each one was named after a deadly sin – though none were so popular as Lust, a strip club in Manhattan that catered to rich, eccentric clientele.

Micah sighed. "I don't know, Tessa."

"Come on. I'll buy you a shot – or three. That way I can get drunk vicariously through you."

Micah pressed his lips together. Alcohol *did* sound pretty good right then to be honest. "Will Jensen be there?" he asked.

"Well, he *is* the man of the hour. But Club Trinity is a big place – two floors, even, I heard. We can say a quick congratulations and disappear into the crowd."

"I'll think about it," Micah finally agreed, if only to get Tessa off his case. He didn't think she'd put up too much of a stink if he decided to back out later. "Now are you planning on actually letting me get any work done today or what?"

She peeked past his shoulder at the computer screen. "Oh yes, damaged mailboxes await no one."

Micah made sure to give her the middle finger as she sauntered away – not that she had far to go. Her cubicle was across from his.

For the next handful of hours, Micah slogged through the files on his desk. The work mostly involved watching grainy surveillance video and running license plate numbers through their recognition system.

When his bladder felt close to bursting from the coffee he'd inhaled – if one still considered it coffee with five sugar packets and three creamers mixed in – he finally got up to use the restroom. He quickly did his business and washed his hands.

Figuring it was time for a break, he intended to find Tessa and tag along with her to her standing lunch date with her husband at the local sandwich shop. Yes, he was that pathetic.

Tessa wasn't at her desk when he returned, however. Figuring she'd gone to the lobby to gab with Dolores – the four-foot, ten-inch tall, sixty-something-year-old who ran the front of the building and who had bigger, brassier knobs than three-quarters of the force – Micah headed in that direction.

He immediately spotted her through the huge glass windows that separated the lobby from the back of the building, where their cubicles and the various offices of their superiors were located. (Plus, the precinct's interrogation rooms and holding cells.) Tessa's red hair was unmistakable even through the blurred glass, and Micah was about to join her where she stood with Dolores and someone else he couldn't recognize through the bulletproof glass – probably a civilian, coming in to report something or another – when-

"I don't give a shit if that information isn't available to the public. You're going to tell me the name of the prostitute that fucking scumbag rapist attacked right the fuck now."

-when a voice, raised and gravelly with obvious upset, but painstakingly *familiar* – had him freezing in place.

Damon?!

What the-

Panicking, Micah immediately ducked behind one of the oversized plants spaced throughout the hallway. (Pretty stupid considering there was no way Damon could see him through the blurred glass – at least, not well enough to make out his identity – but Micah's head was spinning, okay? Cut him some slack.)

What was Damon doing here?

It was easy enough to figure out when his whirling thoughts and galloping heart both settled enough for Micah to register the man's words.

Damon must have heard the news about the Hooker Hunter – not only that he'd been captured, but that he'd been caught in the midst of torturing another victim – a prostitute, like all the rest. In a shady motel in Queens. Not unlike the one Micah had been parked in front of a handful of days ago.

The man was *worried* about him.

Micah didn't know whether to melt in a puddle at the thought of the man being so worked up that he'd marched down to the precinct responsible for the serial killer's arrest or bang his head against the nearest object.

"I've already told you," the cool, crisp voice of Dolores cut through the relative quiet of the hallway, "the young man's identity is considered classified. Not only would it be a horrible breach of privacy if I were to reveal it to you, it is *illegal.* I don't care how

many cuss words you spew at me, the answer is, and will remain, *no*."

A frustrated noise made its way up Damon's throat. Almost like a growl. "Surely you can at least tell me what hospital he's being kept at?"

"I can do no such thing."

A fist hit the top of Dolores's desk so harshly that from where he hid in the hallway, Micah could hear the dish of butterscotch candies she kept there rattle. "How much?" he demanded forcefully.

"What?"

"How *much* to tell me the victim's name?"

Micah could only imagine the amount of cash Damon flashed the woman right then. (Though judging by Dolores's offended gasp, it was quite the lump sum.)

"Excuse me?" Dolores cried. Micah winced at the sound of her shrill voice, shocked no one had intervened yet considering the commotion she and Damon were making. "Might I remind you that you're at a police station? Bribery is a crime punishable by law."

Damon snorted. "Like you pigs aren't corrupted from the top down," he snarled. There was a shocking amount of venom in his voice, and Micah couldn't help but feel stung by it all things considered.

"If you don't leave right this second, you will be escorted out – or thrown in a cell to cool off. *Your choice.*"

Damon didn't immediately respond, and Micah didn't know the man well enough to know whether he would continue his belligerence and push Dolores to make good on her threat or simply turn tail and walk out.

He was surprised when instead of doing either, the man slumped against the woman's desk, his tone desperate as he implored her. "Please, just… can you tell me if his name was Micah?"

Micah's heart stuck somewhere in his throat. Damon sounded *miserable*. Not just guilty for chasing him off. His voice was filled to the brim with some other emotion Micah didn't dare name after the man's clear rejection of him only a handful of days ago.

He wanted to go out there and assure Damon he was fine, of course, he did – he wasn't a monster. But his feet felt glued to the floor, and it was all he could do to internally beg Tessa to *do something*. It wasn't like she didn't know exactly who Damon was.

Somehow, Tessa seemed to pick up on his telepathic pleading because that was enough to get her to (*finally!*) step in. "Like Mrs. Fuller has already reiterated to you, we absolutely can*not* reveal any identifying information about the Hooker Hunter's latest victim."

Come on, Tessa, please…

"However-"

Thank God.

"-I *can* share with you that his name was *not* Micah. He was a young African American whose family has already been notified of what's transpired and are with him at the hospital. Does that sound like whoever you're worried about?"

A long moment of silence, and then… "No, it doesn't." But Damon didn't sound relieved like Micah thought he might have. His voice was still stressed. "Thank you," he added begrudgingly, though he didn't sound nearly as grateful as he ought to have in Micah's opinion, considering he'd just inadvertently called Tessa a corrupt pig.

"So you *are* in possession of some manners, after all." Clearly Dolores hadn't forgiven him for the slight, nor the insult to her moral compass by attempting to bribe her. "If that is all, I think it's time you left – before you cause even more of a scene."

But when Micah dared to peek around the plant he was hiding behind, it was clear he hadn't left. In fact, Damon hadn't seemed to have acknowledged Dolores at all. His attention remained focused on Tessa as he seemed to identify her as the more useful of the two. Or, at least, more sympathetic to his plight.

"How long do you have to wait to report a missing person?" he asked.

Micah felt his stomach drop.

Seriously?

It took a second for Tessa to answer, and although she sounded casual enough when she did, Micah knew she was choosing her words carefully. "Despite what you might have heard on tv, there is no obligatory waiting period. How long has this person been missing?"

Damon huffed, and though he couldn't see clearly through the glass, Micah thought he saw him running an agitated hand down his face. "Three days?"

"You don't sound very sure about that."

A pause. Then, more forcefully: "Three. Days."

"And has this individual been answering their phone?"

Another pause. "I'm not sure."

Tessa must have been making some sort of dubious expression because after a moment, Damon reluctantly added, "I don't have his number."

"Uh-huh. And have you been by his place of residence?"

"I... don't know where he lives."

"Is this some sort of joke?" Dolores interrupted, apparently unable to hold her tongue any longer.

"It's this precinct that's a joke," Damon spat, whipping around to face the old woman and abandoning the strained politeness with which he spoke to Tessa. "You are *utterly useless*. Every single one of you."

"Hey, now-!"

"I'll find him on my own, and when I do, you had better hope my... friend," he decided on after a moment, "is in one piece. Because if he's not, I promise you, this worthless precinct will pay for every little scratch on him, no matter how miniscule, with its own blood."

Micah hadn't realized he was holding his breath until Damon finally turned and stalked out of the building.

Had the past ten minutes really just happened?

Replaying Damon's parting words in his mind, Micah felt his chest tighten with something akin to panic. Had the man really just *threatened* a building full of cops? Micah's *co-workers*?

Micah wasn't a terribly common name. What if Dolores somehow connected the dots between Micah's stint as an undercover prostitute and Damon's visit to the precinct? What if she told Jensen? Worse, what if she told the captain?

Micah's stomach churned.

Feeling the distinct urge to puke, he wasted no time heading back to the toilets. He tried to empty his discontented stomach, but it was empty except for the coffee so nothing came up.

When he eventually gave up, he stared at his pale face in the mirror, pressing the back of his hands to his clammy cheeks before splashing water onto his shell-shocked expression and drying his skin with brown, crispy paper towels until it felt raw. He took a deep breath in through his nose. "Get it together," he ordered his reflection sternly.

No one would put the pieces together. (Probably.) Only Tessa knew the significance of Damon coming to the station, and she would never say anything to anyone.

Speaking of Tessa...

Micah nearly plowed down the pregnant woman when he stepped out of the bathroom. "Sorry, I'm sorry! Are you okay?"

"I'm fine," she assured. "Though I can't say the same for your growly boyfriend." Judging by the shrewd look in her eyes, she somehow knew that *he* knew about Damon's visit. "I've never seen someone get Dolores in such a tizzy before." (That was saying something considering she dealt with more than her fair share of violent criminals.) "Though I think she was equally as turned on as she was annoyed. I know *I* was."

Micah groaned. "Do you say these things just to torture me?" he demanded. Despite Tessa's good humor, he still felt fairly sick about the situation.

Tessa's smile faded, but her eyes remained soft, and her voice assuring as she gazed at him, almost like she thought he was some scared, cornered animal. Micah hated it.

"Are you okay, honey?"

Micah swallowed hard. He didn't bother answering in the affirmative or negative. Instead-

"So... about those shots?"

CHAPTER FOUR

"Ugh. Does she drink ketchup straight from the bottle at home?"

Micah had knocked back two kamikazes, a lemon drop, and was halfway through a vodka soda. His fingers were tingling, and he felt pleasantly floaty.

No amount of liquor, however, could temper his disgust at watching Tessa sip on her *virgin* bloody mary.

Jasper laughed, choking on his drink when Tessa elbowed him in the gut. She flicked Micah on the nose. "Plebeians. It's hardly my fault your taste buds are so underdeveloped."

Jasper shot Micah a look over Tessa's head. It was quite easy considering Tessa barely hit five foot and Jasper easily surpassed six feet. While Tessa was short and curvy, her husband was tall and lanky with narrow shoulders and shoulder-length brown hair he usually kept in a man bun. Tessa teased him endlessly about it.

"If developing my taste buds means I'll suddenly acquire a fondness for pineapple on pizza, I'll pass."

Tessa gasped, mock offended. "Take that back! Pineapple on pizza is the perfect mix of sweet and savory."

"It's an abomination against nature is what it is."

In unison, Tessa and Jasper both turned towards Micah, clearly expecting him to settle what was obviously a regular argument for them. "Um… it's okay, I guess?"

They both looked disgusted by his answer, and Micah tuned them out as the conversation turned towards the many strange cravings Tessa had suffered since falling pregnant, Jasper giving her shit about the time she'd apparently insisted on topping her ice cream with Brussels sprouts.

(*"I was trying to be healthy!"*)

As someone who had seen the woman dip baby carrots into the jar of peanut butter she kept stashed at her work desk more than once, Micah didn't need to know more.

Still, he couldn't help the twinge of envy as he observed the two of them together. A bark of laughter escaped Tessa at something Jasper said, and a moment later he was tucking a piece of wayward hair behind her ear, gazing at her like she was the most precious thing in the world despite the unladylike chortle and the bit of tomato juice she'd just snorted out of her nose. She playfully bit his finger, sucking on the tip for a moment before letting it go, and feeling like a voyeur, Micah turned to stare at his empty-except-for-the-ice drink, poking at the cubes with his straw.

They were so in love with each other it was borderline sickening.

"Hey, Micah, want to dance with us?"

Micah didn't realize he had zoned out until Tessa addressed him. She and Jasper had both stood from the booth they'd snatched, apparently intent on joining the dozens of other people shimmying on the dance floor of Club Trinity.

It was embarrassing enough third wheeling with the couple without having to picture himself gyrating between the two of them. "Uh, I'll pass."

A bit of the melancholy he was feeling must have slipped into his voice because Tessa frowned at him. "You sure?"

"Yup," Micah insisted, making sure to insert more pep into his voice. "Jasper can figure out how to grind against that giant belly all by himself."

Tessa laughed as she flipped him off, promptly dragging Jasper out onto the dance floor. Micah didn't recognize the music playing, but the bass was loud and fast-paced, with some rap flung in here and there – perfect for rubbing yourself up against the nearest warm body.

Except Micah didn't feel like dancing.

As soon as Tessa and Jasper disappeared into the crowd, Micah sighed, resting his face against the table. It was pleasantly cool against his flushed cheek, so he was willing to overlook the fact it was a bit sticky – a sign that he'd perhaps consumed too much alcohol.

He couldn't help but long for a relationship like the one Tessa and Jasper had – someone to share his shitty apartment with and snuggle up with on the cold mornings, putting up with the fact he regularly snoozed his alarm three times before dragging himself out of bed.

Just domestic shit like that.

Micah's mind dredged up handsome features – thick eyebrows, a stubbled jaw, dark hair – paired with a commanding baritone and a sharp sense of humor.

Yup, he'd *definitely* drank too much alcohol.

Micah was pulled from his half-horny/half-morose thoughts by a hand suddenly coming down on his shoulder.

He tensed, sitting up to see a man looming over the booth. He was nice enough to look at, if a bit forgettable, with tidy brown hair and heavy square-frame glasses perched on his nose. He wore a generic white t-shirt paired with straight jeans. The most striking thing about him was the fact he was sporting a worn maroon cardigan over his shirt – hardly on trend for a Friday night out at a club.

"Can I help you?" Micah asked, not quite drunk enough not to be weirded out that the guy's hand was still on his shoulder.

Seeming to pick up on his discomfort, the man quickly removed it. "Sorry. I just couldn't help but notice you seemed a bit down. Sort of a strange place to be depressed. Are you alright?"

"Oh, I'm fine," Micah assured, feeling a bit guilty for pegging the guy as a creep right off the bat. "Just out with friends who are obnoxiously in love with each other. I mean, I'm happy for them – obviously – it's just…" he trailed off.

"…hard to find love in your line of work?" the man guessed.

Micah frowned. *How had he known he worked for the police?* Micah supposed enough of his co-workers were here that someone could have told him. "Um, yeah, I guess. Anyway, third wheeling it with Tessa and Jasper, no matter how much I love them, always makes me want to puke a little."

The man's lips quirked. "Are you sure it's not just the alcohol?" he asked, eyeing Micah's empty glass.

Micah snorted. "I'm not *that* drunk."

"Well, in that case, do you want another?" The man was pulling out his wallet before Micah could respond, flashing crisp hundreds in a way that Micah didn't quite buy was accidental. "What's your favorite? Anything you want, I'll get it for you."

Annnd Micah was creeped out again.

It wasn't that he'd offered to buy him a drink. It wasn't the first time in his life Micah had been propositioned that way – though he never accepted unless he saw the drink being made. (He wasn't stupid.) It was how earnest the guy seemed.

"I'm good, thanks," Micah said, hoping the man would take a hint.

The man frowned, looking taken off guard for a moment before his features evened out again. "Oh, well, do you mind if I sit?"

Dammit.

"Uh, sure," Micah agreed amicably enough – though he stood at the same time. "I'm headed to the restroom, though. Nature calls." He slipped out of the booth before the guy could respond, wiggling through the crowd in the general direction of the toilets.

The place was pretty packed, but most people were on the dance floor or herded around the bar, so Micah only stumbled into a person or two on the way, accrediting his uncharacteristic clumsiness to a mix between the alcohol and the flashing strobe lights.

Miraculously, there wasn't a line, so Micah managed to empty his bladder with little fanfare before shuffling towards the line of sinks. He examined his reflection as he washed his hands. He was wearing a dark green shirt along with a pair of black jeans that felt a size too small, but that Tessa insisted made his butt look "scrumptious" – whatever *that* meant. His mussed hair was also Tessa's doing, but the flushed cheeks and bloodshot eyes were definitely the alcohol's fault.

He couldn't help but wonder what Damon would think of the casual outfit he had on versus the more... *liberal* clothes he'd been forced to wear on the job. He remembered the way the man had looked at his skirt-clad legs before forcing his gaze to settle elsewhere. Maybe Damon would have preferred the fishnet shirt Tessa had attempted to force on him over the green V-neck he had on. (As for why he had a fishnet shirt in his possession in the first place, he'd had questionable taste in college, okay?)

Distracted from thoughts of Damon by the sudden realization that his lips had turned as tingly as his fingers, Micah poked at them experimentally, stifling a giggle at the sensation.

The sound of one of the toilets flushing behind him had Micah quickly lowering his hands. Deciding he'd stalled in the bathroom long enough, he dried his hands before re-entering the loud club.

There was no way he was returning to the booth he'd abandoned, and he didn't particularly feel like dancing, so he made his way to the bar. The closer he got, the louder the music became, and the bass felt like it was a physical force, pounding against his ear drums, by the time he reached the counter. Too inebriated to really care about personal space, he squeezed between two of the bodies crowded around the bar and waited for one of the bartenders to make eye contact with him.

Unfortunately, before the pretty brown woman with the frankly impressive chest or the tall man with the green mohawk – the two closest to Micah – could notice him, one of the people he'd inadvertently wedged himself between was leaning into his space. "Got your license?"

Micah shot him a confused look. "Pretty sure it's her job to ask that," he said, gesturing at the nearest bartender, "not yours."

The man grinned, and Micah was distracted for a moment by the whiteness of his teeth. "Sorry, I guess I was just wondering how it hasn't been suspended yet. You know, for driving all the guys around you crazy."

It took Micah longer than it should have for him to make sense of the man's words. But when he did, he huffed a laugh at the ridiculousness of them. "That line usually work for you?"

The man lost none of his swagger, his smile only growing wider at Micah's obvious amusement. "Usually, yeah. If the person I'm using it on is drunk enough."

Micah snorted. "Charming."

"Yeah, I've heard I'm a bit lacking in that department. But I also have it on good authority that my devastatingly good looks more than make up for it."

Micah rolled his eyes at the absurdity of the man, but he couldn't deny the amusement pulling at his mouth and looked closer at the guy. He was cute enough – clean-cut with classic good looks. Most would probably dismiss him as a typical frat boy, but something about his eyebrows reminded him of Damon, which was probably (*definitely*) what had him seriously reconsidering Tessa's suggestion of a one-night stand.

"So…" the man interrupted his perusal after a moment, "what's the verdict? Not charmed enough? Or not drunk enough? Because I have an easy enough remedy for that second one."

Micah pressed his lips together – they were still pleasantly tingly. "I suppose I could use a drink," he hedged.

The man's eyes lit up. "Tequila shots?"

Micah shouldn't. He had planned on one more vodka soda, figuring he could make it last the rest of the night until Tessa was ready to go home. But the man's genuine excitement was contagious. He nodded.

The man whooped.

Micah let him take care of waving down one of the bartenders, and within a couple minutes two shot glasses along with a pair of lemon wedges and a little bowl of salt were placed in front of them.

Micah took hold of his shot glass, preparing himself for the bite of the alcohol. With his other hand, he pinched a bit of salt, intending on sprinkling it onto the back of his hand.

Except, before he could do that, his wrist was being snatched away by the man who'd bought him the shot. "Wait."

"May I?" he asked, nodding at the juncture of Micah's neck and shoulder.

Micah hesitated, but after a moment, alcohol-induced recklessness had him shrugging. "Sure."

Eyes gleaming, the man took his time sprinkling a healthy amount of salt along the exposed skin of Micah's neck and collar bone. Micah followed his lead, rubbing the salt he'd grabbed into the tendons of the man's neck.

"Who's going first?"

"Me."

Before he could second-guess his own declaration, Micah tipped back his shot, the tequila a painful burn down his throat, setting his esophagus afire. He grabbed the man by the fabric of his shirt, yanking him forward so he could lick the salt off his neck. He tasted like sweat and salt (obviously) and the bitter tang of whatever cologne he must have sprayed on before coming to the club. It was fine – *good* even. But it wasn't Damon.

And fuck, it was so stupid. Micah didn't even know Damon – not really. But the man took up so much space in his goddamn brain that Micah couldn't even enjoy a harmless shot with another guy without the man's absurdly beautiful face, along with his disappointed scowl, flooding his thoughts.

Micah must have hidden his disappointment well enough – either that, or the other guy was as drunk as Micah was – because he looked no less enthused when Micah pulled away and plopped a lemon wedge in his mouth, biting into its supple flesh, the sourness helping wash away the taste of tequila.

"My turn."

Micah braced himself for what was to come next, but he was shocked when before the man could so much as grab his shot glass, he was being tugged backward so harshly by the collar of his shirt that he nearly lost his balance and went tumbling to the club floor.

Within moments, another man filled his space, and Micah could only watch, stunned, as familiar blue eyes drilled into his before the shot of tequila was being tipped back.

Then there were hands on his waist, so warm that the fingers that slipped under his shirt and gripped onto skin felt like brands. A hot tongue lapped at his neck, gathering the salt there before continuing its ministrations on his collar bone, prickly stubble rubbing against his skin as teeth scraped at him.

Micah's alcohol-logged brain couldn't make sense of what was happening.

One second, he'd resigned himself to letting a stranger lick the salt from his neck, and the next Damon was tongue-fucking his collar bone in the middle of the club.

It was positively indecent.

Also, *thrilling*.

Micah's cock, which hadn't so much as twitched when he'd been sucking the salt off the other man's neck, was suddenly rock hard against the zipper of his jeans. It was only Damon's grip on his hips keeping him in place that stopped him from doing something embarrassing like trying to dry hump the man.

When Damon pulled away, Micah had the pleasure of seeing wicked satisfaction flash in his eyes as he stared at the juncture of Micah's neck and shoulder, skin undoubtedly red from beard burn and the borderline vicious tongue-assault.

When Damon's eyes rose from the marked-up skin to meet Micah's gaze, however, his entire countenance darkened, an angry scowl pulling at his mouth.

It did absolutely nothing to discourage Micah's hard-on.

"Where have you been?" the man demanded gruffly. "I've looked all over for you."

Micah was too shell-shocked by what had just happened to respond to the man's question. He stood there, mouth agape like an idiot, and stared.

That was not the case for the poor man whose drink Damon had just stolen. "What the fuck, man? I paid for that shot!"

Damon didn't even glance in the guy's direction, his eyes still drilling holes into Micah's. "I assume this covers it," he said coolly, sliding a handful of bills across the counter.

Micah couldn't see what they were, but by the way the man's eyes widened in disbelief and quickly snatched them up, they probably *more* than covered it. "Uh, yeah." The man shot Micah a guilty look over Damon's shoulder, an apology in his eyes even as he shrugged and backed away, clearly intending on taking the money and fucking off. "It's all yours man," he called before disappearing into the crowd.

Coward.

"Yes, *he* is," Damon agreed, voice so soft and silky Micah wasn't sure if he imagined it in the roar of the music.

Regardless, it didn't take Micah long to break under the penetrating, *judgmental* blue of Damon's eyes. "I should- I should arrest you," Micah said, making sure to empathize his point by jabbing a finger into Damon's sternum.

It didn't come out sounding nearly as intimidating as Micah meant it to. (Drunkenly tripping over your words would do that.) It was annoying, even as his lone sober brain cell was yelling at him to *shut the fuck up*. Damon didn't know he was a cop.

Damon's scowl deepened, but he didn't move to remove Micah's finger. "For taking that asswipe's drink?" he demanded.

"No," Micah denied immediately. "For s-stalking, and being unconstitutionally sexy. It's- it's a *violation* to my eyes."

Damon blinked. "I'm a *violation* to your eyes?" he repeated incredulously.

"Yes," Micah agreed, drunk enough not to be completely humiliated by the words coming out of his mouth – thank God. "And *your* eyes. They're unnaturally blue – they're fucking arresting is what they are. I'm arresting you for- for being arresting."

Micah was sure he could have come up with more ridiculous reasons to bring the man in if he wasn't so distracted by the feel of Damon's hard body under his hands. At some point, the rest of his fingers had joined the one he'd poked into Damon's chest, and they were currently tracing the ridged lines of muscle he could feel through the man's dress shirt. For once, he wasn't wearing a fancy suit jacket.

If Micah wouldn't have been so distracted, he might have noticed the way Damon's features softened at his bizarre declaration, the man's angry scowl drifting away.

As it was, Micah was more focused on exploring Damon's body. He trailed his fingers down his chest and stomach, hands inching to dive into the man's pants, but, of course, Damon was wearing a belt.

Not that that stopped Micah. While one hand fiddled with the buckle, the other attempted to wedge fingers into the waist band of the man's pants.

Micah had the vague, faraway thought that *he* was going to be the one who ended up being arrested – for public indecency. (He was attempting to grope another man in public, after all.)

Luckily – or perhaps, *unluckily* – Damon was still in control of his mental faculties, and he managed to take hold of Micah's wrists and tug them away from his crotch before he could feel anything more than a hint of scratchy pubic hair. "You're smashed, aren't you?" he demanded.

Micah blinked. "What- what gave you that idea?"

Damon's brow furrowed, but the amused tilt of his mouth made it clear to Micah that he wasn't actually mad. "You know, it's much harder to be angry with you this way."

Micah shrugged. "So don't be angry then."

Damon's tongue peeked out and licked his bottom lip, and Micah's eyes immediately latched onto the movement. "Will you come upstairs with me?"

It took a second for Micah to understand the question, and when he did, he had just enough wherewithal to swallow back his immediate response: that he'd "come" anywhere with Damon.

As it was, he hadn't quite consumed enough alcohol to forget the last time he'd agreed to go somewhere with Damon. His mouth had been thoroughly ravaged by the man – and then he'd been swiftly rejected. While it was true that Micah still didn't know the reason for the man's sudden change of heart, it still stung.

"Why?"

Damon seemed displeased that Micah's answer wasn't an immediate "yes", but at least he didn't attempt to drag Micah off like he had the first few times they'd met. "I need to talk to you about something," he said after a pause.

Micah narrowed his eyes. "Is- is 'talk' a euphuism for something else?" he asked. *Oops.* So much for not blurting out whatever came to mind.

"It's regarding a business transaction," Damon replied cautiously.

It was a complete non-answer. And considering Micah was pretty sure the man was still under the impression he was a prostitute… it *could* be a euphuism.

Was he really so desperate that he was going to allow Damon, a man who thought he was a hooker, *use* his body? It was morally questionable at best. Then Micah remembered the kiss they'd shared, the way Damon's fingers had left little bruises on his hips, and how the outline of the man's cock had felt pressed against his own aching erection.

"I…" *Who the fuck was he kidding?* "…okay."

Tension visibly drained from Damon's shoulders the moment Micah agreed. One of the man's hands found its way to Micah's lower back as he led him away from the crowded bar, through the throng of people on the dance floor, and to the spiral staircase that led to the second floor of the club. It was obviously a VIP section – the chained entrance and pair of black-clad bouncers guarding it was a dead-giveaway. He and Tessa, like most of the common folk drinking and dancing on the ground level of the club, hadn't bothered trying to get in.

When they saw Damon, however, the bouncers immediately unfastened the chain and shuffled out of the way – one of the many perks of being rich, apparently.

The tequila must have hit a little harder than he thought because Micah had to focus carefully on the stairs, taking them one step at a time. (After all, no "business transaction" could take place if he fell and broke his neck.)

He only pulled his gaze away from his feet when he'd reached the top of the stairs. The second floor was comprised of a much smaller area than the main floor, taking up about half the space. Micah couldn't concentrate enough to take in the finer details, but there was a private bar and a balcony that oversaw the floor below.

It must have been how Damon spotted him.

Micah was surprised to note that there wasn't much more than a couple dozen people lounging on the expensive-looking furniture clumped together strategically throughout the space. Before he could attempt to take in any more of his surroundings, a woman in a flashy purple dress with a plunging neckline was suddenly marching towards them, her stride (and expression) fierce.

She was tall and beautiful, with lush lips and dark brows and hair – cut just above her shoulders in a fashionable bob. Micah might have been jealous of the familiarity that shone in her eyes as she stared Damon down, if it wasn't obvious to him that they were somehow related. Maybe it was her general attractiveness or maybe it was the scowl, but Micah couldn't look at her and not see Damon.

"Damon, where the hell did you go?" the woman all but snarled. "You can't just take off in the middle of-" she cut herself off abruptly upon noticing Micah.

He raised his hand in something that may have resembled a wave. "Um, hi?"

The woman's frown didn't melt away; rather, her mouth pursed.

Damon carefully took Micah's hand, lowering it back down to his side. "Micah, this is Joelle, my sister – the one Adella told you about. Joelle, this is Micah."

Ah-ha! So he was right!

"This is Micah?" Her bewildered irritation took a turn towards intrigued. Her blue eyes – darker than Damon's, but still pretty – sharpened with interest. For a long moment, she stared, her eyes carefully running down his form – analyzing, *judging*. It probably would have been uncomfortable if Micah currently *had* the ability to be uncomfortable. (As it was, he was much more occupied with the tingliness of his lips, pressing them together again and again to experience the pleasant pinpricks.)

When Joelle's eyes finally left Micah to return to Damon, there was more than a hint of amusement in them. "I hope you remembered to ask him to come with you like a gentleman this time instead of dragging him off against his will."

Micah blinked. Apparently, Damon had spoken about him to his family. Despite the fact that he'd waxed poetry about Damon's ridiculously thick thighs to Tessa, he wasn't sure how he felt about that.

Still, it was nice to know he wasn't the only one to find Damon's controlling tendencies to be on the tyrannical side. (Even if Micah's cock *did* twitch with interest when that commanding tone was directed towards him.)

"He's very bossy," Micah agreed matter-of-factly.

Joelle snickered.

Damon scowled. "Shut up, Joelle. Can you watch him for a second? I need to make a call."

"What? Afraid he'll run off again?" she teased.

Again, Micah probably should have been annoyed – since they were discussing babysitting him like he was some sort of disobedient toddler – but, well, *tequila.*

"Please?"

Joelle waved a hand. "Go on. I think I can handle him for a couple minutes."

Damon nodded, offering her a terse "thanks" before turning towards Micah, putting his hands on his shoulders to make sure he had his attention. "I'll be right back. Stay here with Joelle, okay?"

Micah nodded dumbly, unable to tear eyes away from Damon's magnificent backside as he walked away, in the direction of the stairs.

"It's not right."

Micah turned towards Joelle. "Huh?"

"I practically had to paint this dress on, and somehow, his ass still looks better than mine."

Micah blinked, having no idea what to say. Was it weird for a sister to comment on her brother's ass? He didn't know. He didn't have any siblings. "Um-"

Luckily, Joelle didn't seem to expect an answer. "I hope you know how worried he's been."

The words didn't sound threatening exactly, especially considering the nonchalance they were spoken with, but Micah's hindbrain still screamed *danger!* when the woman suddenly stepped into his space and ran a manicured fingernail down his cheek.

"I – um – worried?" he repeated mindlessly. He'd had an idea, of course, considering the state Damon had been in at the precinct, but Micah wasn't supposed to know about that, so he played dumb. (It was probably easier than it should have been.)

Joelle nodded, allowing her fingers to trail down Micah's neck. She played with the fabric of his shirt. "I don't know *why* exactly, but he thinks you're worth his time despite the fact you work the streets, spreading your legs for anyone who walks by like a common whore."

Micah stiffened. "That's not-" he started, but Joelle wasn't finished.

"It's strange. He doesn't think *anyone* is worth his time, let alone someone like you. Yet here we are." Joelle stared straight into his eyes. "He's going to offer you a deal so good tonight that not even the devil would pass it up, because for reasons I don't understand he thinks you're worth it. For both your sakes, *don't* fuck this up."

Micah swallowed. "You're fucking terrifying," he admitted freely. His mouth wasn't done there though. "Also, hot as hell. I mean, if I wasn't as bent as a- a rainbow-colored pretzel, I'd probably be having to hide a very awkward fear-boner, right now."

Yeah, safe to say his brain-to-mouth filter was completely eradicated at this point.

Joelle didn't immediately react to his word vomit.

After a few seconds, however, her hard expression broke, and she let out a laugh through her nose, her red lips stretching into a huge, Cheshire grin. "You're adorable," she said. "I mean, not adorable enough that I won't fuck you up if you mess with my brother…" she trailed off, leaning forward to kiss Micah on the forehead like he was some precious thing and not someone she'd just called a whore to his face. "But definitely sweet enough that I'll also fuck up anyone who messes with you."

"Uh… thank you? I think?"

She patted his cheek and ran a hand through his hair, almost like she was petting a puppy. "I have a feeling we're going to get along just fine."

"Don't touch him," Damon snapped, stepping between them – suddenly back from wherever he'd disappeared to. There was a thick, black coat in his arms, and Micah was flabbergasted – but too bewildered to protest – when the man tucked it around his shoulders. "I called Geoffrey," he said, much less snarly as he addressed Micah. "The car's around front."

Micah blinked stupidly. "I thought you wanted to talk?" he said

Damon glanced around, a grimace on his face. "This isn't the most... *appropriate* environment for what I want to talk about. I thought we could go back to The Mark..." he paused, as if debating something, "or we could go to my place, if you feel comfortable enough."

Joelle frowned. "Damon, we weren't finished-"

"I'll deal with it tomorrow, Jo," he snapped before his sister could finish whatever it was she was about to say. Damon glanced pointedly at Micah.

Joelle sighed in annoyance and crossed her arms over her chest, but she didn't argue further.

Damon turned back to Micah. "Is my place okay?"

Micah considered his options.

You didn't have to work for the police to know it was the height of idiocy to go to a stranger's house drunk. But Micah couldn't help but feel like Damon was hardly a stranger at this point. Besides, he was curious to see where he lived.

"Your place sounds- sounds good," Micah agreed clumsily. "I've got to text my friend, though, so- so she doesn't freak out when she can't find me."

Damon raised his eyebrows, possibly surprised Micah had someone who'd be concerned if he disappeared for the night – you know, considering his supposed line of work. "Of course. I'm glad you have someone looking out for you."

Micah mumbled something in agreeance as he pulled out his phone. The names of his contact list blurred together, but he was able to find Tessa' s number easily enough – it wasn't like he had many in there. He typed a message that he hoped made sense and pressed send.

"Ready?" Damon asked when Micah pocketed his phone.

He offered a stilted nod.

"Call me tomorrow," Joelle insisted to Damon before turning to Micah and pinching his cheek. "It was nice meeting you, Micah." Micah had a feeling she may have attempted to plant another kiss on his forehead if Damon wouldn't have chosen that moment to drag him away.

He was grateful for the man's sturdy grip around his shoulders as he led him down the steps, back to the main floor. (Honestly, who put a spiral staircase in a club? It was practically asking for a lawsuit.)

Micah was leaning heavily on Damon by the time they made it out the front door of Club Trinity, and he was inebriated enough that he didn't protest as Damon all but lifted him into the back seat of a familiar black vehicle, arranging him so that he was leaning back against the seat.

Damon slid in after him, tapping on the divider after he shut the door so that his driver – Geoffrey – knew it was okay to put the vehicle in drive.

The Rolls-Royce may have been the smoothest ride Micah had ever experienced, but considering the amount of alcohol he'd consumed, the sudden sensation of being in motion still made his head spin. He groaned, but instead of burying his head into his hands in an attempt to stem the dizziness, Micah turned and flopped onto his side, sprawling across the backseat and inadvertently resting his head in Damon's lap, all but burrowing his face into the man's crotch.

Micah didn't have the sense to be embarrassed. Besides, the man's thighs made an excellent pillow.

"Are you alright?" Damon asked stiffly. Hesitant fingers threaded through his hair. They felt *so good.*

"No," Micah said. He frowned. *Wait.* "I mean, yes?" Micah *may* have forgotten the question. "I mean, do- do you still have any of that champagne in here?"

He heard Damon snort somewhere above him. "I'm not sure that's the best idea. We still need to talk. And I want you to actually remember the conversation tomorrow."

That's right. They were supposed to "talk". Heavy emphasis on the quotation marks.

It suddenly occurred to Micah that Damon's dick was literally centimeters from his lips.

His mouth watered at the thought of Damon's warm, thick cock sitting heavy on his tongue. He could picture it perfectly in his mind's eye – the way he'd hollow out his cheeks as he swallowed around Damon, letting the man rut against him until he gagged.

Fuck.

Micah needed the man's cock in his mouth yesterday.

In Micah's alcohol-fueled brain, he could think of no reason they couldn't "talk" right then and there in the car. Sure, there were several layers of clothing between him and his prize at the moment, but that was fixed easily enough.

Which was why, without really thinking about what he was doing, Micah's hands began fiddling with the zipper of Damon's slacks. Almost immediately, his wrists were caught in an ironclad grip. "What are you doing?" Damon asked tersely.

Micah blinked stupidly up at the man. He didn't look mad, exactly, but definitely stiff – and not in the fun way either. "I... I thought you might want a test run of my services before- before talking business."

That made sense, right? It was mostly coherent?

Micah thought so, which was why he decided to resume what he'd been doing before Damon had so rudely interrupted. Sure, his hands were currently occupied, but not his tongue, which was why he decided to nuzzle his face into the man's crotch before *mouthing* at his cloth-clad cock.

"Jesus Christ, Micah," Damon half-snapped/half-yelped, immediately tugging him away. "Why would you-?" he started before suddenly cutting himself off. Micah wasn't sure what he was more fascinated by: the tick in the man's jaw, or the way the veins bulged in his neck. "Is this what you thought I meant when I said I wanted to talk?"

"Um... yes?"

"That's not... fuck, Micah," he snarled, jerking away when he attempted to get at his dick *again.* "Stop that."

Micah pouted, but obliged.

"*This* is not what I meant when I said I wanted to talk business. I promise to explain when we get to my place, okay?"

Damon's tone wasn't mean or even exasperated – in fact, he spoke extremely patiently for someone getting their cock toyed with in the back of a car. That didn't stop Micah's feelings from being hurt for reasons beyond his current cognitive abilities, however.

"Fine," he muttered, refusing to lift his head from the man's lap, but pointedly turning so that he no longer faced the man's crotch. "You- you smell like Christmas trees," Micah said accusingly, his best attempt at an insult at the moment.

(It's what the man deserved for leading him on, and then rejecting him... *again.*)

It didn't succeed in its intended purpose judging by Damon's lack of outrage. But the man's hands returned to his hair after a moment, which Micah considered a win. He leaned into the gentle touch.

"Oh yeah?"

"Mmhm," Micah agreed, allowing his heavy lids to close. "Makes me want to eat you," he admitted after a yawn.

Micah was only vaguely aware of Damon taking a deep, shuddering breath. "You eat Christmas trees, do you?" he said after a moment, voice deceptively light, but Micah could hear something lurking under the surface, something almost... animalistic.

"No, I- I put popcorn strings, and, uh, candy canes on Christmas trees." He paused. "I want to suck you like a candy cane," he confessed brazenly. His mouth was running of its own accord at that point, his brain having shut down a while ago. "But you won't let me."

His ears must have still been working, though, because he heard Damon curse above him in what might have been Italian.

Micah grinned.

He spent his last few seconds before oblivion pulled him under wondering if the man's cock tasted like peppermints.

CHAPTER FIVE

Micah's brain was pounding against his skull like it wanted to escape – a consistent throb behind his eyes that made Micah want to curl up into a ball and never get out of bed ever again.

And why would he when the mattress he was on was so ridiculously comfortable, practically molding around him in an embrace he never wanted to escape? Not to mention the soft, silky sheets and what had to be the cushiest pillow in the world. It was probably filled with exotic bird feathers or something equally asinine.

Wait.

The bed in Micah's apartment consisted of a too-hard twin mattress with a dip in the middle, plain cotton sheets he'd bought from Wal-Mart, and a somewhat lumpy pair of pillows that were several years old and had seen better days.

Micah's eyes shot open, and he sprang up – immediately regretting the sudden movement when his brain protested by attempting to leak out of his eyeballs. Micah balled up his hands into fists and pressed them as hard as he could into his sockets – an attempt to ease the ache before he dared to reopen his eyes and take in his surroundings.

He had to squint because it was so bright.

The entire length of the wall across from the bed was made up of floor-to-ceiling windows, and the sun was shining cheerily, making it difficult for Micah to take in the view it offered of what he was pretty sure was the Hudson River and various skyscrapers of Manhattan.

He turned his attention to the room, instead, which was styled in shades of black and white, the only pop of color the crimson-colored sheets of the California king he was sat on. Micah spotted a bottle of Tylenol and a glass of water on the nightstand nearest him and wasted no time shaking several pills out onto his hand.

He quickly inspected them to make sure they were, in fact, simple pain-relievers, before swallowing them down along with the water. Then he returned the bottle and empty glass to the nightstand, next to the diamond-studded lamp that probably cost more than Micah's rent.

It was tacky and completely superfluous in Micah's opinion – along with the modern art that decorated the otherwise blank walls – but what did he know? His taste was probably as poor as his bank statements claimed he was.

In fact, there was only one person Micah knew who was filthy rich enough to afford a place like this.

Damon.

The events of last night came flooding back to him.

Unfortunately, Micah wasn't blessed enough to be the type to black out when he drank too much. No, he tended to remember every humiliating detail of whatever shenanigans he got up to, and last night was no exception.

Watching Tessa and Jasper being completely adorable with each other and trying not to let the bitter jealousy that stewed inside him show.

A frat boy buying him a shot of tequila, and accepting it in a pathetic attempt to make himself feel better.

Damon intervening. (Micah recalled vividly the feeling of the man's mouth on his neck, tonguing at his exposed clavicle.)

Damon claiming he wanted to "talk" and taking Micah upstairs, where he'd met the man's sister, Joelle – who was somehow just as attractive and even more intimidating than her brother.

And then the backseat of Damon's Rolls-Royce.

Micah recalled babbling nonsensically about Christmas trees and candy canes and… mouthing at Damon's clothed cock like the back alley hooker the man thought he was.

Fuck.

He flopped backward.

Micah was briefly distracted from the mortification he was feeling by the realization that the ceiling of Damon's bedroom was made entirely of mirror tiles.

Huh. Kinky.

But the distraction didn't last long. The humiliation was too intense. Micah closed his eyes. "Lord, I've lived a good life," he intoned seriously. "If you are truly as merciful as you claim, surely you will strike me down now instead of making me deal with the frankly *bewildering* clusterfuck my life as become."

Nothing happened.

Micah sighed, reopening his eyes. The sun continued to shine mockingly through the massive windows.

Was it really too much to ask for some lightning to come down and smite him where he lay? Now he was going to have to drudge up the fortitude to go out there and face the consequences of his actions – face *Damon* – like an actual functioning adult.

Honestly, Micah didn't know what was more embarrassing. That he'd agreed to "talk business" with Damon, fully under the impression that it meant selling his body to the man for a night of passion? Or that he'd somehow failed in closing the deal?

As comfortable as the monstrous bed he was lying in was, Micah couldn't help but feel a bit pathetic waking up in it alone.

He was briefly distracted by his self-inflicted misery by a buzzing in his pocket. Micah frowned, pulling out his phone and cringing when he saw he had three missed calls and half a dozen missed messages.

He didn't know whether to feel relieved or guilty to see that all three missed calls were from Tessa when he unlocked his phone, and all but two of the messages were as well. They were all variations of "call me" and "the stress of being your friend is going to put me in premature labor" and "who the fuck is Don?"

Micah frowned. *Don?* He vaguely remembered texting Tessa before he'd left the club with Damon, so he wasn't sure what had her panties in such a twist. He scrolled to his last message to her.

Going home with a Don is, wants to "talk"

He'd added a cringeworthy amount of winky faces afterwards. Also, a purple eggplant. And a banana emoji.

Ah. That explained things. He was sure he'd meant to type Adonis, which in his liquor-fueled brain, he'd probably assumed Tessa would know meant Damon.

The other two messages were from Jasper – a half-apologetic/half-scolding text, imploring Micah to call Tessa – and his oblivious father, who wanted to know if Micah was going to stop by and watch the football game with him on Sunday.

Neither needed his urgent attention, so Micah returned to his text history with Tessa before quickly shooting off two messages.

A Don is = Adonis = Damon

I'm alive, text you later, keep those babies in your uterus

Then Micah put his phone on silent to avoid being immediately bombarded with questions.

That taken care of, Micah was tempted to go back to what he'd been doing before his phone had distracted him: namely, lie there and continue to feel sorry for himself.

Alas, nature called.

It was only the feeling of an uncomfortably full bladder that finally gave Micah the willpower to drag himself out of bed. There were only two doors not counting the double sliding ones Micah assumed to be a closet.

Saying a prayer, Micah picked one at random, letting out a little sigh of relief when he opened it and an immaculate toilet was revealed. Apparently, the Lord hadn't abandoned him completely.

Micah quickly relieved himself before taking stock of the rest of the bathroom. It wasn't all that dissimilar to the one at The Mark with its fancy marble floors and double vanity. (Although the sinks here weren't jutting out of the countertops like little fountains – which was a plus in Micah's book.) There was both an enormous tub and a shower – and inexplicably, a television mounted in the corner.

Rich people.

Micah was tempted to peek in the shower to find out what sort of products Damon used to smell so amazing all the time, but remembering his fumbling comment about "Christmas trees", he turned to the sinks instead.

Micah washed his face in one of them before running his hands through his cowlicked hair in an attempt to *not* look like he'd just rolled out of bed after a night of ill-advised nonsense. Then he unabashedly ruffled through the vanity's drawers until he found some toothpaste. He squirted the minty concoction onto his index finger before using the makeshift toothbrush to scrub at his teeth until his mouth no longer felt like something had died in it.

When he was finished, he spit in the sink before returning his gaze to the mirror. He took a deep breath. "You have nothing to be ashamed about. Damon said he wanted to talk business with you. As far as he knows, your business involves selling your body for cash. It was perfectly reasonable to assume he wanted you to blow him in the back seat of his car... with his pants still on."

Yeah, Micah really needed to work on his pep talks.

Regardless, he couldn't avoid the inevitable confrontation with Damon any longer, so he forced himself to straighten his shoulders before exiting the bathroom, marching across the bedroom he'd awoken in until he reached the unexplored door.

He pulled it open and stepped out into a living area that looked like it belonged in a Better Homes and Gardens magazine – one that catered to billionaires with a penchant for penthouses.

The space was massive – the huge windows and vaulted ceiling making it seem impossibly larger. There was a walk-out balcony, upon which Micah could make out a set of wicker furniture and... *was that a hot tub?!*

Micah jerked his eyes away from the balcony, back to the inside of the space. Like Damon's bedroom, the place was mostly decorated in monochromic colors. The floors were a gleaming cream-colored hardwood that stretched out across the room, only broken up by a large white area rug near the brick fireplace.

There was minimal furniture – a black leather sofa and loveseat surrounding the rug near the fireplace – and more abstract-looking art hanging on the walls, including a trio of weird (ugly, frankly) metal pieces that were possibly supposed to resemble flowers.

As impressive as the space was, Micah couldn't deny feeling an unexpected wave of disappointment. Sure, the place probably cost more money than what he would make in a lifetime, and the hot tub was awesome, but it was all just so... *impersonal*. He may as well have been at the suite in The Mark for as much as Damon's place told him about the man.

What Micah *wasn't* disappointed by was the heavenly smell in the air – something sweet and cakey that had his stomach twisting in anticipation. He'd avoided looking in the direction of the kitchen until then, his body somehow instinctually knowing that was where Damon was, but he couldn't avoid it any longer.

Sure enough, there he was. His back was to Micah as he focused on the stove, and he hadn't noticed Micah's entrance. Even turned around as he was, however, Micah couldn't help but admire the view.

Damon was in a t-shirt – the most casual Micah had ever seen him dressed – and his trapezius muscles strained against the fabric, his biceps bulging against the sleeves. Unfortunately, a shiny kitchen island equipped with granite countertops blocked the rest of the man from Micah's eyesight.

Micah cleared his throat, taking a step towards the kitchen. "G'morning," he said, voice quiet and a bit croaky yet from sleep.

Damon jerked around at the sound of it, spatula in hand. "You're up." The man sounded surprised. "I thought you'd sleep in longer."

Micah ran a nervous hand through his hair, taking another step closer to Damon. "Yeah, well, I'm used to long nights at the job."

Micah *meant* his job at the precinct, which often required odd hours. Crime didn't sleep, after all, and time-sensitive cases frequently required all-hands-on-deck. It wasn't unusual for him to work evenings and weekends. Take his undercover gig as a prostitute, for example-

Fuck.

"Right," Damon said tersely before returning his attention to the stove.

Could he punch himself in the face, please? Micah took a deep breath in through his nose before bravely taking a seat on one of the

chairs surrounding the kitchen island. Damage control time. "It's a…
um, nice place you have here."

The lack of personal items and boring décor aside, it was an
understatement.

"Thank you," Damon said stiffly, though he didn't turn around
to face Micah. "There's a personal gym and a pool the floor below
this one as well."

Of course, there was.

"That explains a lot," Micah couldn't help but mutter.

Damon glanced over his shoulder, a puzzled frown pulling at
his mouth.

"I mean, no one gets a body like *that*," – Micah gestured
vaguely at Damon's whole person – "what with the arms, and the
back, and the thighs, without working out regularly. I mean, you
could probably bench press *me* if you wanted to. Of course, that
doesn't explain away the face, or the perfectly styled hair, or the
frickin' eyes, but… you know you can stop me at any time, right?"

Micah should have been embarrassed, prattling on about all the
ways he found Damon attractive, but it was hard to feel anything but
proud when the man lost most of the tightness that had gathered in
his shoulders the moment Micah had made that stupid remark about
his "job".

"Speaking of my eyes… you know, someone once told me they
were downright arresting. Threatened to arrest me because of them."
Damon's tone was purposefully flippant, but it was obvious he was
teasing him.

Micah groaned aloud, fighting the urge to hide his reddening
face in his hands. "Yeah, well, that person was probably drunk at the
time. You can hardly hold it against them."

Damon offered Micah a little smirk before transferring
whatever delicious smelling… *thing* he was making from a pan onto
a plate.

There was already a tall stack of what looked like extremely
thin pancakes.

"What are you making?" Micah asked. "Whatever they are,
they smell *really* good."

"Crepes," Damon answered, adding some more batter to his pan. "There's fruit, too, of course," he said, nodding at a platter of strawberries, blueberries, and pineapple. "I also whipped up some fresh cream. Or there's powdered sugar in the cupboards if you prefer that." He paused, his frown suddenly returning. "Unless you want something else? I can always order in."

Micah blinked. "What? No. You already made these."

"But I didn't ask-"

"I will seriously throw a fit if you don't let me try those," he told the man honestly. "Nothing that smells this good could possibly taste bad."

He must have said the magic words because Damon snorted, and his frown disappeared. "Alright. I have enough batter to make a couple more if you want to hang tight for a few minutes."

"Sure," Micah agreed easily.

It shouldn't have been so comfortable, lounging in the man's kitchen and waiting for him to finish cooking (*for him!*), but Micah felt oddly at ease, and before he knew it, Damon was placing a plate of stacked crepes in front of him. Damon grabbed the fruit and whipped cream, along with his own plate and some silverware before taking a seat next to him.

"Eat up," the man instructed.

Micah didn't need to be told twice. He scooped a generous amount of cream atop his first crepe, sprinkled it with berries, and forked a piece of it in his mouth.

Then he fought the urge to moan aloud.

It was like a thin, crispy piece of pancake, that should have been too sweet with the cream and fruit, but somehow wasn't. "I know you told me you like baking, but holy. You know, if being a billionaire doesn't work out, you have some serious skills to fall back on."

Damon snorted. "You're ridiculous," he said, waving off the compliment.

"Seriously, I've never been so happy to have some guy so obsessed with feeding me." For some reason, his mind decided to torment Micah by reminding him how he'd attempted to *eat* Damon the night before, a picture of him mouthing at the man's clothed dick flashing through his mind. "Food, I mean, obviously," he added unnecessarily. "Not, you know…"

Luckily, Damon didn't seem to know. In fact, he seemed distracted by something on Micah's face – his mouth, to be specific.

His heart rate absolutely did *not* ramp up.

"What?" Micah blurted.

"Nothing, you just have a bit of cream-"

"Oh!" Micah quickly wiped his mouth with the back of his hand, feeling like an idiot. Of course, Damon wasn't staring at his lips because he wanted to kiss him. Micah was just a slob. "Did I get it?"

He wasn't wholly prepared for Damon to take him by the chin and thumb the corner of his mouth, running it along his bottom lip. "Got it."

Fuck.

Micah quickly tore his face out of Damon's hand, forking another piece of crepe into his mouth like the uncultured trash he was before an… *unfortunate* situation could develop in his pants.

A semi-awkward silence fell.

Micah cleared his throat. "So-"

"What do you-?" Damon attempted at the same time.

"You first," Micah insisted, plopping a strawberry in his mouth before Damon could object.

Damon eyed him critically. "I was just going to ask what you remembered about last night. You were a little…" he trailed off.

"Plastered?" Micah offered.

Damon's lips twitched. "I was going to say out of it."

"Yeah, well, tequila is *not* my friend."

Damon hummed. "Perhaps you shouldn't be accepting shots of it from strangers then."

Micah frowned. "Are you scolding me?" he demanded.

"No," Damon denied, the liar. "I just can't help but notice you have a habit of making questionable decisions-"

Damon didn't know the half of it.

"-especially those regarding your safety. What if that guy had done something to your drink? Or what if you were so inebriated, you decided to go home with him? He could have hurt you."

Micah had a choice: he could get annoyed at the man's domineering attitude, or he could recognize that, for whatever reason, it was coming from a place of genuine concern. "Well, I didn't go home with him, did I?" he reminded the man lightly, deciding to go with option two – for now. "I went home with *you*."

Damon swallowed. "Yeah, well," he mumbled, seemingly taken off guard for a moment. "I suppose getting drunk isn't the most harebrained thing I've seen you do. Plus, that tequila *did* knock you out pretty good, so at least I didn't have to worry about you running out on me again."

Was Damon... cracking jokes?

Micah furrowed his brow, not sure whether the man was reprimanding him or teasing him. "What can I say? I don't handle rejection well. And you tend to do that a lot – reject me. It's sort of embarrassing considering my profession. I mean, I couldn't even get you to accept a free sample last night."

...

Seriously, *what* was wrong with him?

Damon had done him a solid thus far – acting like a gentleman, and studiously *not* bringing up the fact that Micah had attempted to drunkenly suck his cock in the backseat of his Rolls-Royce. So, of course, like a total ass, Micah had to remind the both of them himself.

It was like his brain was in a competition with his mouth and constantly losing. "Um-"

"You're right. That's because I want to pay you."

Micah's self-depreciating thoughts came to a screeching halt. "... for sex?"

"What?" Damon scowled. "No."

He didn't need to sound so disturbed by the idea.

"Well, I'm sorry for being a little confused," Micah said, not sorry at all. "I've made it pretty clear what I do for a living."

Oh, the irony.

"I'm well aware of your work and the various… undertakings it requires of you." Damon's scowl was back. "It's partly why I wanted to give you the opportunity to work for me instead."

Micah scrunched his nose. "Like as a secretary or something?"

Damon shook his head. "Not quite. I have enough secretaries. What I need is someone accessible to me when I require a companion for social events."

Micah blinked. "So, like a prostitute, but without the sex?" he sought clarification.

"If that's how you choose to look at it," Damon allowed. "I prefer the term escort, or prearranged date."

Micah desperately wanted to ask why the man didn't want sex to be a part of the deal. Micah had made it *more* than clear he was interested, and apparently he was good enough to date – or, at least, fake-date. But the way Damon had backpedaled on him at The Mark – not to mention how quickly he had pried Micah off his dick last night – was still fresh in his mind. He didn't think he could handle another swift rejection at the moment. Besides, there were plenty of other questions to be had, like…

"Why?" Micah asked incredulously.

Damon frowned. "What do you mean?"

"No offense, but you could have anyone you wanted – male, female, young, old, short-term lover, trophy wife. Literally no one would reject you. I mean, not only are you ridiculously handsome – look around, you're loaded."

Micah didn't mean the words as a compliment or an insult – he was just stating facts, and Damon seemed to recognize that. "You're right. Someone with as much money as me attracts a lot of… admirers," he decided on after a moment. "But at least this way, I know you're in it for the paycheck, so there's no mind games or second-guessing your motives." Damon shrugged. "Of course, there are other reasons I'm reluctant to pursue a relationship, but I won't get into that with you."

Micah shook his head in disbelief. "You're an escort's wet dream. You could get on your phone right now and hire one. There are probably thousands in New York alone, and I can guarantee you that every last one of them would be more professional than me."

"I don't want them. I want *you*."

Mica's mouth felt suddenly too dry, and he fought to swallow. "I don't understand," he said honestly. "You're hellbent on paying me to... what, exactly? Hang on your arm at fancy corporate banquets?"

"Making an appearance at work events would be a requirement, yes. So would attendance at family dinners, and pretty much any public event where I would have need of a date." He paused, before hesitantly adding, "Spending time together in private will be necessary as well – at least in the beginning, so we can get to know each other enough to make this look convincing."

Micah should have said "no" immediately; he shouldn't have asked questions or let the man explain.

In fact, he shouldn't have even sat down to eat the man's stupidly delicious crepes. As soon as he'd seen Damon, Micah should have apologized for his behavior the night before and explained that, despite all evidence to the contrary, he wasn't actually a prostitute.

Damon probably would have called him an Uber and sent him on his merry way. In all likelihood, Micah would have never seen the man again.

But he didn't *want* that.

So, Micah had selfishly sat down and eaten the damn crepes.

And now, here he was, so desperate for an excuse to see Damon again that he was seriously contemplating moonlighting as a frickin' escort.

"I... thanks for the job offer, I guess, but I'll have to pass."

It wasn't even the fact that he was secretly a police detective that held Micah back. It was because it was obvious that Damon wanted this to be purely a business arrangement – a monetary transaction, a no-feelings-attached sort of deal. And Micah knew himself well enough to know that he'd be *leaking* feelings by the end of this thing if he agreed.

Damon didn't outwardly show his surprise at Micah's refusal, but he could tell the man was displeased. "It's bad form to reject a man before even seeing his offer," he said before abruptly standing. He stalked across the kitchen, where he rifled through a drawer and retrieved a pen and some scrap paper. He wrote something down on the piece of paper before folding it and sliding it across the kitchen island to Micah.

"What's this?" he asked hesitantly.

"A number."

Micah frowned. He had seen stuff like this in movies before, but didn't think it was something people did in real life. Nevertheless, he carefully unfolded the piece of paper... and his eyes nearly bulged out of his head when he saw what the man had written down. He immediately slapped a hand over the ridiculous number. "I think you accidently added an extra zero," he squeaked out.

"I'm sure I didn't."

Micah shook his head, incredulous. "And, what, this is what you'll pay me for my services every month?"

"Every week," Damon corrected.

This man was *crazy*.

"You can't be serious," Micah denied. "What's the catch? I could understand if this was a one-time payment for some weird sex thing" – a muscle in Damon's jaw twitched – "but you want to pay me *this* amount to what, go on a few dates?"

"You'll have to be available to me on short notice in addition to every other weekend and every Wednesday evening," Damon explained. "At least, those are the days I put in the contract – I'm open to switching the Wednesday evenings to another day if it better fits your schedule."

Micah blinked, mind spinning. *An actual contract?* Damon had clearly put a lot of thought into this.

"I... but I can't just quit my job," Micah said, grasping for an excuse. "I'll lose loyal clientele." There, that sounded like something a prostitute would be concerned about, right?

"The pay is largely to compensate for that," Damon pointed out tersely. (Someone ought to tell the man that prostitutes didn't make a whopping *10,000 dollars a week*.) "You'll also have to sign an NDA," he added.

"An NDA?"

"A Non-Disclosure Agreement. It's to protect both of our best interests," Damon explained. "I won't be able to tell anyone anything I learn about you that you want to keep under wraps, and you won't be able to reveal any of the... sensitive information," he decided on after a moment, choosing his words carefully, "you might overhear when you're with me."

Micah frowned, his investigative instincts pinging. "What kind of sensitive information?"

"Nothing that concerns you," Damon replied, immediately shutting Micah down.

It was a tight-lipped response, but Micah supposed everyone deserved their privacy, as long as their secrets weren't hurting anybody.

Misreading Micah's contemplative silence as upset, Damon eventually added, "It's nothing to worry yourself over. I would never let anything happen to you."

"I'm tougher than you think," Micah bit back. He'd been trained in hand-to-hand, after all, and he had one of the most accurate shots on the force. "I can take care of myself."

Damon looked like he wanted to argue, but after a moment, he only offered a nod. "Well?"

The answer should have still been "no".

A ridiculous 10,000 bucks a week or not, Micah's justifications for denying Damon hadn't changed. Yet, for reasons he couldn't fully explain, Micah found it harder than he should have to turn the man down again.

Which is why instead of a firm rebuff, Micah only feebly protested, "I doubt I have anything appropriate to wear to these fancy events you need a date for."

Damon's eyes sharpened, recognizing Micah's weakening willpower like a shark sensed blood in the water. "That's fine. In fact, I already figured a complete wardrobe overhaul into the offer. We can go shopping as soon as you've finished breakfast. I've cleared my entire schedule until this evening."

It seemed Damon really *had* thought of everything.

"You were that sure I'd say yes, huh?" Micah couldn't help but goad the man.

But Damon surprised him by shaking his head. "No," he said, voice softer than it'd been moments ago, "but I was hoping you would."

Dammit.

Why did he have to sound so infuriatingly sincere? And why did he have to look at Micah like *that*? He'd made it more than clear he had no interest in having sex with him, but Damon still had the nerve to look at him like he was something worthwhile, something precious, and fuck, if it wasn't messing with Micah's head.

Not enough that Micah didn't know that it was a terrible idea to agree to the man's offer, but enough that he almost didn't care how terrible of an idea it was.

Micah's brain screamed "no", but everything else screamed "yes", and… *god fucking dammit.*

"Fine," Micah bit out before common sense could override the burning desire to agree. "But I can't meet up before 5:00 on Wednesdays. I'll try to be available short notice and the weekends you need me – but only in the evenings. And if I say no, you'll have to respect that I have prior commitments I can't get out of and leave it."

There, that ought to cover all the time he was at his real job.

Micah expected Damon to argue, or at least to demand to know why he couldn't always be available, but instead, the man merely offered Micah his hand. "It's a deal."

Mica felt suddenly clammy, but his nerves were alight with excitement. Not sure if he was making the worst decision of his life, or the best, Micah reached forward and clasped Damon's hand, allowing the man's warm palm to engulf his.

"Deal."

CHAPTER SIX

For some reason, when Micah thought of shopping with Damon, he'd pictured strutting through a generic mall with the man – like the popular girls did in teenybopper movies like Clueless or Mean Girls. Sure, he'd argue with Damon about how expensive the clothes he picked out were, but the man would buy them anyway, and in the end, Micah would somehow have transformed from loser outcast to fashion-forward Barbie doll – or, well, a Ken doll in his case.

This would all take place during an upbeat musical montage.

Turns out, the only thing Micah was right about was the arguing.

What shopping with Damon was *actually* like was being stuck in the most prestigious tailor shop in Manhattan – Bianchi's, a beautiful brick and mortar store off Columbus Circle – for hours on end.

Micah had been worried he wouldn't even be allowed in the fancy shop when they'd arrived. While he had taken Damon up on his offer of a shower at his place, they had come to the mutual conclusion that none of the other man's formal wear would fit him, so Micah had been stuck with his black jeans and wrinkled V-neck that still smelled vaguely of liquor.

His worry was squashed, however, when as soon as the pair of store attendants behind the front desk had seen Damon – who, of course, had changed into one of his signature suits – they'd all but laid out the red carpet. The owner of Bianchi's, Miles Bianchi, had even come out the back to tend to Micah himself.

Micah had only ever had occasion to wear a fancy suit twice in his life – once for senior prom and once when his best friend, Scott Larsen, from high school had gotten married. Both times, he'd been able to get away with buying a suit off the rack.

When he'd mentioned this little fact to Mr. Bianchi, the man had turned bright red and sputtered. Then he'd proceeded to take every conceivable measurement of Micah's body sans the length of his dick. Regardless, Micah had felt violated by the time the man was finished, and he knew he would never look at a roll of measuring tape the same way ever again.

He'd then been made to try on roughly twenty different suits. During this process, he'd learned that he had a cool skin tone and was naturally more suited towards greens, blues, and purples versus warmer colors, wide lapels looked clownish on his frame and should be avoided at all costs, and that while he could pull off ties well enough, bowties were "*magnifico*" – Mr. Bianchi's words, not his.

Frankly, Micah never knew so much work went into making people look good, and he didn't know how anyone could stand it. He told Mr. Bianchi as much.

"I can't believe people undergo this torture willingly," Micah muttered, wincing when Mr. Bianchi poked him in the calf with a safety pin. He was tapering the bottoms of some navy pants that paired with the only jacket that fit him well enough to need only minimal alterations.

Damon was custom ordering everything else with Micah's measurements.

"'Tis art, not torture," Mr. Bianchi scolded him. "Look at Mr. Romano, for instance. He is masterful, no?"

Micah couldn't help but scrunch his nose, hearing Damon referred to as "Mr. Romano". Regardless, he glanced Damon's way. The man was busy on his phone. "Well, yeah, he looks good, but have you seen the man in a t-shirt?" Micah had – just that morning. "He'd look just as enticing in a sweatsuit from Costco."

Mr. Bianchi grimaced, looking pained, and Micah had a feeling another poke was coming his way. It was worth it, though, when he saw a hint of a grin pulling at the corner of Damon's mouth – the only sign the man was paying them any attention.

In the end, Damon had ordered eight full suits. Micah had no idea why he needed more suits than there were days of the week, but when he'd attempted to point this out, both Mr. Bianchi *and* Damon had looked scandalized.

Since all the suits except one were being tailored specifically to his measurements, and the one that wasn't still required alterations, he and Damon left the shop with only three boxes of dress shoes. Apparently, everything else would be ready by the end of next week – rushed, of course, for one of Bianchi's most prestigious customers.

Micah had steadfastly refused to look at the bill Damon had signed off on when they'd left, preferring to remain oblivious to the outrageous amount of money the man had undoubtedly spent on him.

Of course, Micah required more than just suits to play boyfriend to a billionaire – or, at least, said billionaire insisted he did, so the man also ended up dragging him to several boutiques, where he purchased Micah a variety of slacks, jeans, dress shirts, sweaters, and, embarrassingly enough, socks and underwear.

Micah allowed the man to have the final say on everything.

He hardly considered himself fashion-forward, and after all, it *was* Damon's money.

The man seemed to take a surprising amount of pleasure in dressing Micah up like a doll. The bossiness in which he ordered Micah to try on this or that wasn't shocking in the least – Micah had grown used to Damon's unique brand of brashness. But the swarm of butterflies that erupted in Micah's belly whenever the man seemed especially appreciative of an outfit or allowed his eyes to linger on Micah's ass in a certain pair of pants made putting up with his effrontery worth it.

Besides, it wasn't like the man didn't take Micah's opinion into account at all. Damon always asked Micah if the clothes he tried on were comfortable, and ordered the store attendant to grab anything he caught Micah eyeing.

Near the end of their excursion, Micah caught sight of a display of woman's pleated skirts and briefly toyed with the idea of asking Damon if he could try one on. (Mostly because he remembered the man's reaction to seeing him wearing one a week ago when he'd been "working".) Ultimately, though, Micah did have *some* sense of self-preservation, and quickly redirected his eyes away from the display before Damon caught him looking.

Thankfully, the store with the skirts was their last stop, and Micah watched, feeling useless, as Damon crammed the handful of bags in the back of his vehicle with the rest of packages he had purchased. Apparently, Geoffrey had the day off, so Damon had been driving them around himself – not that Micah was complaining. The front of his Rolls-Royce was as sweet as the back.

When he was finished, Damon gestured for Micah to hop in the passenger's seat, and he quickly obliged. All in all, shopping with Damon had been bearable – but *only* because the man had been with him the entire time.

The truth was, Micah was tired and ready to go home, where he could collapse onto his bed and sleep the rest of the day away. (What did it matter if it was only late afternoon?)

Micah's stomach gurgled unhappily as he snapped on his seatbelt. He hadn't noticed how hungry he'd gotten from all that shopping until that moment.

Maybe he'd throw a plate of pizza rolls in the microwave before crawling into bed.

Busy daydreaming of cheese-and-pepperoni stuffed goodness, Micah didn't realize Damon had stiffened at the sound of his stomach rumbling. "You're hungry."

Micah blinked at the accusing note in the man's voice, turning to face him. "Um… yeah? I mean it *is* four in the afternoon. We've been shopping for over five hours. I've built up an appetite."

"We missed lunch." Damon seemed disproportionally distressed over this fact.

"It's no big deal," Micah assured, not enjoying the self-reproach he could hear in the other man's voice. "We've been busy. And besides, I had like twenty crepes at your penthouse," he pointed out reasonably.

"Yes, for *breakfast*," the man shot back. "I forgot to feed you."

Alright, Damon's concern had been cute, at first, if a bit convoluted. But *seriously?*

"I'm not a pet," Micah snapped. "I'm perfectly capable of telling you if I'm hungry. Or better yet, feeding myself."

Micah had been good all day, letting Damon boss him around and dress him up as he pleased – he took pleasure in the man's obvious satisfaction even. But enough was enough. Time to remind Damon that despite the weird power dynamics of their relationship – what with the fact that Damon was loaded and obviously powerful and Micah technically worked for him now – he wasn't *actually* dependent on the man. Lest of all for his basic needs.

"In fact," Micah announced cheerily, "to prove it, I'll buy us lunch."

Damon immediately scowled. "You'll do no such thing."

Micah scowled right back. "I may not be a billionaire like you, but I'm hardly desolate. I can afford to buy us a pizza or a couple of hamburgers. Unless you're too good to eat peasant food."

"That's not it," Damon denied, looking offended by the notion while simultaneously trying to smooth Micah's obviously ruffled feathers. "Have you already forgotten about the contract we both signed? Not only am I responsible for your weekly salary and paying for your new clothing, I'm supposed to take care of any expenses we incur while we're out together – that includes food and drink."

Micah shrugged. "So make an exception."

Damon raised his eyebrows. "I'm not in the habit of making exceptions."

That was obvious, but Micah wasn't about to give in. "Make it a habit, then," he said. "Come on. At least let me pretend that I'm contributing. You just bought me thousands of dollars' worth of clothes. It's the least I can do."

"No."

"Please. It would make me happy."

A muscle in Damon's jaw ticked. Then he huffed. "Fine."

Yes!

"But just this once. And nothing expensive. That would go completely against the whole point of our contract."

Micah beamed. "I know just the place."

Twenty minutes later, Micah had finished directing Damon to The Patty Shack, and they were seated at a neon orange booth, awaiting their food. Micah had ordered his usual – a bacon cheeseburger melt with a side of curly fries and a chocolate milkshake. Damon, on the other hand, had gone with a classic BLT, garlic potato wedges, and a glass of water.

Micah supposed he should have known better than to assume the man would turn his nose up at common-people food. He'd dragged Micah to a taco place – a taco place he was invested in – the first time they'd met, after all.

The burger joint was nearly empty – they'd managed to hit the lull before evening rush – so it wasn't long before their waitress, a friendly redhead that reminded Micah of a younger Tessa, returned with their food.

Micah offered her an enthusiastic "thanks" before immediately plunking a straw into his milkshake and greedily inhaling the sweet ice cream. It was *so good*. Micah glanced over to see that Damon's eyes were locked on his lips, where they were wrapped around the straw.

Micah felt his face heat and quickly looked away.

A moment later, Damon cleared his throat from across the table. "Thank you," the man said before picking up his BLT and taking a bite.

Micah blinked, taken aback. "You're welcome." And then the mortification hit him.

Here Damon was, thanking him for buying him a ten dollar sandwich when the man had literally just finished purchasing him a wardrobe that cost more than he'd ever had in his bank account at any one time, and Micah hadn't expressed even the tiniest bit of appreciation.

"And thank you!" Micah said, the words nearly tripping over themselves in their haste to escape his mouth. "For today, I mean – with the job offer, and all the clothes, and taking time off work. No one has ever done anything like this for me before. Just... thanks."

Damon didn't immediately respond, and Micah was surprised to note that the man seemed almost... uncomfortable with Micah's obvious show of gratitude. He couldn't help but theorize that Damon wasn't used to people thanking him, and Micah was taken off guard by how angry it made him on Damon's behalf.

After a moment, Damon seemed to shake off Micah's "thanks" and set down his sandwich. "There's actually one more thing," he said before digging into one of his pockets. He pulled out a small, flat box and slid it across the table towards Micah. "For you."

Micah frowned. "Haven't you bought me enough?"

"Consider it reimbursement for lunch."

Micah shot the man a disgruntled look. He knew damn well that *that* wasn't the point of Micah picking up the tab. Judging by the way Damon crossed his arms stubbornly over his chest, however, he wasn't about to back down, so Micah reluctantly opened the box.

He stared at the iPhone 14 – a phone so new, it wasn't even on the market yet.

Micah wasn't even surprised at this point, but there was no way he could accept the extravagant gift. "I can't take this," he said, informing Damon as much as he slid the phone back across the table.

Damon's face did this strange thing where it was obvious the man was perturbed, but also, somehow unsurprised. (He was probably used to Micah arguing about everything at this point.) "You can and you will," he refuted, making no move to pick up the phone. "Consider it a requirement of the job. After all, I need a reliable way of contacting you."

"Yeah, okay, but I already have a phone," Micah pointed out, pulling it out for good measure.

Damon eyed the three-year-old, outdated phone, with its scuffed phone case and cracked screen.

"I see that. But like I said, I need a *reliable* way of getting ahold of you. I've already programmed my number in under your contacts. Geoffrey's number is there as well if you ever need him to pick you up. Joelle, too, if you can't get through to me for whatever reason. Of course, you're free to add your father and friends or whoever else you want to the phone, or you can keep using your own phone in addition to this one. It's completely up to you."

Micah felt like he was being manipulated into agreeing, but looking at his phone and comparing it to the immaculate model in the box, he couldn't help but acknowledge that Damon had a point.

Besides, it might be nice to have two phones – easier to keep his real life separate from the sure-to-be calamitous rom-com Damon had convinced him to reenact with him.

"I guess that makes sense," Micah begrudgingly agreed after taking a minute to think it over.

"I'm glad you see things my way," Damon said, like he hadn't been truly worried Micah would refuse – like someone who was used to being in charge and getting their way. (It was nearly enough to make Micah reconsider.) "Make sure to keep it charged and on your person at all times."

"Going to be calling me at odd hours, huh?" Micah couldn't help but tease, picking up and examining the phone.

"Just when I need you," Damon assured, and Micah didn't feel disappointed at all – nope.

"So… Wednesday then?"

It was the night they had agreed to get together and attempt to get to know each other, like an actual couple.

Damon offered a short nod. "Wednesday."

CHAPTER SEVEN

Micah had never really bought into the notion that Mondays were inherently awful.

To him, Mondays represented a clean slate – the start of a brand-new week and a chance to start fresh. Sure, it was the first day of most people's work week, but Micah *liked* his job. And besides, the Starbucks a block from the station offered half-off his favorite drink, their white chocolate mocha, on Mondays.

All in all, Micah chalked Mondays up to be like any other day of the week – sometimes good, sometimes bad, but never god awful enough that he lost his will to live and do it all over again the next day.

Not this Monday.

This Monday lived up to its maniacal reputation. If this Monday was a person, it would have been a Karen. Not your typical, run-of-the-mill, asymmetrical hack job, "Can I speak to your manager?" Karen either. No, this was a Karen who left negative reviews on Yelp because "my sushi was RAW" or "the Grand Canyon wasn't as grand as its name implies", and whose husband was probably a lawyer because she was under the impression she needed to exclaim "I know my rights!" at least once per week to meet her monthly quota.

Why was this Monday so goddamn miserable, you ask?

Well, for one, Micah had accidentally muted his alarm when it had blared to life instead of pressing snooze.

For two, when he had catapulted out of bed and into the shower after realizing he'd overslept, Micah quickly discovered that the building's water heater was out of hot water – *again*.

One cold shower and an uncomfortable dash down the hallway in nothing but a towel later, Micah quickly uncovered the third mini-disaster of the morning – the trifecta of Monday suckage, if you will.

Some asshole had pulled his clothes out of the dryer still half-wet in the communal laundry room.

All of this resulted in Micah rushing into work fifteen minutes late in a wrinkled, damp Henley and two-day old jeans *without* his favorite Starbucks drink. Or Tessa's, for that matter.

Micah had planned to buy her some peppermint hot chocolate – she'd been torturing herself trying to cut down on caffeine since finding out she was pregnant, otherwise he'd have gotten her her standard caramel macchiato. It was meant to be a peace offering, an attempt at buttering her up, after having ditched her at Club Trinity on Friday night and then ghosting her the rest of the weekend.

Alas, he'd come into work empty-handed, and pointedly avoided eye contact with the woman as he settled at his desk – quite the feat considering his cubicle was directly across from hers.

It was only half guilt that caused him to avoid looking in Tessa's direction, however. The rest was pure nerves. Micah was unduly paranoid Tessa would somehow figure out the outrageous deal he'd made with Damon just by looking into his eyes.

Regardless, he could feel her gaze burning a hole into his forehead. "How was your weekend?" she asked nonchalantly after a few tension-filled minutes, like he hadn't avoided roughly a dozen texts messages from her over the past two days.

"Oh, you know," Micah answered vaguely, pretending to work, "the usual." He bit back the urge to blather on about the true crime documentary he'd binged on Netflix, which he'd watched while spooning double-fudge brownie ice cream into his mouth and questioning his life choices. (Tessa knew he had a propensity to ramble when he was nervous.)

Tessa leaned back into her chair. "Huh. That's interesting. I didn't think you *usually* had one-night stands with the offspring of Greek gods, assuming the Damon in your message is the one I think it is, anyway. You know, the one who thinks you're a prostitute."

Micah winced.

"I guess I wouldn't know for sure, though, considering you haven't answered *a single one of my messages.*"

Micah forced himself to look up and meet Tessa's judgmental stare. Despite her narrowed eyes and pinched frown, he could tell by the stiffness in her shoulders that she was mostly just worried.

He felt like a jerk – he *was* a jerk. "I'm an asshole, I know," Micah admitted, "and I'm sorry. I should have answered your texts."

"Yeah, you should have," she said, unrelenting, although her frown smoothed at his apology, "so why didn't you?"

Because Micah had known he would end up spilling his guts about agreeing to become Damon's escort if he did. And then she'd tell him how much of a short-sighted idiot he was – which, he already knew, by the way.

"It's... complicated," Micah decided on after a moment.

Tessa wasn't impressed. "So uncomplicate it," she demanded.

Micah groaned, fighting the urge to bury his head in his hands. How exactly was he supposed to explain that he'd literally *signed a contract* to become Damon's personal escort/pretend boyfriend for the foreseeable future? All because the man was operating under the delusion that he was rescuing Micah from his dangerous life as a sex worker?

Tessa leaned in close, a mischievous – *evil* – glint in her eyes. "Did you fuck?"

Micah flushed, a little embarrassed, but mostly relieved Tessa no longer seemed angry with him.

"Why?" he snarked, his first line of defense against potentially uncomfortable conversations. "Want to hear the sordid details?"

"Yes," Tessa said, unabashed, throwing in an eye roll for good measure. "Obviously."

Honestly, anyone operating under the misconception that women weren't just as big of horndogs as men was dead wrong.

"Well, unfortunately for you, I *have* no details to share. Damon and I didn't have sex."

Tessa raised her eyebrows in disbelief.

"I'm serious," Micah insisted. "I mean, not for lack of trying on my part," he confessed reluctantly. That was as close as he was going to get to admitting he had attempted to blow Damon in the backseat of his car despite the fact the man had still had his pants on.

Tessa looked confused. "He rejected you again?" she demanded before her bewilderment turned to anger. "What is his problem? Practically stalking you, but refusing to follow through. He's a cock tease, is what he is." She paused. "Unless he thought you were too drunk to consent and he was just protecting your virtue?" She nearly swooned in her seat. "Oh, please tell me that's what happened."

"Well, I was pretty drunk," Micah agreed, "but I think the main reason is what you said before. Damon, he, um… he still thinks I'm a prostitute."

Tessa's eyes widened. "Still?" she demanded incredulously. "Why haven't you told him you're actually a cop?"

Micah shrugged. Mostly because he couldn't find the words to explain to her that he was afraid that if he admitted to his true profession, Damon would drop him like a hot brick. As far as he could tell, the man's interest in him stemmed from wanting to "save" Micah and little else. If it turned out Micah didn't need to be saved, well… there was little stopping him from kicking Micah to the curb.

And Micah wasn't ready to sever the weird connection he had with the man. As pathetic and desperate as it was, he would take the farce of a relationship Damon had planned over no contact with the man at all.

"You saw him last week," he said eventually. "He didn't seem overly fond of police."

Yet *another* reason Micah had let the misconception about his job linger.

Tessa frowned. "Well, why'd you leave with him then? He didn't pound you into oblivion. You didn't admit to him that you're an undercover detective. I mean… what did you guys even *do*?"

Well, Micah had passed out in the man's car like the light weight he was and then had woken up to crepes – and the vision of Damon in a t-shirt and sweatpants. Then he'd promptly signed his life away.

Okay, so maybe *life* was a little dramatic – but his free time outside of work was about to be obliterated.

Oh, and Damon had bought him what had to be thousands of dollars' worth of clothes.

"It's a long story."

Tessa opened her mouth – no doubt to protest his vagueness – before spotting something – or rather, some*one* – behind him that made her abruptly snap her mouth shut.

That was all the warning Micah got before a hand came down on his shoulder. Fighting the urge to shake off the unwelcome touch, Micah glanced up.

Ah, *Jensen.*

"I've always admired the easy camaraderie between you two. After all, solidarity amongst colleagues is vital in our line of work. But do you know what I find even more important?" He paused, like he was actually expecting an answer, and when neither he nor Tessa responded, he sighed. "Punctuality," he said finally.

Good morning to you, too, fucker.

Jensen continued to stare him down, like he was waiting for Micah to explain why he was late this morning – which was bullshit. He may have been a first-grade detective, but he wasn't Micah's boss. Although Jensen was often in charge of divvying up the cases they were assigned, Micah didn't *actually* answer to him – only to the captain.

It was clear Jensen wasn't about to let up, however, so Micah shrugged – it had the bonus purpose of dislodging the man's hand from his shoulder. "I'll stay late tonight. It's not a big deal."

Jensen pursed his lips, clearly unimpressed, before allowing his eyes to dip down to Micah's wrinkled shirt and generally unkempt appearance. "Of course, cleanliness is an important aspect of the job as well."

Okay, that was just rude.

Micah was a plain-clothes detective. He didn't wear the standard navy uniform of beat cops or the black attire that members of the SWAT team wore. It was basically just expected that he showed up to work somewhat respectably dressed with his badge visible on his person. "Am I in violation of the dress code?" he asked, making sure to keep his tone as innocent as possible. After all, they both knew he wasn't.

Jensen huffed out his nose. "No," he admitted. "But it's still expected that you maintain an aura of professionalism at the station, especially when dealing with clients, and you're pushing the boundaries."

Jensen referred to any civilians they worked with – whether they be victims, witnesses, reporters, or even suspects – as "clients". It was exceedingly rare that he allowed Micah to actually work with "clients", however – preferring to assign him to grunt work, which equated to doing a lot of research, paperwork, and trudging through surveillance footage.

Micah desperately wanted to point out exactly that, but Jensen was still talking. (He enjoyed the sound of his own voice.)

"It really is unfortunate because I have a pair of parents here to report their son missing. I'm swamped with other cases and I was going to assign this particular project to you – even let you take the role of lead detective – but if you can't even be bothered to dress appropriately for work…" he trailed off.

For the first time, Micah noticed the thin manilla folder in the man's hand. He didn't even care that Jensen was *literally* holding the case above his head. Micah had never been assigned lead detective to a missing persons case before. He'd assisted in a handful, sure, but he'd never been in charge.

"I'll tidy up in the bathroom," Micah offered immediately, although there was not much he could do except attempt to smooth down his hair.

Jensen raised an eyebrow, clearly expecting more.

"And… I'm sorry for my tardiness this morning."

That seemed to do the trick. Jensen handed him the folder. "Here. There's not much there. Just a copy of the picture his parents brought in and the form they filled out when they got here. They're in interview room three. And Micah," – Jensen waited until Micah's eyes met his (they were dark brown, almost black, and arguably the man's best feature) before continuing – "don't make me regret this."

"You won't," Micah assured, "I swear."

It was enough to get the man to nod and back up out of his space. Jensen looked to Tessa. "Tessa," he greeted plainly before taking his leave.

She waited until Jensen was out of earshot before…

"You know the only reason that man rides you so hard is because he wants to *actually* ride you, right?"

Good thing Micah hadn't had time to pick up that white chocolate mocha because if he had, he would undoubtedly be spitting it out right now. "Do *not* put that disturbing image in my brain ever again," he ordered. Not because Jensen wasn't objectively good-looking. He was tall, and fit, with the kind of short, but thick beard that Micah generally found attractive on men. He just also happened to be an uptight prick. "He's nearly a decade older than me." And that.

"And here I thought you were into older men."

Micah stood, recognizing Tessa's taunt as the attempt it was to reel him back into the conversation they'd been having about Damon before Jensen had interrupted. But for once, he had better things to do than entertain her with his clusterfuck of a love life. "In case you missed it, I have an important case to get to."

Tessa smiled. "I'm happy for you," she said honestly, "but don't think I'm about to let this go. I know Damon thinks you're a hooker, but you don't *really* expect me to believe that you spent the entire night with a man that looks like he descended from the gods, and you *didn't* have sex? My interrogation skills are top notch, you know. I once made a man piss himself." It was true – she bragged about it often enough. "Lunch time," she intoned seriously. "Your ass is mine."

Micah had no choice but to agree before heading to the restroom. After attempting to make his hair lay flat with the water from the sink, he eyed the folder Jensen had given him.

Maybe his Monday wasn't destined to be horrible, after all. Tessa's anger had been easy enough to sooth, *and* he'd gotten the lead on a case that wasn't cut-and-dry (like the armed robbery with ten witnesses he'd been assigned to earlier in the month) or completely trivial (like the petty property crimes he was often tasked with).

Micah opened the folder. The first thing he saw was the guy's picture. He was young with golden skin that spoke of Hispanic descent, and his hair was comprised of dark brown ringlets that curled over his forehead. Bright hazel eyes shone out at him.

He was cute.

Micah read through the missing persons form his parents had filled out for him. Nico Sanchez was the kid's name. He was nineteen and studying computer science at Queen's College, where he apparently lived in the dorms. His parents didn't know the last thing he'd been wearing, but the last time they'd heard from their son was over the phone on Friday at 7:00 PM. It was now nearing 9:30 on Monday morning, which meant there had been just over 60 hours since last contact. When they'd called campus security to check on their son before coming into the station, Nico's roommate had said he'd been in the dorm on Saturday morning, but that he hadn't seen him since.

So, probably only missing for closer to 48 hours then.

Micah knew immediately why he'd been selected for this case.

It wasn't a particularly glamorous assignment.

Nico was a college student, who hadn't answered his parents' calls over the weekend or returned to his dorm since Saturday. Odds were, he'd gotten shitfaced and crashed somewhere else, possibly losing his phone in the process, but most likely just too wrapped up in his life to realize he was genuinely worrying his family.

Of course, it was nearing December and finals were quickly approaching. It was just as likely the stress had gotten the better of him and Nico had simply taken off – completely of his own volition – for a while.

Either way, the prognosis was good that Nico was alive somewhere – especially if he was the average thoughtless nineteen-year-old who simply just did some very dumb things on occasion.

That's what Micah's limited experience and common sense told him, anyway. Still… for some reason, when he looked at Nico's picture, gazing into hazel eyes not dissimilar to his own, Micah got a heavy, uncomfortable feeling in the pit of his stomach, and he vowed to do everything he could to find the young man, whether he was just off being a typical, reckless nineteen-year-old or not.

It was why he'd become a detective, after all – to help people.

With that thought in mind, Micah determinedly tucked Nico's folder under his arm and made his way to the interview room Jensen had indicated, not wanting to leave Nico's parents waiting.

In short order, Micah was cursing Jensen both in his mind and under his breath. It would have been nice of the man to mention that neither Nico's mother nor father – Juanita and Jorge Sanchez, first-generation immigrants – spoke a lick of English.

Luckily, Manny Rivera – one of the precinct's interpreters, who had helped the couple fill out the missing persons form – was still around, and it was only after a handful of embarrassing attempts to communicate that Micah was smart enough to fetch him.

From then on, the interview ran much more smoothly.

The thrill – the small tendril of joy – that had shot through him at being assigned to Nico's case, however, quickly evaporated. Watching Mrs. Sanchez sob as she described her last phone call with her son was heartbreaking. According to Juanita, they hadn't spoken of anything unusual, and that while Nico had seemed somewhat distracted, he'd been in overall good spirits.

Both Mr. and Mrs. Sanchez went to great lengths to make sure Micah understood that Nico was a "good boy" who was doing very well in his studies – the first of their family to go to college – and that he wouldn't ignore calls from his mother on purpose.

Micah didn't hear a speck of shame in Nico's father's voice when he revealed that his son was gay.

Luckily, because they seemed to have such a close relationship with Nico, they were able to provide Micah with a list of a dozen names of people that Nico was close to, either in the past or present. Included on that list was his roommate and an ex-boyfriend he was still friendly with.

As far as they knew, Nico was currently single.

Towards the end of the interview, Micah found himself tempted to console them – to explain to them that there was a good chance

Nico had simply partied too hard, or perhaps run off – but hearing the pride in their voices as they spoke of their son, Micah knew intrinsically that there was no way they would accept such a simple answer to their son's disappearance, and the last thing Micah wanted to do was minimize their concerns.

So he shook Mr. Sanchez's hand when the interview wrapped up, and accepted a surprisingly firm hug from the tiny Mrs. Sanchez, who was so short she didn't even reach Micah's shoulder.

"I promise I'll do everything in my power to find him," he told them, and he meant it.

The first thing he did after the interview was put out a BOLO (Be on the Lookout) for Nico.

The rest of Micah's morning was spent looking into the list of friends the young man's parents had given him. Only half, including Nico's roommate, picked up their phones – a result of seeing NYPD on their caller ID no doubt. He conducted phone interviews with everyone who'd picked up, and scheduled a time for them to come down to the precinct for in-person interviews later in the week if Nico still hadn't returned by then. He left messages for the rest.

He skipped his lunch break, which Tessa hadn't been too thrilled about all things considered, but she'd brought him back a sandwich, anyway.

He was up to his eyeballs in Nico's various social media accounts, searching for clues to where he could have gone, when Jensen eventually returned to his desk.

"Micah?"

Micah nearly jumped out of his seat at the sound of the man's voice so close to his ear. He turned to see Jensen looming over him. Honestly, hadn't he ever heard of personal space?

Jensen was openly examining the pages he had up on his computer, a little wrinkle forming in his brow at what he saw. (He was probably surprised by how seriously Micah was taking the case he'd assigned him.)

Micah cleared his throat, and Jensen's eyes swiveled back to him. "Did you need something?" Micah asked.

"The captain wants a word with you."

Micah felt himself tense. He blinked in surprise. "Really? I mean, uh, sure. Okay." He closed the tabs on his computer before standing. "Do you know what he wanted?"

Jensen just shrugged. "You tell me."

So helpful.

Fighting the urge to roll his eyes, Micah made his way to the captain's office.

Captain Abram Hart was a busy man – he oversaw the entire 105th precinct, which included dealing with the press, securing their budget, and juggling a slew of other responsibilities that equated to doing a whole lot of paperwork.

Even with all that on his plate, he was a great police captain. He was a firm, but fair boss, and very personable – his face well-known throughout the office. He allowed Dolores and the other ladies who ran the front lobby to host a variety of fundraisers and BBQs whenever they got a bee in their bonnet to boost team morale, and he was honestly invested in the well-being of everyone that worked under him.

It was just... Micah, personally, tended to avoid him while he was at work. For obvious reasons.

Realizing he'd reached the man's office, Micah sighed before rapping his knuckles on the door.

Knock. Knock.

"Come in."

Micah pushed open the door. "Captain Hart, good morning, sir" he greeted.

Captain Hart looked up from some papers he'd been studying on his desk. He was a sturdy man in his early fifties with hair that was full, but almost completely gray, and astute green eyes that peered at Micah behind a set of thick-frame glasses. The handlebar mustache he sported had gone out of style in the 90's, but he'd had it for as long as Micah could remember.

"Hardly morning anymore," Captain Hart pointed out. "Have a seat, Detective Hart."

And did Micah mention that the man was his father?

In Micah's opinion, it was the main reason for Jensen's general animosity towards him. It wasn't a hair-pulling crush like Tessa's romance-inclined mind theorized. The man was just pissed because he didn't think that Micah had had to work for his job. Who cared if Micah had graduated with a double major in criminal justice and sociology? Who cared if he passed police academy training with flying colors, his file filled with comments like "excellent instincts" and "superb reflexes"?

Not Jensen certainly. (Though it was funny how the nepotism Jensen was convinced existed in their precinct didn't sully the man's opinion of his father any. Jensen was up the man's ass any opportunity he got.)

Ultimately, Micah couldn't control what other people thought. He loved his work, and he wasn't about to quit, so he'd taken to giving his father a wide berth at the station, and downplaying their relationship as much as possible. It was a decision his father was well aware of, which was why Micah was surprised to have been called into his office.

"Micah," he snapped, jerking his son from his thoughts. Realizing he'd spaced out, Micah quickly shut the door and sat in the cushioned chair across from Captain Hart's desk.

(Micah tried to avoid referring to him as his dad even internally at work to avoid an unfortunate slip.)

"Is this about being late?" Micah asked. "Because I called ahead-"

Captain Hart waved off his concern before he even finished voicing it. "Jensen already said you planned to stay late to make up for it," he said. "Though I assume you won't make a habit of it."

Micah shook his head, trying not to feel weirded out that Jensen was talking with the captain – *his dad* – about him. "Of course not."

Captain Hart nodded. Then…

"You missed the game yesterday. Giants nearly won it this week."

Micah frowned. He doubted his father had called him into his office to make small talk, let alone about football. While it was true that he watched the game with him most Sundays, Micah by far preferred baseball.

He went along with it, anyway. "Yeah, I know. Sorry about that. It was a... strange weekend," he decided on after a moment.

The captain furrowed his brow. "I'm assuming I don't want to know the details."

Abram fully accepted that his son was gay – and he loved Micah no less for it – but he'd made it pretty clear early on that he didn't want to know the details of his love life. If it was serious, he expected Micah to bring the man home so he could meet him, but that was about it.

Micah knew he'd feel the same way if he was into girls, so he didn't take offense to it.

He thought of mouthing Damon's dick in the back of the man's Rolls-Royce. "That's... probably a safe assumption."

Abram nodded, and a semi-uncomfortable silence descended.

Micah knew his father had more to say, but he clearly wanted Micah to talk – *to crack* – first. It was a tactic he'd used often on Micah when he was a teenager and thought he was up to something devious.

Problem was, Micah had no idea what his father thought he was hiding. Micah licked his lips. "Is that all?"

After a long moment, Abram finally broke eye contact. He sighed. "No, there's more. Dolores informed me about a disturbing incident that happened in the lobby at the end of last week."

Micah froze.

There was no way his dad was talking about what he thought he was talking about.

"As you know, the lobby is equipped with plenty of cameras. At Dolores's insistence, I watched as a man stormed in, clearly troubled, and demanded to know the name of the latest victim of the Hooker Hunter. Dolores was very concerned about his rudeness – not to mention his blatant threats and attempt at bribery. She didn't think twice about the fact that the person he was specifically asking after was named Micah." It was here that Abram dropped his false nonchalance, his stern gaze returning. "But then again, Dolores doesn't have a son named Micah who'd just spent the past week undercover as a prostitute. This man seemed awfully relieved to realize that this Micah person wasn't the perp's victim." Abram raised his eyebrows. "Do you have anything to share that might bring clarity to this situation? Before I start making troubling assumptions?"

Micah was tempted to claim it was all just a weird coincidence, but his father didn't believe in coincidences. Plus, the embarrassed flush he could feel creeping up his neck would probably give him away.

"Damon and I ran into each other while I was undercover," he admitted reluctantly.

Abram's face twisted into a grimace, and Micah immediately understood his mistake. "Not like that! He didn't approach me for... sex... or anything. He actually chased off a potential john for manhandling me. Kind of annoying, actually, but sweet, too, how he was so concerned."

Abram hummed. "He left a big enough impression that you remember his name was Damon, I see."

"He remembered mine was Micah," Micah pointed out defensively – before recognizing the familiarity with which his father had spoken Damon's name. "Wait. Did you already know his name was Damon? Before just now, I mean?"

Abram didn't answer his question. "Yeah, funny how he knew your name was Micah, considering you were undercover with an alias."

Shit.

Micah couldn't even argue that he hadn't given away his name during their first meeting – because that would mean admitting there had been more than one. "Like you said, I guess he left an impression." Micah crossed his arms over his chest. "So, does this mean you're going to bar me from doing more undercover work? Because besides the slip-up with my name, I didn't do anything wrong. In fact, I would argue I did *too* good of a job pretending to be a desolate prostitute considering I made someone worried enough about me that they went to the police."

Abram slammed his fist down onto his desk so hard that the picture frame of Micah's mother shook. "I don't want that man having a single thought about you," he boomed, "let alone worrying enough over you to go to the police."

Micah fought to contain his shock at his father's extreme reaction. "Is this where you admit why you knew Damon's name before I told you it?" he asked.

Abram scoffed. "Do you really think I'd be so concerned if it was just some random civilian who came in asking about you?"

Micah frowned. "I suppose not."

"Damon Romano is *not* a good man. He's dangerous. And if you ever see him again, I need you to promise me you'll run in the opposite direction."

His father wasn't prone to making dramatic statements, so Micah thought it was perfectly acceptable to find he had a sudden stomachache. He swallowed around the lump in his throat. "If he's so dangerous, why isn't he behind bars?"

Abram released a short, sardonic bark of laughter. "I know this will probably be hard for you to accept, Micah, since it's your job to uphold justice and try to keep this world as safe and fair as possible. But some people are untouchable, and Damon Romano is one of them."

Micah licked his dry lips. He wasn't sure he wanted to know, but... "What'd he do?"

"What hasn't he done?" Abram shot back. "He's *mafia*, Micah," he said, finally spelling it out, "and not some underling or lowly gangster. He's the boss. He has his family's fingers in as many illegal projects as legal ones, and whether it's by his own hand or not, the people around him have an unfortunate tendency to wind up dead."

Micah was going to vomit.

"As you can imagine," his father continued, oblivious to the panic attack hovering on the fringes of his son's composure, "he's not a big fan of the police – at least not any that aren't in his pocket. He wouldn't have come here unless he thought it was important – unless he thought *you* were important." Abram paused. "I find it

118

hard to believe he would develop these sort of… feelings for you as a result of a simple run-in."

"What exactly are you accusing me of here, Dad?" Micah snapped. He blamed the fact that his stomach was currently flip-flopping for the slip of tongue – and the emotion that leaked into his voice. "You think we fucked while I was on the clock? That I was *actually* prostituting myself out? What?"

"Of course not!" Abram blustered.

"Because I haven't done anything to encourage whatever interest you're convinced he has in me." *Not during their first encounter, anyway.* "He bought me supper – practically frog-marched me into some Mexican Place called *El Taco Rosa*, but that was it. It's all in the report Tessa wrote up."

"And he didn't make any sort of move on you?" Abram demanded.

Not at that point. "No," Micah said firmly. "I'm pretty sure he thought I was underage, and he was just trying to be a Good Samaritan."

The way his father's face wrinkled made it clear what he thought of *that.*

After a moment, however, he sighed. "I believe you," he said. "But if anything, it makes his fascination with you even more concerning. There's no telling how he'd react if he found out the kid he was hellbent on helping – which I'm still not convinced was his motive in approaching you, by the way – was actually a cop."

Micah was doing his very best *not* the think about that at the moment.

He took a deep breath in through his nose. "Damon probably didn't give our encounter a second thought until the article about the Hooker Hunter being caught broke. While his concern was intense, it was also probably brief. Now that he knows that it wasn't the kid he helped who was attacked, he's probably forgotten all about it – and me."

Abram ran a hand down his tired face. "For your own sake, I hope you're right."

"I'm sure I am," Micah said, wondering how his pants had yet to catch on fire considering he was *such a fucking liar.* "Now that that's settled, was there anything else you wanted to talk about?"

Abram sighed. "No, no, I suppose you can return to work."

Micah took that as the dismissal it was and stood from his chair.

"But Micah…" his father called out before he'd even reached the door.

Micah reluctantly turned. "Yes?"

"Be careful, alright?" It sounded like a warning.

"I always am," he assured, forcing a smile on his face that felt wooden.

Abram returned it with a wince, and Micah couldn't help but wonder if all the stupid, heart attack-inducing stunts he'd pulled as a kid – like that time he jumped from their second story roof and broken his arm because he was convinced he could fly (he was *eight*, alright?) – were flashing through his mind.

After closing the door to his father's office, Micah forced his legs to move at a normal pace as they led him to the bathroom. As soon as he confirmed that the room was empty, however, he hurriedly locked himself in one of the stalls and all but threw himself at the toilet, retching as he attempted to empty the contents of his upset stomach.

Unfortunately, nothing came up since he hadn't had time to eat breakfast that morning. After a full three minutes of dry heaving, all he had to show for his efforts were a sore throat, watery eyes, and a stomach in just as much upheaval as when he'd entered the restroom.

He rested his head against the toilet seat in defeat before immediately regretting the decision and lifting it off. Who knew whose ass had been there last? The thought that it could have been Jensen's – or his father's – made him shiver in disgust.

(Micah was fully aware he was coping with the revelation his father had made about Damon in his office by hard-core compartmentalizing and steadfastly avoiding the topic.)

He reluctantly stepped out of the stall and approached the sink. He splashed some water in his face, but a quick glance at his reflection confirmed it did nothing to perk up his ashen complexion or dispel the red splotches crawling up his neck – something that only happened when he was in extreme emotional distress, and at the moment... well, he was feeling pretty gutted.

What the fuck was he going to do?

Damon – the man who'd kicked the crap out of the guy who had tried to assault him, who was obsessed with feeding him, who worried after him, who was so desperate to get Micah off the streets that he'd bought him thousands of dollars' worth of clothes and wanted to pay him *ten grand a week* to go on dates with him – was, apparently, a mafia don.

He knew that if his father – the fucking captain of the police force – said it, that it was irrevocably true.

Yet, Micah couldn't reconcile the polarizing versions of the man in his head. Damon had been so unflinchingly kind to Micah. Sure, he was bossy, and it was obvious Damon was rich – like ridiculously, *filthy* rich-

Micah's thoughts came to a screeching halt.

Damon *was* filthy rich – and in the police force, it was commonly understood why they called it "filthy": because you didn't accumulate that sort of wealth without getting blood on your hands.

Micah recalled asking Damon what he did for a living to make so much money, and being told he worked in "finances" – that he had his hands in a lot of projects, but mostly real estate. In hindsight, that answer had been shady as fuck.

Micah should have known better – especially as a police detective.

Shit.

What if Damon found out that the "prostitute" he'd hired to be his personal escort was a cop?

The man knew where he lived.

Shitshitshitshitshit. Micah was a fool – a complete fucking idiot.

And worst of all, deep down in the fiber of his bones, Micah knew he still liked him. The attraction he felt towards Damon could be excused. He was a fine specimen of a man, no matter how you diced it – moonlighting as a mafia boss or not. But Micah, honest-to-God, genuinely *cared* about him.

Micah dug the palms of his hands as hard as he could into his eye sockets, willing the disturbing realization to dissipate. He wasn't going to think about it. So his life was a bigger, hotter dumpster fire than he'd thought; he could have a mental breakdown about it later. Right now, he needed to concentrate on his job. There were two parents of a nineteen-year-old kid who needed him to find their son.

It was the thought of Nico alone that staved off the panic attack Micah could feel brewing on the horizon. He yanked several paper towels out from the expender – perhaps more violently then they deserved – and patted dry his face.

Even as he got back to work, however, Micah couldn't help but think he'd been wrong about Mondays, after all.

They truly did colossally suck.

CHAPTER EIGHT

Tuesday was only a hair more tolerable than Monday.

Micah had stayed late Monday evening – much longer than the fifteen minutes he had been late to work called for – but he kept himself busy the entire while, only leaving when dusk had fallen.

He'd carefully scrutinized Nico's online presence and the multitude of social media platforms he and the list of Nico's friends the Sanchezes had given to him used. This involved painstakingly dissecting every picture Nico had posted of himself or had been tagged in over the past year. (This served the dual purpose of unearthing any companions Nico's parents *didn't* know about, and scoping out the young man's usual haunts.)

By the time Micah had clocked out, he knew that Nico's favorite coffee shop was a hole-in-the-wall café near Queen's College named The Tea, that he frequented drag queen bars with his friends on the weekends, and that in nearly every picture, he smiled with his entire face – crinkles near the corner of his eyes and a big, silly grin with shiny, white teeth on display.

In addition to probing his social media, most of Nico's friends had returned Micah's calls, and he'd been able to get a plethora of interviews lined up over the next few days. He'd also made roughly a dozen calls in order to secure permission from Queen's College to search Nico's dorm room.

Micah may or may not have been running himself ragged in order to avoid thinking about the train wreck that was his personal life. (But even if he was, was it really such a bad thing that Nico got the benefit of his fevered attention?)

Micah had been dead tired by the time he'd gotten home, and the theory that if he worked himself to the point of exhaustion, he wouldn't have time to obsess over the clusterfuck of a situation he'd gotten himself into with Damon seemed to prove true.

He'd only experienced a small pang of discomfort when he'd spotted the gleaming, new iPhone 14 sitting innocently on his kitchen counter, the hysteria he'd feel otherwise buried beneath all the fatigue. Pointedly avoiding checking the phone for messages, Micah had merely shut the device off and turned it face down on the counter, determined to deal with the problem it represented another day, before collapsing into his bed and allowing sleep to take him.

Which brought Micah to today – Tuesday.

It was nearing noon, and he'd interviewed three of Nico's friends, including the ex, and not one of them claimed to know where he could have gone – or even why he would have left. They all showed the appropriate amount of concern for Nico, not one of them triggering his bullshit detector.

Two of them had been Nico's study partners, pursuing the same degree in computer science. They'd been adamant that Nico was doing well at school. He wasn't falling behind on his work, like someone overwhelmed by college might have been. It all but killed the working theory that Nico might have taken off because of the pressure of upcoming finals.

It was concerning to them – and to Micah – that he had missed classes yesterday, and now today. Adding to the frustration (and worry) was the fact that there had been no new updates from Nico's social media – which Micah was carefully monitoring. Not once in the past year had Nico gone more than a handful of days without updating his Instagram – until now.

It didn't paint a pretty picture.

Micah had arrived at Queen College's campus a few minutes ago, and he was on his way up to Nico's third floor dormitory to search his room and interview his roommate. He could only hope that something he found – or something Nico's roommate, a freshman by the name of Mateo Flores, said – would shed some light on the situation.

The door he wound up in front of was free of debris, unlike some of the others he'd passed to get there, which were covered in posters, whiteboards, and other miscellaneous decorations.

He raised his hand.

Knock. Knock.

"Mr. Flores – Mateo – it's Detective Hart. We spoke on the-"

Micah didn't even have to finish his sentence before the door was ripped open. Obviously, he'd been expected.

"Hi," Mateo immediately greeted before doing a double take. "Wow, you're younger than I thought you'd be." He blanched. "Not that that's a bad thing!" he rushed to clarify, nervously wiping his hands on his jeans. "I'm sure you're good at your job."

"Uh... thank you?" It was a rare occurrence that Micah met someone more awkward than himself.

Mateo was tall and lanky with close-cropped hair and a pair of hipster glasses perched on his nose that were almost cartoonish.

"It's nice to meet you," Mateo added, thrusting a hand out. "Well, not nice – you know, considering the circumstances. But I'm sure you're a nice person."

"Um, thanks again?" Micah said, accepting the handshake. "I'm here to search Nico's room."

"Oh, right!" Mateo hurriedly stepped aside. "Come in. This is Nico's side," he said, gesturing towards the bed with the maroon-colored bedspread and a cluttered desk.

Micah's first impression was that it was relatively clean for a college dorm. Sure, Nico's desk was covered in an array of books and notes – and a laptop Micah was eager to examine – but there were no dirty clothes littered on the floor or opened Dorito bags lying around. (Though maybe Micah was biased because that was how *his* dorm had looked.) A peek inside Nico's closet revealed a wardrobe many fashionistas would be envious of. Rifling through the immaculately pressed pants and vibrant-colored shirts, Micah spotted names like Alexander McQueen and Dolce and Gabbana.

Micah was no expert, but he knew there was no way he himself could have afforded those brands as a college freshman. (Or as a police detective, for that matter.)

Mateo cleared his throat, bringing Micah's attention back to him. "So, um, should I leave?"

"Let's do that interview we talked about first," Micah suggested, closing the closet door.

"Oh, yeah, of course." Mateo glanced around the room. "Feel free to have a seat... uh, anywhere, I guess."

Not wanting to disturb Nico's desk quite yet, Micah took a seat on the edge of the missing boy's mattress, gesturing for Mateo to do the same on his own meticulously made bed. "Do you mind if I record this?" Micah asked, pulling a department-issued device from the small bag of equipment he'd brought with. He also took out a notebook and pen.

Mateo glanced nervously at the recorder, but he voiced his agreement.

"Okay," Micah said, beginning the interview, "so I know we've been over a lot of this on the phone already, but for the sake of clarity, can you please tell me about the last time you saw your roommate, Nico Sanchez."

Mateo licked his lips. "Uh, it was Saturday morning. He left the dorm sometime between nine and ten, I think. Said he was going out, but didn't say where."

"And was that usual for him?" Micah asked. "To not let you know where he was going when he went out?"

"I'm his roommate," Mateo pointed out, nervously pushing up his glasses, "not his keeper. He meets with his study group sometimes on Saturdays, but it's not like I grilled him about it."

Micah frowned at the almost... *defensive* tone, making note of it before continuing. "Do you know if he was meeting with anyone, in particular, on *this* Saturday?"

Mateo shrugged, and Micah gestured at the recording device.

Mateo flushed. "I don't know."

"What was he wearing?"

"Just a pair of jeans and a long-sleeve shirt. It was red, I think – one of those fancy designer ones."

Micah was grateful for the opening Mateo had unwittingly provided, quickly latching onto it. "Yeah, I saw he had quite a few of those in his closet. According to Nico's parents, he's at Queen's College on a scholarship. How does he afford such luxurious clothes?"

Mateo squirmed in discomfort, once again fiddling with his glasses – an obvious tell that he was nervous. "I don't know."

"Does he have a job?" Micah pressed. "One that his parents might not be aware of?"

"Not- not that I know of."

Mateo was obviously uncomfortable with Micah's line of questioning, and he didn't want to push – yet. So he switched back to questions about when Mateo had last seen Nico. "How did Nico leave when he took off on Saturday? Was he on foot? Did he usually take the subway?"

If he had, subways stations generally had plenty of cameras. Perhaps Micah could look into acquiring the security footage of the one closest to Nico's dorm – before it was eventually erased and taped over, a common occurrence when dealing with CCTV.

Mateo frowned, and then, almost reluctantly… "I think he took an Uber, actually."

"You think?"

"He got a call shortly before he took off. I think it was the driver, saying he was here."

"Was that typical for him to use Uber?" Micah asked.

"Only when he was drunk," Mateo admitted. "It's cheaper to take the subway."

Micah hummed. "Did Nico drink often?"

"Not excessively. Just, you know, as much as any other college student."

"Have you ever seen him use drugs?"

Mateo's eyes strayed to the recorder.

"You won't get in trouble for anything you're about to tell me," Micah assured, making sure he spoke clearly, and gesturing at the recording device to ensure that Mateo understood he had Micah saying so on record if he thought he'd try to pull something later.

Micah wasn't sure if it worked, or if it was just his youth that made him seem trustworthy to Mateo, but it had the young man confessing, "We did pot together once or twice. Nothing harder than that."

Micah nodded. "What about Nico's behavior? Had he been acting strangely before his disappearance? Any out-of-character outbursts?"

"He's been normal, honestly."

"How about the morning he left? Was he acting weird? Nervous, maybe?"

Mateo shrugged, and his hands went to his glasses – *again.* "Not really."

"Not *really*?" Micah pressed. "Care to clarify?"

"He seemed a little... cagey, I guess," Mateo admitted. "Like, sort of excited, but sort of anxious too. I thought that maybe he was going out on a brunch date or something."

Micah quickly jotted that down. "But you have no idea who he could have been meeting," he said – more of a statement than a question since Mateo had already made it clear that he didn't.

"No."

"Can you think of anything else that may be helpful in finding Nico? It could be something small, or something you think is unrelated to his disappearance – anything at all that sticks out in your brain."

Mateo hesitated – it was only for half of a second, but Micah caught it. "No."

Micah turned off the recorder, and Mateo's shoulders slumped in relief.

But Micah didn't let him bask in that feeling for long. He leaned forward, keeping his demeanor serious, but hopefully still empathetic. "Mateo, listen, I think you're holding something back."

The kid sputtered.

"Maybe it's something that you think will embarrass Nico or get him into trouble. Maybe you think you're being a good friend by keeping it to yourself – that it's not your place to tell some random cop his secrets. But it *is* your place, and I'm *not* just any cop. I'm the cop charged with finding your friend, and it's going to be difficult if I don't have all the facts laid out on the table. I'm going to be honest with you. I don't have much to go on at the moment. Whatever you're hiding, it could be the difference between finding Nico alive and… well, *never* finding him."

Mateo was wringing his hands, obviously nervous, but he didn't seem convinced by Micah's spiel.

"Look," Micah pushed – just a little, "I'd hate for you to have the shoulder the guilt of knowing you could have helped find your friend and chose not to for the rest of your life, so whatever it is, just tell me – for your own sake, if not mine or Nico's."

Mateo's gaze, which had been trained determinedly at a spot above Micah's shoulder, wavered – and he seemed to struggle internally over something before his eyes suddenly dropped to the floor. "There is *one* thing," he admitted reluctantly.

Thank God.

"Yes?" Micah pressed.

"I walked in on him once a couple weeks ago when he was… on the computer." Mateo's entire face flushed. "I guess he thought I'd gone home for the weekend. I didn't mean to barge in-"

"Mateo, I believe you," Micah assured, reaching across the small bit of space between them and resting what he hoped was a comforting hand on his forearm. Mateo immediately calmed. "What was he doing on the computer?" Micah asked.

He better not have bothered with all that careful prodding just to be told that Nico was into some weird porn.

"Uh, he was recording himself… *you know*," – Mateo lowered his voice – "polishing the banister."

Micah's eyebrows rose of their own accord. "You mean masturbating? So… you think he was working as, like, a camboy?"

Mateo seemed relieved he didn't actually have to say the words out loud. "Yeah, I think that's what he was doing."

It would certainly explain Nico's extravagant wardrobe, and the fact that he could afford coffee from a place more expensive than Starbucks. He probably had a man – or multiple men – venmoing him money for his performances.

"How often did he pose on his webcam?" Micah asked.

"Uh, I don't know. He didn't do it while I was here, obviously."

Obviously.

Micah pressed his lips together, thinking. "Do you remember when he started accumulating the more expensive clothes in his wardrobe? Maybe there's been extravagant gifts sent to the dorm?"

Mateo frowned. "I remember right before Halloween that he got these super sweet AirPods in the mail. He told me they were a gift from his parents, but if he's really here on scholarship like you said… I'm guessing maybe they weren't?"

Since Halloween – so Nico had probably been doing shows for at least a month.

Micah stood, picking up Nico's laptop, which was still sitting on his desk. "This was the computer he was using to work as a camboy?"

Mateo's already pink complexion grew splotchy at the reemergence of *that* word. "Yeah, that's what he was using."

Micah carefully pried it open. There was still battery life, but the screen saver immediately prompted him for a password.

Fuck.

It was probably too much to hope for, but Micah looked back at Mateo. "I don't suppose you happen to know his password?"

Mateo's brow crinkled. "He called me to e-mail him an assignment from his laptop once, and he had to tell me his password to get to it. If it's still the same, it should be, uh, *3319hufflepuff*. He told me it's his old basketball jersey number, his age, and the Hogwarts house in Harry Potter-"

"-where the hardworking and loyal students are sorted, yeah, I know. I mean, I'm a Gryffindor myself, but I totally stan the Puffs."

Mateo blinked, looking a bit stunned by Micah's unprofessional rambling, but Micah didn't care. The password worked, and Nico's home screen popped up. He grinned. "Thank you, Mateo," Micah said, truly grateful. "You have no idea how helpful you've been."

"Of course," Mateo said, rubbing the back of his neck, "but, uh, you don't think whatever's going on with Nico has anything to do with… *that*, right?"

To be honest, Micah had no idea if the fact that Nico was apparently moonlighting as a camboy had anything to do with his disappearance. But it was a starting point, at least.

Micah offered Mateo a tight smile. "I can't actually answer that without compromising the integrity of the investigation," he pointed out.

"Oh." Mateo retreated a step. "Oh yeah, of course. I'll just, um, get out of your hair then, if you want to look over the room."

Micah nodded in agreement and let Mateo know he could return in an hour. It shouldn't take him longer than that to finish inspecting the room and take a couple of pictures of Nico's more expensive clothes. (Or anything else that happened to catch his eye.) He wouldn't rush the search, but Micah couldn't deny he was eager to bring Nico's laptop back to the precinct for a more thorough examination.

Finally, *a lead.*

CHAPTER NINE

By Wednesday, the excitement of finding his first lead had winked out of existence entirely.

Partially because Micah had actually had to call Mr. and Mrs. Sanchez in to the station and *tell* them that their son was masturbating on camera for extra cash. (He'd promised both them *and* himself that he would keep them up-to-date with any breakthroughs, big or small, in their son's case).

They'd denied that Nico was working as a camboy, of course – *fiercely.*

Micah wasn't fluent in Spanish, but even he was able to pick up on the various (creative) expletives that Mrs. Sanchez, in particular, took to spouting in his general direction. In the span of a half an hour, he'd been called a *"mentiroso"* (liar), a *"puto"* (whore), and Micah's personal favorite: *"inútil como un saco de mierda".*

With an apologetic wince, Manny, the interpreter, had explained to Micah that she'd called him "as worthless as a sack of shit", except she'd went on to add that "even the sack had its uses if one washed it thoroughly enough".

Micah understood their anger.

He'd told them that their son was getting himself off for random men on the Internet for money, and they saw it as an attempt to smear Nico's character – maybe even as an excuse to put his case on the back burner.

Of course, the fact that Nico was working as a camboy didn't make finding him any less of a priority. In fact, Micah had argued to Mr. and Mrs. Sanchez that it made finding the nineteen-year-old *more* urgent since it was possible he'd disappeared after meeting one of his... *customers* from the website.

After Micah had explained that, they'd seemed a tad more open to the possibility that their son had, in fact, been working as a camboy – at least enough to look at the evidence.

A quick exploration of Nico's search history had revealed the website their son had been working for, and when Micah had typed in Nico's location and demographics, he'd been able to find the profile he thought belonged to Nico: *goldenboi19*. There was no face in the naked-except-for-his-underwear profile picture, but the small, barely noticeable birthmark underneath his right pectoral (that the Sanchezes had made note of when they'd filed Nico's papers) had Micah convinced.

Mr. Sanchez had wilted a bit at seeing the picture, but not Mrs. Sanchez. She hadn't been persuaded until Micah had used Nico's laptop to pull up her son's Venmo account. Luckily, Nico had saved his password to the laptop, which made pulling up the account easy. It confirmed Nico had been receiving fairly large amounts of money from seemingly random strangers since mid-October.

That was enough to finally get Mrs. Sanchez to accept the facts for what they were, and she'd gone from cursing Micah's very existence to all but crying in his arms.

Micah *so badly* wanted to find her son for her.

Which brought Micah to the main reason his excitement had faded. Progress on Nico's case had come to a standstill.

He had contacted the website Nico had been working for. There had been no number listed under the customer service bar – a major red flag. There *had* been an e-mail address, however, so Micah had written to them his dilemma. In return, he'd received what he could only conclude was a form letter, which stated that in order to protect the privacy of its clientele, the website's policy was to under no circumstances reveal identifying information of its users.

Venmo, apparently, adhered to the same policy.

Unless, of course, Micah had a warrant. Which he couldn't get without probable cause.

It was bullshit.

And it sucked.

There had been no further useful information on Nico's laptop. Like everyone else under the age of fifty, the nineteen-year-old conducted most of his online activity on his cellphone, which Micah didn't have.

Micah had been forced to rethink his approach to the investigation.

He'd called various administrative members of Queen's College, requesting permission to examine the CCTV footage of the camera he'd noticed situated outside of Nico's dormitory the day before.

Watching the footage verified that Nico had left on foot Saturday morning – in the *opposite* direction of the subway. It all but confirmed Mateo's theory that Nico had left via Uber.

Unfortunately, whatever vehicle he'd gotten into hadn't been caught on camera. And it wasn't like Micah had access to Nico's phone to simply reverse dial the number that had called him before he'd left.

So... despite the fact that Nico had likely met up with someone he'd encountered on the sketchy site he webcammed for (*spankbankboys.com*, honestly), Micah still didn't know who that person was or where Nico was meeting them at or... or even if he was still alive.

The intimate knowledge that with each hour Nico remained missing, the more likely it was he *wasn't* alive, hung over Micah like an ominous cloud, threatening to crush his spirits at times, but he refused to let dark thoughts take hold.

Instead, Micah was using the fact that Nico – and his parents – were depending on him to find him before anything bad happened, as a motivator.

Which was why despite the fact that it was past six in the evening and there was a monster migraine building behind his eyes (probably from staring at his computer screen as he obsessively checked Nico's various social media platforms for updates), Micah was still at work.

He only tore his eyes away from the screen when his ringtone blared to life. He dug his phone out of his back pocket, checking who was calling him.

Tessa.

Micah winced. Shit. He'd forgotten that when she'd left at four, she'd threatened to call him later to make sure he actually got home at a decent time – unlike the previous two nights.

He sighed, accepting the call. "Hello?"

"Can you believe that dumbass's answer to that question?"

It took longer than it should have for Micah's overworked brain to realize what Tessa was talking about: The Family Feud. They often called each other to make fun of the contestants of the popular game show.

He cleared his throat. "Uh, yeah, crazy," he agreed vaguely.

"What would your answer have been?" she demanded.

Fuck.

There was no way she didn't know he wasn't at home. "Um... my spouse, obviously," he said, taking a shot in the dark.

It was a common enough answer to the outrageous questions the host often asked.

A pause. Then... "You're still at work, aren't you?"

Micah groaned. "What gave it away?"

"You mean besides the fact that the question was 'What was the last thing you stuck your finger in?'"

Micah frowned. "Hey, my answer made sense!" he protested.

"Yeah, too bad you couldn't keep the scheme going when I called you out on it."

"You're a witch," Micah accused.

"If by that, you mean intuitive goddess who believes in the power of the earth and karma and senses whenever someone is lying to me, you are absolutely correct." She paused a beat. "But, back to the topic at hand... *why* aren't you at home, Micah? It's well past six, and you promised me you'd leave by five today."

Of their own accord, Micah's eyes drifted to the open folder on his desk. Nico's jovial smile and bright eyes shone back at him. He swallowed. "This is important, Tessa."

Micah heard a sigh, but Tessa's voice was surprisingly gentle when she replied. "Honey, so is getting your rest. You're no good to anyone – *especially* this boy you're looking for – if you run yourself into the ground with exhaustion. You're better off getting some sleep and looking at the case with fresh eyes in the morning than you are slaving away at the station."

Micah knew logically that she was right, but that didn't mean he had to like it.

"Plus," Tessa added, lightening her tone, "I can't in good conscience grill you about what exactly you got up to with Damon last weekend knowing how tirelessly you've been working on this case."

Micah snorted. It was true, despite her threats on Monday, she hadn't nagged him about the man once since then. In fact, Tessa had been helping him with Nico's case. "I'm truly blown away by your selflessness," he deadpanned.

"As you should be," she said, faux-haughtily. Then... "Seriously, Micah, go home, or I'll call your dad."

Micah glowered, even though he knew Tessa couldn't see it. She just had to go and pull *that* card, didn't she?

"Fine," he said, probably more curtly than Tessa deserved. "I'll see you tomorrow."

Ending the call before she could scold him for his tone, Micah pocketed his phone. He glared at his computer screen – probably doing a convincing impression of a sullen teenager – before reluctantly shutting down his computer. He cleared his desk and locked up his files before standing. Ignoring the way his back popped like he was an octogenarian instead of a young, generally fit twenty-three-year-old, Micah shouldered on his coat.

Muttering his good-byes to the handful of personnel working the evening shift at the precinct, he made his way out the door.

It was snowing.

Micah shouldn't have been surprised. It was the first of December, and snow was hardly a foreign concept in New York. If he was in a better mood, he might have even been able to appreciate the beauty of the glistening, white flakes. But there was already an impressive layer of the stuff on the ground. And Micah was tired, with a headache, and now, he was bound to be cold and wet by the time he got home.

His apartment was within walking distance of the station – one of the reasons he put up with his horrible landlord and the complete lack of maintenance. (That, and it was one of the few places he could actually afford on his salary.)

Regardless, Micah was sorely tempted to hail a cab. It wasn't like he'd been getting paid overtime to stay late the past few nights, however, so his internal debate didn't last long before he was sighing, and burying his face as deeply as he could into the neck of his jacket, he began his trek home.

Micah's hair was damp, and he was shivering by the time he was stomping up the stairs to his third-floor apartment. There was a note taped to his door from Mrs. Gregory, the old woman down the hall who owned half a dozen cats despite the strict "no pets" policy of their landlord, and who always cooked for an army and took great pleasure in fostering off her leftovers on Micah.

Sure enough, the note claimed she'd made too much lasagna yesterday and that she had a Tupperware container's worth of it waiting for him in her fridge. Micah's stomach growled in anticipation.

Safe to say, Micah adored the woman.

Fiddling with his keys, he unlocked his door and pushed it open to reveal his dark apartment. He went to flick on the lights-

-and nearly shat himself.

Micah had a studio apartment, which was basically just a fancy way of saying that except for the toilet and shower, everything – the stove and shoddily painted kitchen cabinets, his television, his dresser and mattress – all took up the same space.

And at the edge of his haphazardly-made bed, sat Damon.

Even sitting at the very edge of the twin-size lump, the man made a menacing picture. Like usual, Damon was dressed to the nines in a crisp suit and his hair and short beard was styled to perfection.

Completely wrapped up in Nico's case, Micah would like to have claimed he'd completely forgotten about Damon and the complicated feelings he had for the man, but that wasn't exactly true.

Damon wasn't someone you just forgot about.

But Micah had managed to push thoughts of him to the back of his mind, labeling it a *later* problem. But since the man had apparently broken into his apartment while he was at work, it was safe to say that he was now a *now* problem.

Thankfully Micah's puffy coat hid the fact that he was packing. His hand had automatically gone to his hip – his Glock – when he had spotted the dark figure on his bed, but when he recognized the figure as Damon, he'd played the action off by clutching at the doorframe instead.

He didn't think the man had noticed.

Damon's legs were crossed, and his hands were folded neatly over his knee, looking completely at ease – like he was in some lobby, running a mundane errand, not sitting and waiting for the owner of the apartment *he had just broken into* to get home. Of course, Micah was no dummy, and *even if* Damon's knuckles hadn't been completely white with how hard they were clutching his knee, *even if* the stiff line of his shoulders wasn't radiating tension, *even if* his eyes weren't spitting fire… he would have been able to tell: the man was livid.

And if Micah hadn't had such a shit day, he might have even been scared. But as it was, Micah was just pissed. This presumptuous asshole had broken into his apartment – so covertly that he hadn't even noticed until he'd opened the door, and fuck, if that wasn't going to stick in his craw for a while.

"What the fuck are you doing here?" Micah demanded harshly, slamming the door behind himself even as the part of his mind that actually had operating brain cells berated him for eliminating the only safe escape route from the *proven criminal* sitting on his bed.

"It's Wednesday," Damon replied.

"I'm well aware," Micah shot back. "Is that supposed to mean something to me?"

Even from across the room, Micah could see a muscle in the man's jaw tick. Damon took a deep breath in through his nose, and muttered something to himself. (Probably begging the Lord above for patience, which, *rude*.) Then, more loudly… "Considering it's the day we agreed to meet so that you can effectively do the job I hired you to do, yes, I think it should."

Micah blinked. "Oh."

While he certainly hadn't forgotten Damon, the exact details of their arrangement *may* have slipped his mind with Nico's case taking up the majority of his brain power.

"Yes, *oh*," Damon all but hissed, suddenly shooting up off the bed, all pretense of calm gone. (Apparently that prayer for patience hadn't gotten through the queue.) It only took a handful of long strides for the man to invade Micah's space – although he left a foot or so of distance between them. He stuck his hand in his pocket, and Micah's shoulders tensed in preparation for... well, he didn't know for sure, but all the man pulled out was a familiar-looking iPhone. "Of course, you would have known that if you have bothered to check your phone – you know, the one I gave you and *specifically* told you to have on your person at all times. I sent you *multiple* reminders."

The man sounded nearly as worried as he did angry, and Micah was disturbed to find himself actually feeling guilty. Which was stupid, he told himself firmly. Damon was a *mobster*. He shoved that feeling as deep down as he could.

"I've been busy," Micah said after a minute, doing his best to keep his tone breezy despite the sick feeling in his stomach.

The way Damon's expression twisted made it clear what he thought of that explanation. "You've been... *busy?*" he repeated incredulously, taking another step closer to Micah – it wasn't threatening, exactly, but it only left inches between them. Which was unfortunate, because up close Damon was even more stunning. Micah swore he could count the man's eyelashes if he wanted to.

He tried to swallow, but found his throat was dry. "Um, yes?"
What was the question again?

"With what?" Damon demanded, his entire countenance darkening. Micah swore that even his eyes blackened a shade. "Work?"
Yes, actually, but definitely not how Damon thought.

"No," Micah shot down quickly, before the man got ideas in his head. "Just, you know, some stuff I had to take care of."

Damon's eyes roamed his face, clearly trying to judge if Micah was being truthful. Micah thought for sure he'd insist on knowing what he meant by "stuff". Instead, after an intense inspection...

"Are you on drugs?"

Micah's throat must not have been that dry, after all. How else would he have been able to choke on his own spit? "What? No!" he managed to communicate through the embarrassing coughing fit. "Of course not!"

Jesus, he must have looked more pathetic than he realized if Damon thought he was on drugs. Micah knew he hadn't been getting enough sleep – and that, combined with stress at work, had created some impressive circles under his eyes, but to make the leap to *drugs?* Seriously?

Damon didn't seem convinced by his incredulous denial. "Yeah, because a prostitute strung out on heroin would be so unusual."

"Fuck off, asshole." Micah had called the man a plethora of names in his head since he'd met him – an overbearing ass, a sexy, but bossy jerk, etc. – but this was the first time that he was genuinely upset with Damon. "You broke into my apartment like some kind of fucking stalker, and you think you can demand answers from me? I said that I'm *not* on drugs, and I don't really give a shit if you believe me or not."

Damon stared, and if Micah's face wasn't already warm from berating the man, the intensity of it probably would have made him blush. He was also a little worried for his sanity. There was no way he should have been so comfortable calling a frickin' mafia boss names. Yet Micah could honestly say he wasn't scared that Damon would hurt him.

Yell back, sure. Insult him some more by calling him a liar, okay. Micah thought there was even a slim chance in his stupidly optimistic brain that Damon might finish backing him up against the front door and have his wicked way with him.

"Being busy today doesn't explain why I found the phone I gave you powered down on your kitchen counter while you were clearly out – without it."

Micah wasn't sure if he was disappointed Damon didn't body-slam him into the door, pleased the man apparently believed him about the nonexistent drugs, or annoyed that he'd ignored everything else he'd said to circle back to the phone issue.

Just tell him the truth, the logical part of his brain urged. It sounded an awful lot like Tessa.

What? That I'm not a prostitute?

Not that truth. Just tell him that you've been ignoring the phone because you can't be his gigolo. You know, since he's a frickin' mafia don. Except don't let him realize you know that last part.

Micah took a deep breath in through his nose before purposefully pushing past Damon. Surprisingly, the man let him. "Look," Micah said sternly to his microwave, not quite working up the nerve to turn around and face Damon, "to be honest with you, after having time to think everything through, I just don't think this whole thing is a good idea."

A pause.

"I thought we both agreed you'd carry the phone with you," Damon said, sounding confused.

Fuck.

"I don't just mean the phone." Micah said, turning, but redirecting his eyes to the floor. *Huh.* There was a pizza sauce stain near the stove. That was embarrassing. *Focus, dumbass.* "I mean working as your pretend boyfriend, escort, whatever you want to call it. I'm going to have to retract your job offer, after all."

Another pause.

"So you *have* been working."

Damon sounded pissed again, and it was enough to get Micah to finally look up.

"What? No." Not as a hooker, anyway. "I already told you I haven't been." Micah gestured pointedly at his puffy, formless jacket. "Does it look like I've been trying to pick up johns?"

Damon looked him up and down. "You're actually wearing a coat." It was the first hint of approval in his voice all night.

Micah rolled his eyes. "Yes, thank you, I *can* actually take care of my basic needs on my own despite the opinions of certain others."

Damon reached out and fingered his damp hair. "But no hat," he said, like he hadn't heard a word Micah had just said. He frowned. "I didn't buy you any winter gear on Saturday, did I? We're going to have to go back to-"

Woah, woah, woah.

"I'm sorry. Did nothing I just say compute? I told you; I *can't* work for you."

"Why not?" Damon demanded bluntly. "What's changed between this weekend and today?"

Oh, not much. Micah had just found out that Damon was *a crime lord*, probably supplying a good chunk of the drugs on the street that he was accusing Micah of using, not to mention the countless other violent crimes his syndicate was undoubtedly responsible for.

"It was a bad idea then," Micah protested weakly, his stomach flipping at the thought of the man in front of him doling out drugs, beating someone to a pulp... ordering the murder of a rival gang leader or disloyal underling. "I think I must have still been drunk to agree to it."

Damon scoffed. "You signed a contract," he said.

Examining Damon now, his intimidating stance and rapidly darkening expression, Micah could picture it. He'd make a great mafia boss.

"Yes, but it says nothing about forced servitude," Micah pointed out. (He'd checked.) "The contract contains stipulations about you still paying me out through the end of the month in the event I'm suddenly fired, but there's nothing about me quitting."

Damon scowled. "Is ten grand a week not enough money for you?" he all but snarled in Micah's face. "Because I can guarantee you that no one out there is going to pay you half as much, no matter how prettily you beg."

"It has nothing to do with money," Micah snapped. It truly didn't. He had no intentions of using whatever money Damon ended up paying him in the first place. (He'd secretly hoped to turn whatever *this* was into an actual relationship, no under-the-table payments involved – at least until the whole mafia bombshell had been dropped on him.) "Maybe I just don't want to associate with someone who breaks into other people's apartments like a psycho, or accuses them of doing drugs without any evidence whatsoever – which is especially rich coming from someone like you." Micah ran a disgruntled hand through his hair. "I mean, Jesus, do you always throw a fucking tantrum like this when you don't get your way?"

Damon seemed truly taken aback, little lines of disbelief squiggled in his brow and his mouth even open a little in shock. He probably wasn't used to someone calling him out on his bullshit, Micah thought proudly – what with being a mafia don, and all.

Being suicidally stupid is not something to take pride in, the functioning part of his brain scolded him.

Micah was yanked harshly from his thoughts when Damon's slightly parted lips straightened into a thin, brittle line. "What do you mean someone like me?"

Micah blinked, rewinding back everything he'd just said. *Shit.* He'd all but accused Damon of being involved in illegal activity – drugs, certainly.

"I..." he desperately searched his brain for a logical reason he'd accused Damon of being caught up in the drug trade. "I just meant-"

Damon's hands were suddenly wrapped around Micah's biceps, grip unyielding. "Who told you?" he demanded, the words pushed out through clenched teeth.

"I- it's just, all the money-"

He gave Micah a little shake, nothing harsh or rattling, but certainly enough to put a stop to his stuttered attempt at an explanation. "I said, *who told you?*"

"No one!" Micah shouted. "I frickin' Googled you, okay?" He wasn't even lying. As much as he'd tried to push all thoughts of Damon to the back of his mind as he'd investigated Nico's disappearance, he'd had a moment of weakness Tuesday evening. "Considering your family's checkered history with the law, and the fact you're more loaded than the fuckin' president, I think it's safe to assume you're involved in some pretty shady shit. Drugs at the very least."

Damon stared. His grip on Micah loosened, but he didn't release him. "That's why you cut contact with me? Why you're trying to back out of our deal?"

"*Yes*, okay? I didn't realize you were some frickin' crime lord, super villain, godfather – whatever it is you are exactly – at the time, alright?" Micah knew exactly what Damon was: *a goddamn mafia don.* And regardless of the horrible things it said about his moral compass if he actually entertained the idea of continuing with their unorthodox charade, Micah was *a fucking cop*, and Damon had no idea.

The situation had disaster written all over it.

Micah tore himself from Damon's grip. "I can't believe I actually bought your 'I'm involved in finances' bullshit. Like investing in real estate can earn someone a bank account like yours, regardless of what sort of crazy inheritance your parents left you."

"It's not bullshit," Damon immediately protested. "I *am* involved in real estate, and more legitimate businesses than illegitimate ones."

"Of course, you are," Micah shot back. "After all, you need a good front in case someone actually decides to investigate your ass like they did your father before he died. Let's see, there was racketeering and possession of illegal weapons. According to Google, Anthony Romano was even brought in for questioning regarding *multiple* murders-"

"He was never convicted of anything," Damon snapped, once again stepping into Micah's space and taking him firmly by the chin, "and I'd appreciate it if you didn't speak of things beyond your understanding."

Micah ripped his face from Damon's hands. "Beyond my understanding?" he repeated incredulously. "Believe me, I understand just fine. You invest in startups, like your friend's

Mexican restaurant, to hide the fact that other businesses you finance are a guise for criminal activity. I'm not fucking stupid, Damon, I can keep up."

To Damon's credit, he didn't deny it, although judging by the way his fingers twitched at his side, he was seconds away from reaching out and trying to grab Micah again. "I never said you were stupid," he said instead.

"You didn't have to," Micah shot back. "You treat me like some naïve idiot, like I can't figure out that those 'shipping operations' you mentioned when we met" – Micah made sure to use finger quotes – "was actually just a fancy way of saying you smuggle illegal substances – most likely drugs – into the country. Go ahead, tell me I'm wrong."

Damon said nothing.

"I just want to know what else you're involved in. I mean, if you're not above working with drug cartels, where is the line drawn? You act all high and mighty, turning your nose up at sex work, but who's to say you're not involved in worse shit, like human trafficking-"

"I would *never*," Damon spat, suddenly crowding Micah up against his refrigerator. "People who victimize the most vulnerable members of society – women, children, the homeless – they are *scum.*"

Micah scoffed. "Yeah, because drugs don't ruin the lives of plenty of women and children. And why do you think most homeless people are even out on the streets?"

"People who are addicted to drugs are going to get their hands on them one way or another," Damon argued. "At least I make sure anything coming out of my enterprise is clean, and if anyone tries to tamper with the products... well, they're swiftly dealt with."

Micah swallowed. Damon was so close to him that when he tried to take in a shaky breath and fill his lungs, his chest brushed up against the man's. "Dealt with? What does that mean?"

Did he mean "dealt with" as in fired... *or murdered?* Fuck, Micah felt like puking again – much like he had on Monday when he'd first discovered Damon's real job. Had the man killed someone before? Micah's head was still pounding with a migraine, and the hysterical question was on the tip of his tongue... but did he *really* want to know?

Micah had taken an oath as an NYPD detective to protect the citizens of New York, and if Damon admitted to being a murderer, it made no difference how many NDA's the man had made him sign or how much Micah wanted to grab the man and *shake him*, but also *kiss him* even now... he'd have to arrest him.

"That's nothing you need to concern yourself with."

Fuck. *Fuck.* That wasn't an answer at all.

Micah went to sidestep Damon, badly needing some space, but the man only moved with him, so Micah was forced to take his hands and splay them on the man's chest, intending on pushing him backward. But Damon grabbed his wrists before he could. "I would never hurt you."

The words were said imploringly, an almost desperate edge to Damon's inflection, and as fucked as it was, Micah wanted to believe him – to sink into the man and let him comfort him even. But Damon thought Micah was just some down-on-his-luck prostitute, not someone who worked for the police. And he had no idea what Damon would do to him if he found out. The chilling reminder was like ice water being dumped down the front of his pants. Micah yanked his hands away from Damon – or, at least, he tried to. "Let go of me, and step away – right now."

Several intense seconds passed where Damon did neither. But then, he slowly released Micah's wrists and took two large, purposeful steps back. "You're afraid of me," he accused.

Damon actually had the nerve to sound *hurt*.

"I just fucking accused you of being a stalker, a psycho, a frickin' super villain, and I scolded you for distributing drugs – *loudly*. I'm *not* scared of you. I'm pissed that you lied... and-and I'm disappointed," he admitted, with a bit less steam.

"What's wrong? Not the Good Samaritan you thought I was?" Damon asked, voice tight.

"No, you're not! And I think I'm allowed to be a bit tiffed that the man-" ...*who Micah had been falling for*... "-who offered me this amazing job opportunity – this golden ticket off the streets – is involved in organized crime."

Not just "involved", but the fucking ringleader.

Micah huffed, crossing his arms over his chest. "But I'm also pissed at myself because... because it doesn't even disgust me, not like it should. Because even though my brain is telling me you're a bad, *bad* man, I also can't ignore the fact that you gave me the coat off your back when we first met. Or that you fretted over me every time we ran into each other after that. Or that you told me you wanted to be a baker when you were a kid. Or that you made me the most delicious pancakes-"

"-crepes-" Damon corrected thoughtlessly, seemingly surprised Micah wasn't still berating him.

"-crepes," Micah deadpanned, shooting the man a glare.

Damon looked contrite... and hopeful.

As little sense as it made, Micah didn't want to squash that hope. Yet, logically and ethically, he didn't see how he couldn't. Micah sighed. ""I guess I'm having a hard time differentiating between the two versions of you I have in my head."

Damon shook his head. "You can't. Because I am both of those men. One doesn't exist without the other, but Micah... it doesn't have to change anything between us."

Hysterical laughter threatened to bubble up Micah's throat. "It changes everything," he disagreed.

"I had you sign the NDA in case you overheard anything... unsavory about that aspect of my life when we were together. But my plan from the beginning was to keep you separated – *away* – from all of that," Damon implored. "You only need to accompany me to events associated with my lawful endeavors – charity galas and business trips, mostly – and an occasional family dinner. When you're with me, you'll be protected at all times. I swear to you, I would never risk your safety."

Yes, because *that* was what Micah was worried about. (Although, to be fair, he probably *should* have been – but he'd always played fast and loose with his own well-being.)

"That doesn't change the fact that any money you would pay me is dirty."

Damon clenched his jaw, a sure sign he was losing patience. "I told you; the large majority of my business endeavors are legal."

"Then why not just withdraw from the ones that aren't?" Micah asked, and even he could admit the demand sounded borderline childish.

Damon heaved a sigh of frustration. "That's not how this works. I think you know that."

Micah *did* know that. There were non-monetary consequences to closing communication with drug cartels and other dangerous organizations, after all. And in all likelihood, Damon had inherited whatever shady dealings he had going on with the dregs of society. It wasn't *really* his fault. And Damon wasn't wrong when he said addicts would find a way to get their hands on their meth and heroin with or without whatever dealers Damon had working for him. At least he made sure his supply wasn't laced with anything dangerous – well, not anything more dangerous than the drugs already were, anyway.

…And was Micah really trying to *justify* Damon's actions? What the hell was *wrong* with him?

Micah obviously wasn't doing a very good job covering up his mixed emotions, because Damon must have seen a crack in his armor when he said: "One event."

Micah frowned. "What?"

"Just keep up your end of our deal for one event, and I'll pay you through the end of December."

Micah opened his mouth to protest, but Damon steamrolled right over him.

"I would prefer you use the money to find a safer place to live, and maybe buy yourself something pretty, but if you really think the money's dirty, you can donate it to charity for all I care. Just one event – *one* outing. And if you still want to withdraw from our arrangement after that, I won't pursue-… it."

Micah's brain really must have been fried from the awful week he'd had so far because he could have sworn Damon was about to say "you" at the end of that spiel, but that the man changed it to "it" at the last second instead. Micah was too tired to contemplate what that could mean, so he remained silent.

"Micah, *please.*"

Fuck, it was like that polite, little word coming from this bossy, domineering man's mouth was his kryptonite. Micah let out a half-despairing/half-frustrated sigh, fighting the urge to pull at his own hair. "What kind of event?" he hedged.

"Just a small gathering," Damon assured, "a family dinner to ease you into things. My sisters and I try to get together every weekend that we're all in town." So the whole criminous family would be there. *Great.* "But if we're going to do that, we'll have to continue with tonight's original plan… you know, getting to know each other."

"You mean there are hidden layers to your personality beyond secret mafia boss?" Micah sassed. He'd been avoiding using the actual word "mafia" until now, and he had to say, he was impressed by Damon's lack of reaction to it. Though Micah stiffened when the man once *again* reached for him, taking him by the wrists and flipping his hands palm-side up so that he could rub his thumbs soothingly over Micah's pulse points.

"Since we're being upfront with each other, I feel like I should also tell you…"

Micah's stomach clenched.

"…I greatly enjoy pistachio ice cream."

Was… was Damon cracking a joke?

Micah stared him down, but the man's mouth didn't so much as twitch. The glimmer of amusement in his eyes gave him away, however. "You monster," Micah accused, deciding to go along with Damon's blatant attempt to deescalate the situation. "Now I know the real reason you can't get a date." (Micah wasn't entirely feigning his disgust. Anyone who chose pistachio ice cream over hot fudge or caramel had to have been a direct relation of the devil.)

Of course, the *real* reason Damon was still single probably had more to do with his choice of… extracurricular activities than his favorite flavor of ice cream. Which brought Micah back to Damon's proposal.

He blamed what happened next on the hypnotizing motion of Damon's thumbs on the thin skin of his inner wrists.

He took a deep breath in through his nose. "Fine," Micah said, biting out the word before he could change his mind. "*One* event, but that's it."

And then he was cutting off contact with Damon. He *had* to.

Damon sighed in relief. "Thank you," he said, gratitude evident in his voice.

Micah nodded, and in a desperate bid to do something with his hands before he *did something with his hands*, he shook Damon off before turning and opening his refrigerator. "Want something to drink?" he asked before taking in the contents of his fridge and realizing all he had to offer was a couple cans of his favorite energy drink and a carton of milk that's best by date had passed three days ago. "Uh... I mean, I have a water softener, so the stuff that comes out of the tap is passable. Sorry, if I had remembered you were coming, I would have gotten some refreshments or something."

When Micah peeked over his shoulder, he saw how horrified Damon looked at the sad state of his fridge. Understandable, considering how empty it was. Some sandwich meat, a carton of eggs, various condiments, a half a jar of pickles, a bag of shredded cheddar, and some wilted greens that had looked crisp when he'd optimistically bought them a week ago at the store, but now appeared to be on death's door, was all there was taking up space in the vintage appliance.

Still, Micah didn't want to encourage the "poor, desolate prostitute" image Damon already had in his head of him.

"I haven't had time to go shopping," he said, a bit waspishly, even though Damon hadn't actually said anything. (He didn't need to. His expressive eyebrows spoke for him.)

"Too busy with all that... 'stuff'?"

It was a reminder that the man hadn't forgotten his vague explanation for why he hadn't been home when he'd gotten there.

"Yes," Micah said airily, making it clear he didn't plan on elaborating.

Damon seemed to understand that judging by the way he ran a frustrated hand through his hair. After a moment, he merely sighed and pulled a phone out of his pocket, typing a quick message. "That's ok. Geoffrey's downstairs. I can have him pick up a few things and bring them here."

Micah frowned. "Geoffrey's here? I didn't see your car when I came up," he pointed out. Damon's Rolls-Royce would have been hard to miss in his neighborhood.

"I took a different vehicle." *Of course, the man had multiple cars.* "And I had him park a couple blocks down so as not to attract attention."

Micah narrowed his eyes. "Just admit you wanted to scare the shit out of me," he accused.

Damon threw his hands up, but he didn't deny it. "I thought you were ghosting me, like a little brat."

The pang that snarly word – "brat" – sent through his dick made *zero* sense. Micah clenched his thighs, fighting to ignore the inappropriate reaction. "Excuse me? For all you knew, I could have been dead under a bridge somewhere."

"Well, I'd hoped not," Damon said, "because then I would have had to burn the entire city to the ground."

It was said nonchalantly enough, but the fire in Damon's eyes made Micah suspect there was more than a grain of truth to the threat... and *fuck*, did the man not realize that statements like that messed with Micah's head?

You didn't say things like that unless you genuinely cared about someone.

Yet Damon had made it clear it was purely a business relationship between them. It was confusing, and Micah's dick was already confused enough about the situation without his brain starting to question things as well.

Micah cleared his throat to break the somewhat awkward tension that had fallen after Damon's declaration. "So," he said, clapping his hands together. "Since you've already let yourself in, I might as well give you the tour." He gestured vaguely at the oven and microwave. "We are standing in what I like to refer to as the kitchen." He pointed at the card table surrounded by mismatched chairs he'd picked up from various thrift stores. "Dining room." Finally, he waved in the direction of the bed Damon had been crouched atop of when he'd walked in. There was also a corduroy couch and a flat screen tv situated on top of a nearby dresser. "And lastly, what I affectionately call the bedroom/living room."

"And the bathroom?" Damon asked, like he hadn't inspected the entire space while Micah had been gone.

"The bathroom's through there," Micah answered regardless, pointing at one of three doors. The two others led to a small closet and, of course, the exit. "It's nothing fancy. There's a toilet, a sink, and a shower stall. I know it's not much," he said, referring to the apartment at large, "but it's mine, and it's home."

Truth was, as much as he disliked the landlord of the building, and annoying as it was dealing with cold showers most mornings, Micah was proud of his tiny apartment. Even with a full time job, living on your own at twenty-three was nothing to scoff at in a city as expensive as New York. Sure, the space was small and cramped even with the minimal amount of threadbare furniture he owned, but Micah liked to think of it as homey.

It certainly wasn't as impressive as Damon's monochrome, clean-cut penthouse with its stainless steel appliances and balcony with a hot tub, but at least Micah's personal touches – the family pictures he'd hung on the wall, various band posters, his Mets flag, and, of course, the novelty throw pillows Tessa had bought him for his birthday – a fuzzy, rainbow-colored one, and a classic "Sounds gay. I'm in." in black and white – gave the space personality.

Micah was torn from his thoughts when Damon approached the pictures he had on display.

Micah had the presence of mind to be grateful that none of the photos featured his dad in uniform. Especially when Damon plucked one off the wall to examine it more closely. It was a picture of Micah with both his parents. He was eleven and decked out in a youth baseball uniform, tan from the sun and freckles standing out starkly across the bridge of his nose as he smiled brightly at the camera. His mom and dad were on either side of him, each with an arm slung around his shoulders. It had been taken only a month or so before his mother had unexpectedly passed.

Damon must not have had any personal run-ins with Micah's father because no recognition sparked in his eyes as he examined the picture. "You were a cute kid," Damon offered, gaze drifting to another photo, this one featuring a wiggly toddler version of Micah in his mother's lap, face smeared with chocolate.

He was probably wondering how the happy kid in the pictures had ended up working the streets.

"Yeah, well, I didn't have a trio of sisters to force me into dresses, but I'd like to think I still turned out okay."

Damon shot him a half-hearted glare, but he returned the picture to its place on the wall, which Micah was grateful for. Whether Damon recognized his father or not, Micah didn't need him looking *too* closely into his life.

"So how do you want to do this exactly?" Micah asked when it seemed like Damon was finished inspecting his décor. He plopped down on one side of the couch, leaving the other half available for the man. "Did you make, like, flash cards or something? You know, for all the things I need to know before this dinner?"

Damon raised his eyebrows. "I was hoping to go about this more… organically, I suppose?"

"No flashcards then, okay." Micah bit his lip, thinking. He had an idea, but Damon would probably think it juvenile. Still, it was worth a shot. "Want to play twenty questions?"

Damon frowned. "What's twenty questions?"

It wasn't a "no".

Perking up, Micah patted the seat next to him. Damon obediently sat, and Micah turned to face the man, folding his legs pretzel-style and ignoring how one of his knees pressed up against Damon's thigh. "It's pretty much what it sounds like. We take turns asking each other questions, and the other person answers."

Damon's frown didn't ease. "What if you ask a question that I don't want to answer?"

"Well, it's not like I can *make* you," Micah pointed out reasonably, "but I thought the whole point of this rendezvous was for us to get to know each other."

When Damon still didn't agree, Micah sighed. "How about we're both allowed to pass on any questions we don't like, but if we do, we *have* to answer the next question we're asked – provided it's not just a reworded version of the original question."

"Okay," Damon agreed reluctantly after taking a minute to contemplate the ground rules Micah had laid out.

Micah smiled – and though it had no right, it was the first one in days that actually fit his face – it didn't feel forced or strained or fake. It felt *real*. "Okay, since it was my idea, I get to ask the first question."

Damon's dubious expression made it clear what he thought of *that*, but he didn't protest, so Micah took a moment to think about what he wanted to ask. He supposed he should probably ease Damon into the game, so nothing that would make him use a pass right away. Still, it ought to be something he actually *wanted* to know the answer to.

Micah grinned. He had just the question.

"Do you think I look pretty in a skirt?"

CHAPTER TEN

Over the next handful of hours, Micah learned a plethora of information about Damon.

Apparently the man was a Yankees fan, his favorite cuisine was Italian, he identified as bisexual, and he had a tattoo. When Micah had immediately used his next question to demand what the tattoo was of and where it was located, he'd been treated to the erotic sight of Damon stripping off his suit jacket and unbuttoning his shirt.

Micah was able to take in a muscled chest covered in dark hair and two dusky pink nipples before Damon turned and showed off his back. Spanning across his shoulders was what Damon claimed was his family emblem, which looked like a shield and pair of swords superimposed over the wings of a regal-looking bird, perhaps a species of eagle or hawk.

Micah had been sorely tempted to reach out and touch it – trail his fingers across the inked skin. He wasn't sure if he was relieved or disappointed when Damon shrugged back on his shirt before he could give in to the urge.

Regardless, it provided a smooth transition for him to ask more questions about Damon's family. Micah learned that Damon's sister's names were Caprice, Joelle (whom he'd already met), and Sophie. Caprice, the oldest at thirty-four, was married to a man named Jason Vitali, who – as Damon put it – was "in business" with him. Joelle, the second oldest, was described as the most "free-spirited" of his sisters. Apparently, she had an unconventional, on-again-off-again, open relationship with a man Damon simply referred to as "Fernando". And finally, there was Sophie, the youngest at twenty-two – only a year younger than Micah – who was still in college, and unattached as far as Damon knew.

Micah had eventually worked up the nerve to ask about his parents and how they had died, and while Damon had briefly hesitated to answer, he'd ended up telling Micah that their names had been Anthony and Natalie, and that they had died in a car accident when Damon was just twenty.

In an effort to ask about Damon's "job" without actually asking about Damon's "job", Micah had also asked if the man had ever fired a gun (he'd gotten a terse "yes"), and what the worst injury he'd ever sustained was.

Micah had been relieved when Damon had answered he'd gotten his ribs and nose broken in an ill-advised fight in his youth.

Of course, turnabout was fair play, and Micah had had to tell Damon the embarrassing story of how he'd broken his arm in an attempt to fly off the roof of his childhood home when the man shot the question back at him. (He'd seemed as assuaged by Micah's answer as Micah had been by his.)

Micah had had to give up other information about himself as well. Surprisingly (*thankfully*), Damon seemed as leery of asking Micah about his "profession" as Micah had been of asking Damon about his, so he hadn't even had to lie.

Most of Damon's questions had been fairly tame, like asking Micah his favorite food (anything that could qualify as dessert), or his favorite color. (Micah had immediately blushed after blurting out the word "blue", avoiding Damon's deep *blue* eyes for a while after.)

The only questions that had made him uncomfortable were the ones about his family – his father, specifically – which he'd tried to answer as vaguely as possible.

It was only about a half-hour after Damon had left his apartment – after Micah had showered and collapsed onto his bed – that he realized he'd legitimately enjoyed getting to know Damon. It'd been *fun* playing twenty questions with the man, and worst of all – even though he had seen Damon less than an hour ago – Micah found that he already *missed* him.

It was pathetic, and if Micah wasn't already concerned about his mental facilities, he certainly would have been then. All sorts of alarms were going off in his brain. It didn't matter how charming or devilishly handsome or sweet (in a convoluted, pushy way) Damon was, he was a fucking mob boss, and Micah had no business *enjoying* himself around him.

Micah had gone as far as typing in "therapists near me" into the search bar of his phone, because clearly there was something drastically wrong with his psyche, when he heard a buzzing sound coming from the kitchen. When he'd gone to investigate the noise, he saw a "new message" alert on the iPhone Damon had gifted him.

It could only be from one person.

Despite the instant spark of curiosity, Micah was proud to say he lasted an entire minute before swiping to see what the message said.

Who's your favorite musician?

Thank God no one had been there to see the loopy grin that broke out across Micah's face. (The answer was Queen, obviously.)

That was how Micah ended up exchanging text messages back and forth for two entire days with New York City's most notorious mafia don. At least, that's what he was doing when he wasn't working Nico's case at the precinct.

Call Micah paranoid, but there was no way he was bringing the phone Damon had given him to the station. Even if Damon hadn't installed any nefarious devices on the iPhone – a big *if* – there were plenty of other ways to track a phone. Hell, there were even apps for it.

Thankfully, Damon had yet to ask why Micah didn't answer his texts between the hours of 8:00 AM and 4:00 PM, and if he did, Micah was fully prepared to lie – something, surprisingly enough, he hadn't had to do so far.

Regardless, Micah only ever responded to Damon's texts when he was at home, which is where he was at right now. It was inching past ten o'clock, and last Friday's debacle aside, it was where Micah spent most of his Friday evenings. Because Micah was lame.

Also apparently a glutton for inevitable tragedy, since instead of using his miniscule downtime to find some tv show to binge on Netflix – or better yet, sleep – he was exchanging texts with a mobster.

It was downright idiotic.

So why did he light up from the inside whenever the iPhone buzzed with an incoming message?

Speaking of… the phone vibrated in his hand, and Micah quickly swiped right.

Telepathy. (Micah had asked Damon what superpower he'd choose to have if superpowers existed.) **I have a feeling you'd say flying if I asked you in return-**

Damon wasn't going to let the jumping off the roof when he was a kid thing go, was he? Micah had been *eight*.

-so, instead, when's your birthday?

Micah squinted suspiciously at the question. It seemed innocent enough on the surface, but so had Damon's late Wednesday night question about whether Micah preferred silk or cotton.

Guess who had called Micah at work around noon the next day because "some tattooed ruffians with a huge mattress are trying to break into your apartment"? That's right, his elderly neighbor, Mrs. Gregory.

Because Damon had taken it upon himself to buy Micah a new bed – fluffy pillows, cobalt blue comforter, *silken* sheets, and all. And he'd paid an undoubtedly outrageous sum to have them delivered to Micah's apartment that day.

Micah had had to use his lunch break to rush back to his place and let the movers in (one of whom he'd recognized as Geoffrey) – but not before he'd called Damon and hollered at him for the presumptuous gift. Damon didn't sound contrite about his actions at all; in fact, he seemed pleased to endure Micah's testy telling-off.

At least until Micah had convinced him to begrudgingly agree to take the price of the bed and accessories out of his weekly paycheck. (It wasn't like Micah actually had any designs on the money, anyway.) Then Damon had just sounded put out.

At least the man had had the good sense to get him a queen-size bed and not a king. There wouldn't have been much floor space left otherwise. Micah was reluctant to admit it, but the bed was actually *really* nice – an unparalleled improvement over his lumpy twin. He'd slept better last night than he had in ages. (Not that he was about to tell Damon that.)

Micah grabbed a cookie from the sleeve of peanut butter patties he'd grabbed from his pantry, careful not to get crumbs on the new sheets as he munched on the treat.

That was the other thing.

Damon had bought him a ridiculous amount of groceries on Wednesday.

When the man had said he was sending Geoffrey off to pick up a few snacks, Micah hadn't expected Damon's chauffeur to return to his apartment with *five* loads of groceries. His refrigerator and pantry were fuller than they had ever been, stuffed to the brim with expensive, organic foods that were probably much better for him than the frozen pizzas and processed mac and cheese he usually bought.

His cupboards had enough dry goods to easily last him through December.

It was ridiculous, and between the clothes, and the groceries, and the luxury bed, Micah was beginning to think that Damon had a bit of a sugar daddy kink. It's what caused Micah to eye Damon's question about his birthday with such suspicion. After all, what went hand-in-hand with birthdays? Gift giving. And Damon seemed to get off on flustering Micah with expensive presents.

Luckily, Micah's birthday wasn't anytime soon.

I'm a Leo.

Did Micah leave his answer vague to be purposefully annoying? Perhaps. But it served the dual purpose of keeping identifying information to a minimum.

After all, if Damon ever decided to run a background check on Micah, he was well and truly fucked – and not in the fun way.

I get major Capricorn vibes from you, maaaybe Scorpio.

Micah was one of those people who unapologetically sent out multiple text messages to his friends, one after the other, as thoughts occurred to him, versus someone who sent out well-reasoned paragraphs.

Micah debated what question he wanted to ask Damon in return. He supposed he could play it safe and ask something simple.

They were talking about birthdays... maybe the favorite gift Damon had ever received?

But for some reason, Micah's brain kept circling back to all the gifts Damon had given him. Even if the man *did* have a sugar daddy kink... what else got him off?

Micah hesitantly typed out a message: **What are your kinks?**

Then he stared at the "send" button.

Are you seriously about to ask Damon what gets his cock hard? The sensible part of Micah's brain was *not* impressed. After all, Damon had made it abundantly clear that whatever this... *thing* was between them, it was to remain purely professional.

Sure, but if Micah really was his boyfriend/significant other/lover/whatever, wouldn't it be expected of him to know what... tipped Damon over the edge, so to speak?

And who the hell would ever ask you that?

Micah immediately thought of Joelle. It'd been pretty clear the woman didn't have much in the way of boundaries when they'd met last weekend. Would it really be outside the realm of possibility that she – or one of Damon's other siblings – would ask something outrageous like that?

Sure, Micah could always make something up, but for the sake of professionalism...

Have you ever heard of such a contrived, blatantly untrue excuse?

Micah hit send.

The butterflies in his stomach that always seemed to pop into existence whenever Micah was texting Damon, turned into ravenous monsters, batting their wings unforgivingly against his insides until he felt vaguely ill.

Which was just silly. Asking about the man's kinks – for the sake of *professional* curiosity – was a far cry from sexting with Damon, or sending the man *nudes* or something.

Micah hadn't felt nearly so nervous after demanding if Damon had enjoyed the sight of him in a skirt on Wednesday. (Although he'd felt himself flush when Damon had unabashedly said "yes" before asking Micah if he had any allergies. Micah had frowned in confusion before answering "some shellfish". The reason Damon had asked became evident, though, when he had immediately relayed the answer to Geoffrey, who was shopping for groceries.)

Micah recalled being oddly touched by Damon's thoughtfulness.

But back to the point… if Micah hadn't felt nervous then, why were his nerve endings positively alight with anxiety now?

Micah tensed when the phone buzzed where he'd hastily thrown it down on the comforter after pressing send. Telling himself to stop being such an overthinking dunderhead, he took a deep breath in through his nose before opening Damon's response.

His answer did nothing to alleviate the beasts wreaking havoc in Micah's stomach.

Edging. Light bondage. Pretty panties on even prettier boys.

Micah wasn't sure what he'd been expecting. Maybe a light scolding for asking such a personal question. He thought Damon might even finally use one of his passes and refuse to answer. Whatever Micah had been expecting, it wasn't *this*.

Micah's own sexual experience was pretty vanilla. He hadn't moved past mutual blowjobs in high school, except for one particularly memorable incident when the quarterback of the varsity football team, Garrett Ferguson, had eaten out his ass until he'd cried. (Although the prick had all but ruined the experience when he'd gone and threatened to beat Micah black and blue if he told anyone about it afterwards.)

In college, he'd experimented more, and while Micah was far from a virgin, the most sexually deviant thing he'd probably ever done was let a guy in the same criminal justice program as him use a pair of cuffs to secure him to his headboard. The guy had wanted to "dominate" him, and Micah had lost track of the times he'd called him a "dirty slut" as he'd pounded into him. It had been… weird, and while Micah had gotten off (*eventually*), he'd quickly concluded that he didn't particularly care for being cussed at and called vulgar names and *spat* on during sex.

Micah couldn't help but feel being with Damon would be different.

Sure, Damon was a bit domineering, but he was also considerate and sweet. Micah had a feeling the man was a very generous lover, and certain parts of his body couldn't help but react as he reread the words the man had sent again. Especially that last part.

Pretty panties on even prettier boys.

It wasn't *that* much of a shock Damon had a thing for crossdressing considering how he'd tried and failed to hide the way he'd eyed Micah in that schoolgirl skirt two weeks ago. But the words felt oddly targeted – like they were meant specifically for Micah.

But that couldn't be right... could it?

Feeling like a pervert, but unable to muster up the wherewithal to fight the urge, Micah leaned back in bed and allowed his hand to slink down his body until it was inching past the waistband of the loose sleep shorts he was wearing. His cock was already half-hard, and it took an embarrassingly few amount of tugs to get it all the way there.

Micah closed his eyes, working his prick as he pictured Damon doing the same thing to his own cock. Micah had never been particularly self-conscious about his dick. It was a decent size – proportionate to the rest of his body – and smooth with a pink mushroom head. He generally kept himself well-maintained, with blonde pubic hair leading from his belly button to the base of his cock, but the rest of him carefully manicured.

He couldn't help but imagine what Damon's cock was like. If it was anything like the rest of him, it was bound to be big. Micah tried to picture it in his head. A monstrous cock with an engorged head so angry it was almost purple. Heavy balls nestled in dark hair.

Fuck.

Despite the fact that he was on top of his covers, Micah felt almost unbearably warm, and he knew his entire body was flushed even as all his blood flowed south.

Dropping the phone, Micah used his free hand to yank down his shorts. His cock sprang free, and Micah let out a breathy little moan as he brushed a thumb over the urethra.

What did Damon think about when he masturbated?

Pretty boys in pretty panties, like he'd said? What about *Micah* in a pair of panties?

Struck by a sudden idea, Micah all but catapulted out of bed. Kicking off his shorts, he hurried to his dresser. He dug through the underwear drawer until he found what he was looking for buried at the very bottom.

A few months ago, for Tessa's baby shower, Micah had gotten the woman a gag gift: a package of granny panties fives sizes too big for her. In retaliation, Tessa had "gifted" Micah his own pair of women's underwear in front of all of their colleagues.

Instead of granny panties, however, she'd opted for something much more... risqué.

Micah examined the black, cheeky panties with lace trim. There was even a tiny, frilly bow atop the waistband.

Micah didn't know *why* he hadn't thrown them out, exactly, but they were certainly serving a purpose now.

He almost lost his balance as he slipped his legs through the appropriate holes, pulling the panties up until they *mostly* covered his junk. Surprisingly, they fit pretty well. Even more surprisingly, they weren't exactly *un*comfortable. Micah would even describe the brush of satiny fabric against his cock as erotic.

Micah grabbed the iPhone he'd been using to communicate with Damon and mindlessly took a picture. He wasn't stupid enough to include his face in the shot, so it only showcased him from the neck to just below his knees.

In the picture, Micah's chest was splotchy with arousal, but it was the underwear that stole the show. The fabric stretched across the outline of his cock, a little spot of dampness towards the top where precum must have stained the fabric.

If one looked closely, they could see a little hint of his cock head peeking out.

Looking at the picture, Micah couldn't help but wonder if *this* was what Damon imagined when he got off.

Fuck.

The thought of Damon masturbating to Micah was too hot to handle, and dropping the phone back onto the bed, Micah returned his attention to his dick. One leg hoisted up on the mattress, Micah used his unoccupied hand to shove the frilly fabric to the side so he could roll his balls between his fingers, then reached back further still until his fingers were brushing up against the pucker of his entrance.

Micah closed his eyes, imagining it was Damon's hands touching him like this, worshipping his body and whispering dirty things in his ear, telling him what a "good boy" he was, and how "pretty" he looked for him like this, satin fabric twisted around his thighs, as he worked himself to orgasm.

Micah set a punishing pace, yanking on his cock as he toyed with himself. He pushed against his hole, breaching the hot channel with little more than a fingertip, but it was enough. Micah's stomach clenched, and he half-grunted/half-whined as he came, spurting against his stomach as stars exploded against the black of his eyelids.

Jesus.

Heaving, Micah allowed himself to collapse backward onto his new bed, careful not to get his spunk on the sheets, even in his delirium.

Maybe it was the post-orgasm bliss, or maybe he really *was* just a complete dumbass, but for some reason, when Micah picked up the iPhone and saw the picture of himself in panties again, some part of his hindbrain decided it would be a good idea to share the photo with Damon.

Still dazed from his release, and working mostly on autopilot, Micah sent the picture to the man.

He'd even included a cheeky caption: **Panties like these?**

It wasn't until Micah's breathing had slowed, and the post-orgasm high had worn off, that Micah really comprehended what he'd done.

He tensed all over. Then sat up, ramrod straight.

What the fuck? *Why?!*

Why the hell would he *do* that? Ignoring the fact that it was a jerk move to begin with, it didn't take a genius to realize that sending an unsolicited dick pic to the man who was essentially his employer was the epitome of unprofessional.

Micah fumbled with the phone. Maybe by some miracle, it hadn't sent. Reception in his apartment was sometimes spotty. But, of course, the state-of-the-art iPhone Damon had given him for work purposes (*not sexting purposes, you moron!*), had had no issues sending the picture message.

Worse, it had already been "seen".

Fuck. *Fuckfuckfuck.* There was no taking it back now.

Grabbing a towel from the bathroom, Micah quickly cleaned himself up from the... *activities* he'd been partaking in only moments before. He shucked off the underwear and pulled back on his shorts. Then he began pacing his apartment. (Unfortunately, it wasn't a large enough space for it to be very satisfying, but Micah's nerves wouldn't allow him to sit still.)

He couldn't help but think what Damon's reaction must have been to receiving the photo. Had he been shocked? Annoyed that Micah was blurring the lines between business and pleasure yet again? Maybe even disgusted?

Or... had the man *liked* it? Like he'd admitted to liking the sight of Micah in a schoolgirl skirt?

Was it wrong that Micah felt arousal stirring in his nether regions again?

Fuck! Get it together!

Damon already thinks you're a prostitute. Is it that big of a deal if he thinks you're a slut, too? I mean, judging by the fact you're already half-hard again, you kind of are.

"Shut up," Micah muttered to himself.

As much as Micah wanted Damon to ignore the inappropriate photo he'd sent, the longer he went without getting a reply, the more out of control Micah felt.

Was relocating to Mexico an overreaction or a legitimate response to what he'd done?

Upwards of twenty minutes later, it was almost a relief when he heard the phone buzz across the room from where he was standing in the kitchen, shoveling chocolate ice cream into his mouth straight from the carton. (He was a comfort eater, okay?)

Forcing himself to walk over to the phone and face the consequences of his actions, Micah picked up the device and reluctantly swiped open the message from Damon.

It's not your turn to ask a question.

CHAPTER ELEVEN

Micah hadn't known how to respond to Damon's message, and the man hadn't followed it up with any more texts, so he just... didn't.

His first instinct after reading the message had been... *that's it?*

Micah supposed he had expected more of a reaction to the lurid photo. Was Damon mad? Upset?

Micah had no idea, and he couldn't exactly ask Damon, as the man had so eloquently pointed out: *it wasn't his turn to ask a question.*

Micah hadn't been able to sleep well, even on the pristine mattress Damon had bought him, huddled in silky-smooth sheets. Instead, he'd spent his night tossing and turning, thoughts chasing each other around in his head.

While he couldn't be sure Damon had meant to punish him with that succinct response, Micah felt suitably chastised by the next morning when he woke up with a headache pounding behind his eyes and nervous energy buzzing beneath his skin where it had gathered with nowhere else to go.

He swallowed down a couple Tylenol before attempting to get some off-the-book work done at home. He managed to put the ... *inciden*t aside long enough to concentrate for a couple of hours, using the time to send messages to the dozen or so regular subscribers to Nico's webcam show. (Not that he expected them to respond.)

Micah hadn't been able to dig as deeply into Nico's missing persons case at work as he would have liked since Jensen had allotted him other assignments – nothing more interesting than vehicular theft – on top of Nico's case. They couldn't use "all of their man hours" on a "simple missing persons case", after all. (Insert eyeroll here.)

Regardless, it wasn't until Damon texted Micah around noon, reminding him that he was picking him up at five, that Micah's anxiety truly began to ebb.

At least the man was still talking to him. That meant he couldn't be *too* mad? Right?

Damon had failed to tell Micah where they were having this family dinner at in the message, however, so Micah had no idea what he was supposed to wear. He started typing out a message to simply ask the man, but halfway through, Micah remembered that *it wasn't his turn to ask a question.*

In the end, he rifled through the clothes Damon had purchased him last weekend and settled on a pair of gray wool slacks and a collared dress shirt, over which he pulled on a navy sweater. Micah hoped it was formal enough that he wouldn't be stared at if they ended up at a high-end restaurant, but casual enough that he didn't look like a try-hard at what Damon had described as a perfunctory family dinner.

Fifteen minutes before five, Micah couldn't contain his nervous energy any longer, and he threw on his coat before locking up his apartment to wait for Damon down on the curb.

Micah was drawing nonsensical squiggles in the slush that had gathered on the sidewalk with the tip of his shoe, wondering if he should have worn boots instead of the loafers he'd decided on, when a familiar vehicle rolled up at exactly 5:00.

Micah hurried to the Rolls-Royce, opening the nearside passenger's door and sliding into the back seat before either Damon or Geoffrey could bother getting out to greet him.

Micah felt Damon's eyes on him immediately, his gaze burning a hole through the side of his head as Micah brushed out the dozens of tiny snowflakes that had fallen into his hair. Micah fiddled nervously with the zipper of his coat, not sure what he was expecting.

Perhaps a joke about his supposed profession because he'd been waiting for Damon on the side of the street like a common prostitute? Or maybe the man would simply launch into whatever lecture he had prepared over the unsolicited picture Micah had sent him.

Regardless, it wasn't until the vehicle was moving again that Micah finally gathered the nerve to offer the man a tight-lipped smile. "Hey."

He pulled his shoulders tight to his neck, preparing himself for the inevitable scolding, but instead...

"You look nice."

Micah was glad his cheeks were already stained red from the chill. "Um, thanks. You too. I mean, you always look good," he rushed to add. "What with the clothes, and the hair, and the... you know, everything." He gestured awkwardly at Damon's entire person.

Micah couldn't help but wonder what it would feel like to go an entire five minutes in the man's presence without making a fool of himself. Obviously, he wasn't about to find out today since he *couldn't. stop. talking.* "I hope I'm dressed okay. You didn't say where dinner was going to be, so I went with some slacks and a dressed-up sweater." Don't say anything about your underwear. *Do not.* "I'm not wearing panties underneath, just regular briefs. In case you were wondering. Not that you were, obviously... just, you know, to clear the air."

In case anyone out there was wondering if it was actually possible to die of embarrassment, Micah could confidently say no. It only *felt* like your insides were shriveling away into nothing.

Damon's eyebrows had disappeared into his hairline halfway through Micah's spiel. "Consider it cleared," he said after a beat of incredulous silence.

"I'm sorry about the picture, by the way," Micah added, since apparently his mouth had gone on strike from his brain. "I don't know what I was thinking. I shouldn't have-"

Micah was cut off when Damon placed a hand over his mouth, warm fingers pressed against his lips. (It shouldn't have been as distracting as it was.) "Micah," Damon said, tone even, "calm down. The picture..." Damon trailed off, like he wanted to say something about it, but thought better of it a moment later, "don't stress about it. It's fine." Damon slowly removed his hand from Micah's mouth. "And don't worry, we're eating at my penthouse, so I'm sure whatever you picked out to wear is acceptable."

Micah couldn't help but wonder if Damon would feel the same way if he'd donned one of the outfits Damon had first met Micah in. Regardless, he offered the man a hesitant nod. "Okay."

"Okay."

Micah worried his bottom lip. "So... are all of your sisters going to be there?"

Damon had mentioned it was hit-or-miss if they all showed up any given weekend.

"They already are," Damon answered. "Joelle called a few minutes ago to let me know they were waiting for us. My uncle came too."

Micah blinked. "Your uncle? You never mentioned that you had an uncle."

"His name is Marco; he's my dad's younger brother. He's heavily involved in some of my... financial endeavors."

He was a mobster, in other words. That explained why Damon hadn't spoken of him. Micah debated whether or not to dig deeper. "So, is he like a partner, or an enforcer, or...?"

"Both," Damon said, which explained exactly nothing. "He usually doesn't show up to family functions."

Micah frowned. "Did one of your sisters tell him you were bringing someone? Do you think he came specifically to meet me?"

Damon's gaze drifted to his tinted window, and for a second Micah didn't think the man was going to answer. And then, so quietly Micah almost didn't hear: "Unfortunately, that is undoubtedly why he came."

Micah was about to crack a joke about how reassuring *that* was, when he stopped to really *look* at Damon. He was a fairly stoic person, and he didn't have a lot of obvious tells, unlike Micah, who tended to ramble or fidget when he was feeling skittish. But taking in how stiff the man was – Damon's shoulders radiated tension and his jaw looked almost wired shut – Micah knew. Damon was *nervous*.

Without thinking twice about what he was doing, Micah reached across the space between them and took hold of Damon's hand. Damon glanced down in surprise, but turned to look at Micah without ripping his hand free, which Micah counted as a win.

Micah squeezed in a way he hoped was comforting. "Everything's going to be fine."

Damon didn't verbally respond, but he squeezed back, and he didn't let go of Micah's hand until they reached their destination.

It was stupid, but Micah felt almost bereft when the man finally loosened his hold after Geoffrey parked and opened the door for him. Micah didn't bother waiting for Geoffrey to come open his door; he just got out on his own.

The skyscraper Damon lived in was as intimidating as Micah remembered. If Micah were to hazard a guess, he'd say the impressive building had about sixty floors, and in many ways, it was similar to The Mark.

Micah allowed Damon to lead him through the glass double doors and the fancy lobby with its glossy, marble floors and iridescent chandeliers. There were bodyguards situated near the doors and a middle-aged receptionist behind the front desk, but they all merely nodded at Damon as he strode past.

They passed another pair of bodyguards near the elevator, where Damon used an electronic key card to buzz them inside. There were no floor numbers to punch in on the elevator. Instead, each tenant's card was keyed in to a specific floor for optimal privacy and security.

Damon actually owned two cards: one for his penthouse, and one for his gym and pool on the floor below.

It was silent as they rode up to Damon's floor, and Micah used the time to silently peruse himself in the shiny reflection of the elevator doors, attempting to contort his face into the same stonelike expression that Damon could effortlessly pull off.

It didn't work.

Before he knew it, the elevator doors were chiming as they opened, and Damon's pristine entryway was staring back at him.

"Damon, is that you?" a familiar voice called from further in the penthouse.

Micah looked past the entryway into the living room, and he was able to count six heads before the one with the familiar bob of brown hair shot up from the loveseat, rushing to greet them.

Joelle was dressed much less provocatively than the last time Micah had seen her. Instead of an electric purple dress with a plunging neckline, she wore a black pencil skirt and a flowy, red blouse that showcased her tanned arms. She looked no less lovely for it.

"Who else would it be?" Damon muttered, but Joelle ignored him to showcase the deceptive strength in said arms by tugging Micah into a tight embrace.

"You actually brought him!" she said, speaking to Damon before turning her full attention on Micah, whom she was all but nestling in her arms. She pressed a kiss to his cheek. "Micah, darling, you're even more exquisite than I remember."

"I should hope so," said the Hispanic man with a well-groomed beard and flashy neon shirt who had followed Joelle into the entryway. "You were four whiskeys deep and as high as a kite the last time you saw him."

Micah stiffened at the reference to drugs, but Joelle merely rolled her eyes. "Don't listen to him. I don't do drugs – well, nothing besides a little ganja here and there, and who doesn't do that? The *only* thing I'm high on is life."

"It's scary, but true," the man agreed, offering Micah a little wave. "Hi, I'm Fernando." So this was Joelle's on-again-off-again boyfriend. "I'd offer you a handshake, but since Joelle seems intent on suffocating you with her admittedly impressive breasts-"

"That's enough," Damon interrupted, rubbing the column of his nose like he was staving off a headache. "Joelle, can you release Micah, please? He hasn't even had the chance to take off his coat."

Joelle huffed, but complied. "Sorry about that, Micah. I was just so excited that my brother has *finally* brought someone to these family dinners, that I forgot myself for a second."

"That's alright," Micah said, "I don't mind." And surprisingly, it was true. Sure, Joelle's greeting had been a bit much, but Micah was an only child who'd always wondered what it would be like to have siblings.

He shrugged off his coat, and Damon hung it up before reluctantly leading him into the living room, where the rest of the party had seemed content to sit back and watch the scene in the entryway.

Damon waited until Joelle and Fernando followed them into the room before introducing Micah. "Good evening, everyone. As I'm sure you heard Joelle exclaim, this is Micah." He placed a burning hand on the small of Micah's back. "I expect you all to treat him with the utmost respect. Any slight against him *will* be viewed as a slight against me, *capiche?*"

It was an enhanced version of "be nice or else", which Micah hadn't been expecting. He couldn't help but notice that Damon's eyes had remained locked on one specific person throughout the little speech. Classically handsome, but with gray sprinkled in his hair and beard, he was probably a decade or two older than everyone else gathered, and could only be Damon's Uncle Marco.

"You say that like we are a bunch of heathens," the man in question pointed out shrewdly as he stood from the couch. The smile he offered Micah was all teeth, and he was reminded vaguely of a shark. "I'm not sure what my nephew has told you about us," – Micah didn't think he imagined the peculiar look the man shot Damon at that – "but I assure you, that *that* couldn't be further from the truth." He took Micah's hand before he could think to offer it. "I'm Marco, Damon's uncle. It's a pleasure to meet you, Micah." Micah blinked in surprise when Marco actually brought his hand to his mouth and kissed the back of it. "I think I speak for all of us when I say I look forward to getting to know you. Damon's quite picky, and I aspire to unearth what makes you so special." Marco squeezed his hand once, so tightly it was almost painful, before letting go.

It was a greeting, thinly-veiled insult, and warning, all in one.

Micah didn't know how to react to it.

Thankfully, he didn't have to, because the only other unnamed man in the room, a clean-cut looking fellow with slicked back brown hair and green eyes, stood to introduce himself next. "Hello, Micah," he said, offering his hand to shake, like an actual *normal* person, "I'm Jason Vitali. It's great to meet you."

"Likewise," Micah said, quickly taking his hand.

Jason turned and gestured behind himself. "And this, of course, is my stunning wife, Caprice."

Caprice, Damon's oldest sister, was the only blonde in the room – well, besides Micah. Her pixie cut accentuated her high cheek bones, and her blue eyes were a shade lighter than Damon's. She was wearing a beautiful floral dress with a cinched waist. An impeccable leg peeked out from the high-waisted slit from where she sat, cross-legged, on the couch.

She offered no greeting to Micah and remained sitting, merely eyeing him critically from behind a large glass of wine.

"Uh, hello, Caprice. You look lovely. Damon's told me a lot about you." That was a stretch, but he had told Micah *some* things about her, at least: that she was smart and had an eye for fashion, but that she could also come across as cold, and she had only gotten frostier over the years as she and her husband continuously tried and failed to have a baby.

Caprice took a long, slow sip of her wine, and for a second, Micah didn't think she would respond, but then...

"That's funny, considering I've only just heard about you last week."

Ouch.

"Oh, um-"

Thankfully, Micah was saved from having to come up with a response by the last woman in the room coming to his rescue. She sprang up from her seat and thrust her hand forward. "Hi, I'm Sophie."

Micah had known by process of elimination that she could only be Damon's youngest sister, Sophie, even before she'd said so, but he still found himself a bit taken back. Because while she was just as beautiful as her siblings, she also didn't quite look like the rest, whose angular features and blue eyes marked them as obviously related. Sophie had a softer look, a more rounded face, and big doe eyes. Not to mention the fact that her skin was brown.

Damon had talked a lot about Sophie to Micah. Apparently, she didn't run as hot as Joelle or as cold as Caprice, and was fairly even-tempered. She was a college student still deciding on what she wanted to do with her life. (According to Damon, she'd changed her major about half a dozen times since she started at Columbia three years ago.) The way Damon spoke of her made it clear he had a soft spot for her, and that he was protective of her in ways that he wasn't of his older sisters.

But Damon had never once mentioned the fact that she was adopted. There was no conceivable way she shared both biological parents with her siblings.

"Hi, Sophie," Micah said, offering her a grateful smile, and hoping his surprise didn't show on his face, "I'm Micah." He immediately flushed. "Obviously."

Micah didn't think it was his imagination that Sophie's smile grew a tad more genuine at his obvious lack of grace.

"Great!" Joelle said, clapping her hands together. "Now that introductions are out of the way, let's eat. Micah needs some fattening up, and it smells absolutely heavenly in here." Joelle wasn't wrong. The smell of freshly baked rolls, along with something more savory, filled the air.

Micah allowed Damon to lead him from the sitting room to the formal dining area. It was the only room in Damon's penthouse that was somewhat closed off from the rest. (Damon had given Micah a tour last Saturday after he'd woken up in the man's home and agreed to his unorthodox proposal.)

He'd wondered at the time why Damon needed such a long, magnificent table with a dozen fancy, upholstered chairs – all identical, of course, not like Micah's mismatched chairs that surrounded his dingy table at home.

Now he guessed he knew.

On the table laid a magnificent spread of food. Micah supposed he shouldn't have been surprised it consisted of mostly Italian cuisine: creamy chicken and broccoli alfredo and meat-stuffed ravioli in some kind of mushroom sauce in fancy glass platters, two baskets of flakey rolls, fruit galore, and last but not least, a platter of what looked like chocolate cannoli. Damon hadn't seen fit to go over any special dining etiquette on Wednesday, so Micah was relieved to see that there was only one set of silverware sitting at each fancy table setting.

Damon steered Micah into the chair that was directly to the right of the head of the table before taking that seat for himself. Once everyone was sitting, he bowed his head – sending Micah a quick look to make sure he followed suit – and said a short prayer.

Micah hadn't realized the man was religious.

Micah was confused when Damon took it upon himself to dish up Micah's plate when he was finished with the prayer, scooping both kinds of pasta onto his plate as well as two dinner rolls and a generous helping of fruit.

It wasn't until he set the dish down in front of Micah and began filling his own plate with food that the others began serving themselves.

Sophie, who had taken the seat on the other side of Micah, must have noticed his confusion because she offered him a kind smile as she explained, "It's because you're the guest of honor."

"Oh."

Seeing as he couldn't avoid it any longer, Micah forced himself to ignore his nervous stomach and stabbed a bit of ravioli with his fork. He thought his nerves would make the food tasteless, but he was pleasantly surprised by the burst of tangy flavor that hit his tongue, and he fought the sudden urge to groan aloud.

Joelle had no such reservations, the moan she let out practically pornographic. "Delicious as always," she declared.

"It's adequate, I suppose." Micah assumed that was a high compliment coming from Caprice. "But where's the lobster risotto?"

"Micah's allergic to shellfish," Damon explained from his spot at the head of the table.

The look Caprice shot Micah made it clear she thought Micah's allergy existed only to inconvenience her.

"I'm allergic to cats," Fernando offered, commiserating. "My mother had a particular fondness for them, and she was quite upset when I puffed up like a marshmallow after being scratched by one of her favorite tabbies when I was *un niño pequeño*. She had to rehome the poor things."

"I'm surprised she didn't rehome you."

Fernando merely laughed off Caprice's quip. "She probably would have been happier," he agreed.

Micah had no idea if he was being serious or not, but judging by the way Joelle curled a comforting hand around the back of his neck and nuzzled the side of his face, there was at least a grain of truth to it.

"I've known about my shellfish allergy since I was old enough to understand what an allergy is," Micah said, hoping to distract the man. "But that didn't stop me from trying the fried shrimp at my friend's birthday party when I was a kid. It seemed like a good idea at the time – until five minutes later and my face was as swollen as one of his Hulk balloons."

Fernando let out a bark of laughter.

Micah smiled. "Luckily, my friend's mom was a nurse, and she had a spare EpiPen that she injected me with before I could go into full anaphylactic shock."

"You never told me about that," Damon said, looking somehow stiffer than when he'd sat down.

Micah shrugged, biting into one of the buttery rolls on his plate. "I was ten and reckless."

"And what about now?" Marco asked. He'd taken the chair directly across from Micah and his stare was piercing. "Have you managed to curb your... impulsivity now that you're older?"

If only he knew.

Micah thought over his answer carefully before opening his mouth. "I'd like to think I'm a mindful person, but I'm not adverse to taking risks if the rewards are comparable."

"An excellent way to approach business *and* life," Jason praised, "the two of which are often intertwined."

Marco merely hummed, his eyes – blue like the rest of his family's – never leaving Micah's.

Desperate to divert the attention from himself, Micah turned to his right. "Sophie," he blurted, "Damon told me you go to Columbia. That's a really prestigious school."

Sophie blinked, taken off guard for a moment by the sudden change of subject, but she nodded anyway, playing along. "Yeah, it's great. They have a great fine arts program. When I started, I thought I wanted to major in something creative like photography or interior design, but lately I've actually been looking into teaching."

"Teaching? *Really?*" Joelle asked.

Apparently, this was a new development.

"How… quaint," Caprice offered.

"Teaching is one of the most noble pursuits there is," Micah said, not quite able to keep the defensiveness out of his voice. (His mom had been a teacher.) "That's great, Sophie," he assured.

Sophie smiled. "Thanks, Micah. What about you?" She froze. "I-I mean I know you didn't go to college, or anything-"

"Jason," Damon cut in before she could embarrass either of them further, "how was Canada? I didn't have time to check in earlier, but I trust the trip went as expected?"

"Everything ran smoothly," Jason answered promptly. "Business took less time than either of us anticipated." He looked to his wife. "Caprice and I even had time to visit Notre-Dame Basilica. It's architecture is breathtaking."

"It's not nearly as beautiful as the original in Paris," Caprice disagreed, "and a complete tourist trap. Hardly worth the hassle of enduring the cold to get there."

"Must we discuss work at the dinner table?" Joelle cut in before Caprice could find something (or someone) else to disparage. "Micah doesn't need to hear the details of a boring business trip any more than I do, and I, for one, would much rather learn about Micah and his exploits." She turned to him. "Go on, sweetie, entertain us with stories of your travels."

Micah blinked. "Oh, um, I've never actually been out of the country."

Joelle's brow crinkled. She was clearly perturbed by this revelation.

"I mean, my parents took me to the Grand Canyon when I was, like, five, I think," he added, like that would somehow soften the blow.

"Well, that's just sad," she said bluntly after a moment, before shaking it off. "No worries, though, I'm sure Damon will take you with him to the family estate in Italy this Christmas; it's tradition, after all. Let me tell you, the European countryside is beautiful in the winter."

Micah shot Damon what he hoped was an inconspicuous look. He doubted the man planned on taking him on some grand vacation, and Micah had no intention of leaving the country with him even if he did. "That sounds lovely," he said, anyway, because what else was he supposed to do?

Joelle beamed.

"Of course, there's plenty of exciting things to get up to without ever having to leave the country," Fernando pointed out. "We live in New York City, after all, the greatest metropolis in the world."

"Of course," Joelle immediately agreed. "There are plenty of adventures to be had in the city. So, what do you get up to in your free time, then, darling? I mean, besides making poor schmucks like my brother fall head over heels in love with you?"

She shot the man a teasing grin at that before returning her gaze to Micah.

Micah felt heat creep up his neck despite the complete inaccuracy of her statement. "Nothing that interesting," he said, pushing the last couple of bites of food around on his plate. "I like to exercise to stay in shape. My friend drags me out sometimes, but mostly, I stay in. I follow the Mets and binge a lot of documentaries on Netflix."

All in all, his life sounded pretty pathetic when summed up like that. But the truth was, until he'd met Damon, Micah's life had basically revolved around work – just not the type of work anyone at the table thought he did.

"What sort of documentaries do you watch?" Sophie asked politely.

"True crime, mostly. Some historical stuff, too."

Marco raised his eyebrows in interest, but it wasn't until a second later, when he began asking questions, that Micah realized he may have made a mistake. "Crime documentaries?" He shot Damon a particular look. "What kind of crime documentaries?"

Shit.

"Oh, you know," Micah said, waving his hand in a way he hoped looked casual, "just the typical stuff: serial killer interviews, mysterious disappearances, infamous cold cases." He made sure to make no mention of organized crime.

Marco looked him up and down. "You're one of those people who romanticize crime then?" he pressed.

Micah couldn't help it; he snorted. "Hardly. I mean, the criminal mind is fascinating and all, but I'm actually more interested in the investigative process... you know, examining the presented evidence and making a judgement for myself about what I think happened."

Marco narrowed his eyes. "So you don't just mindlessly believe whatever the police tell you?"

Micah frowned. "No one's infallible, but I think they are generally on the right track." He paused, hesitating a moment before adding, "I actually wanted to be a cop when I was younger."

Micah glanced at Damon, wondering if he would be upset he had made such an admittance to his family considering... *everything,* but his stoic expression offered no insight.

"A cop? Really?" Luckily, Marco looked more amused than anything. (After all, who would suspect an *actual* cop to admit to a family of mobsters that he had wanted to be a policeman when he was younger? It was probably the only job they viewed in a worse light than what they *thought* Micah did for money.) "So, you're inquisitive then?"

Micah shrugged. "I prefer the term 'naturally curious'."

"Curiosity killed the cat, you know," Marco pointed out, before taking a sip of his wine.

"Good thing they have nine lives then," Micah shot back.

Marco grinned his shark-like smile. "Perhaps. Alas, people like you and me are only blessed with one, and it's always a tragedy when one's life is… cut short."

"Micah doesn't have to worry about such things," Damon snapped, breaking up Micah's strange back-and-forth with his uncle. "Not when he's under my protection. Or have I not made that clear?" he demanded crisply.

Marco merely regarded Damon silently for a moment before offering an acquiescing nod. "Of course."

The tension in the room was cut by the sound of Jason clearing his throat. "How about that cannoli, then?"

Damon glanced down at Micah's plate at the man's suggestion, frowning when he saw Micah hadn't quite cleared it. To be fair, though, Damon had been generous when he'd filled it, and there were only a few bites left.

"Cannoli sounds great," Micah agreed.

Damon's frown didn't diminish, but he nodded before reaching for the platter of pastries, holding it in front of Micah and insisting he take what he wanted before serving himself and then allowing the others to help themselves.

"Rosetta's really outdone herself this time," Joelle said as she popped a piece of cannoli in her mouth. "These are divine."

She was right.

The outer layer of the pastry was crisp and sweet, and the chocolate cream filling was as smooth as silk with just the hint of cinnamon. Although Micah was a tad confused. "Who's Rosetta?" he asked, after swallowing down the cannoli.

He didn't realize it was an odd question until, almost simultaneously, everyone's head swiveled as they turned to stare at him.

"Rosetta is Damon's maid and personal chef," Joelle said after a moment of awkward silence. "She made all the food tonight. With how close you and Damon seem, I figured you'd have met her by now."

"We don't live together," Damon pointed out reasonably.

"I guess I just figured Damon was so good in the kitchen that he didn't need a chef," Micah added, hoping to help Damon smooth over his misstep. "I mean, the crepes he made for breakfast last weekend were the best I've ever had." Also the *only* ones he'd ever had, but it wasn't like *they* knew that. "But with how busy he is, it makes sense, of course, that he would need to hire someone to cook for him."

Micah hadn't realized until he'd finished talking that the stares were not abating at all. In fact, if anything, they'd grown more intense.

"Damon made you crepes?" Sophie asked hesitantly after a moment.

"Uh, yes?" Micah glanced at Damon for help, but the man was staring resolutely down at his plate. "They were very good," he added reassuringly.

"We know Damon's crepes are good," Caprice retorted, voice positively scathing. "We've only been begging him to make them for us – make *anything* for us – for the better part of a decade."

"It's great that Damon's baking again," Joelle quickly interjected, shooting her brother a glance before redirecting her gaze at Micah. "We're glad you got to try some of his food. You're right, his crepes *are* very good. I'm honestly jealous." She paused. "It's just... well, we haven't seen Damon in front of a stove since our parents passed."

Oh.

Shit.

"You must give excellent head."

Micah was glad he didn't have any cannoli in his mouth, or he was sure he would have choked in addition to instantly turning as red as an heirloom tomato.

"Caprice!" Jason exclaimed, sounding aghast.

"I'm just pointing out the obvious! It's not like Damon made a point of trying to hide how they met, and I'm tired of dancing around the subject. As a whore, Micah *must* be good." Her eyes were blue ice as they drilled into Micah's, daring him to contradict her.

But Micah couldn't. Because while he wasn't *actually* a prostitute, Damon thought he was – and it was the story he'd fed his family. (Although Micah still didn't understand why Damon couldn't just tell them that they were faking their relationship, and that he had essentially only hired Micah as an escort.) And Micah wasn't about to come out as a frickin' cop, which really only left one option.

"Well, I have been told I have a talented mouth. And I've got to admit, there's nothing quite like the taste of another man's cock sitting heavy on your tongue as he unloads into the back of your throat."

Never let it be said that Micah backs down from a challenge.

Caprice looked shocked. Sophie looked about as mortified as Micah probably *should* have felt. Joelle cackled. Marco merely took a sip of his wine, staring at Micah like he was a specimen under a microscope who'd just done something particularly interesting. And Damon... well, Micah didn't dare look at him.

Caprice recovered first. "You uncouth, little-"

"Oh, put a lid on it, Caprice," Joelle snapped. "No one wants to hear your holier-than-thou bullshit. You're the one who brought up giving head at the dinner table. And besides, working in the sex industry is a perfectly valid profession."

Micah couldn't help but wonder if Joelle had forgotten than she, too, had called him a whore when they'd first met – although, looking back on it, he supposed it had been more of a test than a show of any true maliciousness on her part.

"You *would* say that considering your boyfriend's a stripper."

"Um, ex-stripper, actually," Fernando pointed out, though neither woman paid him much mind.

"And you talk about people like Fernando – people like Micah – like you don't personally profit off of them. Or have you forgotten that part of the monthly allowance Damon gives you is financed by the clubs *I* run? The Seven Deadly Sins are the most successful clubs in all of New York, none of them more so than Lust, and the reason for that is simple: sex sells."

When Micah had found out that Damon was a mafia boss and started doing research on him, he'd discovered pretty quickly that the man was the main financier of The Seven Deadly Sins, one of the city's most popular (and notorious) set of night clubs, but he hadn't realized that Joelle was so heavily involved in them.

"There's a world of difference between visiting a tasteful club like Lust-"

"You *would* say that considering your husband frequents the place, wouldn't you?" Joelle asserted.

"Hey!" Jason piped up. "You know that certain aspects of my work-"

Caprice steamrolled over both of them like she couldn't hear them.

"-and picking up a desperate hooker off the street, dressing him up, and parading him around at what is *supposed* to be a family dinner. Yet here we are, forced to pretend that he's someone actually worth getting to know, and not some random whore that Damon is paying for unlimited access to his hole-"

Smack.

Damon's fist came down so hard on the table that *Micah's* plate rattled. He didn't dare look at the man, but he knew it couldn't be good when he saw Jason pale out of the corner of his eye. "Jason, take your wife, and *leave.*"

Caprice, however, didn't seem cowed at all. She shot out of her chair. "Seriously, Damon? You're taking *his* side" – she jabbed her finger at Micah – "over your own sister's?"

"I don't see any sides," Damon snapped at her, standing from his own chair, and shoving her fingers out of Micah's face. "All I see is you bullying Micah, a guest in my home – a guest who I warned you not to disrespect. You're lucky the only thing I'm doing is throwing you out."

"Come on, Caprice," Jason said, standing and taking her by the elbow, "let's just go."

Caprice shrugged him off. "Did I say something untrue?" she demanded. "Or does the truth – that he's nothing more than a whore – just hurt? Are you really going to deny you're paying him for the 'pleasure'" – the air quotations around the word were obvious – "of his company?"

Damon said nothing.

"That's what I thought," she said nastily.

"Like Damon doesn't pay *you*," Joelle snapped.

"That's different; I'm his sister," Caprice shot back.

"But I'm more than just your brother, aren't I?" Damon's voice was deceptively calm, but his eyes were swirling with anger, and so dark they almost looked black. You'd have to be blind not to see the danger that lurked beneath the surface. "Or do you need a reminder that I'm also the food in your belly and the roof over your head? The designer dress on your back, and the commas of your bank balance?" He sneered. "You live a very comfortable life, Caprice, but it's at my behest. The more you speak, the more quickly you fall out of favor. For your own sake, I suggest you listen for once in your life, and *get the fuck out of my sight*."

Micah was impressed Caprice managed to hold Damon's gaze for as long as she did before her eyes finally fluttered to the ground. Spinning on her heel, she fled.

Micah didn't know if was possible to look graceful while stomping out of a room in a fit of ill-temper, but somehow, she pulled it off.

"I'm so sorry, Damon," Jason said, grabbing the blazer he'd slung over the back of his chair.

"It's Micah who deserves your apology."

"Of course." Jason nodded eagerly before turning his sights on Micah. "Please, forgive my wife, she's hormonal, and it's been a long week-"

Micah had always found public apologies uncomfortable. He didn't know if it was *that* or that the "hormonal" excuse Jason used rubbed him the wrong way – it smacked of masculine condescension – but he cut the man off before he could say more. "It's fine," he assured. "Don't worry about it."

Jason gave him a tight-lipped smile before turning to Damon and offering him a weird sort of bow. Then he hurried after his wife. Not a moment later, the distant chime of the elevator doors sounded.

Despite Caprice and Jason's exit – or maybe because of it – the air was filled with a thick sort of tension, and Micah could feel the weight of everyone's stare on him. He cleared his throat and turned to Damon, but kept his gaze trained just above the man's shoulder instead of meeting his eyes. "I think I need some air."

He didn't wait for Damon to rebuke him or grant permission, Micah merely stood from his chair and walked in a brisk, but controlled pace to where he knew the balcony was located. (He didn't want to look like he was running away, even though he definitely was.)

A burst of cold air hit him as soon as he opened the glass balcony door, but Micah didn't care. He sucked in the crisp air greedily. Ignoring the hot tub and wicker furniture, Micah grasped the railing of the balcony and rested his head against it, closing his eyes and willing himself to just *not think* for a while.

Dissociating is unhealthy, a voice in the back of his head couldn't help but point out, but Micah ignored it, forcing himself to breathe and feel the cold metal against his forehead and *that's it*.

An indeterminable amount of time later – it could have been five minutes, or it could have been twenty – the sound of the door opening behind him finally broke Micah from his stupor. He turned, unsurprised to see Damon.

"Everyone's left."

Micah nodded, leaning back against the railing. He didn't blame them for not wanting to stick around after that clusterfuck. He bit his lip. "I'm really sorry-"

"I apologize-"

Micah stopped mid-sentence. He and Damon had spoken at the same time.

Damon frowned. "Why are *you* sorry?"

Micah pulled his shoulder up to his ear in a shrug. "I shouldn't have egged your sister on like that. I mean, her concerns about me are valid. You *are* paying me. Not for sex, like she thinks, but still. She doesn't want me taking advantage of you."

Damon snorted. "Caprice knows how unlikely it is that anyone would ever be able to pull the wool over my eyes enough to take advantage of me."

"Perhaps," Micah allowed, "but it's natural for her to have questions and be protective, especially considering my job…"

Damon had *no* idea how accurate that statement was, evidenced by the scowl that transformed his face. "Don't make excuses for her. Caprice had no right to speak to you the way she did, and I… I had no right letting her behavior slide for as long as *I* did." Damon ran an agitated hand through his hair. "Goddammit," he muttered under his breath.

Micah couldn't help but notice how much more expressive – more animated – the man became when it was just the two of them, and even though he had no right to feel any kind of way about it, satisfaction warmed his insides that Damon felt so comfortable around him, anyway.

Then the man spoke. "This entire dinner was a mistake."

Micah stiffened.

Just like that, the warmth was gone, and he could suddenly feel just how cold it was, standing outside on Damon's balcony. The words were a harsh reminder of the deal they had struck in Micah's apartment on Wednesday evening.

One event. One dinner – as a test run. That was it. And then this… this quasi-relationship, or whatever it was he had with Damon, had to end. For both their sakes. Micah just never thought that Damon would be the one ending it.

Ignoring the fact that it felt like his heart was being squeezed in a vice, Micah pushed himself off the railing. "You're right," he said, trying to sound cavalier, "this isn't working."

"What?" Damon looked startled, and then a bit panicked. After two long strides, he was within arm's length of Micah. "No. I know I fucked up, but that's no reason to end our arrangement."

Micah was confused, but he refused to let himself feel that spark of warmth again. "You just admitted yourself that this dinner was a mistake."

Damon frowned. "Yes, but only because I didn't think things through. I should have had you meet my family one at a time, or planned to host the meal at a restaurant where Caprice would have been forced to be civil. I never should have subjected you to her vitriol. It's my fault. I... I didn't protect you."

Damon sounded truly heartsick over it, and as endearing as that was, it was also a little ridiculous, in Micah's opinion. "She said some mean things," he pointed out. "It's not like she stabbed me with her dinner fork. I'll get over it."

Damon's frown didn't dissipate. "So... you're not upset, then?"

"Not really. I mean, sure, the thing with Caprice was embarrassing, and your uncle's obnoxious, but the rest of your family was pretty nice. That doesn't change the fact that we only agreed to one dinner, however. Or did you forget about the deal we made at my apartment?"

Judging by Damon's expression, he hadn't forgotten, but he'd hoped that Micah had. "I'll do better next time," he said, taking another step forward so that there were only inches between them. Their proximity only made the man's eyes more blue, more penetrating. "You don't have to see Caprice or Marco again if you don't want to. I'll even give you a raise. You can have Caprice's weekly allowance in addition to-"

"It's not about the money," Micah cut in before Damon could add even more ridiculous terms to their agreement. "Or your family," he said when Damon opened his mouth to continue arguing.

But the wrinkles in the man's brow only grew more pronounced. "Then why?" he demanded.

Because you're a mafia don and I'm a police detective.

Because our pseudo-relationship isn't real, but my feelings – and dick – don't seem to understand that, and I have to protect my heart from what is almost certainly inevitable devastation.

But Micah couldn't admit to the first, and he didn't know how to verbalize the second. So...

"It's a big time commitment," he said, keenly aware of how lame the excuse was, especially considering Damon had made him quit his "job". "And I feel weird lying all the time. Not only to your family, but to my friends, too. I mean, how do you expect me to explain where I got all these clothes?" He hadn't worn any of his new wardrobe to work for this reason. He was lucky Tessa had left him alone for as long as she had about the Damon situation as it was. "And what about the fact that I'm not... selling myself anymore?"

Damon scowled. "Just tell them you got a new job," he suggested after a moment. "It's the truth, after all."

Micah rolled his eyes. "Yes, because a cashier or a waiter could afford these." He gestured at the pressed slacks and fancy cashmere sweater he was wearing.

"Tell them you got a new boyfriend then, and that he's rich. It's close enough to reality. Just don't tell them my name, and be vague when you describe our dates."

Damon had no idea the irony of him explaining to Micah how to muddy the truth to deliberately mislead someone.

"I don't know," Micah hedged.

"*Please*, Micah." Damon reached forward and took him carefully by the shoulders, pulling him into what *could* be construed as a hug. Micah's nose brushed Damon's chin, and he stared stubbornly at the man's mouth.

Fuck.

"You can have anyone you want," Micah protested weakly, but he could already feel his resistance crumbling. (Why did Damon's lips have to look so soft and inviting? Micah had been outside for all of thirty minutes and his were already chapped.)

"But I want *you*."

Just not the way Micah wanted him to want him, as fucking idiotic as it was. He said nothing.

"There's leftover cannoli in kitchen," Damon coaxed.

Micah frowned, finally allowing himself to glance up and look Damon in the eyes. "Are you seriously bribing me with more dessert right now?"

"Well, you already said no to the extra money," Damon pointed out seriously, but with a hint of a grin pulling at his mouth. (Probably because Micah hadn't outright refused him.) "I also have ice cream in my freezer."

Micah wrinkled his nose. "Let me guess, it's pistachio."

Damon actually laughed at that, though Micah wished he hadn't – because the sound reignited that stupid, self-satisfied warmth in his belly. "There's strawberry, too.

Micah bit his lip. "Will you make me some more crepes?" he asked hesitantly, having learned the significance of Damon making them only an hour ago.

Damon tilted his head to the side and examined Micah carefully, likely trying to decide if he was serious. "Will you agree to attend another event with me?" he asked.

Say no, his brain screamed.

"Yes," Micah agreed immediately, his relationship with his brain well-established by now, "but I demand crepes *and* ice cream."

Damon smiled, and for the first time that night, Micah didn't think there was any tension in his shoulders. "Crepes and ice cream, it is." The man pivoted to go back inside, but he kept one hand on Micah's arm to pull him along with him.

But Micah locked his legs and stayed in place. Before he went back inside, he had to ask. "Damon?"

The man, who was already frowning at Micah's refusal to budge, turned around. "Yes?"

Micah took a deep breath. "If I said no – to another event, to another deal, to *you* – would you have let it go? Let *me* go?"

Damon's grip tightened almost imperceptibly around his arm, and for a long moment, he didn't answer. But eventually... "Let's just be glad we don't have to find out."

* * *

Bad boys, bad boys, whatcha gonna do? Whatcha gonna do-

Micah woke to the blaring of his ringtone. The blasting of that particular song meant it could only be work calling. (Tessa had chosen it for him, okay?) It was probably the only reason he was able to muster up the energy to push himself up onto his elbows and answer the call.

"Hello," he said, voice groggy with sleep. He cleared his throat and tried again. "Hello, this is Detective Hart."

"Micah," Jensen said, his voice loud and jarring in his ear, "I'm going to need you to come down to the station."

Micah pulled the phone away from his ear and glanced at the time – 6:43. He frowned, but obediently stumbled out of bed, anyway. "It's still dark," he pointed out, like the other detective had somehow missed this crucial detail, even as he started looking for a clean pair of pants to pull on. "And it's Sunday. I have the day off."

"It concerns the missing persons case I assigned you."

That definitely caused the remaining fog of sleep to dissipate. Micah's thoughts felt suddenly clear. "Nico?" he asked immediately. "What happened? Did he show up? Did someone find him?"

There was a short pause on the other side of the phone, and then firmly, yet carefully, Jensen said, "They found a body."

The phone slipped from Micah's hand.

CHAPTER TWELVE

The shoulder of Micah's shirt was damp with tears and his sternum stung where Mrs. Sanchez had struck him with her tiny fist when he'd delivered the news to her.

She'd taken Nico's death about as horribly as he expected any mother would. Micah knew the five stages of grief – had been forced to learn about them during his training as a detective for situations like this. But knowing the stages and watching someone live them out right in front of you were entirely different things.

She'd been in denial until Micah had shown her the pictures. (He couldn't take her to the body as it was still being processed for evidence.) She'd flown into a fit of rage when she saw the photos – the waxen pallor of her son's face, the rope burn that encircled his wrists and ankles, the undeniable birth mark on his chest. She'd turned on Micah then, cussing in Spanish, and with nothing else to take her anger out on, she'd punched him with her small, wrinkled fist over and over again.

Manny, the translator, had been concerned, and had fled to get help, but Micah was more than willing to be an outlet for her justified fury. Besides, it wasn't long until she'd dissolved into tears, clinging to Micah like he was a lifeline, no longer her personal punching bag, as she cried.

Micah just held her. Mr. Sanchez had been in a state of shock since Micah had shown them the pictures, silent and staring into the distance – hardly in a condition to help his wife.

Micah didn't think acceptance would come for either of them for a long, long time.

Manny eventually returned with Jensen, who'd had to physically pry Mrs. Sanchez off of him. It was only when Micah had promised he would find who'd done this to her son and make them pay that she reluctantly released him.

He watched through a two-way mirror as Manny introduced them to the precinct's grief counselor.

"Have they found anything substantial at the crime scene?" he demanded as soon as Jensen joined him.

Micah had already been there – where a garbage man had discovered Nico's body near a dumpster in a rough part of Queens. He'd defied Jensen's orders to head straight to the station that morning and had gone there instead.

Jensen had scowled fiercely when he'd arrived, but Micah was already pissed enough that the man had taken charge of the scene when *Micah* was the lead detective of Nico's case.

Nico had been naked, with obvious rope burns around his wrists and ankles. There had also been bruises around his neck, and his abdomen had been colored black and blue from what looked like a vicious beating. Nico's face, however, had remained almost entirely untouched. If not for his ashen skin and the smudges under his eyes, he could have been sleeping.

Micah could recall vividly the nineteen-year-old's hazel eyes from the hundreds of pictures he'd gone through on Nico's Instagram. They'd always been sparkling with life.

(He'd had to excuse himself from the crime scene to vomit around the corner of a nearby abandoned storefront before forcing himself to return.)

Nothing around Nico had looked obviously disturbed, indicating the young man had probably just been dumped there, not killed.

Still, thoroughly searching the area and processing evidence would probably take the rest of the day. Micah had only left to break the news the Nico's parents. Jensen had insisted on coming with him, asserting that Micah looked "pale", but Micah knew the man was still in contact with the policemen at the crime scene, hence the question.

Jensen frowned. "They're finishing up, but it doesn't look promising. More than likely, it's just a dump site," he said, confirming what Micah already suspected. "We just have to hope the perp left evidence somewhere on the body."

The body.

Just yesterday, he'd been Nico. Micah swallowed hard, forcing himself to focus on what else Jensen had said. "Hope?" he repeated incredulously, shaking his head. "That's not good enough. We need to nail whoever did this; I promised Mrs. Sanchez I would."

Jensen frowned. "I heard. You know it's against policy to be making guarantees like that. We'll do our best, of course, but you shouldn't-"

Micah didn't have the patience to let Jensen finish his reprimand. "I know we can't get an autopsy done until..." Micah hesitated, "*the body* is ready to be moved from the scene. Still, I think it's pretty obvious our cause of death is strangulation."

Jensen nodded. "Probably."

"You know what that means, right?"

Jensen raised his eyebrows, clearly at a loss. "That our victim died of asphyxiation?"

Micah fought the urge to tear at his hair. "You're kidding me, right? The rope burns? The fact that Nico was found naked on public property? That he likely died of strangulation? This has the Hooker Hunter written all over it."

The more evidence Micah listed, the stiffer Jensen grew, and by the time Micah had finished – and had actually said the serial killer's name aloud – Jensen's expression was completely closed off.

"We caught the Hooker Hunter over a week ago," he said. "Or have you forgotten that we got an actual confession from the guy?"

Micah shook his head. "You know as well as I do that people admit to crimes they don't commit all the time, sometimes simply for the notoriety."

"Normandy fits the profile," Jensen argued staunchly.

"Maybe, but his latest victim didn't," Micah pointed out, "not exactly. None of the others that the Hooker Hunter took were raped – at least not so blatantly."

Jensen snorted. "Oh, and this guy – this Nico – *does* fit the profile of his victims? The Hooker Hunter killed gay prostitutes, not random college students."

"Nico was homosexual," Micah shot back, "and the right age. Not to mention the fact that he had a webcam show where he masturbated for money. Nico's roommate said that he thought he was going out to meet someone the morning he disappeared. Who's to say it wasn't one of his patrons?"

Jensen pursed his lips. "Even if that *was* who he was meeting, running a webcam show is *not* the same thing as working the streets. You're stretching."

"Maybe the Hooker Hunter used Normandy's confession as an opportunity to switch things up," Micah reasoned. "Or maybe he was growing bored of the easy prey that prostitutes provided and wanted to up the ante a little?"

"That's a lot of maybes. And regardless, none of the other victims were beaten as badly as Nico," Jensen pointed out. "This is much more likely to be a result of gang violence or even a hate crime."

"Or," Micah said, refusing to let the subject drop, "the Hooker Hunter didn't count on Nico being difficult." He knew he was being stubborn, but something deep down in Micah's gut was telling him he was right. "Like you said, Nico *wasn't* a prostitute. Maybe he didn't take as kindly to… whatever the Hooker Hunter says or does to his victims before killing them. Maybe Nico fought him." Micah chewed his bottom lip. "Look, I'm not saying it's a sure thing, but it's something we at least have to consider." He shrugged. "Besides, Normandy's confession never sat right with me."

Jensen scoffed, crossing his arms over his chest. "So, what? You want to reopen a closed case and cause hysteria because a criminal's confession *doesn't sit right with you*? Over a hunch? The blowback the department would face alone is enough reason to deny a request like that."

Micah found himself subconsciously mirroring Jensen's defensive stance. "It's not a hunch," he disagreed. "There's evidence to back the theory up. And the blowback would be much worse if the department doesn't reopen the case and it turns out the Hooker Hunter is still out there, posing a threat to society – *killing* people.

You're just biased because *you're* the one who pulled the confession from Normandy."

Micah knew it was the wrong thing to say even before he said it, but his control over his mouth wasn't great at the best of times.

Jensen closed his eyes and pinched his nose, clearly holding back his frustration with Micah, and for a second, Micah was so strongly reminded of Damon that the dormant butterflies in his stomach came to life and fluttered. But then Jensen opened his mouth, and all thoughts of Damon fled. "I'm sorry, Micah, but I'm going to have to pull you from Nico's case."

Micah's entire body went cold. And then a flash of heat. "What?" he demanded hotly, knowing he was being loud, but hardly caring. "You can't do that. This is *my* case. You assigned me lead detective."

"That was back when Nico was merely a missing person. This is a homicide investigation now. You don't have the experience to take the lead on a case like this, and you're obviously too close to it." He pointedly eyed the wet spot on his shirt where Mrs. Sanchez had been sobbing against him.

"That has nothing to do with anything. You're just pissed that I might be right about the Hooker Hunter."

Jensen took Micah by the arm and crowded him against the wall. "Keep it down, would you?" he said, glancing around. "Look, if I thought for a second that your theory might be right, I would be the first in line to reopen that investigation." He released Micah's arm. "As it stands, your opinion on the matter is no longer consequential. We're done here."

Micah had never liked Jensen, but he'd always at least thought the man was decent at his job – refusing to give Micah any interesting cases aside. Which is why for the first time, Micah contemplated doing something he never wanted to do, something he swore to himself he would never do when he got this job.

"If you try to pull me from Nico's case, I'll go to the captain."

Use his relationship with his father as a threat.

Jensen stiffened. "Excuse me?"

"You heard me. I'll go to Captain Hart. I'll lay out all the evidence, like I just did for you, and let him decide if it's worthwhile to reopen the investigation."

For a long moment, Jensen just stared at Micah. Then...

"Fine," the man snapped. "You can stay on Nico's case, but *I'm* taking the lead, and we're *not* reopening the Hooker Hunter investigation unless you can provide me with enough evidence – *hard* evidence – to justify doing so, understand?"

Micah was tempted to argue further. Despite his threats, however, he really didn't want to go to his father. Not only would it be a hard hit to his reputation, he honestly wasn't sure who the man would side with – him or Jensen. "The case stays close – for now," he agreed reluctantly, "but we *both* take the lead on the case. I... I promised Nico's parents."

Jensen looked him up and down, likely trying to sense if this was truly a sticking point for Micah. "Fine," he said tersely after a moment. "In that case, put in a request for a warrant that you can serve to Nico's cell service provider while I finish up at the crime scene. That site he webcammed for, too.""

Micah was pretty sure partners weren't supposed to boss each other around, but he nodded anyway, not up for more arguing. "Sure. That shouldn't be an issue now that there's..." *A body. Because Nico was dead.* "...proof of foul play."

Jensen frowned. "Yeah, murder." He continued to eye Micah. "Take lunch when you're finished filing for that warrant. You look like shit." With that parting shot, Jensen turned and stalked off.

When he disappeared around a corner, Micah slouched against the wall, his head making a dull *thunk* when he closed his eyes and allowed it to fall backward against the plaster. It may have been a shitty thing to say, but Micah had zero doubts that Jensen was right about him looking like garbage.

Along with a pounding headache, his stomach had been in knots all morning (the vomiting earlier hadn't even helped all that much), and his eyes felt sore even though it hadn't been him sobbing until he was choking on his breath in interview room three – it had been Mrs. Sanchez.

Because Nico was no longer just missing; he was dead.

Because Micah hadn't been able to find him in time.

Instead, he'd been off fucking around with a frickin' billionaire mafia boss, having the time of his life while-

Stop.

Micah knew he had to stop the onslaught of self-flagellating thoughts before he drove himself crazy. And he knew from experience that the best way to shut his brain off was to keep busy, so after taking a deep breath in through his nose, he pushed himself off against the wall and got back to work.

He went to his desk, intending on filing the paperwork for a warrant like Jensen had suggested, but before he could get started, he was all but tackled by Tessa.

Micah was deeply impressed by the fact that even though it looked like she'd somehow stuffed *two* basketballs up under her shirt, she was somehow able to squeeze both her arms completely around his middle. "I heard the news," she mumbled into his chest. "I'm so sorry, honey."

Tessa had assisted him with Nico's case over the past week, helping him comb through the nineteen-year-old's social media profiles and just generally acting as a sounding board for Micah's theories about where he had gone.

Micah returned her embrace, but he was surprised that when he went to speak, his throat felt too tight for words, so he simply nodded before gently prying her off him. He cleared his throat. "Yeah, it… it sucks."

It somehow described the situation completely, yet didn't touch the awfulness of it at all.

"Anyway," Micah said, sliding into his desk chair and powering on his computer, "I have to get a warrant from the judge so I can track Nico's cellphone data."

Better to be doing something useful than just sitting there and dwelling on the misery of it all.

Tessa frowned over his shoulder, but he paid her no mind. "Okay," she said, "but you know it usually takes a couple hours for low-priority warrants to get approved. So file for it, but afterwards, I'm taking you out for lunch."

Micah's stomach twisted in protest. "I'm not really hungry-"

"Nope," Tessa asserted before he could shrug her off. "You look like a stiff breeze could take you in a fight right now – and you carry *a Glock* for fuck's sake. You need to eat something."

Micah sighed. "Jensen *did* say I look like shit," he allowed.

"Well, loathe as I am to agree with him, he's right. Finish filing for that warrant, then we're out of here."

That's how, half an hour later, Micah found himself huddled in their usual booth at the sandwich shop a block from the station. It was where they usually wound up whenever Micah deigned to join Tessa and her husband for lunch.

Speaking of Tessa's husband... "Where's Jasper?" Micah asked as he picked at his turkey sub.

Tessa waved a hand as she dug into her own cheesesteak sandwich. "I told him to shove off today – that you and I needed to have some girl time to chat."

Micah scowled at her over the table, but his heart wasn't really in it. "Not sure how it's escaped your notice this long, but I'm not a girl."

Tessa huffed. "Yeah, yeah, you're all man. It's an expression, Micah. The point is that you need someone to talk to."

"Do I really? Or do you just have the insatiable need to be a listening ear?"

Tessa raised two unimpressed eyebrows.

Micah sighed. "Seriously, I'm perfectly fine, Tessa."

"Really? You're perfectly fine?" she parroted. "Is that why you're pushing around your curly fries – curly fries you love so much, you once made up an embarrassing haiku about them that one time we were drunk – instead of, I don't know? Actually eating them?"

Micah's face reddened. "Sorry if my appetite's trash because I was busy processing a dead body this morning," he snapped.

Instead of snipping back at him, Tessa merely nodded sympathetically, and Micah realized he'd been had. His shoulders slumped. "Sorry," he muttered.

Tessa reached across the table and took him by the hand. "It's okay, Micah."

And just like that, all of Micah's pent-up emotions started spilling out. It wasn't like a dam flooding, where everything came bursting out at once, but rather a slow, messy leak where his hands started trembling and his eyes filled with tears of their own accord.

It would have been embarrassing if Micah wasn't so upset.

"It's just... his body was *fresh*, Tessa," he said, voice hushed. "The autopsy will take a few days to complete, but there's no way Nico was dead for more than a day – two, at most – before he was dumped."

They both knew what that meant.

"You don't know that for sure," Tessa pointed out reasonably. "It's below freezing outside. It's possible for a body to be preserved-"

Micah shook his head. "I *know*, Tessa. I know Nico was still alive when I got his case."

"Micah," Tessa started, voice careful – it was very unlike her. "It's not your-"

"I know I didn't kill him, okay?" Micah interrupted before she could finish the asinine sentence. "But you didn't see his body. He was *naked*, Tessa. And beat to all hell. There were rope burns around his wrists and ankles." Micah knew he shouldn't be giving out this information to someone not working directly on the case, but he couldn't help himself. "Who knows what the sick fuck was doing to him while I sat there... doing what exactly? Chatting up his roommate? Scrolling through his Instagram? Outing him as a porn star to his parents, who, by the way, are fucking devastated that their son is dead?"

"Micah-" Tessa tried again.

"*No*, Tessa! I don't want to hear it. Do you know what I was doing this weekend while Nico was being tortured by some psycho?

I was fucking around with Damon, meeting his family and binging fancy Italian cuisine. I didn't even think of Nico *once*-

"Micah, stop it-"

"I didn't kill him, okay? I'll acknowledge that. But *please* don't tell me it's not my fault. Because I didn't save him either."

Micah was breathing hard by the time he was finished – which was stupid, he hadn't even gotten up from his seat.

Tessa waited until Micah had a handle on his panting – had a handle on *himself* – before speaking. "Are you finished?"

Micah nodded.

"Good, because it's my turn to talk now, and I need you to listen to me very closely." She was still holding his hand and gave it an authoritative squeeze. "You did everything you possibly could for Nico. You talked to *dozens* of people. You literally filed for the same warrant you requested an hour ago, but the judge denied it – as he was bound to do with the lack of evidence you had to work with. You're *not* omniscient; you're *human*. It doesn't matter what you were doing this weekend – there is *nothing* you could have done."

Micah swallowed. "It hurts," he admitted quietly.

"It hurts because you care. That's a *good* thing. I wouldn't change a goddamn thing about you. But you can't internalize it. You can't take others' pain and make it your own. It doesn't do anyone any good in the end, and it'll burn you out faster than anything else about this job."

"You're right," Micah said. And he knew she was. But that didn't make it any easier to deal with. Although her easy understanding and staunch support *did* take away some of the burden of Nico's death.

"I don't like seeing you question yourself. You're a good detective, Micah."

A little of the doubt that had been looming over him since he'd gotten the news about Nico that morning drifted away. Feeling a bit lighter, Micah nodded, and maybe even meant it. "Thanks, Tessa."

Tessa smiled, popping one of her fries into her mouth. "Also, you're a secretive little fuck."

Micah froze. "I-... *what?*" He jerked his hand out of Tessa's grip.

"Don't get me wrong," she said, munching on another fry. "You're allowed to have a life separate from work. I encourage it even. But not only have you gone out with Damon *again*, you're meeting his family now? And you haven't told me? What the hell, Micah? The last I knew, he thought you were a prostitute, and you were still denying the fact that he was fucking you up the ass?"

Micah's face burned, and he threw a fry at Tessa. As good as the salty morsels were, it was a sacrifice he was willing to make. "He isn't," Micah hissed.

"Oh, so you're fucking him up the ass?"

"*No!* Not that either!"

Tessa *still* didn't look like she believed they weren't screwing each other's brains out. "Well, does he at least realize you're not a hooker now?"

Micah opened and closed his mouth, floundering for a second. It immediately gave him away.

"*Seriously?*" Tessa just looked annoyed now. "I repeat: what the hell, Micah?"

"It's... hard to explain."

"Try me," Tessa ordered. "I promise I'll do my best to keep up."

Micah groaned. "You did this on purpose," he accused. "Inviting me to lunch under the guise of being concerned so you could ambush me about this."

"I am concerned," Tessa protested, "just about more than one thing. I've held back for over a week now. First because you threw yourself so wholeheartedly into Nico's case, and then because Jensen was bogging you down with extra work besides. But you've been acting off long before today. I mean, you were as white as a sheet last Monday, and walking around with these big, sad eyes – like a kicked puppy. And then, towards the end of the week, you were all smiley and daydreamy. It was weird. *You've* been weird. So, please, for the love of God, just tell me what's going on."

Micah would like to claim he'd held out a little longer, but the fact of the matter was, he broke pretty much immediately.

He had bottled up all his strange, little interactions with Damon – and the feelings that went along with them – and had corked them somewhere inside him. They'd been festering there with no one to unload them on. So it was almost a relief when it all came pouring out, like an actual broken dam this time.

Micah told Tessa about the blowjob that wasn't in the back of Damon's car, about the man's ridiculous penthouse, about the crepes, and the fucked up deal they'd made. The shopping trip, and the phone, and the game of twenty questions they'd been playing – the reason for all his smiling late last week. He even told her about the unsolicited photo he'd sent Damon of himself in women's panties. (Tessa had nearly choked on her sandwich, she was laughing so hard – especially when Micah had told her the photo had featured a pair of underwear that *she* had bought him. Tessa had demanded to see the picture, but luckily, he'd had the good sense to delete it after sending it.)

All in all, Micah thought his friend had taken everything pretty well. ("I told you when you two first met that this had Pretty Woman written all over it.")

There was just one thing she couldn't seem to wrap her mind around. Well, *two* things.

"It makes no sense. I mean, why would a man like that – filthy rich, and with a face *and* ass of a god – need to pay someone to *pretend* to date him?" She dragged the last of her fries through the puddle of ketchup on the side of her plate. "I mean, no offense, babe, because you're gorgeous – you can join Jasper and I in the sack any time, it's an open invitation-"

Micah groaned, burying his face in his hands. "Tessa-"

"-but it's sketchy as fuck. Especially since he's paying you *that* kind of money. I mean, have you checked your Venmo to see if he's actually sent you anything?"

Micah still hadn't worked up the nerve to do that, in fact, afraid he'd see a ridiculous number in his account and freak out over it.

Besides, he had no intention of actually using any of the money. He told Tessa so.

She frowned, but shrugged. "That's your call, I suppose. Though I still don't know why you won't tell him you're not actually a prostitute."

"I actually have a very good reason for that."

Micah had told Tessa nearly everything there was to know about his situation with Damon. But there was one thing he'd purposefully avoided mentioning, and it was finally the moment of truth. Where Micah told her that the deal he'd struck with Damon was even more fucked up than she thought.

Tessa wiped her greasy fingers off on a napkin before giving him her full attention. "Let's hear it then."

"It's his job," Micah revealed hesitantly. "It's dangerous. It's also why he pays me to be his escort instead of finding someone he actually likes to spend his time with."

Tessa sent him a disbelieving look. "He seems to like you just fine. *More* than fine, actually."

Micah waved away her words, even if they did make his heart flutter a little. "The point is, with his job being… what it is, I can't tell him that I work for the police."

Tessa frowned. "But I thought he worked in finances," she said.

"That's *technically* true," Micah hedged.

Tessa crossed her arms over his chest, resting them pointedly on her swollen belly. "Do you plan on telling me what the man *actually* does for a living before or after I pop these two out?" she demanded.

Micah sighed. Then he braced himself. "Damon's a mafia don."

CHAPTER THIRTEEN

Tessa took the news better than he thought she would.

And by that, Micah meant that she had only yelled and scolded him for about twenty minutes instead of the solid hour he'd been expecting. *("What sort of mental gymnastics did your brain manage to perform that you thought for even a single second that this was a good idea?!")*

Sure, it was only because they were already late getting back to work that she'd had to stop, and yeah, she had sent him looks filled with varying degrees of exasperation and worry for the rest of the day, but Micah was counting it as a win.

Regardless, he had to put it out of his mind as much as he could to focus on Nico. He'd gotten the warrant from the judge and had served it to the cell service provider Nico used. He hoped to receive tracking information by the end of the week. In the meanwhile, he had a dozen interviews to reschedule now that Nico's case had been updated from a missing persons inquiry to an active murder investigation. That took up the majority of his afternoon.

It was nearing five o'clock, and Jensen had already left for the day, with strict orders for Micah to do the same. (That was an hour ago.) He was surprised Tessa was still lingering around, considering it was a Sunday, and he knew for a fact that she had the day off.

Her motivation behind staying late became clear, however, when she clocked out immediately after him and looped her arm around his elbow. "Drive me home, would you, Micah? I'm not feeling well." She placed a hand over her belly to emphasize her "fragile" state.

It was all a ruse, of course, to rebuke him over the Damon situation some more.

"He's a criminal and you're a cop," she all but hissed at him as soon as he got behind the wheel of her beat-up, red Toyota. "You realize how stupid that is, right?"

Micah didn't have to ask who or what she was talking about.

He sighed, but begrudgingly started Tessa's car, knowing he was in for a *long* fifteen minute drive. "I know, okay?"

"Then why did you agree to something so... so brainless? You said yourself that it isn't about the money, and I know the man is built like a horse, but no dick – or ass, for that matter – is worth putting your life on the line over-"

"I *know*, Tessa," Micah said, hoping that if he repeated himself the woman would understand he knew how ill-advised the weird, little relationship he was building with Damon was. "I just *like* him, okay?"

"And what exactly is it that you like so much about him that you're willing to play chicken with your life?" she demanded, looking skeptical. "Not to mention what it would do to your career if it got out that you were dating a professional criminal."

Micah winced. He hadn't considered that.

"Is it that he makes you feel special?" she continued. "That he's rich and important, and drops thousands of dollars on you without blinking an eye?"

"That's *not-*"

"Hey, I'm not judging," she cut in. "I'm just saying that there are tons of rich, attractive fish in the sea – just like Damon, sans the criminal history – that would love to have a pretty thing like you hanging off their arm, and that would pamper you with attention, and all sorts of gifts-"

"I don't want gifts and attention, alright?" Micah snapped. He huffed. "I mean, it's nice, obviously – especially the attention. But... I just- I want *him*, alright?"

It was a thought that had been lurking in the back of his mind for a while now, but it was the first time he'd voiced it aloud.

"Are you trying to say you're in love with him?" Tessa demanded incredulously.

"What? No!" Micah exclaimed. "I mean... I don't know. What is love, anyway?" He glanced at the speedometer, wondering if 30 MPH was slow enough that he'd dodge any life-threatening injuries if he just yeeted himself out of the car right then and there.

Tessa, for her part, looked like she might shove him out the door herself. She probably hoped he would hit his head on the way down, and the blow might trigger his brain to regenerate some of the critical thinking cells he was obviously lacking.

"Micah, you hardly know him, and what you *do* know is that he's a criminal." That seemed to be her go-to argument. "And not some petty vandal or small-time arsonist. If Damon's a mafia don as you claim – that means he's violent, and he's dangerous, and that he's got more blood on his hands than most blood banks even have in storage at any given point in time."

Micah did *not* want to hear this.

"Obviously, he thinks you're a catch – and you *are* – but what happens if he finds out you work for the police? He knows where you live, Micah, and he's so rich, I wouldn't be shocked if he wiped his ass with hundred dollar bills. He could find you out *so* easily if he wanted to. And what if when he does, he hurts you? Or worse?"

Micah's knuckles were white where his hands gripped the steering wheel. "Damon wouldn't do that." He didn't realize how much he actually believed it until he was forced to say it out loud.

"But it's a risk you're willing to take?" Tessa pressed.

"Yes, okay?!" Micah snapped, slamming on the brake when the light in front of him turned red. He turned to face Tessa. "I get it. I'm a reckless moron who's putting everything on the line for a man who doesn't even *like* me – not how I want him to, anyway. It doesn't make sense, and I can't explain my decision-making away with logic because it's *not* logical. I know that; I *do*. But I'm doing it anyway."

The drinker behind him honked their horn, and seeing that the light had turned green, Micah eased off the brake.

Tessa was quiet while they drove down the road. Then...

"Okay."

Micah blinked. "Okay?" he repeated. "That's it?"

Tessa shrugged. "I mean, I agree with you – you *are* a reckless moron. Most of me thinks you've lost your mind. But there is a tiny part of me – and I mean miniscule – that also thinks that this whole convoluted mess you've gotten yourself into is sort of *a little bit* romantic.

Micah glanced her way, surprised. "Really?"

"I mean, it's definitely a romantic comedy, but yes."

Micah huffed.

"Like I said, it's a *tiny* part, and I'm probably wrong. I'm an eight-month-pregnant, hormonal mess, for fuck's sake. Regardless, *all* of me loves you, so if you're set on doing this no matter what I do or say, who am I to stand in your way?"

Micah let that sink in. "Thanks, Tessa," he said quietly after a moment.

"And besides, if he hurts you, I'll just kill him. I mean, I'm a police detective. It's not like I don't have the resources."

Micah snorted. "You know, I think you'd get along very well with Joelle – that's Damon's middle sister. She's a fan of death threats, too."

Tessa pursed her lips. "To be clear, I don't give a rat's ass about Damon or his family. I care about *you*. So, you're going to be smart about this from now on, and at least text me when you're going to meet up with Damon, telling me where you're going, and letting me know when you get home."

Micah was tempted to tease the woman about practicing her parenting skills on him, but he restrained himself. It was an easy compromise to make, after all. Tessa was one of the most important people in his life, right up there with his dad, and he didn't want to lose her. "That sounds reasonable."

"Of course, it is. I'm not the one who's lost his damn mind." Tessa reached across the middle console and flicked him on the side of the head.

All in all, for what had been one of the toughest days of work he'd ever had, it ended on a pretty contented note.

The rest of Micah's week progressed in a similar pattern.

The majority of his days were spent reinterviewing the important people in Nico's life and performing a much more thorough search of his dorm while he waited for the tracking information from Nico's cell service provider to arrive.

The official autopsy report on Nico's body had come back mid-week, prompting another mini-row between Micah and Jensen when minute levels of chloroform were detected in his system – something he had in common with some, but not all, of the Hooker Hunter's victims.

In the end, Micah had begrudgingly agreed to keep the case closed as there had also been foreign skin cells detected under Nico's fingernails. There was no proof that any of the Hooker Hunter's victims had ever had the chance to fight back, like Nico clearly had.

Unfortunately, when they ran the DNA provided by the skin cells through the system, no matches popped up. It meant that whoever had murdered Nico wasn't in their database.

Ultimately, they were no closer to finding Nico's killer at the end of the week than they were at the beginning.

Despite the lack of progress at work, there had been some bright spots in his week – specifically when Damon took him out to eat at a fancy restaurant on Wednesday for what Micah had taken to calling their "weekly bonding session" in his head.

He would have preferred to just hang out at one of their apartments, but Damon insisted he needed to learn proper dining etiquette. Micah couldn't deny that the food had been delicious. (Though the way Damon had watched him eat with dark, hooded eyes had made him squirm in his seat, clenching his thighs together in an attempt to stop any other bodily reactions.)

Micah was wholly certain that the quartered garlic potatoes he was eating were delicious, but he couldn't enjoy the taste of them with Damon staring at him like that.

The man had hardly touched his own food. Instead, his gaze was laser-focused on Micah, seemingly enraptured as he watched Micah stab a potato, bring it to his mouth, and chew – then repeat, occasionally pausing to lick the buttery sheen from his lips.

"Am I doing it wrong?" Micah asked, unable to take the intense scrutiny after a while. He was only being a little sarcastic. He knew he was using the correct fork – Damon had ensured that – and he was making sure to chew with his mouth closed, but for all he knew, he was committing some other social faux pas.

Damon dragged his eyes away from Micah's mouth and cleared his throat. He didn't seem at all abashed at being called out for staring. "You're doing fine," he assured.

"Are you sure?" Micah asked. "I mean, I've only been feeding myself for twenty-three years now, but if you think you can do a better job of it..." Micah held out his fork, teasing the man.

But to his immense surprise, Damon snatched it from his hand. Instead of using it, however, he put it down, and picked up one of the glazed baby carrots on his own plate with his fingers, holding it to Micah's mouth.

Micah sputtered, pushing the man's hand away. "What are you doing?"

"You offered to let me feed you," Damon pointed out the obvious. "Or did you change your mind?"

It was said blandly, with an air of nonchalance, like it made no difference to Damon what Micah decided. But Micah could hear the dare in the words anyway. Micah blamed his stubborn streak and his inability to back down from a challenge for what came out of his mouth next. "No, I haven't changed my mind."

Damon brought the carrot back to his mouth and raised his eyebrows, his cue for Micah to open up.

Micah's face blazed, but he obeyed, and Damon carefully fed him, pushing his fingers against his lips, almost inside. The carrot was earthy and sweet, and Micah tongued the bit of glaze that got caught on the corner of his mouth. Damon's eyes tracked the movement before he picked up another bit of carrot. "More?" he asked.

Micah nodded.

By the time they'd finished their meal, Micah's stomach had felt heavy and sated with something that had nothing to do with the amount of food he'd eaten. (His cock had also been straining against the zipper of his pants.)

Of course, his erection had quickly wilted when Damon revealed at the very end of dinner the reason he was so insistent that Micah learn proper dining etiquette ASAP. It had everything to do with the next event he was expected to attend with Damon.

A fancy charity gala on Saturday evening.

And unfortunately for Micah, Saturday evening had arrived.

CHAPTER FOURTEEN

Micah stared at himself in his dingy bathroom mirror, feeling like an utter imposter in one of the ridiculously expensive suits Damon had bought him two weeks ago exactly.

The man had called and suggested Micah wear the gray ensemble with the leather suspenders and navy bowtie. Micah may have kicked up a fuss about it if he thought it was an order, but Damon had asked nicely enough, so he'd obliged.

He'd also attempted to style his hair, so it looked purposefully messy instead of the regular messy it usually was. Then, in a moment of inspiration, he'd dug out the eyeliner and mascara he'd used to play hooker with when he'd first met Damon. The black was a little smudged around his eyes – he wasn't nearly as skilled at applying makeup as Tessa – but he thought the end-job was passable.

No amount of fiddling with his hair or messing with makeup could banish his nerves, however. Micah felt clammy in his suit despite the winter weather, and the bowtie around his neck felt more like a noose than a clothing accessory.

He was relieved when his phone finally chimed, announcing that Damon was outside. He slipped on a pair of loafers before shrugging his arms through the fancy trench coat Damon had bought him specifically to be worn over suits and headed out.

Spotting Damon's vehicle immediately – it stuck out like a sore thumb in this part of Queens – Micah opened the back door and scooted inside.

Like every time he got into the man's car, Damon couldn't seem to stop himself from staring.

"What?" Micah asked as Geoffrey pulled the Rolls-Royce back into traffic.

Damon didn't look away. "Are you wearing makeup?" he asked.

Micah felt his shoulders tense defensively. "Is that a problem?"

Damon blinked. "No. You always look beautiful," he said simply.

Micah's face burned. He'd been called a lot of things before: hot, sexy, and on one particularly memorable occasion, "a pretty boy with a mouth that looks like it's made for sucking cock". But Micah struggled to remember a time he'd been called beautiful.

Micah supposed that most people considered it a feminine term. Regardless, he grappled with how to respond. "Stop," he finally muttered, willing the blush on his cheeks to vanish as he pressed the back of his hands to them.

Damon frowned. "Why? We're going on a date. It's standard procedure to compliment your partner."

"Yeah, but it's not a *real* date, is it?" Micah pointed out.

Damon reared back at the reminder, his jaw clenching as he glanced away. "Right."

Micah was nearly overcome with the impulse to apologize, which was dumb. He was only stating the truth. Regardless, he had to bite back the urge for the remainder of the drive, which was quiet and tense – at least in Micah's own head.

All thoughts of having unintentionally offended Damon fled his mind, however, when they pulled up to the event in question.

The charity gala was being held at Gotham Hall, a building in Midtown with grand columns and an intimidating facade. It was renowned for its luxuriousness and timeless beauty on the inside, and an extremely popular venue for the scant percentage of the population able to afford to rent it out.

But Micah had been warned about the location of the event, so it wasn't *that* which took him off guard.

No, what had Micah blanching was the fact that there was a red carpet rolled out outside of Gotham Hall, complete with a throng of reporters holding flashing cameras.

"Damon," he hissed, "Is that a red carpet?"

"Well, it isn't purple."

Damon sounded so unconcerned that Micah couldn't resist glaring.

"What? I told you that there would be one."

"I thought you were joking!" Micah exclaimed. "And *the press* is here." The last thing Micah needed was his picture in the newspaper, arm in arm with an infamous mobster, for all of his co-workers, or worse, *his father* to see.

Damon frowned, finally seeming to have caught on that Micah was actually upset. "Does it make you that uncomfortable to be seen with me?"

"Yes!"

Damon's face did this strange thing, like he was debating whether or not he ought to be offended by the ferocity of Micah's exclamation or not.

Micah sputtered. "Not- Not like that! It's just…" – he fought to think of a valid reason for his meltdown – "didn't you say it was dangerous to be associated with you?" he finally settled on. "What if your enemies, or rivals, or whatever, see us together and assume I'm important to you?"

Damon immediately softened. "You *are* important to me." *Do not read into that, Micah, do not,* his brain warned him. "And I'm perfectly capable of protecting you." The man must have been able to see that *that* didn't ease Micah's concerns at all, however – mostly because they weren't Micah's *actual* concerns – because he sighed. "But if you're that worried about it, just turn into me when we step out of the vehicle. Hide your face in my shoulder, and we'll walk quickly, okay? There are plenty of people attending the gala tonight more interesting than a real estate mogul like me. The press isn't as likely to print my picture as, say, Beyoncé's."

Micah gaped. "*Beyoncé* is here?"

The corner of Damon's mouth twitched, and Micah's eyes narrowed. "You're fucking with me."

Damon shrugged. "You're going to have to go in to find out."

At that point, Micah realized they were the next car in the line of fancy vehicles dropping off the gala's guests at the start of the red carpet. He took a deep breath in through his nose to calm himself. "Fine."

Following Damon's instructions to shed his outer coat, he waited impatiently for the man to walk around and open his car door for him so Micah could hide himself as the man had suggested. Damon curled an arm around his shoulder, and Micah all but nuzzled his face into the man's armpit.

They walked quickly.

There were lots of flashes in his peripheral vision and people shouting out for "Mr. Romano!", but (thankfully) Micah only heard a handful of reporters demand to know who Damon's date was before they were inside Gotham Hall, which was closed off to the press.

An attendant, or server – Micah wasn't really sure how it worked, but the young man was wearing a burgundy vest and black tie that matched the rest of the staff he could see meandering around – greeted them. As soon as Damon said his name, he was leading them through the long entryway that opened into the grand hall.

It was breathtaking.

He and Damon must have been some of the last guests to arrive because the place was bustling with mingling people in fancy dresses and impressive suits. But they didn't take away from the marvel of the room at all.

It was *huge*, and circular, with a ceiling that had to be at least four or five stories tall and featured a chandelier that probably took up more square feet than Micah's entire apartment.

Micah didn't know if it was the unique architecture or the mood lighting, but something about the place made Micah feel more like he was in a medieval cathedral, or even a castle, rather than a posh building in New York.

The marble floors were a warm brown, and the interior walls were made of multicolored brick. Most of the space was taken up by round tables with ornate floral centerpieces, but there was also an area which Micah assumed was meant for dancing, as well as a large podium, which featured a band playing soft jazz music. Of course, there were also two bars on either side of the circular room, which seemed to be popular spots for guests to congregate.

The grand hall also featured multiple archways, which Micah assumed branched off into other rooms, such as lounges and restrooms. He knew one of the rooms must have showcased the items for sale in the gala's silent auction.

It was one of the ways – besides the ticket prices, which Micah assumed were quite exorbitant – that the gala was raising money for a charity called Dare to Dream – a foundation that helped youth in foster care by offering education and resources for families in need.

One of the only reasons Micah had agreed to attend the gala with Damon at all was because he thought it was a worthwhile cause.

"Alright?" Damon asked, pulling Micah from his reverie. He hadn't realized he'd stopped walking as he stared, wide-eyed at the grandeur of Gotham Hall.

Micah nodded, allowing Damon to pull him along after the attendant, who was showing them to their table. He didn't see Beyoncé anywhere, but he *did* see a head of hair that looked suspiciously like Dolly Parton's.

"Don't worry," Damon assured, his lips tantalizingly close to Micah as he spoke softly in his ear, "we only have to stay for the meal and the results of the auction. Then we can leave."

As awed as Micah was by the splendor of the place, leaving sounded awesome.

It wasn't long after they were seated that the rest of the chairs around their table began to fill. Micah wasn't sure if he was relieved or dismayed to recognize most of the faces.

There was Damon's Uncle Marco, dressed pristinely in a gray suit a shade darker than his own. He chose to sit in the free chair next to Micah.

Micah was taken off guard to also see Caprice and her husband, Jason – and he wasn't the only one surprised judging by Damon's reaction. "Caprice, I didn't expect to see you here."

He sounded pissed.

Jason, at least, had the sense to look apologetic.

Caprice, however, remained unruffled by Damon's displeasure. She merely took a sip of her drink before offering her brother a lazy smirk. "You wouldn't, would you? Not since you've stopped taking my calls." She gestured at the woman beside her. "Renata invited me."

Which brought Micah to the people he *didn't* recognize.

"Hello, love," the woman said, taking the free seat on the other side of Damon, but not before pressing a kiss to the man's cheek, leaving a little red smudge of lipstick behind.

Micah's eye did *not* twitch at the action.

And he didn't care at all when the tall, leggy woman with loose, black curls cascading down her back, mysterious dark eyes, and a pair of tits so perky Micah was pretty sure he would have popped a boner if he wasn't as gay as gay can be – this "Renata" person – offered Damon a tumbler full of amber liquor. "I got you a whiskey. They had your favorite."

It wasn't any of Micah's business how this *gorgeous* woman knew Damon... even if she apparently knew him well enough to know his favorite brand of whiskey – something Micah had no clue about.

"Well, don't be rude," Caprice demanded when Damon didn't immediately drag his glare away from his sister to greet the other woman. "Thank Renata for the drink."

Micah didn't know how Caprice withstood the heat of Damon's glare – lots of practice, probably.

After a moment, he turned to Renata, his gaze immediately softening. "Thanks, Renata. That was considerate of you." He took the proffered whiskey.

Micah's stomach did *not* twist with something akin to jealousy *at all*.

So why did his insides untangle when Damon returned his eyes to Micah. "Would you like anything from the bar?"

It was a complicated question. As tempted as Micah was to guzzle whatever alcohol he could get his hands on to ease the tension he could feel building in his shoulders, he didn't want Damon fetching him a drink and leaving him with these people.

Sure, the middle-aged couple that took the last of the table's seats didn't seem so bad – they appeared content to let whatever drama was unfolding before their eyes finish before introducing themselves – but besides them (and Damon, obviously), Micah didn't think a single other person wanted him there.

Luckily, a waitress strode past just in time to solve his dilemma. "Excuse me, Miss, but do you have any-" Micah cut himself off, glancing around at what everyone else was drinking. "Do you have any wine?"

"What kind of wine would you like?" the woman asked.

"Red is fine."

The woman frowned, a confused wrinkle appearing on her forehead. "Yes," she said, making sure to keep her voice carefully neutral, "but what kind of red, sir?"

Micah was many things, but an expert on wine was not one of them. As far as he was concerned, there were three kinds of the stuff: red, white, and rosé.

"Um…" Micah couldn't help but glance Damon's way for help.

Quickly catching on to Micah's plight, the man interjected. "*Recioto della Valpolicella*, if you have any, please."

The waitress seemed relieved to get a specific answer. "Of course, sirs, I'll be right back."

Micah's shoulders relaxed.

"*Recioto della Valpolicella* is a sweet wine made with dried grapes from northeastern Italy," Damon explained. "I usually find it too honeyed for my tastes, but it's a passable aperitif, and perfect for someone with a sweet tooth."

Micah fought to stave off a blush. He'd assumed Damon had just rattled off something random, not ordered something specifically for him.

"Honestly, do you know nothing of wine?" Caprice demanded from her spot across the table, ruining the moment.

"I think it's cute," Renata offered, offering Micah a smile, but there was a glint in the woman's eyes that Micah couldn't read. Did she actually think it – *he* – was cute? Or did she mean it the same way a southern belle said "bless your heart", and she actually thought Micah was uncultured swine, like Caprice so clearly did? "Where did you find this one again?"

The question was asked sweetly enough, but the way Renata immediately looked to Caprice made it clear. She didn't just think Micah was uncultured swine, she *knew* he was uncultured swine. Or, a prostitute, anyway. Well, *ex*-prostitute. (*Pretend* ex-prostitute to be precise, but there was no way she was privy to *that* part.)

Caprice's eyes gleamed. "Well-"

"I apologize if my lack of knowledge when it comes to wine is offensive," Micah hurried to spit out before Caprice could say anything more. He turned to the woman in question. "But I'm sure you'd make an excellent teacher if you could find it in your heart to take me on as a pupil. Every time I see you, you seem have a glass in your hand, after all."

Caprice's face reddened. "E-excuse me?" she sputtered even as her husband choked on a bit of surprised laughter.

Though no one chortled as loudly as the man of the unknown couple at their table. "He's calling you a lush, dear," the man said. "Nothing to be ashamed of. Most of us here are." He took a pointed swig of his drink and winked. "Mr. Romano, you must introduce me to your entertaining… companion."

"This is Micah Gallagher, my date for the evening."

Micah may have been a sucker for Damon, but he wasn't stupid enough to give the man his *real* last name, which is why he'd signed all the NDA's using the name Gallagher instead of Hart. (He'd borrowed it from Tessa.)

"Micah, this is Jonah Sullivan and his wife. Mr. Sullivan is the founder and CEO of Sullivan and Sons."

The name sounded familiar, but Micah couldn't place it until Mr. Sullivan added, "We're one of the top-earning weapons manufacturers on the east coast. We're especially known for our semi-automatic handguns."

Micah perked up. "Oh, yeah! The NYPD uses Glocks made by your company." *That's* where he'd heard of them before.

Damon shot Micah a look that was half-baffled/half-concerned – actually, probably *mostly* concerned – like he was wondering how he could have possibly known *that*. (Which, in hindsight, it'd been a spectacularly stupid thing to say.)

So preoccupied with Micah, Damon totally missed the nervous glance Mr. Sullivan cast his way. "Yes, well, a customer is a customer, of course. Though, it's your date here that owns the patent on our newest batch of hammerless revolvers, so I highly doubt any of those will wind up in police hands."

Micah stiffened. "Oh."

Sure, he'd known Damon was at least *vaguely* involved in the drug trade, but he hadn't realized he also dealt in weapons.

Damon frowned. "Are you alright?"

The unpleasantness of the realization sat heavy in his stomach. "Fine. I... I just didn't realize you were invested in anything other than real estate."

"A smart man like Mr. Romano?" Mr. Sullivan interjected. "He knows there's money to be made in just about any industry – and the gun industry is one of the largest."

Micah pressed his lips together. "Maybe. But don't you think we have enough guns in this country?"

He dealt enough with the result of gun violence at his job to know.

If Micah thought Mr. Sullivan would take offense to the question, he was wrong. The man merely laughed, his robust stomach shaking so hard Micah was surprised it didn't jostle the table. "That's not for me to decide, sweetheart; that's up to the people. It's a simple matter of supply and demand, something I know might be hard to wrap your pretty head around."

The condescending asswipe.

"But don't you think there's a certain moral responsibility for weapons manufacturers to *limit* the supply?" he demanded. "I mean, there's more guns than people-"

Damon's hand was suddenly on Micah's thigh, squeezing warningly.

It distracted him enough for Mr. Sullivan to interject. "That's what makes this country so great! And we're all patriots here, aren't we?"

"We most certainly are," Damon assured. "And I appreciate your business, Mr. Sullivan, but I'd *really* appreciate if you showed a little more respect towards my date."

Nothing about Damon's icy tone was subtle. And if Micah had any lingering doubts that Damon was a powerful man, they were well and truly washed away when Mr. Sullivan – a powerful figure himself – blanched. "Of course. I'm a passionate man, you see, and I forget myself at times. My apologies if you took offense."

The apology was directed at Damon, but Damon merely turned towards Micah.

Why did it feel like he had a man's life in his hands?

Micah cleared his throat. "None taken."

Before the tension could grow any more stifling, Marco interjected with a question about the hammerless revolvers Sullivan and Sons was working on, and talk turned towards business.

At least for the men.

Caprice and Renata appeared to be gossiping, shooting furtive looks Micah's way every few minutes, with a resigned-looking Jason caught between them. As for Sullivan's wife, she hadn't uttered a word since they'd sat down. Her eyes were somewhat glazed, and Micah suspected she may have been high on something. (Micah didn't blame her considering her husband.)

He tried not to feel disappointed when Damon's hand drifted from his thigh.

He was beyond relieved when the waitress finally returned with the wine, pouring it expertly into a glass. "Thank you," he said, truly grateful as he took a sip of the *Recioto della Valpolicella*. Damon was right – it was sugary sweet, and probably the best wine Micah had ever tasted. "Leave the bottle, would you?" he asked.

"Of course."

Shortly after that, the jazz music lulled, and the lighting dimmed. Everyone still lingering around the bars found their seats, and the chatter at their table quieted as the host of the gala took center stage.

He was an older gentleman, but not *old* old. His gray hair was slicked back, and he wore a simple three-piece suit with a black and gold striped tie. Micah recognized him immediately as Senator Andrew Wilcox.

Micah's father detested the man. He considered him one of the main congressmen responsible for New York City's shrinking police budget.

Micah listened with half an ear as he introduced himself and thanked everyone for attending the gala. He talked about the charity they were raising money for, Dare to Dream, at which time he invited his son on stage.

It was well-known that Senator Wilcox and his wife had adopted the boy out of the system. The twelve-year-old's boxy suit hung off his adolescent frame, and the smile he wore looked forced.

Micah imagined it got old being paraded around as proof of his father's generosity and supposed altruism. He tuned out as the boy returned to his seat and Senator Wilcox spoke of some of the "wonderful, unique" items they had available for auction in the east wing of the venue.

The man must have made a joke at some point because Micah nearly jumped out of his seat when Renata suddenly laughed out loud, going so far as to grab Damon's arm and press her face into the man's shoulder as her boobs shook with mirth.

It was at that point Micah refilled his glass with wine and redoubled his efforts to ignore not just Senator Wilcox, but the occupants of his table as well. (Even if he couldn't help but subtly eye the way Renata *not-so-subtly* eyed Damon.)

Thankfully, Senator Wilcox didn't seem to be as longwinded as most politicians because he managed to wrap up his speech fairly quickly, and soon enough, the same waitress that had brought Micah the wine returned with a round of appetizers for everyone.

If the trio of tiny bites on his plate could be considered appetizers.

The waitress explained each hors d'oeuvre. There was smoked salmon wrapped in the thinnest cucumber Micah had ever seen, drizzled with some kind of white sauce. In the middle, was a goat cheese-stuffed fig topped with a bit of pancetta. And on the end of a fancy white spoon, there was the only bit of food Micah recognized on sight: a deviled egg. Except it featured a cluster of tiny, black beads on top, which Micah belatedly realized was caviar.

The food was fine. Probably even fantastic to be honest, but Micah couldn't concentrate on the flavors, too busy making sure he held his knife and fork correctly as he cut into the tiny portions of food he could just as easily have picked up and plopped into his mouth.

The main dish was served shortly after the hors d'oeuvres, and was much more hardy. Each guest received one of three meals: prime rib with a side of baked potato, chicken in a bed of wild rice, or a vegetarian option, depending on what preference they checked on their ticket.

Thankfully, Damon had chosen prime rib for both of them.

As tender and juicy as the meat was, however, Micah found it difficult to enjoy it. How could he when Renata seemed to find an excuse to touch Damon every other minute? At the moment, she had a hand resting on the man's forearm for absolutely no reason that Micah could discern.

Not that it was any of Micah's business.

(Except it sort of was. It wasn't like Renata knew his relationship with Damon was a farce, after all.)

Micah picked up his wine glass on autopilot, frowning when he discovered it was empty... again.

"More wine?" Marco offered innocently across the table.

Except Micah doubted the man did anything innocent in his life. He didn't know what Marco's motive was in offering him more to drink, but he imagined the man would greatly enjoy watching a dunk Micah make a fool of himself.

Still... the idea wasn't completely without its merits.

Micah was about to nod and offer the man his glass when Damon's hand was suddenly back on his leg, even higher this time – only inches from his crotch. "I think Micah's had enough wine for now, yes?"

Micah could argue – cause a scene. But he wasn't *that* inebriated yet – not even buzzed, really, with all the food he'd been mindlessly shoveling into his mouth, so he just nodded. "Water's fine," he said, reaching for the fancy decanter that looked more like a vase than a water pitcher.

He did not care at all when Damon squeezed his thigh in approval. And he especially didn't care when Damon allowed his hand to linger on Micah's leg, even as dessert was served.

Dessert was similar to the first course, except instead of a trio of hors d'oeuvres, it was a trio of tartlets. One tartlet was filled with lemon meringue and topped with whipped cream, one was made of jam and decorated with raspberries sprinkled with powdered sugar, and the last, Micah's favorite, was a chocolate tart, topped simply with chopped walnuts.

It was easily the most enjoyable part of the meal. Because Micah had a sweet tooth, obviously. Not because Damon's hand remained on his leg the entire time, rubbing soothing circles against the inside of his thigh.

As people finished with their dessert, the music started up again, and gala guests began to wander from their seats. Some returned to the bars, but Micah saw many meander out the east-side archway, presumably to go check out the various items that were up for auction.

Micah couldn't deny he was curious as to what sort of things people rich enough to be invited to a gala like this bid on, and he agreed easily when Damon suggested they go explore the auction themselves.

He tried not to let his irritation show when Caprice invited herself along – with Renata, of course. He must not have been able to completely mask his distaste judging by the perturbed look Damon shot him.

In the end, everyone sans the Sullivans, trailed after them into the east wing, Renata practically hanging off Damon's arm.

It was sickening, and Micah had had just about enough of it. Even if their relationship wasn't real, he and Damon were supposed to be on a date, and if the man was going to let some (gorgeous, dazzling) *desperate* model hang off his arm, Micah wasn't going to torture himself by making himself watch.

"I'll be right back," he said, ignoring the flash of alarm in Damon's eyes and the way he immediately reached for him. Dodging the man's hand, Micah disappeared into the crowd. Ignoring the hint of guilt he felt, Micah forced himself to concentrate on the items set up on fancy tables and pedestals.

It took a bit of wandering to figure out they were organized by category.

Micah wasn't surprised by the vintage bottles of aged wines and whiskeys – each probably worth well over a thousand dollars – on display towards the back of the room. Neither was he taken off guard by the quantity and quality of art on display – mostly paintings, but there were some charcoal drawings and sculptures up for auction, too. There were also designer handbags and jewelry, including a particularly impressive pendent necklace featuring huge a sapphire that reminded Micah of Damon's eyes.

What Micah had dubbed as the "experience" section was probably the most interesting. Up for auction included things such as luxury resort stays and Broadway tickets. You could even bid on hot air balloon rides and cooking lessons from Gordon Ramsey himself.

Micah's favorite area, however, was definitely the sports memorabilia section. It was amongst the autographed balls, baseball cards, and athletic shoes, that Micah found the holy grail of Mets fan collectibles: a 1969 Mitchell and Ness jersey signed by Tom Seaver himself. It was the year that the Mets had first ever won the World Series. (They'd only won it one other time, in 1986, and Damon often brought up that fact whenever they'd have their half-playful/half-serious debates about the Yankees versus the Mets. Damon couldn't seem to comprehend how Micah could be a fan when the Mets hadn't won the World Series once since Micah had been alive.)

Micah must have been staring at the jersey, in awe, a bit too long – ignorant of his surroundings and clogging up the space – because somebody bumped into him.

It wasn't a hard knock, but large hands immediately reached out to steady him anyway. "I'm so sorry," a masculine voice apologized, and Micah turned to see a man about his height, but with broader shoulders and probably fifteen pounds of more muscle on his frame.

"That's okay," Micah assured. "It was probably my fault. I was a little distracted…"

As cute as the guy in front of him was – with his dark green eyes and twin dimples in his cheeks – Micah found his gaze trailing back to the coveted Tom Seaver-signed jersey.

The man followed his line of sight. "Ah, a Mets fan, I take it?"

"Well, I *am* from New York, and I *do* have a soul, so…"

The man laughed. "I think the majority of people in this room would take offense to that."

Micah snorted. "Probably. Rich, successful assholes with plenty of money, but very little character, cheering for a rich, successful team with even less scruples…" Realizing he was on the verge of ranting (also, probably insulting the man), Micah forced himself to stop. He rubbed the back of his neck. "Sorry."

Luckily, the man seemed to take his social blunder in stride. If anything, his smile grew. "That's okay. I may be a rich, successful asshole, but even I don't deign to cheer for the Yankees." He stuck out his hand. "I'm Ashton, Ashton Albrecht."

Fighting off a blush, Micah took his hand. "I'm Micah. I'm *not* a rich asshole, just a regular one. It's my date who's the hyper-successful, mega-rich, *colossal* ass."

"And do I happen to know this colossal ass?"

Micah shrugged. "Maybe. His name's Damon Romano."

Ashton's easy smile slid off his face. He seemed disbelieving. "You're here with *Romano?*"

Micah blinked. "Er-"

Like he'd somehow heard his name, Damon was suddenly upon them. He swooped in, hands grasping Micah by the arms. "Micah, there you are. I've been looking all over for you," he said, a borderline scolding quality to his voice.

"Sorry," Micah said lightly, not sorry in the least. "I was just admiring the items up for auction. Look, a Mets jersey signed by Tom Seaver himself!" Micah gestured at the jersey, and Damon reluctantly turned to look. He also finally seemed to realize Micah had been talking to someone. He stiffened when he saw Ashton. "I also ran into another Mets fan, someone who actually understands baseball is about more than just salary cap."

"Albrecht," Damon greeted coolly.

"Romano," the other man said succinctly in turn.

"Do… you two know each other?"

"We're old schoolmates," Damon said after a moment of tense silence. "It doesn't surprise me at all you're a Mets fan, Albrecht. Seems your tastes run the same way as they always have."

Damon was calling him a loser, basically, from what Micah could gleam.

Albrecht snorted. "Mates is a strong word," he said, referring to the first part of what Damon had said. "And I'd say the same for your tastes… except they've clearly improved since school." His eyes pointedly scanned Micah. "It was lovely meeting you, Micah," he said, voice noticeably softening before his eyes hardened again, offering Damon a terse nod before he took his leave.

"Good riddance," Damon muttered. Placing a hand on the small of Micah's back, he ushered him along, making a show of examining the remaining items up for auction as he spoke. "How do you manage to find trouble wherever you go?"

"Trouble?" Micah repeated incredulously. "Ashton was perfectly nice until you got there and insulted him for no reason."

Damon just grunted, pretending to examine a basketball autographed by what looked like nearly the entire Knicks team.

Micah sighed, deliberately taking a step to the side so Damon's hand was forced to fall off his back. Damon looked up, a frown etched on his face. "Besides, I didn't think you'd miss me. You seemed occupied enough when I left."

Damon's frown deepened. "What are you talking about?"

Micah huffed, glancing around. There were still a lot of people meandering about, taking in the various luxuries up for auction, so he grabbed Damon by the cuff of his sleeve and pulled him to the corner of the room where it wasn't so crowded. And then it all came spilling out. "Renata," he hissed. "She was putting her hands all over you. Honestly, the woman's so horny for you, I half-thought she was going to rip off her dress, get on all fours, and beg you to give her the D right there in front of everyone."

Damon stared. But after a moment, a little smirk tugged at the corner of his mouth. "Are you jealous?"

"W-what?" Micah sputtered, face flushing. "No! I'm *annoyed*. And insulted. I mean, she thinks you're here on a date with another person, but she's trying to climb you like a tree anyway – right in front of my eyes, no less. And worst of all, you're letting her."

Damon crossed his arms over his chest, and Micah tried not to be distracted by the way the fabric strained against his biceps. "Yeah, but it's not a *real* date, is it?"

Micah froze.

Maybe it was incidental, or maybe it was completely on purpose, but Micah was pretty sure those were the exact same words he'd said to Damon in the car. And fuck, they *hurt*.

The reminder that it was all pretend gnawed at his insides, and Micah could feel his disappointment swelling. He swallowed it down and took a step backward. "You know what? I have to pee."

"What?" But he'd already snuck away from Damon once, and apparently, the man had caught onto his antics, because he grabbed Micah by the elbow before he could lose him again. "Hold on."

Nevertheless, Micah wasn't about to let himself be held against his will. He ripped his arm out of Damon's grip. "I'm just going to take a piss. I'll be back in five minutes, just... go talk business with Mr. Sullivan or find a dark corner to shag Renata or something."

Wow. That wasn't bitter at all.

Micah ignored his inner voice's sass and didn't stick around to see Damon's reaction to his comment. He just hightailed it out of the east wing. As he bustled through the main hall, he noticed that some of the couples had taken up dancing, but he didn't stop to watch or talk to anyone.

He hurried through the west-side archway, which led to a fairly deserted lounge, and a bit further in on the left-hand side: the men's restroom.

There was no line, thank Christ. Even better, the bathroom was empty.

Although the main reason he'd left Damon high and dry was to hide before the hurt he could feel filling his chest cavity showed on his face, Micah also *did* have to pee, so he quickly took care of business in one of the vacant stalls.

He must have been lost in tumultuous thoughts because when he stepped out of the stall, he nearly shat himself when he ran straight into Damon's Uncle Marco, of all people. (Which was strange, since he hadn't heard the door open or any footsteps.)

"Jesus, you scared me," Micah said, bringing a hand to his chest, under which his heart pumped double time. "It's all yours," he added, gesturing behind him at the open stall before stepping up to the line of sinks.

When he glanced up into the mirror after soaping his hands, Micah's heart rate sped up even more when he realized that instead of using the toilet, Marco had apparently decided to stand creepily close behind him instead.

"How much?" the man demanded.

Deciding he wasn't going to show his alarm – whether he was actually intimidated or not – Micah made a show of carefully washing and drying his hands before turning around to face Marco. The man had left only a foot of space between them. "How much… what?"

Marco frowned. "Don't play coy; it doesn't become you. How much money to leave Damon alone?"

Micah could admit to being caught flat-footed. "Does Damon *want* me to leave him alone?" he asked. "Because he's a big boy, and I'm pretty sure he'd tell me himself if he did."

Marco's eyes narrowed. "What Damon wants is of little consequence," he said after a moment. "I'm not about to let him be taken on a ride by some pretentious, money-grabbing hussy no matter how prettily you bat your eyes at him." He paused, eyeing Micah up and down. "Or me, for that matter."

Ew.

Micah didn't have to fake being insulted. "I'd rather get ran over by Damon's Rolls-Royce – no, whatever pretentious vehicle *you* drive – than let your old-man cock within ten feet of me." He paused. "And I didn't even know Damon was rich when we met, so you can fuck right off with that gold digger bullshit."

"Met?" Marco raised an eyebrow, ignoring the first part of what Micah had said. "Is that what they call picking prostitutes up off the street nowadays?"

Micah rolled his eyes. "Fuck you."

He went to step around the man, but Marco immediately copied his movement, apparently not ready to let Micah escape. In fact, he took the opportunity to crowd Micah further up against the sink, until it was digging into his lower back.

"I don't think you understand. I'm doing this for you as much as I am for him."

Micah fought the urge to snort. "And yet somehow, I get the feeling that your motives aren't entirely selfless."

"Think what you want. But the way Damon acted tonight – snubbing a business partner, trailing after you like a lost puppy – it's obvious you're a glaring weakness, *his* weakness. I'm assuming you know what happens to weaknesses in our line of business?"

Micah could imagine.

"Like I said," Marco continued, "I'm doing you a favor. Now, I don't know what Damon's been paying you, but despite his obvious infatuation, his favor is much more easily lost than it is won… so, keeping in mind that your free ride can end at any time, how does $100,000 sound?"

What the fuck?

Micah knew, objectively, that it was probably a drop in the bucket for someone like Marco, but *still*. "You're crazy."

Micah flinched when Marco abruptly scruffed him by the back of his neck, yanking him forward and holding him there, so that there were mere inches between their faces. "And you think you've hit the jackpot with Damon – that he's an all-expenses-paid ticket to a worry-free life in a gorgeous penthouse and vacations to the seaside whenever the urge strikes, but in case it hasn't sunk in yet… the lifestyle Damon lives is rife with danger." He stared pointedly into Micah's eyes. "He's a dangerous man who keeps dangerous company."

It was more of a threat than a friendly warning. Micah swallowed. "I'm not afraid of you."

Marco tilted his head to the side, examining Micah. "You know? I believe you. But all that tells me is that you're a poor judge of character. Because, darling... you *should* be."

Whether he was afraid of Marco or not, Micah couldn't deny he was relieved when the door to the restroom suddenly opened. A man with a distinguished goatee and bloodshot eyes stumbled in, taking in the sight of them and blinking.

Marco had Micah crowded up against the sink, a hand gripping the back of his neck, and their faces were definitely closer than socially acceptable. From an outsider's perspective, Micah wasn't sure whether you'd be able to tell Marco had been threatening him, or if it looked more like they'd been caught in an... *intimate* position.

"Is there a problem in here?" the man asked after taking a second to gain his bearings.

Marco released Micah and smoothly stepped out of his space. "Of course not," he said at the same time Micah blurted, "No!"

They eyed each other for a moment.

"I was just leaving," Micah announced to the room at large, though he couldn't resist turning around and adding a parting shot in Damon's uncle's direction. "Damon will worry if I'm gone too long."

A lesser man may have frowned or gritted his teeth, but Marco merely smiled benignly. "Of course."

Micah had mixed emotions when he returned to their table to see Damon there, apparently waiting for him. Most people seemed to have congregated back into the main hall, and were either crowding the bars or waltzing on the dance floor.

The stress from his showdown with Marco must have shown on his face because Damon shot up from his seat as soon as he saw him, a frown pulling at his mouth. "Are you alright?"

Micah debated telling him about his uncle's threats, but quickly dismissed the idea. It wasn't worth the potential drama it would cause. "I'm fine," he assured instead. "Just had to pee, like I said —

you see, it's a perfectly normal bodily function for us *ordinary* people."

Okay, so maybe he was still feeling a little jilted from earlier.

Damon raised his eyebrows. "What does *that* mean?"

Oh, just that Damon was as far from ordinary as it gets. Micah still wasn't completely convinced he was an actual human being – more like a godlike entity sent down from above (or more likely, *below*) whose sole purpose in life was to fuck up Micah's moral compass and wreak havoc on his libido.

Micah just sighed. "It's nothing."

Damon didn't seem convinced. Regardless, he didn't push it. Instead, he nodded towards the dance floor. "Would you like to dance?"

Micah was taken off guard by the question, but a quick glance at the graceful, almost synchronized dancing made the answer obvious. "Considering the only dancing I know how to do is erratic grinding, I'll have to pass."

Damon snorted. "Waltzing is easy if you have a competent partner. I'll teach you."

Micah shook his head. "I can't. Just... go ask Renata or something. I'm sure she'd leap at the chance."

Annnd Damon's frown was back. "I don't want to dance with Renata." He paused, examining Micah. "Nor do I want to rip off her clothes or 'give her the D', just to be clear. In fact, there's only one person here I'm interested in fucking, and possessive asshole that I am, I'd never let anyone's eyes but my own see them in such a vulnerable state."

Had it suddenly grown about fifty degrees hotter in here or was it just Micah?

His face was burning hot, and his dick had taken approximately .5 seconds to go from soft to rock hard in his pants at Damon's near-vulgar words. There was no way the man was referring to him, right?

But why would he say it to him then? And more importantly, what was Micah supposed to say *back?*

In the end, Micah took a deep breath in through his nose in an effort to calm himself and opted for what he considered a safe response. "Well, as long as it's not Caprice you're so passionate for, I'm not about to judge."

It worked as Micah had hoped, and Damon laughed.

Even as the sexual tension between them dissipated, Micah couldn't bring himself to regret it – not when he was treated so rarely to the sound.

"No," Damon assured as his laughter trailed off, "definitely not." And then more seriously: "I really am sorry about Renata. If I knew it bothered you, I would have told her to stop. I didn't even know she was going to be here."

"She just acts so familiar with you," Micah said, feeling the need to explain his discomfort with her behavior even though Damon hadn't asked for an explanation. "Not even your sisters are so touchy-feely... well, maybe Joelle," Micah mollified. He tilted his head to the side. "I mean, is Renata an ex or something?" He realized it was a personal question as soon as he'd asked it, but before he could open his mouth to backtrack-

Damon sighed loudly, running a hand through his hair. "Renata isn't an ex. More like... a mistake."

As annoyed as he was with the woman, Micah still winced. "Ouch."

"I didn't mean it like *that*. It's just... she's one of Caprice's best friends – a model and influencer she met while traveling after university." *Of course, the hot, leggy brunette was a model.* "She's had a thing for me as long as I can remember-"

"Yeah, she doesn't exactly hide it, does she?"

Damon quirked an eyebrow. "Anyway, one night, shortly after my parents died, I was in a bad place, and well... I slept with her. It should have never happened," he rushed to add. "I used her, basically, and I feel terrible about it. And ever since, well... her infatuation hasn't exactly ebbed, has it?"

Wow. That explained a lot, actually. He'd probably be acting just as thirsty for Damon as Renata if he'd gotten a taste of the man and had to let him go afterwards.

Micah shrugged. "Okay."

Damon seemed disbelieving. "Okay?"

"Well, it's not like I agree with using people for sex, but you were both consenting adults – and it was long before we met, obviously – so why would I be mad?"

"So… you'll dance with me then?"

Micah snorted. "Renata had nothing to do with why I said no to dancing." (Although, admittedly, it *had* had a lot to do with his bratty attitude.)

Damon crossed his arms over his chest, sizing Micah up. "So you'd rather stay here at the table and talk then?"

Micah shrugged. "Sure."

But before he could pull out his chair, Damon was intercepting his hand. "Okay, maybe you can tell me how you happen to know what kind of Glocks the NYPD uses then."

Micah froze. He knew Damon didn't know he was a cop – he'd be looking a lot more murderous than concerned right now. But that didn't mean Micah wanted to have to make up some lie. So he sighed. "Fine, one dance."

Damon nodded. "That's all I ask."

Liar.

Micah and Damon danced to one song together – and then a second, and then a third. The first song, Micah had made an honest attempt to waltz. But after stepping on Damon's feet countless times, and somehow managing to elbow him in the ribs when the man tried to spin him, they made the executive decision to downgrade to a simple box step halfway through the second song, and by the third song, they weren't even pretending to do anything but sway back and forth in each other's arms.

They were one of the few couples not waltzing on the dance floor, and maybe Micah should have been embarrassed, but he wasn't. He would gladly make a fool of himself in front of everyone in the room if it meant having Damon's undivided attention and the man's warm hands on his waist. (Caprice's quietly shocked expression – which she quickly hid behind an unaffected visage – and Renata's put-out pout, when he caught sight of them on the side of the dance floor, were an added bonus.)

It must have been getting later than Micah thought, because it was after their *fourth* song dancing together that the band took a break and the host of the prestigious gala – Senator Wilcox – returned to the stage and called for everyone's attention.

"I'm pleased to announce that the silent auction is officially closed, and thanks to everyone's unbelievable generosity, we've managed to raise a very impressive estimated $425,000 for Dare to Dream."

Everyone clapped, with a couple of the more inebriated guests cheering loudly.

"Yes, yes, it's very impressive," Senator Wilcox affirmed. "As tradition dictates, we will be revealing the three top-earning items of the auction and presenting them to the winning bidders. All other items can be picked up in the east wing during the remaining hours of the gala. So, without further ado..." the senator paused, nodding to one of the servers waiting on the wings, who quickly delivered three envelopes to him. He opened the first envelope. "The third-highest earning item was the beautiful diamond-encrusted sapphire pendent necklace designed by Stephanie Berlusconi, and the winner of the necklace... Mrs. Rosalie Walsh."

Everyone applauded as the spotlight found Rosalie, an elderly woman with a head of impressive white curls and lips painted a bright red. One of the gala's workers, delicately handling the necklace, delivered it to her.

"The second-highest earning item was an all-expenses-paid trip to Cabo San Lucas, Mexico, and the winner of the trip... Mr. Ashton Albrecht."

Micah blinked, surprised that the man he'd met earlier – Damon's old school rival – had bid on and won such an extravagant prize, but he clapped politely with the rest of the crowd (sans Damon) when the spotlight found him.

"And last, but certainly not least, the highest-earning item of the auction – and this one came as a bit of a surprise. With an extremely generous bid of $50,000, the winner of a Mets jersey signed by Tom Seaver himself... Mr. Damon Romano."

Micah couldn't have been more shocked if he'd been strapped down to an electric chair (illegal in most states, by the way, including New York). He turned to Damon in disbelief. "You hate the Mets," he hissed, but he forced a strained smile on his face when the spotlight found Damon and the man pulled him into it along with him.

A worker, carefully carrying the folded jersey, handed it off to Damon. It wasn't until the spotlight left them and Senator Wilcox began wrapping up his speech, that Damon spoke. "I don't hate the Mets," he said. "They aren't impressive enough to draw such a passionate response from me." He turned to Micah, holding out the jersey. "But I think we both know it's not for me, is it?"

Micah shook his head in denial, going so far as to take a step backward. "No way. I can't... no, *you* can't-"

Micah nearly jumped when the music started up again, and Damon had to pull him off the dance floor. "I can't accept this," he said after taking a moment to *just breathe* and gather his thoughts. He tried his best to sound resolved.

"But it'll just collect dust at my place," Damon pointed out reasonably.

"So return it," Micah said, like he was talking about some t-shirt from Walmart, and not a jersey signed by frickin' Tom Seaver. (Micah offered an internal apology to the deceased man.)

Damon raised an eyebrow. "That's not how this works."

"Just say you accidentally added an extra zero or something," Micah insisted.

"But then the kids will miss out on all that money."

Fuck. *Fuck.* Micah knew Damon was just baiting him, using the kids as an excuse to get him to agree to take the jersey, but... it was signed by *Tom Seaver.* And it wasn't like the money wasn't going someplace worthy... *shit.*

"Fine," Micah said, all but snatching the jersey from Damon. "But only because it's for the kids."

"Of course," Damon agreed diplomatically.

It suddenly occurred to Micah that he was being an ungrateful ass. Damon had done something obscenely *nice* for him –

completely unsolicited, but that almost made it *more* sweet – and here he was, mucking it up.

Micah didn't question the urge.

He just launched himself at the man, throwing his arms around Damon's shoulders and squeezing tight. "Thank you," Micah murmured into the heat of the man's neck, feeling Damon's beard brush against his temple and trying not to think about how it would feel elsewhere.

Judging by the way Damon stiffened in his arms, he was as taken off guard by the hug as Micah had been by the gift. After a moment, however, his hands slowly came up and returned Micah's embrace. Damon's breath was but a rustle in Micah's hair when he whispered, "You're welcome."

CHAPTER FIFTEEN

"I'm just going to have to dress up as a hooker and work the streets again."

Tessa sighed, shooting Micah an irritated glance over the sandwich she was eating at her desk. To be fair, she'd been listening to him complain about the idiosyncrasies of Nico's murder investigation for the better part of a month.

It had been three weeks now since Micah had first been assigned to Nico's missing persons case, two weeks since the young man's body had been discovered, and one week since they'd received the tracking data back from Nico's cell service provider.

At first, it had looked promising.

The last tower Nico's cellphone had pinged at was one in downtown Queens.

Since Micah already suspected Nico had been going on a breakfast date based on his previous detective work, he'd quickly zeroed in on the dozen or so restaurants in the area covered by the tower.

Only about half of them served brunch. One of which was a café called The Tea.

Micah recognized the logo immediately – from all the Styrofoam coffee cups Nico liked to pose with on his Instagram.

It had been his first stop, and Micah had gotten lucky. The barista working behind the counter recognized Nico as a regular when he'd shown her his picture. She even recalled that he'd come in on the day in question. She remembered because Nico had arrived with a date, and she'd been fairly devastated since she'd had a bit of a crush on him.

(Though not nearly as upset as she'd been to learn she'd been one of the last people to see Nico alive.)

Unfortunately, she couldn't remember much about the man Nico had come in with – just that he was white with dark hair, "probably" around six feet tall, and that he'd been "plain-looking". Her description probably matched about a fourth of all the men in New York, and Micah had known immediately that bringing in a sketch artist would be a pointless endeavor.

There was no paper trail either.

When the girl had gotten her manager to look up the receipt for the day and time Nico and his unknown companion had visited, it'd turned out they had paid in cash.

It wasn't a complete bust, however.

Like most businesses in the city, The Tea had street-facing security cameras – which Micah quickly gained permission to bring into the precinct.

He had felt his lungs constrict when he recognized Nico stepping out of a dark-colored van on the Saturday morning he'd disappeared. But the man who got out and entered the café with him – Nico's mysterious date – *must* have known where the cameras were stationed, because he didn't turn to face them once.

Micah had felt like punching his computer.

Instead of giving into the urge, however, he'd handed the grainy surveillance video over to Tessa, who was an expert at enhancing CCTV footage. She was able to clear it up enough to make out the van's license plate. She'd also been able to snag the license plate of the cab that Nico and his date had left in approximately an hour later.

Which left Micah with two new people to interview.

Much like the barista, the Uber driver who had dropped Nico and his date off at The Tea vaguely remembered Nico when he was shown a picture, but he couldn't recall much about the man Nico had been with. The man had paid him in cash.

Micah's interview with the cab driver had gone even worse. The man seemed distrustful of police in general, and he'd barely even glanced at the picture Micah tried to show him of Nico, claiming he taxied a lot of people around the city, and *he could hardly be expected to remember the faces of every one of them, could he?*

All in all, Micah felt like he'd spent the past several weeks chasing his own tail, where all leads led absolutely nowhere.

It was frustrating and damn near crippling on his self-esteem. Each day that passed, he grew less and less confident that they'd find Nico's killer and bring him to justice. The worst part was having to give Mr. and Mrs. Sanchez daily updates – something he'd promised them *and* himself he'd do. Having to admit every day that they were no closer to arresting anyone then when they'd first found Nico's body was taking it's toll on his mental health.

Micah, for his part, remained convinced that whoever killed Nico was also responsible for the string of murdered prostitutes that came before him, but with no new evidence to support his theory and with the Hooker Hunter "officially" in custody, the cases remained unrelated in everyone's minds but his own.

It's what prompted his half-assed idea to go back undercover as a prostitute.

"What good would working the streets do?" Tessa demanded. "Even if Nico's murder *is* the work of the Hooker Hunter – and that's a *big* if – he's clearly moved on to more sophisticated targets. If anything, you should be considering starting your own webcam show." The woman wiggled her eyebrows.

Micah glared. "You'd like that, wouldn't you? A video of me shimmying around in a pair of women's panties or, I don't know, stroking a dildo, so that you could have something to hold over me forever."

Jensen, who'd happened to be walking past their desks while nursing a cup of coffee, choked and had to spit the caffeinated beverage back out into his cup. He shot Micah an incredulous look, a flush crawling up his tan neck.

Micah fought off his own blush. "Sorry," he blurted, holding up his spoon with one hand and his chocolate pudding cup with the other, "we're taking lunch."

Jensen merely shook his head and stalked off.

Tessa snorted in amusement, waiting until the man had turned the corner to wherever he was headed before refocusing on Micah.

"Well, since you refuse to show me the dick pic you sent to Damon…"

Micah winced at the reminder of *that* particular blunder. "Trust me," he said, remembering how his cock had strained against the silky panties, a little drop of precum staining the top, "our friendship would never recover."

"Do I need to remind you that I've seen you naked?"

"I was drunk!" Micah protested. "And strip poker was Jasper's idea!"

Tessa ignored him. "Speaking of Damon… how are things going with, you know, *all* that?"

Tessa wasn't particularly subtle about pressing for details when it came to Micah's pseudo-relationship with Damon. She claimed it was purely because she was concerned for his safety, but Micah failed to see what his safety had to do with demanding to know if they'd finally fucked each other yet every other day. (And he wasn't about to ask and open himself up to jokes about whether or not he could "safely" handle Damon's undoubtedly impressive girth, thank you very much.)

"Fine," Micah said blandly, just to be irritating.

"So you haven't heard from him since Wednesday and the hot tub incident?"

"I'd hardly call it an incident," Micah said, wondering why he'd even told her about it in the first place. (Probably because Tessa knew they met up every Wednesday in an effort to make their charade of a relationship as convincing as possible, and she nagged him until he gave up the details every time.)

Micah had agreed to go to Damon's penthouse two days ago for their latest meeting, but only on the condition that Damon let him try out the hot tub. Micah was delightedly surprised when the man had given in, but he'd been unprepared for the sight of Damon in nothing but his swim trunks.

He'd seen the man shirtless on only one other occasion, and that was just to show Micah the tattoo on his back. At the time, Micah hadn't been able to fully appreciate the view, but he'd nearly drooled at the broad shoulders, developed biceps, and defined stomach all out on display on the man's balcony. Not to mention that dark patch of hair on Damon's chest, and the small, but no less wiry-looking trail of hair that disappeared into the waistband of the man's trunks…

Micah lost his train of thought.

Oh yes, Damon's trunks. They had been scandalously short, and even if Micah could have somehow withstood the sight of Damon's shirtless chest, his brain had all but short-circuited upon seeing the man's huge, meaty thighs on display. In fact, only one part of Micah's body had remained working at maximum capacity at that point.

You guess the body part.

It was nigh impossible to hide a hard-on in a pair of swim trunks. And instead of being able to enjoy the heated water of the hot tub, or the view from the balcony, or anything at all about the experience of soaking with Damon – the entire time, Micah had sat cross-legged, as far away from the man as the tub allowed, tense as can be as he willed his painful erection to *just go away, already*!

Damon had noticed his discomfort, but not the cause of it, and the poor, sweet, *cruel* man had offered Micah a massage to help him unwind.

And idiotic, horny Micah had *agreed.*

It had been both the most and least satisfying fifteen minutes of Micah's young life. (Pathetic, he was aware.)

"Oh, I know!" Tessa exclaimed, yanking Micah from his poorly thought-out reverie. (He was getting hard – *again.*) "The next time you and Damon get together, you can just have a sleepover – cuddle in your underwear in Damon's bed and explore each other's bodies in case anyone asks what either one of you look like naked."

Micah frowned. "Why does that just sound like an excuse to feel each other up?"

Tessa rolled her eyes so hard it looked physically painful. "Gee, I don't know, maybe because everything you two get up to together seems like it's just an excuse to spend time together, or touch each other, or almost, but not quite, screw each other's brains out?"

Micah crossed his arms over his chest. "Damon's made it clear this is a business arrangement. I can't... I *won't* let myself think otherwise." It left him open to too much heartache.

Tessa sighed. "*So* oblivious," she muttered.

Micah shifted in his swivel chair, fiddling with his pudding. "Although, I should let you know, Damon did text me yesterday and ask me to pack an overnight bag."

Tessa's eyes lit up with a wicked sort of glee. "So you *are* having a sleepover? I frickin' knew it. Though I don't know why he bothered to tell you to pack anything. He probably wants you naked the entire time; I know *I* would."

Micah chose not to respond to that. "He, uh... he also asked me if my passport was current?"

Tessa stiffened, her expression going from teasing to hard in a second. "Jesus, Micah. You said no, right? Because no one asks that unless they plan on going out of the country and taking *you* along with them. And I know you have enough self-preservation to never agree to that, no matter how wound up Damon gets you."

"You either greatly overestimate my self-preservation or greatly underestimate my libido," he admitted reluctantly.

"Micah!" Tessa yelled, glancing around after Micah shushed her, but then sitting up and leaning into his space as much as her swollen belly allowed. She hissed at him like a snake. "What if he found out you're a cop, thinks you're a narc, and he's planning on burying your body somewhere on his family's countryside estate, huh?"

Micah shook his head. "I would be able to tell if he knew," he argued, although he wasn't completely sure he was right. Micah *thought* he had a good read on the other man, but Damon had a better poker face than any hardened criminal Micah had ever met.

"Even if he doesn't know, Damon's still not a good person, Micah. He's a mafia don. It would be the definition of foolhardy to trust him. Lord knows I don't."

"I know that, okay? I do. But, at least when it comes to my safety, I *do* trust him. So, call me a reckless idiot or whatever, but... I'm still going to go wherever he wants to take me."

Tessa stared. "You're a reckless idiot," she said. "A feckless, inconsiderate donkey, who's going to put me into early labor."

Micah winced. Though he shouldn't have been surprised. She wasn't one to let an opportunity to insult someone bypass her.

Then Tessa sighed. "*But* I'm glad you told me. Keep your phone on you the entire time, and you better respond to all my texts in a timely manner or I'm going to call the U.S. Embassy of whatever foreign country he's taking you to-"

"Italy, I'm pretty sure. He's mentioned a family house there."

"-and get Damon tarred and feathered, got it?"

Micah grinned. "You're going to be the coolest mom," he said, offering her what remained of his pudding when he saw her eye it with interest.

"Yeah, well, my kids better not be little assholes like you." She leaned back into her chair and dug into the pudding. "So, is this trip supposed to be like an early Christmas present or something?"

Micah blinked. "Huh?"

"I mean, Christmas is, like, a week away," she pointed out. "Did I tell you I booked a vasectomy for Jasper as his gift? I am *not* doing this again." She pointed down at her belly with her spoon. "Did you get Damon anything?"

Fuck.

CHAPTER SIXTEEN

What do you get *a frickin' billionaire* for Christmas?

Micah had had a minor meltdown at the station about it much to Tessa's amusement.

Of course, it didn't help matters that Damon was picking him up early the next morning for their impromptu trip – 2:00 AM to be precise – which left only a handful of hours to pick out a present for the man.

Micah had racked his brain about what he knew about Damon.

He was a mafia boss, and a workaholic. He loved his family, but still kept them at arm's length. His hobbies included working out (*obviously*), baking, and hanging out with Micah. He liked the Yankees (puking emoji) and pretty boys in pretty panties (insert purple devil emoji here).

Tessa was of the opinion that Micah ought to buy a lacy thong, bend over, and present *himself* as Damon's gift. Micah had shot that idea down immediately. Even if the man didn't outright reject him, Damon thought he was an ex-prostitute, and Micah suspected the man would interpret such a gesture as Micah offering to have sex with him in exchange for bringing him on a mysterious trip, which... *no*.

In the end, Micah had gone shopping in downtown Queens after work and had managed to find an adorable apron in a boutique with the caption "Don't be afraid to take whisks!" printed in bold font along the front, atop a picture of a whisk. The fact that the apron was adorned with blue frills around the edges, nearly the same color as Damon's eyes, was a bonus.

Micah loved it, and he may or may not have spent a chunk of his evening picturing Damon wearing the apron (and nothing else) as he fried Micah up a stack of delicious crepes.

Still, Micah couldn't help but feel self-conscious about the gift. Damon was a billionaire, after all, and he could buy himself anything that struck his fancy. What made a punny apron special?

Hoping it got a laugh out of the man if nothing else, Micah wrapped it in some holiday wrapping paper he'd purchased from the same shop as the apron and packed it away in his bag Friday night, planning on giving it to Damon sometime during their trip.

Saturday morning – if 2:00 AM *could* be considered morning – saw Damon arriving at Micah's apartment to pick him up as promised. Damon must have taken luggage and trunk space into consideration because instead of the usual Rolls-Royce, Geoffrey drove them to the nearest airport in an elongated Cadillac Escalade.

Micah was too tired to be as impressed as he probably should have been.

He woke up quickly though when they reached the airport, and after a quick stop at customs, he and Damon were escorted straight to the airstrip to the boarding ramp of *a private jet*.

Micah had been expecting a commercial flight – first class, sure, because it was Damon – but *a frickin' private jet?* He knew he looked like an idiot, standing there on the tarmac, gawking at the plane with wide eyes as he tried to collect himself.

"Of course, you have your own plane," he said to the man beside him, aiming for petulant, but sounding awed despite his efforts.

Damon, for his part, seemed amused by Micah's dumbstruck expression, and he took great pleasure in leading Micah up the ramp, and showing him around the plane – which featured both a mini-bar and a big screen television – before they were informed by the pilot, a man Damon merely referred to as "Miguel", to strap on their seatbelts for take-off.

Once they reached the correct altitude, they were allowed to roam as they pleased, but Micah was still tired – it was barely 3:00 AM – and Damon was already sitting beside him on one of the plane's couches, working on something on his laptop, so Micah merely unbuckled, got comfortable, and allowed himself to doze.

He must have managed to fall completely back under sleep's spell because an indeterminable amount of time later, he was being gently shaken awake. "Micah?"

"Hm?" he mumbled incoherently.

"Wake up. The sun is rising."

Micah peeked an eye open. "What?" he asked, confused in the way one could only be in the first seconds after being suddenly awakened from deep sleep. He vaguely noted that he'd somehow wound up curled against the man's side, his head resting on Damon's shoulder.

That was enough to startle him awake. He hurriedly straightened, mortified to see a damp spot on Damon's dress shirt where he'd been *drooling.* Why hadn't the man woken him up?

He didn't even look like he cared that Micah had been slobbering on him, his expression uncharacteristically soft as he took Micah in – which, was silly. Because Micah knew how he looked like in the mornings. His hair was probably sticking up at all ends, there was sleep crusted in his eyes, and undoubtedly, there were crease marks from the collar of Damon's shirt pressed into his cheek.

"I said the sun is rising," Damon repeated himself.

Micah blinked, unsure why that called for waking him. "It tends to do that?"

Damon raised an amused eyebrow. "I thought you'd might like to see it? It's a novel experience watching it from within the sky."

Now *that* made sense. "Oh, yeah, definitely."

Micah allowed Damon to lead him to a window, and let Micah just say, the man completely undersold the experience. Witnessing the stunning pinks and yellows blossom across the sky from within the clouds itself wasn't just novel – it was breathtaking.

"Wow." It was the only word Micah could manage.

"Yeah, wow."

Micah turned to face Damon, but he froze when he saw the man was looking at him, instead of the sunrise... like somehow he found Micah even more mesmerizing than the view out the window.

Micah's entire body flushed, his heart somehow in his throat and yet galloping against his ribs at the same time.

Say something, you idiot!

"I-"

"Mr. Romano, sir, are you or your guest hungry?"

Micah jolted when they were suddenly interrupted by the lone flight attendant on the private jet. (It wasn't like they needed more than one with just the two of them and the pilot.) He wasn't sure if he was annoyed or relieved by the disruption, but he offered the young, pimply kid – he looked like he was fresh out of high school – a smile, anyway. The small nameplate pinned to his chest declared that his name was "Paul".

"I'm good, Paul," Micah said. Thanks, anyway."

When Micah turned back to Damon, it was to discover a scowl had taken over his face. Whether it was due to the interruption, or he was simply frowning at Micah's answer to Paul's question, Micah didn't know. "We'll have something light for breakfast," he informed Paul after a moment. "Please bring a cheeseboard out to the couch.

"Of course, sir, right away, sir."

A minute later, they were sitting back on the couch, and Paul was setting an intricate platter of food in front of them that could in no way be considered a mere "cheeseboard". The tray was covered in a variety of not only delicately cut cheeses and meats, but also an assortment of crackers, clumps of green and purple grapes, a split-open pomegranate, and to the side of everything… sushi.

Shit.

Micah felt Damon stiffen beside him. "What is this?"

Micah knew Damon well enough by then to recognize the flat, almost soft, tone as dangerous. Paul did not. He did, however, appear taken off guard by the question. "It's the cheeseboard you asked for, sir." He paused. "It features aged cheddar, Swiss, and Pepper Jack, as well as a variety of cold-cut meats and-"

"And what is *this?*" Damon interrupted, cutting Paul off with a hiss, gesturing at the perfectly formed sushi rolls.

"It's… sushi, sir?" It came out as more of a question, and Paul looked nervous now, like he realized he'd done something wrong, but he wasn't sure what.

"And you dare serve us sushi when Micah's *allergic* to shellfish?"

Paul paled upon realizing the severity of his mistake.

"I explicitly told Morgan that everyone on staff was to be informed of Micah's shellfish allergy. Did she fail to tell you?"

Micah could only assume this "Morgan" person was Paul's boss.

"No, I- I just forgot. I'm so sorry," Paul blathered, grabbing the sushi with his bare hands in his desperation to fix his blunder. "Here, let me-"

Damon snatched Paul by the wrist, and squeezed hard enough that the man yelped and folded in on himself.

"Damon," Micah hissed, having had about enough of Damon's hissy fit, "stop it. It's fine. *I'm* fine."

It was like the man didn't even hear him.

Micah had seen Damon pissed before. He'd watched him kick a man's ribs in during their first meeting, after all. But Micah's adrenaline had been pumping at the time, and he had never thought that Damon looked *scary*. But he certainly looked the part of menacing mafia don *now*.

"What would have happened if Micah had eaten the shellfish and suffered a reaction?" he demanded in a tone that promised violence. "All the way up here? Away from all possible medical care?"

"Actually, I have an EpiPen in my bag," Micah appealed reasonably, glancing first at Damon and then the ghost-like Paul. "And I'm sure there's an extra one in whatever first-aid kit the plane is equipped with."

Neither paid him much attention.

"It will never happen again," Paul whimpered. "I swear."

"No, it won't," Damon hissed, "because by the time I'm done with you, you won't be fit to clean toilets let alone work at another airline again. Consider yourself blacklisted." He – *finally* – let go of Paul's wrist, shoving him backward. "Take this tray away – all of it, everything's contaminated now – and get out of my sight. I don't want to see you for the rest of the flight."

Micah tried to catch Paul's eye as he hurriedly scooped up the tray – to offer him a sympathetic smile, at least – but the kid steadfastly refused to meet his eyes. Micah could only watch as he cleaned up the coffee table and disposed of the food before... locking himself in the bathroom?

Honestly, Micah didn't blame him. He might have pissed himself in Paul's shoes.

He took a deep breath before turning to Damon. "Was that really necessary?"

Micah had the pleasure of the man turning his glare on him. "He almost *poisoned* you."

Micah's eyebrows shot up. "That's an extreme interpretation of events. It was an innocent mistake. You didn't need to-"

"He got off easy," Damon interrupted, voice little more than a snarl. "If you'd have eaten anything on that tray, no amount of his stammered apologies or *your* misplaced mercy would have been enough to bring him back."

Micah frowned, prepared to argue, but suddenly realized just how tense Damon actually was. The man's hands were gripping his knees so tightly that his knuckles were white... almost like he was trying to stop them from shaking.

It was only then Micah realized that Damon hadn't just been angry... he was *scared.* And whether it *should* have affected Micah or not, he felt himself immediately soften.

"Hey," he said, taking Damon's hands and prying them off his knees. Half-surprised the man allowed it, Micah brought one of Damon's hands up to his face, placing it against his cheek. "No facial swelling." He put the man's other hand on his chest and took a pointed breath. "My breathing's fine. You don't have to worry. I'm safe, okay?"

The man swallowed hard enough that Micah saw his Adam's apple bob, but he didn't say anything and seemed in no hurry to escape Micah's touch, so Micah took a chance and rested his head on Damon shoulder – *consciously* this time. "So," he asked, gesturing at the tv, "does this thing have Netflix?"

The tension in Damon's body slowly ebbed as they watched a random rerun of Love It or List It on HGTV, and thankfully, the remaining hours of their flight were uneventful. They arrived at their destination around noon.

"Welcome to Siena," Damon said as he helped Micah off the plane at what appeared to be a private airport.

"So we *are* in Italy," Micah said, unable to resist the urge to glance around. The runway of the airport they'd landed at appeared modern, but small – and Micah could see towering mountains covered in snow-capped trees in the distance.

Damon frowned. "Didn't I tell you where we were going?"

Micah shrugged. "Not specifically. You just asked about my passport, so I assumed we were headed somewhere out of country, and I know you're from Italy so…"

Damon didn't seem impressed by Micah's deductive reasoning. "You didn't know where I was taking you, but you went with me anyway? *On a plane?*"

Well, it sounded moronic when he put it that way. "I trust you," Micah said simply.

Damon's expression softened at the admission, but that didn't stop him from scolding Micah. "Don't ever get in a car – or on *a goddamn plane* – with anyone ever again if you don't know where they're taking you, got it?"

Micah rolled his eyes. "It's not like I've got men lined up around the block, dying to fly me out to Italy," he pointed out.

A muscle in Damon's jaw twitched. "Still. You need to be more careful."

Not in the mood for arguing about whether or not he could take care of himself, Micah sighed. "Yeah, sure. I promise not to get into any more cars, planes, trains, or pirate ships with any strangers, alright?"

Damon's mouth twitched at that last one. "Thank you. And I apologize for not telling you sooner where we were going. We're in Siena right now, but my family's estate is about thirty miles south, nestled in the Tuscan hills. We'll be driving there in a rental." He pointed at the black Lincoln Town Car waiting for them on the tarmac.

A customs agent greeted them on the runway, and after a quick conversation, wherein another employee of the airport loaded their bags into the vehicle, he and Damon were on their way.

Micah couldn't help but marvel at the view out his window, hardly believing that he was in *Italy*. The airport was located on the outskirts of Siena, so Micah didn't get to see much of the city – only blurred images of tall buildings that seemed to be made entirely of brick, red and bronze colors dominating the landscape.

The vast majority of the ride was through the countryside. Having lived in New York City for the majority of his life, Micah hadn't been exposed to much nature outside of Central Park and the occasional tree planted here and there along the sidewalks, but the Italian countryside... it was beautiful.

Micah felt like he was in a winter wonderland. Evergreens were everywhere, and even the snow here was somehow prettier. Instead of being gray from smog and other air pollutants, it was so white, it glittered in the sunlight.

As they drove, Damon explained that while most of his business was conducted in America, he also owned a handful of restaurants throughout Italy and the third largest vineyard in the country. Despite this, he generally only visited his family's Italian estate a handful of times a year. Apparently. the house was "pretty big", and he kept a team of housekeepers and landscapers on payroll to upkeep it throughout the year.

Micah probably shouldn't have been surprised at that point when they pulled up to a wrought iron gate, beyond which extended a gravel drive that led to a house that Micah could think of plenty of better adjectives to describe than "pretty big". And more apt nouns than "house", for that matter.

Like "mansion", for example, or if Micah was feeling particularly dramatic, "castle".

"Is this the part where you tell me you're actually Italian royalty?" Micah demanded as he took in the colossal, three-story structure. (It had a pair of *steeples*, for fuck's sake.) Much like the buildings in Siena, Damon's ancestral home appeared to be made of brick, but of a much richer, darker variety. Almost more black than red, really.

Damon merely shot Micah a fond look before parking the car. "I asked the staff to clear out for the weekend," he explained as he removed both his own and Micah's luggage from the trunk, "so we have the house to ourselves."

"This place is so massive, I doubt I'd even notice if someone besides us was staying here," Micah joked, steadfastly ignoring the way his heart sped up at the implications of them being alone. Especially since he still wasn't completely sure why Damon had decided to bring him here. Perhaps as more proof to his family that their "relationship" was serious?

"Don't worry," Damon said as he unlocked the front door. "I'll give you a tour."

And after dropping their bags off in the foyer – which was a massive room with vaulted ceilings and a duel staircase that led to the second floor – that's just what Damon did.

Starting on the first floor, he led Micah to the west wing, which featured the kitchen and formal dining room. The huge, ornate table in the middle of the latter room put the one in Damon's penthouse to shame.

The east wing featured a drawing room, which was essentially just a fancy living room adorned with extravagantly patterned couches, a billiards room, and a room Damon referred to as "the winter study" – which, living up to its pretentious-sounding name, was basically a frickin' library disguised as a den.

Damon led Micah to the second floor next, walking him through all *eight* bedrooms. He explained that the third floor was used mostly for storage, but they did venture up a secluded staircase so that Damon could show off what he called the "observatory" – which was a circular room with huge glass windows for walls and a massive telescope for looking out of them.

Damon told Micah that his grandmother had had a penchant for astrology, and that she would take him and his sisters up there when they were young to read them their fortunes in the stars – before she'd eventually passed on.

"What did she tell you about your future?" Micah asked curiously, half-wishing it was dark already, and not mid-day, so that *he* could see the stars – a special treat when you lived in a smog-filled city.

Damon shrugged. "Just the typical horseshit that all fortune tellers spew," he said. Despite the harshness of his words, his tone was fond. "That I'd experience great strife, but also boundless joy, in life."

"And what about your love life?" Micah teased, feeling brave. "Did she say you were destined for loneliness or a love story that would put Hallmark to shame?"

Damon pinned Micah in place with his gaze. "Nanna said I'd meet someone who would challenge me in every way possible – someone who would test my self-control, but lend me great strength." A frown tugged at Damon's mouth. "She also said I'd lose them without sacrifice."

Micah raised his eyebrows. "Nanna sounds dramatic," he pointed out.

"You have no idea," Damon muttered in agreement, but his mouth remained in that miserable, little half-frown.

"You know, I find it hard to believe that the stars said *all* that," Micah said, in an attempt to cheer him up. "Nanna probably just knew what a stubborn ass you were and wanted to hammer home the fact that *all* relationships require compromise."

Damon snorted in amusement, his lips twitching upwards, and Micah took a selfish sort of thrill in the fact that he was able to pry the sound and tiny smile out of the man. Damon wrapped his arm around Micah's shoulders and squeezed. "Maybe," he agreed, "but that doesn't explain how she knew you'd be a hooker."

Micah poked him hard in the side in retaliation.

It wasn't until they went back to the main floor to retrieve their bags that he realized the man had all but alleged *Micah* was the great love his grandma had seen in his future.

He didn't mean it like that, Micah immediately scolded himself before his brain could fixate and get ideas. *He was just making a joke.*

Except instead of showing Micah to the room he'd be staying in, Damon ushered him into the same bedroom he dropped his own luggage off in, taking Micah's duffel bag from him and placing it with his belongings on the carpet.

The room wasn't anything like Damon's bedroom back in New York. While Damon's entire penthouse was the definition of modern with its hardwood floors, monochromic color scheme, state-of-the-art appliances, and impersonal wall hangings, Damon's bedroom at his family's estate was like something from back in time.

The walls were a warm yellow, the windows adorned with heavy red drapes, and the floor was covered in a plush rug featuring an elaborate configuration of pale blues and creams. There was no sign of electronic gadgets, the fireplace in the corner looking like it took *actual* wood to get it going.

In the center of the room was a massive king-size, four-poster bed, its curtains pulled back to reveal a dark green bedspread and more pillows than Micah had ever seen on a single bed barring that one time Tessa had dragged him into a Bed, Bath, and Beyond.

"So… what do you think?"

Damon seemed oddly nervous for someone who had looked and sounded so smug while showing him around the house. (Almost like he was trying to impress Micah. But that was silly.)

"I think this whole place is awesome," Micah said honestly. "*Why* do you live in New York again?"

Damon smirked. "Business, mostly. Although, I have to admit, I've grown a certain… fondness for the people there. Well, a few people." Micah was *not* going to read into that at all. "Do you really like it?" he pressed.

"Damon, it's basically a castle," Micah pointed out. "What's not to like? I would have been impressed with a one-bedroom cottage." He paused, glancing around. "Although, I'm not sure where I'm supposed to sleep?"

Damon frowned. "Here, of course." He gestured at the bed.

Micah chewed his bottom lip. "Yeah, okay, but what about you?"

Damon blinked. "I... I suppose I thought the bed was big enough for the both of us." He shook his head. "But that's absurd to think you'd be comfortable with that. I'll just-"

But Micah didn't get to hear what Damon was going to do.

"I'm comfortable with it!" he practically shouted at the man. "That's *totally* fine with me. I mean, the bed's huge, and it'll be less mess for housekeeping to deal with when we leave, so yeah... let's just do that."

Jesus, try not to sound too eager or anything.

"As long as you're okay with it," Damon hedged.

"Trust me, I'm *beyond* okay with it."

Seriously, could you sound any more desperate?

Luckily, before Damon could question why exactly Micah was so keen to share a bed (like the answer wasn't obvious), Micah's stomach decided it was time to gurgle loudly. He offered Damon a sheepish smile. "Sorry, I didn't have breakfast. You know, because of the sushi incident."

Damon looked horror-struck. "Fuck, you're hungry. I should have fed you as soon as we landed. You're probably starving."

"You didn't have breakfast either," Micah pointed out. He couldn't help but feel the man was being a bit hard on himself considering Micah was a full-grown adult, perfectly capable of procuring food for himself if he so chose.

"It's two in the afternoon," Damon stressed, like he'd committed some unforgivable sin. He shook his head. "Anyway, the pantry and refrigerator should be fully stocked," he said, taking Micah by the hand and pulling him out of the bedroom, presumably leading him towards the kitchen. "I can make you anything you want."

Micah shrugged. "Anything is fine," he said honestly.

Damon shot him an unimpressed look over his shoulder.

"I mean, pizza sounds good, I guess," he said, figuring it'd be easy enough to pop a frozen pie into the oven.

"Pizza it is."

Micah wasn't prepared for Damon to sit him in a chair before filling the countertop with various ingredients and begin making what appeared to be *homemade pizza dough*.

"Don't you have anything frozen we can throw in the oven?" he asked.

Damon shot him a half-offended/half-disgusted look before returning to his dough-making. Not that Micah was complaining. The man had shed his suit jacket and rolled up the sleeves of his dress shirt, and Micah didn't even bother trying to disguise the way he eyed Damon's strong forearms, watching the way his veins bulged as he worked the dough.

Micah offered to help, but after he managed to dump a tablespoon instead of a teaspoon of black pepper into the sauce (forcing Damon to start the sauce over), and then sliced his finger open on the cheese grater while shredding the mozzarella, Damon gently, but firmly, forced him to sit back in his seat.

About thirty minutes later – fifteen minutes after Damon had put the pizza into the oven – Micah was scarfing down what he could honestly say was the best pizza he's ever eaten. (And he lived in New York, he'd eaten *a lot* of pizza.) His stomach felt close to bursting by the time he was finished.

"You've ruined pizza for me for life," he complained as he patted his slightly distended stomach. "How am I ever supposed to eat takeout again?"

"You're ridiculous," Damon said, waving off the compliment.

"I'm serious." Micah tilted his head in consideration. "Although, it's probably a good thing you aren't around to cook for me every day. I'd gain twenty pounds the first month."

"You'd look cute with a little belly."

Micah flushed at the unexpected comment. Judging by the hint of red crawling up Damon's neck, *he* hadn't anticipated the words coming out of his mouth either.

Time to change the subject, Micah.

He cleared his throat. "So... what's on the agenda for today?" he asked, figuring he probably ought to know *why* exactly they were at Damon's ancestral house – in *Italy*. "I mean, I doubt you flew me all the way out here just to show off your family's countryside estate."

Except that when Micah plucked up the courage to look up from his empty plate, it was to see Damon glancing off to the side, not quite meeting Micah's eyes. "My sisters and I plan to spend Christmas here next week. I didn't want to intervene with any holiday plans you may have, but I still wanted you to be included, so I thought we'd fly over this weekend to make sure the estate was in acceptable condition for next week."

That was a lot of words to basically confirm that Damon *had*, in fact, dragged Micah all the way to Italy just to show off his family's countryside estate. Maybe Micah should have been irritated, but instead, he felt oddly light, and warm, and giddy.

"That's... actually really sweet."

Damon's eyes darted back to his. "Next time I bring you here, it'll be for more than just the weekend," he assured. "I'll take you skiing in the Alps, or we'll visit the Carnevale. Of course, if you'd rather go in the summer, the beaches are beautiful."

Micah didn't know if it was how uncharacteristically earnest the man sounded or the fact that he assumed he and Micah would still be "together" come summer, but his throat felt suddenly tight. "That sounds amazing," he said, voice a bit croaky. "But, I mean, this is good too. I don't have to see the Alps or walk some beach to enjoy spending time with you."

Too much, Micah, a voice in his head warned. *Too honest.*

Luckily, Damon didn't comment on it. "Of course, we don't have to spend the entire day in this musty, old house. They are some hot springs in the woods, about a mile southeast of the courtyard, that I wanted to show you if you're up for it."

Private hot springs in the middle of the woods with Damon?

Honestly, it sounded like an invitation for another "hot tub incident" all over again, and if Micah had any sense in his brain, he'd turn Damon down.

"Sounds fun."

Internal sigh.

Micah hadn't packed anything but a coat and hat, but after digging through a handful of wardrobes on the third floor, they found enough winter gear for both of them to make the mile-long hike in the woods. (Micah also managed to dig up some old baby pictures of Damon that he'd spent an appropriate amount of time "oohing" and "ahhing" over.)

The sun was already setting by the time they finally ventured outside, dusk settling upon the winter wonderland that was Damon's backyard. Damon led Micah through white-speckled evergreens, assuring him that he knew the way by heart as they trudged through the snow, no path in sight.

Apparently, he and his sisters visited the springs every year, and when they were younger, they used to search the forest for mussels and the perfect Christmas tree, which their father chopped down and dragged to the house so they could decorate it together.

Sure enough, it didn't take long for the telltale sound of running water to hit their ears, and Micah spotted steam rising above the trees. The evergreens opened up to reveal a small clearing, the cluster of hot springs nestled there making Micah's eyes widen in wonder.

There were about a dozen small pools of water encased by slabs of pale stone, the water flowing from a small, rocky cliffside some distance away – all of it surrounded by the white and green landscape that was Tuscany in winter.

Maybe it was the city boy in him, but Micah couldn't help but feel awed by the natural beauty of the springs.

"The water flows down all the way from Mount Amiata," Damon explained, gesturing at the squat waterfall from which the water gushed. "It stays a balmy 99 degrees all year long."

Micah wasn't *so* awed, however, that he didn't notice when Damon unzipped his coat and began shrugging it off, along with the rest of his winter gear. Then his shirt came off over his head.

"What are you doing?" Micah managed to find his voice when the man began unbuttoning his slacks. His brain could not compute the fact that Damon seemed to be *stripping* in front of him.

"Well, you can't go in the springs in full gear," Damon pointed out reasonably.

"You're going *in*?" Why did his voice sound so much more high-pitched than usual?

Damon glanced his way. "Why else would we come all the way out here?" He seemed amused by Micah's confusion as he hooked his thumbs over the waistband of his pants and unceremoniously pulled them down.

He didn't seem self-conscious at all to be standing in front of Micah in nothing but a pair of boxer-briefs.

And why *should* he be?

Between the muscled pectorals sprinkled with hair, the corded biceps, the bulging thighs, and the outline of what appeared to be a *ridiculously* massive cock behind a pair of *absurdly* tight underwear, Micah's eyes couldn't seem to pick what to focus on.

After an awkward thirty seconds where his eyes *feasted* on the buffet of prime masculinity presented before him, Micah somehow managed to muster up the willpower he didn't know he had to jerk his gaze away.

Thank God his face was already tinged pink from the cold.

Damon didn't comment on his ogling. He merely lowered himself into one of the larger springs before turning back to Micah and asking, "Aren't you coming in?"

Micah swallowed hard. "I- I don't have my swimsuit," he stuttered.

Damon raised an eyebrow, not bothering to voice how ridiculous that excuse was considering he had just hopped into the spring in nothing but his underwear. "You know, you're acting awfully shy, considering..."

"Considering what?" Micah snapped, finally regaining some of his footing with the perceived offence.

Considering that he'd supposedly worked as a prostitute? That he'd attempted to drunkenly blow Damon through his pants? That he'd sent the man a picture of himself in nothing but a pair of cum-stained panties?

...okay, so maybe Damon had a point.

Instead of finishing his sentence, however, Damon merely covered his eyes with his hands. "Is this better? Will you come in now?"

Asshat. Micah ought to refuse just for that.

But then again, was he really going to pass up the opportunity to lounge in a natural hot spring in the middle of Italy?

Throwing his hands up in defeat, Micah quickly rid himself of his winter gear before stripping down to his underwear. (*Why* in the name of all that is holy had he chosen to wear his superhero-themed briefs today?) Before Damon could open his eyes and tease him for it, he sank down into the water – as far away from the man as the spring allowed.

And, *Jesus*, what an experience it was.

He felt himself melt into a pile of goo as the warm water hit his cold, stiff muscles, and he couldn't resist the urge to groan aloud. "Okay, so this *is* pretty amazing," he admitted after a moment, opening his eyes as he'd involuntarily closed them upon entering the water. "Tessa is going to be so jealous."

"Who's Tessa?"

Micah froze. God, he could be so *stupid* sometimes. What was even more concerning than the slip-up, however, was that Micah's first instinct was to just *tell him the truth*.

Micah shrugged in a way he hoped looked casual. "Just a friend from work who looks out for me."

It was true in the technical sense, if not in spirit.

Damon tended to shut down and distance himself at any mention of Micah's "job", but to his surprise, the man actually shifted *closer* to Micah – so close that their knees touched under the water.

Fuck.

"I'm glad," he said, his *thigh* pressing up against Micah's now. "But you don't need anyone looking out for you anymore. It's my job now."

Micah laughed, but it sounded forced to even his own ears. "I thought I was the serf in this relationship," he joked.

Damon snorted. "You're… something," he admitted, turning to face Micah so that their noses – their lips – were mere inches apart. Was… was he really going to *kiss* him?

Micah thought his heart might beat out of his chest in anticipation, and his cock was already straining against the waistband of his briefs at the thought. And yet…

He couldn't let it happen.

Was it everything Micah had ever wanted from Damon? *Yes.*

Would he have already been straddling the man and attempting to suck his soul out through his mouth a month – hell, maybe even a few weeks – ago? *Also yes.*

But that was before the feelings Micah had for him became all-consuming. Sure, he'd have been brokenhearted if they'd fucked and then things had gone sideways weeks ago, but now? If he let Damon kiss him – *fuck* him – he knew he'd be ruined if (*when*) everything went to hell.

And they *would* go to hell.

Because Damon ran a crime syndicate, and Micah was a cop, and there was no way they could make a *real* relationship work between them.

So instead of leaning forward and meeting Damon halfway as he inched closer, Micah did the only thing he could think of to salvage the situation. He swept his arm through the water and splashed the man in the face.

Damon froze, his expression so flabbergasted as water dripped from his hair into his eyes that Micah couldn't help but let out a real laugh despite the gravity of the moment. "Oops," Micah offered.

Damon glared, and so distracted by the way water clumped in his eyelashes, Micah didn't even see the tidal wave of water coming for his own face until it was too late.

Micah sputtered, choking on the warm water of the springs as it got into his mouth and nose.

What ensued was the most erotic water fight Micah had ever participated in. They half-splashed/half-wrestled each other in the little pool of water, Micah trying to climb the man and dunk him underwater at the same time as keeping the fact he had a borderline painful situation in his briefs under wraps.

By the time they were finished roughhousing, they were both soaked and red in the face from a mixture of strain and laughter. It was the happiest Micah had ever seen Damon, his white smile so blinding it was almost hard to look at.

Micah wanted to kiss it – kiss *him* – desperately. His resolve *not* to was hanging on by the barest of threads when a loud *howl* suddenly pierced the air.

Micah shot Damon a nervous look. "What was that?"

Damon shrugged, a smile still playing at his mouth. "Probably just a wolf."

"*Just* a wolf?" he repeated incredulously. "Gee, try not to sound so concerned."

"Lots of wild animals live out here – wolves, deer, wild boar. We hear them – even see them – on occasion, but they've never bothered us."

Despite Damon's reassurance, Micah was still spooked, so they agreed it was time to call it a night and head back to the house.

Thankfully, the cold air put a damper on his erection so Micah wasn't completely mortified when Damon helped haul him out of the water. Despite Damon's earlier teasing, Micah wasn't actually body shy, but anyone would feel inferior next to a near-naked Damon.

The hike back to the house was dark, the stars twinkling madly in the sky. The sight drew Micah's admiration, but it wasn't enough to completely take his mind off how much colder it felt outside with damp underwear and wet hair. Micah couldn't seem to stop shivering, and Damon frowned at the way he continued to shake even after they were inside the warm house.

"There's a bathroom attached to our room. You shower first while I get a fire stoked."

Micah wasn't about to argue with that plan. After indulging in a hot shower and throwing on a pair of pjs – fleece pajama bottoms and an oversized Mets t-shirt – he felt much better. True to his word, Damon had gotten a fire going in the meantime. While Damon went to grab a shower for himself, Micah took his phone from his bag and curled up on the couch in front of the wood fireplace, figuring he'd better text Tessa and give her an update.

Physically safe, but on the verge of emotional catastrophe.

He didn't get a response before the din of running water coming from the bathroom quieted and Damon returned to the room. He was dressed casually, in a pair of comfy-looking sweats and a plain white t-shirt, sleeves tight around his biceps. His damp hair stuck to his forehead, and Micah spotted a little bead of water dripping down the side of his neck, where it disappeared into the collar of his shirt.

Micah was so busy trying not to swallow his tongue that he forgot to hide the phone.

"I see you're still using that decrepit, old thing."

Micah quickly tucked the phone away under his thighs, smiling sheepishly. "Yeah, sorry."

Damon shrugged. "I said you could." He tilted his head to the side. "But that *does* remind me. I have something for you."

Before Micah could ask what that meant, Damon was unzipping a compartment of his luggage and pulling out a present. It was rectangular, and fairly small, pristinely wrapped in gold wrapping paper with a festive bow on top. Damon all but thrust it into his hands.

"If it's another phone…"

Damon shook his head. "It's not. Besides, why would I give you another one when you hardly use the iPhone I already gave you?"

Micah chewed his bottom lip. "I have something for you too," he admitted before pushing himself off the couch and digging through his own bag to pull out the gift he'd gotten Damon.

It was shabby-looking compared to what Damon had given him, a wrinkled mass of Santa Claus wrapping paper, but Damon didn't seem to think so. He seemed shocked to be receiving something, and carefully took the proffered gift from Micah's hands like it was something precious.

It made nervous butterflies sprout in Micah's stomach as he reclaimed his seat next to the man on the couch. "Should I go first or...?"

That seemed to snap Damon out of whatever strange daze he'd fallen into. "Yes, please, open it."

Under Damon's watchful gaze, Micah untied the bow before tearing into the wrapping paper to uncover an unassuming box. Opening the box, Micah revealed a watch.

Micah felt his stomach cramp in disbelief. Because, of course, it wasn't just any watch. It was a platinum *Rolex*, complete with a diamond-encrusted dial and even larger, shinier gems serving as the numbers.

"Damon, I don't even want to know how much this is worth," he said faintly.

"So don't ask," the man said simply.

Micah shot him an unimpressed look.

Damon sighed. "Look, I know you don't use the phone I gave you outside of your apartment because you think it's bugged, or that I'm spying on you with it."

"You realized you all but confirmed this belief just now, right?"

Damon ignored him. "So this is my solution to the problem. It's not a smart watch, so you know it's not loaded with tracking apps, *but* I did have a panic button installed." He gently took the watch from Micah and showed him the small, nearly imperceptible button on the side. "Press this three times if you're ever in trouble, and your coordinates will be sent to me immediately."

Micah was both impressed and touched. However, he'd been uncomfortable just *holding* such an expensive timepiece, he couldn't imagine wearing it around. And besides, what if he accidentally triggered the panic button and sent Damon his coordinates while he was at the precinct?

Damon held out his hand, clearly expecting Micah to lay his own in it so he could help him put on the watch. Micah gnawed the inside of his cheek in indecision.

"Please," Damon implored, a little crinkle of worry forming in his brow. "It's disconcerting for me to know that most of the time you're out of reach with no form of protection. It distracts me from work. I know I presented it as a gift, but it's as much for me as it is for you."

And fuck if Micah wouldn't do anything to make that little crinkle of worry fade away. Ignoring the foolishness of what he was doing, Micah sighed and laid his hand in Damon's, allowing the man to carefully fasten the watch around his wrist. It was light and surprisingly comfortable, feeling not at all like the shackle Micah had pictured in his mind.

"Thank you," Damon breathed out, and before Micah could snatch his hand away, he pressed a little kiss to the inside of his wrist, right abut the clasp of the watch.

Micah snatched it away as if he'd been electrocuted, his brain feeling a bit as if he *had*. He cleared his throat. "Your turn," he said, nodding towards the gift in Damon's lap. He felt his nerves return as Damon carefully unwrapped the crinkled paper. "It's nothing expensive," he babbled. "I mean, you probably won't even like it-"

"If it's from you, I'm sure I'll love it," Damon assured before Micah could get carried away. And then he was delicately holding up the apron Micah had got him, staring at it for several long moments. "I take it back. You are incorrigible." But he had a grin tugging at his mouth and his eyes were sparkling.

Relief and a wicked sort of satisfaction battled inside Micah when he saw how inexplicably pleased Damon was with the gift. It made him bold. "Wear it for me tomorrow when you make breakfast," he demanded.

Damon raised his eyebrows. "Excuse me?"

"Wear it for me *please?*" Micah said, rewording his earlier demand, softening his voice so it sounded more like a plea. "After all, I'm wearing your gift, aren't I?" He pointedly held up the wrist with the watch.

Damon hummed, and when they had gotten so close, Micah didn't know, but he could feel the vibrations of the sound in his own chest. "I suppose I could be convinced."

It was an invitation if Micah had ever heard one. And fuck if Micah didn't want to take him up on it. But he *couldn't* because he knew devastation would follow. So instead of leaning the rest of the way into Damon's space, or crawling into his lap, or just making a grab for the elastic waistband of the man's pants and shoving his hand inside like the uncouth harlot he was... Micah discreetly scooted over, leaving a respectable foot of distance between them.

"So... it's not the worst Christmas gift you've ever received then?"

Damon frowned – whether at the change of subject or the change in his demeanor, Micah couldn't tell – but he tactfully played along. "Definitely not. That honor belongs to Joelle. Last year, she got me a lifetime supply of Viagra, and if I recall correctly, the year before that, it was candy nipple tassels – used ones, mind you, since half the candy was missing."

Micah couldn't help it – he snickered. He imagined that was the point of the gifts, to make Damon laugh. He didn't do it nearly often enough. "I wish I had siblings to torment me at Christmas." The holiday just hadn't been the same since Micah's mom had passed. His father had tried, of course – at least the first few years – to make Christmas time as magical as she had – but after a while, they didn't even bother with a tree, let alone presents beyond gift cards stuffed in old envelopes. "Although I think I'd take a brother over three sisters."

"They're awful," Damon complained, but you'd have to be deaf not to hear the fondness in his voice. "Stone-cold bitches, to be honest – Caprice and Joelle, at least. You've seen that firsthand. Sophie, though... she's a bit sweeter, softer than the others."

The mention of Damon's youngest sister roused Micah's curiosity, which had lingered, but laid dormant inside him since his first meeting with the girl. "Can I ask you something?"

"You just did," the man pointed out.

Micah huffed. "It's about Sophie," he said, "I mean, you obviously don't share the same birth parents...?" he allowed the half-statement/half-question to trail off when Damon stiffened beside him. "Never mind," he hurriedly backtracked. "I'm just being nosy."

After a moment, Damon sighed, but the tension didn't leave his shoulders. "No, it's only natural to be curious, I suppose. We're half-siblings, technically. We don't share the same biological father."

Micah blinked. "Oh."

"My mother didn't cheat on my father," he added swiftly (*defensively*), perhaps misreading the surprise in Micah's voice as disdain. "She was assaulted by one of my father's men, someone he trusted. I was ten when it happened. It was the first time my father took me out with him on a job."

Micah did *not* like the sounds of that, his stomach twisting in apprehension.

"He told me on the way what the sick son of a bitch had done. When we got to the warehouse, he was already strapped to a chair, his face bloodied and eyes swollen shut. My father handed me a crowbar."

Micah felt sick, and he didn't know what to say, so he said nothing.

"But you know what my mother did when she found out what happened to the man?" Damon asked. "She *cried*. Maybe it was just relief that he was dead and gone, or maybe it wasn't... but it always made me wonder." He shook his head. "Either way, my parents' marriage was never the same after that. They grew distant. I'm not even sure if they were still talking to each other when they died."

Was Damon implying that his mother, in fact, *wasn't* raped, and that the tryst she'd had with the man who fathered Sophie was consensual? Micah couldn't tell.

Either way, taking in Damon's curled shoulders and the clear self-loathing that rang through his voice, Micah hated Damon's father – a dead man – more than he'd ever hated anything or anyone in his life. More than he hated the vicious criminals he worked to arrest on a daily basis, more even than the freak aneurysm that had taken his mother away.

Micah's feelings didn't matter at the moment, however, only Damon's. So he needed to get his act together, and *fucking say something*.

So Micah took the man by the face and forced him to look into his eyes. "None of it was your fault," he said, words firm and unyielding – they left absolutely no room for argument. Micah couldn't imagine how confused and scared Damon must have been at only ten years old, seeing a bloodied man tied to a chair and being handed a frickin' crow bar. "Whatever happened, you were only a kid – just doing what was expected of you."

Damon swallowed, and Micah saw his Adam's apple bob. "And what about now?" he asked. "I'm thirty-two, and I'm *still* doing what's expected of me. Does that make me a monster?"

Micah took a deep breath in through his nose. "Maybe," he admitted. "But it doesn't change how I feel about you."

Damon's eyes, a hypnotizing blue, drilled into his own. "How do you feel?"

Micah couldn't resist anymore – he just *couldn't*. Not when Damon looked at him like that, like he was some precious, implausible thing.

Fuck the fact that heartbreak was imminent, and that Micah would probably never recover when things inevitably went south, that he would probably wander around as a husk of himself for months afterwards… Damon needed him, and that was all that mattered.

So, carefully cradling the man's face in his hands, Micah leaned forward and kissed him.

CHAPTER SEVENTEEN

So, carefully cradling the man's face in his hands, Micah leaned forward and kissed him.

It was just a mouth pressed to another mouth at first, soft and unassuming, but then Damon relaxed against him – he grew *pliant* – and Micah became braver, sucking and nipping at the man's lips until he opened up. Then Micah found himself *licking* into the other man's mouth and sucking on his tongue as his hands – which had been holding Damon's face at the beginning of the kiss – grasped at his hair.

Micah had the presence of mind to think the man tasted good – like coffee and mint – before he suddenly found himself being hauled into Damon's lap. Fingers dug into his hipbones as the man held him by the waist, practically grinding him against his crotch. Micah's breath hitched when he felt the evidence of Damon's arousal – huge and hard in his sweatpants – pressed against his own pajama-covered cock.

Damon took advantage of Micah's distraction by dragging his mouth down his chin and along his jawbone, kissing and nipping and leaving a trail of love bites Micah doubted he'd be able to hide in the morning. Damon sucked on the ticklish spot right beneath his ear and Micah whined.

He felt needy and out of control, and *why the hell did they still have their clothes on?*

Micah tore away from Damon – not *all* the way off his lap, the ironclad grip Damon had on his hips made it clear he wasn't going anywhere unless the other man allowed it – just far enough so he could haphazardly pull his shirt off over his head. Then he turned his attention to Damon's shirt, tugging at the hem. "Off," He demanded sharply.

Damon leered. "You're a bossy, little thing when you're wound up, aren't you?"

Micah glared, tugging again at Damon's shirt. "You'll have to excuse me when I've been fantasizing about getting my hands on your cock for fucking weeks-"

Micah hadn't even finished his sentence before Damon suddenly had him by the chin, his grip firm as he tugged Micah's face forward. His breath against his ear sent a shiver down Micah's spine. "You're not going to be able to speak with that filthy mouth of yours by the time I'm through with you."

Micah wrenched his face out of Damon's grip. "Is that a promise?" he asked cheekily.

"It's a warning."

Micah barely withheld an unmanly squeak when Damon suddenly stood, hooking his hands under Micah's thighs to make sure he wouldn't fall. He couldn't help but be impressed with the ease at which Damon carried him – a full-grown man – across the room, before tossing Micah onto the bed.

Sure, being manhandled so effortlessly was a little emasculating, but also *a lot* hot.

Micah didn't have time to ponder about what may be a newly discovered kink, however, because seconds later, Damon was pulling his shirt up over his head. And then tugging his pants down his legs, kicking them into a discarded pile on the floor.

He wasn't wearing underwear.

Micah had spent an embarrassing – frankly *unhealthy* – amount of time fantasizing about Damon's cock. What it might look like, how it might feel – against his hand, in his mouth, in his ass, he wasn't picky.

Reality didn't disappoint.

Huge and hard, it jutted proudly against the other man's toned stomach, its wide mushroom head colored an angry purple. Massive, heavy balls, sprinkled with hair, hung below the alluring display, and Micah probably would have sold his soul just to have been able to roll them between his fingers and suck them into his mouth.

Micah's mouth literally watered at the thought, and he knew he was staring, but he didn't think anyone on God's green Earth could blame him. "Your turn," Damon said, crawling onto the bed so that his knees caged Micah in.

Micah instinctively lifted his hips up off the bed to help the man roll his pajama pants down his legs. Damon chucked them next to his own on the floor before returning to deal with Micah's briefs. He fiddled with the elastic band of the underwear.

"May I?"

Not trusting his voice, Micah nodded, the action stilted.

"I'm going to need you to use your words, Micah."

Fucking overbearing, domineering (*stupidly considerate*) asshole. Micah sucked in a breath. "What happened to making it so I couldn't talk?"

Damon smirked. "Soon," he said, still not making a move to pull down Micah's underwear.

Micah groaned. Fuck. What did the man want? For him to beg? Micah was just desperate enough in that moment to do it. *"Please."*

Damon's face twisted at the word, almost like he was in pain (*or incredibly turned-on*), and then he was yanking Micah's underwear down his legs. Micah's cock sprang free, so hard it *thwacked* against his belly button, sticky precum already smeared across the head.

Micah had never been particularly self-conscious about his cock (see: unsolicited dick pic). Sure, he wasn't as long or as thick as Damon, but he'd always thought he was a respectable size – proportionate to the rest of his body.

But there was something so intimate about the way Damon sat back and stared – completely unabashed. It made Micah squirm, stuck between wanting to preen under his watchful gaze and cover himself with his hands.

"Fuck."

Micah's cock twitched. "That's the idea," he gritted out.

Damon's eyes flickered to his when he spoke, and Micah could see how dark they were – almost black, like his pupils were threatening to completely overcome the irises. He looked unquestionably... *hungry.*

Micah licked his lips.

Damon's eyes followed the movement of his tongue. "Brat," he muttered, and then he was on him, crushing Micah's body with his own as he crashed their mouths together. It was an unsophisticated clashing of teeth and a frenzied battle of the mouths. Damon's tongue forced itself between his lips, and Micah was all to willing to suck it inside his mouth.

He was running short on oxygen by the time Damon finally let up, but he didn't have much time to regain his breath before the man buried his face into Micah's neck, lavishing the skin there with attention, and coaxing breathy moans out from the back of Micah's throat.

He dragged his mouth down the plane of Micah's chest, and Micah jolted when he grazed one of his nipples with his teeth before sucking the pink bud into his mouth. His breath hitched at the sensation.

"You like that?" Damon teased, releasing Micah's nipple with a wet *pop*.

Asshole.

"Fuck you," Micah said, breathless. "Also, *yes*, okay? But there are other parts of my body absolutely dying for attention right now." He emphasized his point by arching his hips off the bed, attempting to rub himself up against the man hovering over him.

But quick as lightening, Damon's hands were on his hips, pinning him to the bed. "So impatient," he scolded lightly before leaning down and pressing an airy kiss – a mere brush of the lips – to Micah's belly button.

Micah felt vaguely lightheaded and dragged in a shaky breath through his nose. It immediately escaped him in a *whoosh*, however, when Damon buried his nose into the crease of Micah's thigh and inhaled. Damon's mouth was mere inches from his cock. He only had to turn his head, and-

Damon had the nerve to moan like *he* was the one with a mouth so tantalizingly close to his dick. "You smell so good."

Fuck.

It took every ounce of Micah's self-control not to lift his hips up off the bed like a wanton whore.

"Damon," he whined feebly instead, remembering how well begging had worked a few minutes ago, and not caring if he was being a manipulative, little shit. "Please, Damon, I'll be good, just-just *please*-" Micah fisted the sheets in an effort not to grab the man by the roots of his hair and show him exactly where he wanted his mouth.

But he didn't have to, because-

"Of course, *tesoro*," Damon agreed, breath warm against Micah's already flushed skin. "Whatever you want." Then he turned and fucking swallowed Micah whole.

He was glad Damon still had him firmly by the hips because his entire body jerked when he was enveloped in the tight heat of the man's mouth. Add to that the mesmerizing sight of Damon's lips stretched around his cock, his head bobbing as he worked Micah expertly, and Micah knew he wasn't going to last long.

Damon tongued his slit, and Micah cursed.

Thoroughly distracted, he didn't even notice that Damon had slipped a hand between them until there was suddenly a finger pressed right *there* – against the pucker of his hole. It wasn't doing anything other than sitting there, a tiny pressure against his most intimate place, but it was enough that Micah had to tense his thighs and lock down on the pressure building behind his cock. "Fuck, Damon, fuckfuck*fuck*."

Micah could have cried when the man pulled himself off his cock. "Hm, you're still talking."

That's all the warning Micah got before the man was suddenly flipping him over onto his stomach and guiding (*manhandling*) him onto his hands and knees. "Wh-what-?" Micah asked, but he choked on the rest of the words – whatever they were going to be – when Damon palmed the globes of his ass and separated the cheeks.

"Beautiful."

An involuntary shudder made its way down Micah's spine at Damon's breathy proclamation.

And then a hot mouth was right there.

Micah yelped at the sensation, knowing it was coming and yet wholly unprepared for the feeling of a broad tongue lapping at the crack of his ass. Overgrown stubble brushed against his cheeks as Damon buried his face into Micah's ass, sucking the little pucker of his hole into his mouth.

Micah's stomach swooped at the sensation.

"Oh, Jesus, God, fuck, frickin' Pope Francis," Micah babbled, mindlessly throwing out whatever religious figures his strung out mind could conjure, "don't stop."

Damon didn't stop.

He wriggled his tongue into Micah's asshole, spearing him with it until Micah was an absolute mess, barely holding himself up on shaky legs while making half-moan/half-gasping sounds that would have been embarrassing if he wasn't in the midst of getting his ass eaten out by someone with a tongue as talented as it was wicked.

"You taste like fucking candy," Damon breathed against him, and Micah moaned helplessly at the words. Then something a little firmer than a tongue was probing at his hole. A finger, Micah recognized dazedly, when he felt the tip of it push inside him. And then Micah gave up on thinking all together because the finger slipped all the way in, and Damon was fucking *slurping* around it.

"Damon, *please!*"

"Please what?" Damon asked, voice like gravel, his finger still knuckle deep.

If Micah could concentrate on anything other than *that* and the fact his dick was a hard, unyielding ache between his legs, he would have attempted some snarky remark at the blatant teasing. As it was, he'd been reduced to mere one-word responses. "*More.*"

Micah thought he might die when instead of giving him what he wanted, Damon withdrew his finger, and backed away. He let out a truly pathetic whimper. "No…" he said, whining into the mattress. He wasn't even sure when he'd buried his face in it.

"Hush," Damon said, soothingly, still looming over him, running a hand up and down his back in a reassuring motion. "I just need to get the lube so I don't hurt you. But I want you to stay just like this for me. Can you do that?"

Micah groaned at what seemed like a Herculean task.

"Can you do that for me, Micah?" Damon repeated, giving his hip a little squeeze to ensure he had his attention."

Was there any alternative?

"Y-yeah, yeah, I can."

"Thank you, sweetheart." Then his hand was gone.

Micah heard rustling behind him, but he didn't even turn around to look. Instead, he stayed perfectly still, just like Damon had asked.

It felt like an eternity, but it was probably only half a minute later, that the man returned. "Such a good boy." A kiss was pressed to his tailbone, right above his ass.

Micah didn't have time to process that – or how he felt about being called "a good boy" – before a lubed finger was rubbing at his hole and carefully entering. Then there was another finger – slowly, painstakingly – joining the first. And then another, until he was stuffed full.

Micah could feel himself bearing down on the digits, and he knew he was making noises as Damon pumped his fingers in and out of him – desperate, high-pitched whines – but he couldn't bring himself to care. He was so close; he knew he was.

If only he had something to rub up against...

That's what your hands are for, genius.

As soon as his brain made the suggestion, Micah attempted to slink a hand underneath himself.

Unfortunately, strong fingers wrapped themselves around his wrist before he could succeed. "None of that now," Damon chastised him.

But Micah wasn't exactly in the state of mind to listen. Taking advantage of the position of their hands, he decided to try to bring *Damon's* hand to his dick instead.

Unfortunately, the man merely ignored his attempt, using his superior strength to press Micah's wrist back against the bed.

A frustrated noise bubbled up Micah's throat at the blatant denial.

"Hush. You don't need that hand. You're going to come for me just like this. That's what you want, sweetheart, isn't it? To come like this? Untouched? That's what *I* want."

Micah moaned helplessly at the thought, but...

"I don't know if I c-can," he admitted.

"You can. Let me show you."

A moment later, Damon's tongue joined the fingers in his ass, and he was *curling* them – pressing them up against his prostate without mercy. Micah's vision whited out, and God, Damon was right, because a moment later, he was coming, his shout muffled by the mattress as thick, milky spurts spilled all over the sheets.

Micah's strength fled him all at once, and he would have collapsed right into a puddle of his own jizz if Damon hadn't had the sense to haul him off to the side of the mess, arranging himself between Micah's legs on the bed. He pressed open-mouthed kisses to Micah's face, his neck, muttering sweet nothings against his slick skin.

"-did so well-"

"-so fucking perfect-"

The words made his stomach flip, but high as Micah was on his own orgasm, he was painstakingly aware of the fact that Damon was still hard, his cock standing proudly between his legs, huge and angry-looking. And fuck if Micah wasn't desperate to touch it.

Giving into the urge, Micah reached forward and took the man's cock into his hand. Damon's girth was such that his thumb didn't even meet his other fingers where he wrapped them around the bottom of the shaft.

Ignoring Damon's shocked inhale and the stream of cuss words that catapulted out of his mouth – "shit, fuck, *Micah*" – Micah stroked him once, twice-

Damon caught his wrist in an iron-tight grip before Micah could do it a third time. Despite the pulse that Micah could see beating rapidly in the bulging veins of the man's neck (his cock, too), when Damon pinned his hand down onto the mattress, it was with careful, gentle fingers. He rested his forehead against Micah's. "You wreck me, you know that, right?"

Micah licked his lips. "Pretty sure it's you who's going to wreck me with that... thing."

Thing, Micah? Christ.

So he was a bit ineloquent fresh off the best orgasm of his life and with a massive cock in his face. Cut him some slack.

Shockingly, instead of teasing Micah, Damon merely leaned forward and kissed him. It was sweet, borderline chaste, but Micah could *taste* himself on Damon's tongue, and he felt his dick give an interested twitch, already half-hard despite the fact he'd just blown his load all over Damon's sheets.

"Are you sure you want to do this?"

Damon was a living, breathing contradiction. He was a violent mafia don, but spoiled Micah rotten, treating him like some precious, breakable thing. He was pinning Micah's hands above his head, grip unyielding, and yet was asking permission to fuck him. It made no sense, and maybe it should have scared Micah that someone so hot-and-cold – so unpredictable – had so much power over him.

But Micah wasn't scared. "Please," he begged, practically choking on the word with how much he wanted it.

That was all the confirmation Damon needed to line his cock up with Micah's asshole, still glistening with saliva and lube.

Micah craned his neck to watch, entranced as Damon pressed the tip up against the tiny pucker. He was prepared for it to hurt – at least a little – regardless of how loose the man had gotten him beforehand. (It was unavoidable with how large Damon was.) But as the man pressed forward – agonizingly slow as he stuffed in inch after inch – Micah realized he wasn't prepared for how... *full* he'd feel.

By the time Damon was all the way in, heavy balls pressed against the crack of Micah's ass cheeks, he felt like he was close to bursting – like a doll stuffed with too much cotton, seconds away from unraveling.

Damon was panting with restraint from where he hovered above him. "Okay?" he asked through clenched teeth.

"Fucking m-move," Micah said bossily, gasping when Damon immediately responded to the demand by carefully pulling out until just the tip of his cock remained inside him... and then ramming it back in.

Micah *keened*.

"Like that?"

Did this motherfucker *really* want to banter with Micah while his monstrous cock was shoved up his ass? Fuck *him*. "B-barely even felt it," Micah managed to stutter out breathily, lying through his teeth.

"Oh? Maybe I should pull out then – let you take care of yourself."

It was an empty threat – it *had* to have been. Damon was buried balls deep inside of him, his pupils were blown so wide they were practically *black* with desire, and Micah could see the veins popping in his arms and neck with how forcefully he was restraining himself.

But that didn't mean Micah was about to risk it. "No, *no!* I'm sorry. You feel amazing. I'm so full, I feel like I'm falling apart. P-please."

"You're pretty when you beg. But the time for talking is over."

That was all the warning Micah got before Damon pulled out and then thrust forward, bottoming out inside of him – *again*.

Fuckfuckfuck... *"Fuck!"*

It was like being split open, but in the best kind of way. Damon speared him on his cock again and again, setting a punishing pace. Micah's dick remained trapped between them, so hard it ached, and he writhed helplessly, lifting his hips to try to create friction, but his hands remained trapped above his head in Damon's unrelenting grip, so ultimately, he could do little but lie back and *take it*, cuss words catapulting out of his mouth between breathy moans and punched out grunts.

"Shit!"

"Fuck!"

"Shit!"

(He really needed to work on expanding his vocabulary.)

When Damon released his wrists after a particularly violent thrust, Micah thought the man was finally having mercy on him.

He was mistaken.

All the man did was throw Micah's knees over his shoulders before resecuring his hands, resuming the furious pace. The position ensured that Micah was practically bent in half, and when Damon thrust forward, impaling him on his cock, Micah *wailed.*

Damon didn't stop. He pounded into him, battering Micah's abused prostate with his mammoth dick, and Micah's thoughts became muddled things, his brain unable to process much beyond the pleasant burn of his hole, the wet *smacks* of Damon's balls slapping against his ass, and the pressure building behind his cock.

Damon's hands squeezed around his wrists as his thrusts became more erratic, and for a second, Micah imagined how it would feel if the man had actually tied him up – with a silken scarf, some rope, or maybe even a pair of kinky handcuffs. Fuck, Micah's *own* cuffs.

For some reason, that particular thought made his stomach clench, and his balls throb.

"Damon, please," he croaked, wrung out, and desperate. "Please, please, pleasepleaseplease," he begged, the words slurring together at the end. He wasn't even sure what he was begging for – but somehow Damon seemed to know. He released one of his wrists and wrapped his fingers around Micah's cock, pumping once, twice-

And that meager touch was all Micah needed for his (*second!*) orgasm to come careening to the surface.

He came so hard his vision whited out, and when he returned to consciousness a few moments later, Damon was shuddering above him, groaning from where he had buried his head into Micah's shoulder, the sound long, low, and broken.

Micah's insides felt hot, and he could feel Damon's dick, spent, but still trapped in his ass. A shiver racked his body at the realization he was full of the man's cum – almost like a post-orgasm aftershock – and Micah whined.

Truly, the orgasm he'd just had *must* have been otherworldly because he seemed to fade in and out of awareness for the next few minutes. He allowed strong, capable hands to clean him (since he'd come all over himself... *again*) and wrap him in a blanket. Once he was suitably bundled, Damon pulled him into his arms, tucking Micah up under his chin.

"You still with me?" Damon asked, his chest rumbling softly beneath Micah's cheek.

Micah didn't blame him for asking. Despite promising Micah he wouldn't be able to talk by the time he was through with him, Damon hadn't actually managed to silence him until now.

It was strange.

Micah was used to his mind running a mile a minute, his mouth usually operating only a beat behind, but for once in his life, his thoughts were quiet, and he didn't feel the need to fill the silence with needless babble. He felt content, and warm, and just... cared for.

Still... strung out on his own orgasm as he was, Micah figured he ought to muster up the energy to say *something*, at least.

I love you. IloveyouIloveyou*Iloveyou*.

Micah was shocked by the fierceness with which the words popped into his mind. Thankfully, he was cognizant enough not to actually say them. Instead, Micah settled for muttering: "If you try to Venmo me for this, I'll fucking murder you in your sleep."

Damon stiffened... then he chuckled, a hand coming up to half-ruffle/half-tug at his hair. "Brat," he murmured, pressing a kiss to the crown of Micah's head.

But from the way Micah's stomach warmed, he might as well have just said "I love you, too".

CHAPTER EIGHTEEN

"Excuse my language, but what the ever-loving fuck, Micah?" Tessa's face was almost as red as her hair, and she was gesticulating wildly with her fork, a bit of spaghetti still hanging limply from the prongs. "Did you really just wake up and think, you know what? Today, I choose self-destruction."

Micah, for his part, was caught off guard by the intensity of her reaction. He'd been looking forward to telling her the nitty-gritty details of his trip to Italy with Damon for days. He's wanted to explain the house (mansion) in detail, and tell her about the springs, and most importantly, describe the mind-blowing sex he'd had with the man.

(He couldn't believe he'd actually *lost time* after that second orgasm – like he'd transcended onto an entirely different plane of reality, where everything was beautiful and nothing hurt.)

Micah had been a ball of nerves the morning after. Especially when, despite having fallen asleep in Damon's warm embrace, he'd woken up to a cold, empty bed. He'd attempted to brace himself for the worst after that, crawling out of the covers and tugging on his abandoned briefs.

Different scenarios had run through his mind.

Maybe Damon wanted to pretend that nothing had happened, and he'd be distant with Micah until he got the hint.

Or maybe Damon would sit him down and flat out tell him that the night before had been a mistake. Perhaps he'd be nice about it, or perhaps not, but either way, the man's obvious regret would kill him.

Maybe Damon would even finally *fire* him.

Micah's stomach clenched at the thought.

Thankfully, before his spiraling thoughts could grow too catastrophic, Damon had surprised him.

By waltzing into the bedroom, wearing nothing but the apron Micah had presented him with the night before, holding a platter of stacked crepes in his hands.

"Why aren't you in bed?" Damon demanded, a frown on his face as he spied Micah standing in the middle of the room, naked but for his underwear.

Micah blinked. "Why aren't you in bed?" he shot back when his brain finally recovered from the sight.

Micah had seen Damon in a variety of expensive, fitted suits, and on a handful of other occasions, casual sweats and t-shirts, and he always looked hot. But this… never had the man ever looked so delectable. (Except, perhaps last night.)

Damon held up the tray like the answer to Micah's question was obvious – which, it was. His frown didn't dissipate. "Where did you think I was?" he asked after a moment.

That Damon had abandoned him in a fit of regret, or embarrassment, or maybe even disgust. That he was avoiding him somewhere in the house. (Micah had even entertained the notion that the man was so sickened by what they'd done, that Damon had fled the country, leaving Micah there, content on letting him find his own way back to the States.)

Not that Micah was about to admit to any of that.

Ultimately, he only shrugged before crossing his arms over his chest. "I don't know."

Damon carefully set the tray of food down before turning back to Micah. He fingered a bit of Micah's cowlicked hair, his other hand running up and down a tense bicep. "How is it that you're even prettier in the morning?"

And just like that, all of Micah's self-doubt fled. His shoulders loosened, and he leaned into Damon's touch. "You're the one in a frilly apron," he pointed out, mumbling the words into Damon's shoulder.

Not that Micah was complaining.

"You asked me so nicely yesterday. What kind of monster would I be to deny such a simple request? Especially when you were so good for me last night."

His words made Micah feel warm all over, and he hummed, feeling more confident. "Well, I suppose it's only proper that I find a way to thank you then."

Damon pressed a kiss into his hair. "Only if you want."

Oh, Micah wanted.

And to prove his point, he slowly lowered himself onto his knees, untying the apron and bunching it up out of the way. Damon's cock was already at half-mast, and bracing one hand on the man's thigh, Micah wrapped the other around the bottom of the shaft.

Damon sucked in a breath above him, stiffening when Micah leaned forward, giving the slit experimental, little kitten licks before stretching his lips around the ridged head of Damon's cock and suckling on it like a baby at its mom's teat.

Damon groaned. "That's it, sweetheart. Take what you can."

Micah nearly rolled his eyes.

He planned on taking much more than just the tip, and he proved it by suddenly devouring Damon whole – until his cock hit the back of his throat, until he was practically gagging on it – before backing off again.

"Jesus, Micah," the man above him all but snarled. Fingers dug into his scalp, entangling in his hair. "Fuck, is this okay?"

Instead of verbally answering, Micah merely went back to work, taking as much of Damon in his mouth as he could, and making sure to wrap his hands around what he couldn't, jerking him in time with his mouth as he bobbed his head up and down, rubbing at the veiny underside with his thumb.

Shutting out all other thoughts, Micah focused only on the feeling of Damon's cock, heavy on his tongue, and the dark, musky scent of him in his nose where it brushed up against wiry pubic hair.

He gorged himself on the man's cock, gag reflex threatening to trigger over and over again, until his eyes were watering and drool was dripping down his chin. Until the man above him was gasping out praise between intelligible moans and cuss words.

Damon's thighs were trembling with the effort to hold back, and Micah was hard in his underwear – convinced he could come from the heady sense of power that came with knowing it was him pulling those wanton moans from the man above him alone.

It wasn't long before the hands on his head were tugging forcefully at the roots of his hair. "Micah, tesoro, I'm going to come-"

Micah knew he meant the words as a warning – Damon was telling him to disengage now or live with the consequences.

Micah wanted the consequences – badly. And just in case his refusal to budge wasn't enough of a hint for Damon to understand that, the way he hollowed out his cheeks and hummed around the man's dick certainly should have been.

Micah heard Damon shout, his body shuddering at the force of the orgasm that took hold of him, and spurt after spurt of the man's hot cum shot down Micah's throat.

Micah couldn't get enough of it, slurping it down like the whore Damon thought he was.

When he was finally spent, Damon heaved Micah up by the armpits before cupping his face and kissing him unabashedly on the mouth. "Thank you."

Needless to say, the crepes had been cold by the time they had gotten to them. They were still delicious, though – and totally worth it.

Unfortunately, Micah hadn't seen Damon since their flight back to New York. He'd had to fly back out to Italy – with Uncle Marco and his sisters this time – a few days later. Tessa had been gone, too. She'd taken vacation from work so she could spend Christmas with her mother out in Idaho, and had left before Micah had gotten back from his impromptu trip.

This meant that Micah had spent a low-key Christmas at his dad's place, watching football and scarfing down Chinese takeout. Which was fine, but he'd been practically dying to go over the details of his trip to Italy with Tessa. He thought she'd be excited for him, or possibly smug.

He hadn't expected for the woman to be *mad* at him.

"You *wanted* me to have sex with Damon," Micah accused. "I don't know how many times you practically begged me to just fuck him. What was that one particularly ridiculous thing you kept saying... ah, that's right, you told me to 'just board the beef bus already'." Micah made sure to use finger quotations for that gem.

Impossibly, Tessa's face grew redder. "That was before I knew he was a fucking mob boss," she all but snarled at him. "Who knows how many crimes – *deaths* – he's responsible for? And forgetting about the ill-advised tumble in the sheets for a moment, I can't believe you're actually wearing this around." She grabbed Micah by the forearm attached to the wrist that wore the watch Damon had gotten him for Christmas.

Micah yanked his arm out of her grip. "He promised it wasn't bugged. And it's not like it's a smart watch, so he couldn't have downloaded any weird tracking apps on it."

"Oh, you mean like that phone he gave you?" Tessa pointed out primly. "The one he practically admitted was a tracking device?"

Micah hunched his shoulders defensively. "He only did that because he was worried about me."

"Yeah!" Tessa agreed loudly, a hysterical edge to her voice. She clearly didn't care that they were in public, having stopped at an Olive Garden to eat after Micah had picked her and Jasper up from the airport. (Damon would have a fit if he knew; he despised Olive Garden.) "Because he thinks you're a fucking prostitute, Micah. Not a goddamn cop – but *you are*. And I don't care how much faith you have in him, there's no telling how Damon will react when he finds out." She took a deep breath in through her nose, as if attempting to calm herself. "I know there's no way you've been wearing that to the precinct."

"So what if I have been?"

Tessa slapped her fork down on the table, spaghetti and all. Sauce splattered on the tabletop. "Shit, Micah. Do you *want* him to find out?"

Of course not.

Except... maybe a tiny part of him *did*. He was tired of lying to Damon, and hiding such a big part of his life from him. He felt sick about it when he thought about it too long... so sue him if he no longer thought it would be the worst thing in the world if Damon discovered his real job.

When he didn't immediately answer in the negative, Tessa had apparently had enough of his bullshit. "Jesus Christ, Micah, I know you're not this fucking obtuse. I swear, it's like he fucked the brain right out of your skull-"

"Hey!"

She slapped her hands down on the table, pushing herself up. "Look, I don't care how good-looking, or generous, or sweet on you Damon is, it doesn't mean you can trust him. You claim he won't hurt you, even if he finds out you're a cop, but what if he does, Micah? You have people who care about you. *I* care about you." To Micah's horror, tears sprang into the woman's eyes. "It's like you don't even give a shit. I can't believe you're being so careless, and so... so selfish!"

With that parting shot, she marched off, away from their table and out of the restaurant, presumably to the car.

As instinctual as it was for him to defend Damon, Micah had to admit... Tessa wasn't exactly wrong in her assessment or out of line with her concerns. And he'd just brushed them off – *had* been brushing them off for weeks – because it was easier to theorize the size of Damon's cock versus whether or not the man had killed anyone before.

Suffice to say, Micah felt like an asshole.

Glancing up from his bowl of uneaten alfredo, Micah spotted Jasper – who'd been serenely watching his and Tessa's blowout – munching on a breadstick, seemingly unbothered by his wife's abrupt exit. "Well," Micah snapped, annoyed, "aren't *you* going to scold me now? Or, you know, at least go after your wife?"

Jasper snorted. "Does it look like I have a death wish to you? She'll ream me worse than she did you if I attempt to coddle her before she's calmed down." The man shrugged. "As for scolding you, well... I guess I just got to trust that you know what you're doing when it comes to this guy."

Micah frowned. "Really? Because Tessa clearly doesn't." The fact stung despite the validity of her concerns.

Jasper sighed, finally putting down the damn breadstick. "Look, Micah, Tessa's just stressed. You know how she's like after having to spend time with her mom, and I don't want to be that asshole who blames everything on hormones, but, I mean, she *is* nearly nine months pregnant with twins." That was a fair point. "It goes without saying that she loves you," he continued. "We *both* do. She's just worried. And, I mean, you can't exactly blame her considering."

And that tiny bit of fight that was still in him fled. Micah's shoulders deflated. "Yeah, I know."

"Good." Jasper slapped him on the back. "So, buy her a Butterfinger and tell her you're sorry tomorrow morning at work, and it'll be like this never happened, alright?"

Micah nodded.

After that, Jasper flagged down a waitress, who quickly returned with to-go boxes for their pasta. Micah shrugged off Jasper when he tried to drag him out to the car, telling him he'd grab an Uber so Tessa could have some space to cool off.

That night, for the first time since Damon bought him his new bed, Micah had trouble sleeping.

He was disheveled and grumpy when he walked into work, a mood that only worsened when he presented Tessa with not only a king-size Butterfinger, but also a family-size bag of Sour Patch Kids, only for her to snub him when she spotted Damon's watch on his wrist.

She snatched the candy from his hands, not even offering a "thank you".

Multiple times after that, he tried to engage her in conversation, but she flat out ignored him unless it was work-related. And even then she only offered clipped, one-word responses.

It didn't seem to matter to her that Micah had already been wearing the watch to work before she'd returned from Idaho, and Damon and his cronies had yet to storm the place. It didn't seem to matter that if Damon *really* wanted to, he had plenty of other avenues available to him to find out Micah's true identity. The man had his address, for fuck's sake. It wouldn't be all that hard to unearth his real last name, and from that information, discover his career as a police detective.

Tessa was determined to be pissed at him and give him the silent treatment.

Unfortunately, the same could not be said for Jensen.

He stopped by Micah's desk late morning, a frown pulling at the corners of his mouth. "Micah, a word, if you please."

Micah glanced up from his computer, where he was recording the results of his *sixth* phone interview of the day. The owner of *spankbankboys.com* had finally responded to the warrant they'd served him after the discovery of Nico's body. (A task that was difficult in and of itself as the only means of contact the website offered was an e-mail address.)

The day before Christmas, he and Jensen had received an extensive list – it specified every user who had ever watched one of Nico's live shows, messaged Nico, or sent money to Nico's Venmo account.

The list had contained well over a hundred individuals, so they'd decided to prioritize Nico's paying clientele first, of which there were only a dozen or so "regulars".

Of course, the website couldn't give them the *actual* names of Nico's customers, as they weren't required to identify themselves to use the site – just usernames and the IP addresses associated with them. But that was nearly as good.

After running the IP addresses through police software that traced them back to the physical addresses of their respective routers, Micah quickly discovered that only two of them were located in New York. He and Jensen had immediately honed in on those.

Unfortunately, each had resulted in dead ends.

The first address had belonged to a married man whose wife had begrudgingly alibied him. Apparently, they'd been on a family vacation to Florida at the time of Nico's disappearance.

The second address had belonged to an eighty-year-old widow. Miriam Murphy was a retired school teacher and church secretary who lived alone.

Micah seriously doubted that the money coming from the user account associated with her address was coming from the old woman – especially since all the money had been uploaded from prepaid Visas. More likely, someone had simply been using her Internet connection to communicate with Nico and send him money.

Unfortunately, with a dead husband and no brothers or sons who lived nearby, they couldn't zero in on anyone in particular.

It didn't help that when they'd told Miriam exactly what sort of crime they were investigating and why they needed to speak with her, she'd immediately become agitated, snapping at them that "no one she associated with would waste their hard-earned money on good-for-nothing whores with no sense of morals" and refusing to cooperate further.

Yeah.

Micah was convinced they were close – that they needed to probe deeper and maybe even case Mrs. Murphy's house to see if she received any regular visitors who would have access to her Internet.

But Jensen wasn't convinced.

He wanted to cast a wider net and investigate the rest of the names on the list the website provided before focusing in on Mrs. Murphy.

So, Micah was forced to start investigating the out-of-state user accounts, hence the phone interviews. He was only halfway through the list of Nico's paying customers, and he'd lost track of how many angry wives and mothers (and on one particularly memorable occasion, a husband) he'd spoken to.

Honestly, he was a little relieved to be interrupted by Jensen. Or, he would have been if it weren't for the frown. Micah knew from experience, he was likely to walk away from whatever discussion Jensen wanted to have in a foul mood.

"What's up?" he asked, anyway.

"We'll talk in my office," Jensen clarified before turning on his heel, expecting Micah to follow.

Sighing, he quickly closed out of his document before doing just that. After shutting the door behind himself, Micah sat in the chair Jensen indicated, trying not to be annoyed when instead of sitting behind his desk, Jensen sat on top of it, so that he was looming over Micah, only about a foot of distance between them.

He didn't immediately speak.

It was an obvious power play, but Micah wasn't in the mood for games, so he cut right to the chase. "Is this about Nico's case?" he asked. "Has there been a breakthrough?"

Jensen's frown deepened. "It's come to my attention that you've been calling Mr. and Mrs. Sanchez and giving them daily updates on their son's case."

Micah blinked.

Whatever he thought Jensen wanted to talk about, it hadn't been *that*. "Well... yeah. Nico was their only son. I want to make sure they know we're doing all we can to bring his killer to justice."

Jensen nodded slowly. "That's great, and we are doing that. *You're* doing that. But you realize that there are certain aspects of Nico's case that need to remain under wraps, even from Nico's family, to ensure the integrity of the investigation."

Micah stiffened. He didn't appreciate being spoken to like he was an idiot. "You say that like I've told them anything compromising. My reports to them are all different variations of assuring them that we're doing our best and that their son's case remains our top priority." Micah frowned. "What else could I have told them? They already know we're investigating his association with *spankbankboys.com*. Unless... unless you're concerned I might tell them we think Nico might have been another victim of the Hooker Hunter?"

A muscle in Jensen's jaw ticked, giving him away.

Micah couldn't believe this. "Don't worry. I've kept mum about the fact the serial killer we supposedly captured a month ago might still be out there." He didn't even try to disguise the bitterness in his voice.

Jensen crossed his arms, clearly unimpressed with his tone. "That's good, since there's no evidence whatsoever to support that particular theory of yours."

"No evidence?" Micah repeated incredulously. "You've conceded that Nico was probably killed because of his association with that website. Sure, webcamming might not be prostituting in the classic sense of the word, but it's *still* sex work. That, combined with the chloroform found in his system and the marks around his wrists and ankles – not to mention, the manner in which his body was found – I, for one, think the connection is obvious."

It was part of why Micah was so annoyed having to conduct all these out-of-state phone interviews. In his mind, there was a sizable chance Nico had been killed by the Hooker Hunter, who was obviously a New York native.

"You're stretching," Jensen refuted, "taking the evidence and trying to make it fit your theory. If Nico's murder was the work of the Hooker Hunter, then where's his next victim? He never went more than a month between slayings when he was at large."

"You say that like you *want* there to be another victim," Micah snapped.

And then immediately felt guilty about it. Jensen may have been an overbearing jerk, but he'd never actively root for people to get hurt. "Sorry," he muttered.

Jensen made no indication he'd heard the apology, too busy pinching his nose in obvious frustration. "No more contact with the victim's family," he said sternly. "From now on, I'll be taking any calls from the Sanchezes."

Micah froze. "You *can't* do that. You're not my boss – at least, not on this case; we're *partners*."

Jensen nodded patiently. "And partners look out for each other. We step in when we see that our colleague is doing something unhealthy for the case – unhealthy for *themselves*. I'm just looking out for you, Micah."

"More like you're looking out for your reputation," Micah retorted, wanting to argue further, but knowing it was pointless when Jensen got *that* particular look on his face.

Not giving the man a chance to respond, Micah stood and rounded for the door. He made sure to slam it shut behind him, ignoring the half-curious/half-wary looks his co-workers shot his way as he stomped back to his desk.

Not Tessa, though. She didn't even look up from her computer despite Micah's obvious upset.

Needless to say, his day didn't improve from there.

Stuck at a standstill on Nico's case and his friendship with Tessa in turmoil, Micah felt like he was hanging on to his sanity by a very frayed thread by the time he got home from work. It seemed ironic to him that the only aspect of his life that *didn't* suck at the moment was his relationship with Damon.

Unfortunately, the man wasn't due home from Italy until the next day.

"Tomorrow," Micah muttered to himself as he flopped into his bed that night. "Tomorrow will be better."

There was no way it would be as unbearable as today had been – not with Damon finally back in the city. At least, there was no way it could possibly be worse.

(In hindsight, *ha-ha-motherfucking-ha.*)

CHAPTER NINETEEN

You're invited to my place this evening – 6:00 sharp – so we can plan Damon's birthday party over wine.

Micah stared, flummoxed at the message he'd received on his iPhone while he'd been at work.

He'd practically sprinted home from the precinct to check it, hoping he'd had a text or missed call from Damon, letting him know the man had caught up with work since his flight in earlier that morning, and that he was able to see Micah tonight.

Micah *really* wanted to see him. And hug him. And kiss him. And suck his cock until his belly was full of the other man's cum. (That escalated quickly.)

But he'd had no new messages from Damon, just *this*.

Not only did Micah have no idea Damon's birthday was coming up, the message – timestamped at 10:25 AM – was from an unknown number. Judging by the brisk, but relatively polite wording, Micah might have guessed it was from Sophie, or perhaps Joelle's fiancé, Fernando.

Which is why the message immediately beneath it was even more mindboggling.

Well? Can you make it? This is Caprice, by the way. Timestamped a mere five minutes later.

(He'd accidentally kept her waiting for hours. Whoops.)

As far as Micah knew, Caprice hated him. Micah couldn't say he felt quite the same ire towards her, but he'd be lying if he said he wasn't still pissed about the charity gala and how she'd tried to hook Damon up with her friend – right in Micah's face.

It was more than a little suspicious that she was suddenly inviting him to her place.

Maybe she and Damon had had a heart-to-heart over the holidays?

Yeah, or maybe he threatened to take away her allowance if she doesn't play nice.

Micah had to admit, the second option seemed more likely. But that didn't mean he didn't want to improve his relationship with the woman. And if Caprice was going to offer an olive branch, he'd be a fool not to take it.

Especially with the whole birthday curveball.

Christmas had been stressful enough. He had *no* idea what to get Damon for his birthday. Surely, one of his sisters would throw him a bone and give him an idea.

Although, if not, he supposed he could always revert back to Tessa's suggestion, back when he'd asked her what he should get the man for Christmas, and just cuff himself to Damon's headboard in nothing but a pair of lacy panties.

Now that he was sure he wouldn't be brutally rejected, the idea had some merit.

But first, apparently, Micah had a party to co-plan.

I'll be there. But... I don't know where you live?

He wasn't surprised when she answered within minutes.

You know El Taco Rosa on 69th Street.

It was a statement, not a question. Micah wondered if Damon had told his family it was where they'd had their first "date".

I do.

I'll pick you up there in an hour. Don't be late.

Which was how Micah found himself loitering a small distance away from the alleyway where he and Damon had first met an hour later. Back then, he'd been undercover in a canary-yellow crop top and an obscenely tight pair of leather pants.

Today, he couldn't be dressed more differently – in clothes Damon had bought him. He was wearing black slacks and matching penny loafers along with an oversized plum-colored cashmere sweater that was constantly threatening to fall off his shoulder. (Not that anyone could see that considering Micah had layered a heavy jacket over the ensemble. He'd even put on a hat and gloves, knowing Damon got huffy when Micah didn't dress appropriately for the weather.)

Micah had no idea what sort of car Caprice drove, and she hadn't seen fit to tell him over the phone, so he leaned nervously against the brick exterior of El Taco Rosa, keeping an eye out for what he assumed would be some ostentatious vehicle – a bright red Ferrari or maybe a flashy Cadillac.

He was surprised when a discreet, black Volvo pulled up in front of him. Doubly so when the passenger's window rolled down to reveal Caprice's husband, Jason, behind the wheel.

"Hey," he said, offering Micah a friendly grin as he stretched over the seat and opened the door. "Caprice told me you needed a ride to our place."

It figured she couldn't be bothered to come get him herself. "Uh, yeah, thanks," Micah said, hopping into the car and making sure to shut the door behind himself. "I hope she didn't strong-arm you into picking me up. I could have just taken the subway or gotten an Uber if I'd known she didn't feel like getting me herself."

Jason raised his eyebrows incredulously as he carefully rejoined traffic. "Damon allows you to take public transport?"

Micah felt a twinge of annoyance at Jason's obvious disbelief. "I'm not sure what you think you know about my relationship with Damon, but he's not actually in charge of me." He lifted his arm and flashed Jason his watch. "Besides, he got me this – panic button and all."

Jason stiffened, seemingly surprised by that – for all of a second, anyway – before his shoulders loosened and his face morphed back into its default benign expression. He was quiet for some minutes. "I didn't mean it as an insult," he said eventually. "Damon is just well-known for his... protective streak," he settled on eventually. "I would know, seeing as I married one of his sisters."

"My condolences," Micah muttered under his breath – though not quietly enough judging by Jason's sudden bark of laughter.

"Caprice is... a handful," he admitted cautiously after regaining control of himself.

"That's *one* way of putting it."

"She's like her brother – overly protective of those she loves. She thinks you're only with Damon for his money and that you're bound to leave him heartbroken," Jason said, surprisingly candid.

"Is that what *you* think?"

Jason shrugged. "Doesn't matter what I think. Damon obviously cares for you so her behavior is unacceptable. I'm sorry."

Micah frowned – at the non-answer and apology both. "You shouldn't apologize for other people's actions."

Jason hummed. "Maybe I'm apologizing on my own behalf."

Micah side-eyed Jason. "Why? You've been polite to me – nice even."

The man shook his head – the motion so miniscule, Micah barely picked up on it. "If I was nice, I'd have told you a long time ago to run as far away from this family as humanly possible – while it was still a viable option."

Micah crossed his arms over his chest, his earlier annoyance making a reappearance. "I had that talk with Uncle Marco already."

"Really?" Jason's eyebrows shot upwards again. "Huh. He must like you then."

Micah snorted in disbelief. "He tried to bribe me into leaving Damon, and when that didn't work, he resorted to threats. Does that sound like he likes me to you?"

"He wouldn't have given most people a chance to respond to threats."

He would have just killed them, in other words.

Micah rested his head against the seat. "I can handle myself," he muttered, not sure if he was trying to convince himself or the man beside him.

It didn't matter. Jason didn't argue with him, and they fell into silence until entering a gated community on the upper east side of Manhattan. Micah had assumed Caprice and Jason resided in an upscale high-rise like Damon, but to his surprise, Jason parked in front of a classic brownstone.

The house was on a corner lot, four stories tall, and easily twice the size of any of its immediate neighbors, but what made it truly stand out was the fact that it had a fenced-in yard. It was snow-covered at the moment, but Micah could imagine how vibrantly green the grass looked in contrast to its muddled brown and gray surroundings in the spring.

"Nice place," Micah said, truly meaning it as he stepped out of the vehicle. Micah imagined it was easily worth millions – probably well into the eight figures. (Hell, Jason had probably had to sell his soul to get his hands on an actual yard in the city.)

"Caprice wants our kids to a have a place to play as they grow," he said, seeing how enviously Micah eyed the plot of land.

That's right. Damon had mentioned they were trying for a baby – without much luck so far, unfortunately.

Unsurprisingly, Jason and Caprice had an excellent security system in place, with Jason having to scan his thumbprint before they were even allowed entrance.

Their home was as lavish on the inside as Micah expected. Taking in the dark wood floors, monochrome color scheme, and oddly familiar metal flower-like decorations on the wall, Micah suspected Caprice had had a hand in decorating Damon's penthouse.

Their house was open concept, and Micah only had to remove his shoes and coat and take a few steps inside to get a full view of the state-of-the-art kitchen, the dining room with its grandiose chandelier hanging above a mahogany table, and the living room filled with cream-colored furniture. Off to the side, there was a spiral staircase that Micah assumed led to the upper floors of the house.

The place was spotless, and Micah wondered if Caprice had a maid or cook like Damon, despite seemingly not having a job herself. (*Probably.*)

In addition to being spotless, the house was empty. Quiet.

Micah frowned, and for the first time since Jason picked him up, he felt a trickle of unease slither down his spine. "Where's Caprice?"

No sooner had he asked the question did he feel the bite of cold metal against the back of his head. "I'm afraid Caprice is… out."

Micah swallowed hard, thoughts running through his head at the speed of light as he debated how to play this because… *what the fuck was happening right now?*

Except Micah knew exactly what was happening. Jason had the barrel of a gun pressed against the back of his head, digging into his scalp. He just didn't know *why*.

Without permission from his brain, Micah's mouth decided the best way to deal with the situation was denial. "Oh? What's she up to?" he asked, shocking even himself with how nonchalant he sounded. "Shopping?" *For bleach to get out the bloodstains, perhaps? The rug in the living room did look awfully expensive – it wouldn't do to ruin it with brain splatter.*

You've been trained for shit like this, Micah, get it together!

Grasping valiantly at any piece of knowledge he'd retained from said trainings, Micah turned to face Jason. After all, most people had more qualms about shooting someone point-blank if they had to look their victim in the eye.

But "most people" weren't mafia-hardened criminals, and Jason's expression didn't change. His eyes remained a cold, unyielding green. Micah had a stray thought that they weren't nearly as intimidating – or pretty, for that matter – as Damon's when he was mad.

But the revolver Jason wielded more than made up for that. "Give me that watch," Jason ordered.

Fuck.

"Is it even Damon's birthday?" Micah asked in a desperate bid to distract him.

His brain was assaulted with the mental image of a smug Caprice presenting Damon with a shiny, bow-adorned box, Micah's severed head lying inside. Micah quickly pushed aside the morbid image, forcing himself to focus. He couldn't give Jason the watch – not when it was his best shot to get out of this – whatever *this* was.

But it didn't seem like Jason was going to give him a choice. He dug his gun so hard into Micah's forehead that he was sure it'd leave indents. "The watch. *Now.*"

Seeing no other option other than to comply, Micah unclasped the watch from his wrist – hands surprisingly steady as he gave it to Jason, who immediately pocketed the timepiece.

"Now your cellphone," Jason said.

Moving slowly and nonthreateningly, Micah did as he was instructed. But Jason only frowned, confused when Micah handed over his cracked phone – the state-of-the-art iPhone Damon had gifted him left behind in his apartment as usual.

"What the fuck is this?"

"My phone." Micah didn't actually say *"duh"* – he wasn't suicidal – but his tone certainly implied the word.

Jason scowled. "Don't be a smartass. There's no way Damon allows you to strut around with only this piece of trash for communication."

Micah shrugged. "Like I said in the car, you don't know shit about mine and Damon's relationship."

Micah became intimately acquainted with Jason's gun – a semi-automatic revolver, he was pretty sure – when the man jammed it into his side.

Micah winced, but he forced himself to remain as still as possible as Jason patted him down and turned out his pockets, all the while digging the barrel of his gun into his ribs, threatening to blow apart his insides.

"Damon will murder you, you know. If you go through with this." It wasn't even a threat – it was a fact.

Jason didn't respond, but he seemed satisfied that Micah didn't have any other communicative devices on him because he removed his gun from Micah's side and took a step backward.

"Sit down," he said, gesturing at the couch in the living room. Micah imagined blood would be a nightmare to get out of the cream-colored upholstery.

"You don't have to do this," Micah said, even as he hesitantly obeyed and lowered himself onto the couch.

Assuming he intended to kill him, Micah wasn't sure why Jason hadn't just shot him already. He'd had plenty of opportunity. Whatever the reason, it gave Micah hope that maybe – just *maybe* – Jason didn't *actually* want to kill him, and perhaps he could salvage the situation without bloodshed.

That didn't mean Micah didn't have to force down the urge to thrash or kick out when Jason pulled out a pair of zip ties and used them to bind his wrists and ankles together. Reminding himself that he'd been trained how to get out of zip ties, Micah forced himself to remain calm, pushing the panic he could feel threatening to rise in his chest as deep down as he could, even as the plastic wire dug into the thin skin of his wrists.

Still, he couldn't quite bite his tongue. "Why do you need to tie me up if you're just going to shoot me?"

"Jesus, do you ever shut up?" Jason snapped. Maybe Micah should have been scared at the man's obvious displeasure, but mostly, he was just glad to have finally prompted a reaction from him. "You're nearly as fucking annoying as Caprice."

"Is that why you're doing this?" Micah pressed, sensing an opening. "Caprice? Does she really hate me so much?"

"Caprice has nothing to do with this," Jason denied. "Well, not nothing," he acquiesced. "She may not know what I'm doing, but it *is* almost entirely her fault. I, for one, actually like you, Micah."

Micah was pretty sure it was frowned upon to hold people you liked at gun point, but he swallowed down that observation. "Then let me go," he said simply instead. He still wasn't sure why Jason seemed set on killing him in the first place. "We'll talk through whatever's bothering you... and Caprice," he tacked on.

Jason smiled. "That's sweet. I can see why Damon likes you. And like I said, I was willing to let you be. I thought you were a good match for Damon even, especially since you came equipped with a dick instead of a pussy." Jason's features transformed into a scowl. "But then my bitch wife couldn't keep her damn mouth shut. She's nearly ruined everything with her irrational hatred of you. Did you know Damon has already halved her monthly allowance? He's threatened to strike her from his will, even demote me – thinks I'm some pussy-whipped bitch."

As relieved as Micah was that the man was talking, the more he spoke, the more confused Micah grew. "I-I'm sorry Damon did that," he eventually managed to stutter. "He shouldn't have. Family's important, and you're obviously very good at what you do. But I can talk to him," he quickly added. "I'll convince him to restore her allowance and whatever else." Micah debated for a second whether he ought to keep going and address what else Jason had said – that shit about being relieved Micah was a guy and not a girl – but in the end, curiosity won out. "Why were you so happy I have a dick, and not, you know…?"

Jason snorted. "Why do you think? Two men can't exactly have children, can they?"

Well, not in the traditional way, but there were obviously other options, like surrogacy or adoption. Not that Micah was about to point that out. "Why would you care whether or not Damon has babies?"

Jason took a seat on the coffee table directly across from Micah, gun still in hand, but it was fairly relaxed by his side. "Because if Damon ever procreates, his children will automatically inherit the family business," he spoke slowly, like Micah was dense. "If, however, Damon remains childless, his sister's sons are first in line to inherit. Caprice is the oldest. Why do you think I married such a frigid bitch in the first place?" Jason shook his head. "Of course, if I had known the useless whore would take so damn long to get pregnant, I probably would have passed her up for Joelle. But what's done is done. She'll have my son eventually." Jason eyed Micah pointedly. "Not that any of that will matter if she's cast off before the boy is even conceived. Thus, the source of my problem – the cause of her feud with Damon – needs to be eradicated."

Micah needed to be eradicated, is what he meant.

Micah was stuck between feeling bad for Caprice because she was married to a manipulative, power-hungry psychopath who obviously didn't care about her beyond her reproductive organs, and annoyed with the woman that her irrational hatred of him had put Micah in the guy's crosshairs to begin with.

"If you're so convinced that I need to be 'eradicated', then why haven't you shot me already?" Micah asked sharply, because, apparently, he was an idiot.

"Don't think that I won't," Jason snapped back, fingers tightening noticeably around the gun. "But I prefer not to. Shooting people… it's a messy business, and there are plenty of other ways to off someone without spraying the evidence of the crime all over your house." With that, Jason stood, pulling something out of the pocket of his suit jacket and placing it on the coffee table.

Micah stiffened when he recognized the items. A small vial of clear liquid and a syringe with a needle.

"You're a prostitute," Jason said, tone indifferent. "They overdose all the time. Hookers live harsh lives, after all. I imagine they're constantly haunted by all the things they've been forced to do to survive – even those being pursue by surprisingly soft billionaires. Heroin provides a tempting temporary escape. Though, of course, it won't be so temporary for you."

Micah took a deep breath in through his nose, knowing he would have to make his move soon if he wanted to get out of this alive. "Damon will never believe it," he protested, carefully rotating his hands as much as the zip ties allowed, attempting to gradually shift the locking mechanism of the makeshift cuffs so that it was positioned exactly in the tiny space between his wrists. "He knows I don't do drugs."

Micah was forced to stop his wriggling when Jason once again lifted his gun and pointed it at his head. The man scrutinized him with shrewd eyes, and Micah thought for a moment that he'd successfully popped a hole in his plan. But after a moment, Jason only shrugged. "Maybe," he said, unscrewing the vial of heroin with his free hand and expertly filling the syringe with the liquid drug. "But then he'll assume your death was the work of his enemies – of which he has many. The guilt will eat away at him – he'll *drown* in it, and maybe even get so depressed that he'll save me the hassle of having to off him and do it himself."

If possible, Micah's alarm magnified. "You're going to kill Damon?" His voice came out more panicked then he intended.

Jason shrugged, cool and collected as he answered. "Eventually, yeah. After all, what's the point of being next in line to the throne if the throne's occupied?" He took a step into Micah's space, looming over him with the syringe. "Now be a good boy, and stay still for me, won't you?"

Maybe it was the fact Jason had implored him to be a "good boy" – something only Damon had ever done.

Maybe it was because his mind was screaming that Damon might die if he didn't somehow get out of this situation to warn him.

Or maybe it was simply that the syringe was inching too close to his arm for comfort.

Whatever it was that ultimately prompted Micah, he acted.

Micah's ankles may have been tied together, but that didn't mean he couldn't move this legs. As soon as Jason got close enough, he leaned backward and thrust his legs up, nailing the man in the crotch with his knees.

Jason howled, his gun-free hand instinctively going to cup the family jewels.

Taking advantage of the man's momentary occupation with his balls, Micah lifted his hands up above his head and then brought them down as forcefully as he could, elbows out. The momentum, along with the weight of his arms, was enough to snap the zip tie – just like it had been in police training.

That didn't mean it hadn't hurt. Micah's wrists were inflamed, and stinging fiercely from the maneuver, but he didn't have time to focus on that. Instead, he leapt forward as much as his bound ankles allowed and tackled Jason to the ground.

He fought for control of the gun, knowing possession of the weapon was all he needed to turn the tables.

Speaking of tables... the coffee table had toppled with the force of Micah's tackle, the glass surface shattering upon impact, and Jason cussed up a storm as Micah wrestled him in the splintered remains.

"-going to kill you, you stupid cunt-"

"-goddamn wily whore-"

Judging by stature alone, Micah guessed they were about equal in strength. He may have even been stronger than Jason with desperation on his side, but the fact of the matter was, Micah's ankles were still bound together. Focused as he was on getting the gun, it wasn't all that surprising Jason managed to knee him in the gut hard enough to knock the breath from his lungs.

Micah sucked in oxygen, resisting the urge to curl into himself, but the split-second distraction was all Jason needed to bring the gun down hard onto the side of his head.

Stars burst behind his eyes, and Micah had barely comprehended the fact that he'd been *frickin' pistol whipped* before the gun was coming down again, just as hard, and connecting with his temple once more.

Micah blacked out for what was probably only seconds, but seconds was all the time Jason needed to climb atop his prone form, knees on either side of Micah's torso, caging him in. Jason continued to cuss him out even as Micah bled sluggishly from the head, dazed from what was probably a concussion in the making.

Looking back, it was a miracle Micah even heard it over Jason's temper tantrum and the ringing in his ears: the sound of the front door creaking open and the telltale *click clack* of high heels against the wood floor.

Jason heard it, too, stiffening above him.

Micah turned his head from his spot pinned beneath the man just in time to see Caprice, sharp features uncharacteristically expressive in their shock, drop a bottle of wine onto the floor.

Crash.

Its shattered remains joined the rest of the glass on the floor.

For a moment, all was quiet. Then-

"What the fuck is going on here?"

CHAPTER TWENTY

"What the fuck is going on here?"

Caprice's voice was dangerously soft, but Micah had to give Jason credit – the man didn't flinch. In fact, he recovered from her unexpected arrival rather commendably.

Giving Micah a quick once-over, and apparently deciding he'd scrambled his brains enough that he was no longer a threat, he climbed off him. "I thought you were having a spa day with Renata."

Jason sounded awfully accusing for someone who'd just been caught red-handed in the middle of a murder attempt.

"Renata got sick so we had to cut it short." A pause. "Why is Micah tied up in our living room, bleeding out on my Martin Brudnizki rug?"

On one hand, she sounded more pissed about the rug than the fact that Micah was hurt. On the other hand, Micah was pretty sure that was the first time he'd ever actually heard her say his name when referring to him – so maybe she did care... at least a little.

"And what the fuck did you do to the coffee table?"

You know, probably.

"I'll clean it up," Jason hastily assured her. "And I'll replace the rug. I was just scaring Micah, roughing him up a bit to warn him away from your brother." He glanced around at the mess. "Things got a little out of hand."

"A *little* out of hand?" Caprice repeated incredulously.

"I did it for you," Jason shot back. "Everything I do is for you." *Fucking liar.* "But I'll clean it up – make everything as good as new."

"And are you going to make *Micah* as good as new?"

"He-he wasn't just roughing me up," Micah finally managed to speak, pleased that his words weren't overly slurred despite the fact his tongue felt heavy in his mouth and he could taste the coppery tang of blood. "He means to kill me." Micah wasn't super sure

Caprice would care, to be honest, so he made sure to add, "He's going to kill your brother too. As soon as you conceive."

"Shut up!" Jason barked at him, taking a threatening step towards where Micah was attempting to push himself up off the floor. (It would help if the walls would stop spinning.)

"H-he's only with you for your uterus. He wants to use your baby to usurp Damon's spot as head of the family."

"You can't listen to this crazy, gold-digging whore, baby. He'd say anything to turn us against each other – to turn *Damon* against us. He just wants us out of the picture so that he can have Damon and all his money to himself."

Micah fought the urge to scoff. *As if.* He turned to Caprice, begging Damon's sister with his eyes to believe him – someone she'd hated at first sight – over her husband. "Please, Caprice."

"How stupid do you think I am?"

Micah's heart sank.

But then, miraculously, she reached into her purse and pulled out her cellphone, and her eyes were pure ice as they turned and met Jason's head-on. "Damon's going to fucking slaughter you for making him bleed."

Thank Christ.

Unfortunately, before Micah's colossal gratitude even had a chance to sink in, Jason was moving. "Fucking bitch!"

He slapped the phone out of Caprice's hand and grabbed her by the hair, tugging at the roots and yanking her head backward so that her neck was bent at an awkward angle. He dug the barrel of his gun into her head, much like he had to Micah earlier.

"Hey! Leave her alone!" Micah forced himself onto wobbly feet, his ankles still connected via zip tie.

"Stay the fuck back!" Jason shouted, cocking the gun. "Or I'll blow her brains out."

Micah froze.

With his plan falling to pieces in front of him, it seemed Jason was no longer adverse to using the gun. And he had it aimed at Caprice – Damon's sister. Feuding or not, the man would never forgive Micah if he allowed her to get hurt.

"There's no logical way out of this, Jason," Micah said, hoping to appeal to his common sense. He carefully shuffled closer to the pair. "Just let her go – let *us* go – and skip town while you still can."

Caprice sneered from where Jason had her by the hair, apparently not cowed at all despite having a loaded weapon pressed against her head. "Even if he flees the country, Damon will *never* let him go. He won't stop until he's hunted down, and he'll make him *beg* for death before granting it."

Micah shot the woman an incredulous look. "Yeah, not helpful, Caprice," he hissed.

"Don't worry your pretty head about it, Micah," she said in response, sounding entirely too calm considering. And it was only because he was looking at her that he noticed her sink her hand into the inside of the blouse she was wearing. "He's not going anywhere."

Before either Micah or Jason could ask what the fuck *that* meant, she was yanking a tiny bottle of some sort of aerosol can out from between her breasts and spraying Jason full in the face with it.

Jason screamed, hands automatically releasing Caprice and going to his eyes.

Pepper spray, Micah realized dazedly.

Figuring that was his cue, he half-leapt/half-fell into the man, and took him down to the floor – again. This time, though, Micah had the advantage. Jason couldn't even open his eyes to fight back, and before the man could react, Micah grabbed him by the wrist of the hand that held the gun and thwacked it repeatedly against the floor until Jason was forced to release the weapon.

The revolver skidded across the floor. "Caprice, get the gun!"

She didn't need to be told twice. Moving faster and more gracefully than any woman had the right to in heels like the ones she was wearing, Caprice snatched the gun up off the floor.

"Quit your blabbering before I spackle the kitchen with your viscera," she snapped at the wailing Jason.

"Do you have anything to hold him with?" Micah asked as he flipped Jason onto his stomach and wrestled his hands behind his back. "Some more of these handy-dandy zip ties, maybe?"

Caprice pressed her lips together. "Hold on," she said, digging through a drawer in the kitchen before tossing Micah a massive roll of... duct tape?

Micah blinked. "That works."

He made quick work of restraining Jason's hands, and then figuring it was better to be safe than sorry, returned the favor of binding his ankles together.

Only once the immediate threat had been neutralized, Micah turned back to Caprice. "Got anything to cut these with?" he asked, pointing to his own restricted ankles.

She frowned before shuffling back into the kitchen, returning with a steak knife this time, which she immediately handed over.

"Thanks."

Caprice picked her phone up from where Jason had smacked it onto the floor as Micah sawed himself free. "I'll call Damon," she offered.

Micah tensed. "No!"

Caprice raised an unimpressed eyebrow. "No?"

Micah licked his lips nervously. "I... I mean, you said yourself that Damon would murder him."

"Eventually," she agreed coolly – seemingly uncaring that it was her husband they were talking about. (Then again, the man had just threatened to kill her, so fair.) "This fucker will be begging for the sweet release of death by the time my brother is done with him."

And therein lie the dilemma.

Allowing Damon to torture this man – letting him *kill* him – went against everything Micah stood for and believed in as a member of law enforcement.

Sure, Micah had known for months now that Damon was up to his eyeballs in crime – he was a mafia don, for fuck's sake – but Micah had never been a direct witness to anything.

He'd been privy to vague conversations, full of connotation and suggestion... but overhearing Damon hissing what sounded like threats in Italian and occasionally Spanish over the phone was different than permitting the murder of another human being.

Willfully ignorant as it was, Micah had been able to separate Damon (the violent mafia boss) and Damon (his doting… boyfriend?) in his mind, so much so that he practically considered them two entirely different people. But they weren't… they were the *same*. And Micah's two versions of Damon were fast fusing together. Which left Micah with a decision to make.

Could he really allow Caprice to call Damon with a clear conscience, knowing that it would lead to Jason's inevitable murder?

Sure, Jason had tried to kill him. He'd tied Micah up, held a gun to his head, and had attempted to bash his skull in with that same gun. Was it really *so* unreasonable if he wanted Damon to dish out his own brand of justice to the man in retaliation?

Oddly, it wasn't what Jason had done to Micah that made a dark, twisted part of Micah whisper *no, it's not unreasonable at all.* It was what he'd *threatened* to do to Damon.

Then there was the fact that Micah's identity would almost certainly be revealed if he did what he ought to do – what he was morally and legally obligated to do – and called the police.

Did he really want to blow up his own life – put his career on the line, ruin irrevocably his relationship with Damon – over some violent criminal who had just tried to kill him? Who undoubtedly had dozens, if not hundreds, of other illegal acts under his belt? For all Micah knew, Jason had *successfully* committed murder before.

Was it worth it? Was *he* worth it?

Caprice certainly didn't think so, judging by the half-confused/half-disgusted way she was eyeing Micah. She probably thought he was suffering from some sort of brain trauma from being hit one too many times on the head. He could feel blood still sluggishly leaking down the side of his face – and he knew that *that*, combined with the badly chafed wrists and the undoubtedly wild look in his eyes, probably made him look quite… brittle.

Eventually, Caprice returned her attention to her phone. "I'm calling him," she said authoritatively. "I'll be sure to tell him to bring a doctor."

"Let me do it!" he blurted before she could finish making the call.

She glanced back up, clearly skeptical. Micah must have looked really pathetic, though, because after a moment, she sighed. "Fine," she snapped, handing Micah her phone. "Hurry up then."

She already had Damon's number pulled up on the screen. All Micah would have to do was hit the "call" button. And he wanted to – *so* fucking desperately. His fingers hovered above it in indecision.

Then, taking a deep breath in through his nose, Micah made a choice that he knew had the potential to destroy *everything* – and hit three familiar digits.

"You've reached 9-1-1. What is your emergency?"

Micah cleared his throat. "Hi, yeah. My name is Micah Hart, and a man just tried to kill me."

Caprice was still holding Jason at gun point a few feet away, and he saw in his peripheral vision the way she stiffened, but he refused to look at her despite the fact her eyes burned a hole through him. That didn't stop her from hissing at him like an angry cat. "What are you doing?" She took a furious step forward. "Who did you call?"

Micah shuffled backward in case she tried to snatch the phone away.

"What's your location, Micah?"

Micah rattled off Caprice's address, and the woman cursed.

He did his best to ignore her – and Jason, who still bleated pathetically every few minutes – and simply focused on answering the 9-1-1 operator's questions. It helped that she had a calm, even voice.

"Are you safe?"

Micah glanced at Caprice. "Relatively." (The operator hadn't liked that.)

"Is your attacker still on the property?"

"Yes, but he's restrained. I duct taped his arms and legs together."

A bewildered pause. *"Okay. Does he have a weapon?"*

"A gun – some sort of semi-automatic revolver. But we got it away from him."

"We? Is there anyone else there with you besides the perpetrator?"

Micah winced. "My... friend? Her name's Caprice." The woman in question scoffed, shaking her head in obvious derision.

"Are either of you hurt?"

"No. Well, my head is bleeding," he amended, "but it's nothing life-threatening."

"I'll dispatch an ambulance," she assured. *"In the meantime, if it's safe to do so, I want you and Caprice to go outside to meet the officers who are on their way to you. Make sure the gun is in plain view when they arrive, okay? Stay on the line with me, and let me know when you hear the sirens."*

Micah turned towards Caprice. "She wants us to go outside," he reiterated.

Caprice pursed her lips at the news, but after a brief stare-off with Micah, she merely huffed and led the way.

It was cold outside without his jacket or even his shoes on, the snow quickly wetting his socks, but Micah could barely feel it. (*Probably the shock*, said a voice in his head that sounded an awful lot like Tessa.)

Tears sprang in his eyes at the thought of his friend. Maybe the totality of the situation was finally catching up with him – he'd almost *died* – but at that moment, Micah would have given just about anything to be on the receiving end of one of Tessa's bone-crushing hugs.

He cleared his throat. "What precinct is responding?" he asked the woman on the phone.

"Um, let's see... that would be the 9th precinct, stationed in east Manhattan."

"Can you contact Detective Tessa Gallagher of the 105th precinct in Queens and inform her of the situation? Tell her to get here – if you can, *please*."

Micah didn't get to hear the operator's response before the phone was abruptly taken from him. He watched numbly as Caprice hung up on the woman, glaring at Micah so harshly he was shocked he didn't combust on the spot.

"We were supposed to stay on the line," he said dumbly.

Micah knew, logically, that it was her husband, Jason, who'd just tried to kill him – but in that moment, he found Caprice much more intimidating.

She didn't respond to his stupid remark. "You said you were calling Damon," she accused bitingly instead. "What the fuck?"

Anything Micah could say in response – any excuse or reason he could possibly come up with – got stuck in his throat.

"Well?" she snapped. "Just how hard did that idiot inside hit you on the head that you somehow mixed up Damon, my brother who runs a goddamn illegal empire, and the fucking police? Do you have any idea what you've done?"

Micah could only nod. He *did* know – but she didn't, not yet.

"Well, what do you have to say for yourself?"

"I'm sorry."

"You're sorry?" Caprice scoffed. "You didn't seem very sorry a minute ago on the phone. And asking for some detective by name? Since when the hell are you friends with anyone on the force?"

Micah swallowed. "Since my dad is the captain."

They may have been standing outside in the tail end of December, but somehow, Micah still felt it drop about ten degrees at his confession.

"What did you just say?"

Something inside Micah screamed for him to stop – to fucking *take it back* – before he ruined everything. But he'd known what was going to happen – what was inevitable – when he'd made the call, and it was only a matter of time until Caprice did too. Until *Damon* knew. "My father's the captain of the 105th precinct in Queens."

And I'm a police detective.

Micah was too much of a coward to admit that part out loud.

Unfortunately – or maybe, *fortunately* – he didn't get a chance to see how Caprice would react to the revelation about his dad, because a moment later, the sound of sirens filled the air, and there simply wasn't time.

"Listen," Caprice all but snarled at him, grabbing him by the front of his sweater. "I invited you over to my place to... to-"

Realizing she was attempting to come up with a cover story, Micah quickly finished for her, "-to help plan Damon's birthday party."

Caprice scowled, but acquiesced. "I invited you over to help plan Damon's birthday party. Jason walked in on us in a compromising position and assumed we were having an affair. In a jealous rage, he went mad – tied you up and beat you bloody. Eventually, I was able to take him off guard, and we flipped the tables on him. That's the story. If you know what's good for you, you won't stray from it."

"I won't," Micah assured. It was the least he could do.

The flashing red and blue lights visible down the block were quickly approaching.

Intimately familiar with police procedure, Micah plucked Jason's gun from Caprice's hand before she could protest and kicked it down the sidewalk a good distance away from them. He had his hands in the air above his head before the first cop even got out of his patrol car, Caprice reluctantly following his lead.

From there, things were a blur.

Micah was led to the back of an ambulance, where his head wound was examined. The medic, a lovely middle-aged woman named Tracy with a prominent streak of gray in her hair and an excellent bedside manner, made him lie back on a stretcher so she could shine a light in both of his eyes. He winced at the brightness, his brain screaming in protest.

Diagnosed with a mild concussion, he was given an icepack and told he would be allowed to stay on the scene as long as he permitted her to put several stitches into the side of his head where the butt of Jason's gun had broken skin. "You're lucky," she said, expertly sewing him back together, "the cut's right along your hairline, so even if it scars, it won't be noticeable."

Micah didn't have the energy to explain to her that the last thing on his mind was whether or not he'd acquired a new scar.

He wasn't sure where Caprice had disappeared to when the police had arrived, but he was given a front row seat to two officers leading a cuffed (they must have removed the duct tape) Jason to the back of a squad car.

The man had finally managed to pry open his eyes, but they were redder and more bloodshot than any junkie's Micah had ever seen, and tears were streaming down his face – whether an involuntary reaction to the pepper spray or an honest response to the bleak future he faced, Micah didn't know.

Once they had their perp in custody, the remaining policemen and women seemed content to focus their attention on Micah. "Are you Micah Hart? The one who made the call?" a burly officer with an impressive orange beard asked as Tracy fussed over his inflamed wrists, dabbing antiseptic on his broken skin.

Micah nodded.

The officer – "The name's Bernard Judson, just call me Bernard." – had just begun questioning him when he looked up, and suddenly, Tessa was there.

He didn't even get the chance to greet her before frizzy hair was suddenly in his mouth, and he was being squeezed so hard he was half-afraid the woman was going to send herself into early labor. But that didn't stop Micah from squeezing her right back. Sitting on the stretcher, he was able to bury his head into her neck, her curly hair a curtain, hiding him from the world.

Tessa's presence was like some sort of switch, and all his backlogged emotions suddenly broke free, and Micah found himself holding back a sob, his fingers curling desperately into her shirt.

"Be careful," he heard Tracy caution somewhere behind him. "He has a concussion and fresh stitches."

Tessa ran a soothing hand through his hair, careful to avoid where blood had congealed. "I can only pray it was enough to knock some sense into him."

A sound that was half-laugh/half-cry escaped Micah's mouth unbidden.

"Um, excuse me-" That was Officer Judson.

Tessa turned to face him. "Give him some space, would you? He can answer your questions later." She literally shooed him, and Micah may have found the situation funny – Tessa chasing a man twice her size away even with the pregnant belly – if a million other emotions weren't trying to make themselves known to him at the exact same time. Micah felt nauseous.

"Uh, it's my job to-"

"I know all about your job," Tessa snapped. "I'm a detective with the 105th precinct, and so is *Micah*," Tessa stressed, all but squashing him to her bosom, "so kindly back off."

Whether it was morally right or not to use their status as members of the force to get Officer Judson to back off, Micah wasn't about to stop her.

Especially since it worked. The man raised his hands in the air in the universal signal of surrender. "I didn't know," he assured before turning to Micah. "We can speak later."

Micah nodded, the "thanks" he wanted to offer stuck somewhere in his esophagus. After he left, Tessa asked Tracy, the medic, if they could have some privacy.

Then it was just them.

"What happened?" she asked immediately, finally releasing Micah from her crushing grip, only to relocate her hands to his shoulders. "Did Damon-" her breath hitched "-did he...?"

It took him a moment to realize Tessa was asking if Damon had hurt him.

"What? No!" he said, not able to get the denial out fast enough. He shook his head, immediately regretting it when a sharp pain shot through his skull. "*No*. He has no idea what happened."

Unless Caprice had told him already. (Micah had spotted the woman on the phone, some distance away, shortly after Tessa had arrived.) In that case, Damon was probably on his way to... to... Micah didn't know what the man was going to do.

"What *did* happen?" Tessa demanded.

"Not here."

Tessa looked like she wanted to protest, but Micah glanced pointedly at their surroundings – the place was still crawling with police – and she dropped the subject. "I told your dad as soon as I got the call," she said instead. "He was fifteen minutes behind me."

Micah fought the urge to groan. He was grateful for the warning, however, when the man arrived a short time later, with Jensen, of all people, in tow.

His dad loved him, Micah knew this. Captain Abram Hart just wasn't always very... tactile in his affection. This resulted in him hovering awkwardly over Micah, looking torn between wanting to hug his son and drag him into the nearest interrogation room and ask him what the hell had happened.

He seemed to settle for fussing over his injuries.

Jensen – Micah still wasn't sure *why* the man had come – had no such qualms. "What were you even doing in this neighborhood?"

Micah's mind shot to the story he and Caprice had come up with. "My boyfriend's sister lives here. We were planning a party for his birthday."

"You have a boyfriend?" Jensen repeated doubtfully, which... *ouch.*

"Why can't Micah have a boyfriend?" Tessa demanded, coming to his defense like the faithful friend she was. "He's hot as fuck *and* adorable. Not to mention he's sweet, and smart, and loyal, and kind. He's a damn catch."

Micah's and Jensen's cheeks were both tinged pink by the time she was finished. "It's not that. It's just..." He turned to Micah. "You're always so busy with work."

"And whose fault is that?" Tessa snapped.

That shut Jensen up. Micah's father, however, looked confused. And *maybe* a tad hurt. "You never told me you were dating anyone. Who's this mysterious boyfriend?"

That was his cue. The time had come for Micah to tell his dad, a frickin' NYPD police captain, that his son was dating a known mafia boss.

Sensing his nerves, Tessa grabbed his hand and squeezed. Micah held on for dear life.

But it appeared the universe had it out for him. Because before he could even open his mouth to admit anything, a dreadfully familiar Rolls-Royce was speeding onto the scene.

Micah knew immediately that it wasn't Geoffrey behind the wheel – not at the speed at which the vehicle was traveling, not with the way it was hastily thrown into park after the front wheels hopped the curb.

He was proven right when Damon jumped out of the front seat.

Micah didn't know what he was expecting. He had no idea what Caprice had told Damon, but one thing was certain as the man scanned the scene before spotting Micah in the back of the ambulance and making a mad beeline for him: Micah had never seen Damon like *this*.

Damon had an aura of power that no one could deny. But composed as he usually was – dressed to the nines and hair perfectly styled – that power had always seemed contained. Yes, he was a predator – a dangerous one, at that – but a controlled predator.

Not so tonight.

He was like an animal unleashed, the energy around him wild and chaotic and *dark*. His hair was messier than Micah had ever seen it – like a tornado had landed in it (or he'd been gripping at it in a panic since his sister had called him) – and his eyes were bright, dangerous, *worried* – and focused entirely on Micah.

"Fucking Christ," the man spat when he reached him, hands grasping either side of Micah's face, turning it this way and that – either not noticing or not caring that Micah was surrounded by a trio of police detectives. "What the fuck happened?"

Micah gnawed his bottom lip. "Jason had a gun," he said, voice small and tinny.

Damon rested his forehead carefully against Micah's. "I'll kill him," he vowed, tone gentle, but eyes mad.

Micah felt his own fill with water.

"*This* is your boyfriend? Damon fucking Romano?" Abram's voice was loud and incredulous, spearing through the serenity of the moment. Micah's father seemed stuck between disbelieving and horrified.

Damon tensed at the man's outburst. "What the fuck is it to you, pig?" he demanded, turning in Micah's father's direction. That's when he seemed to realize they were surrounded by cops, and all of them were staring. "What are you looking at? Quit standing around and do your fucking jobs."

It was then that Micah realized Caprice hadn't told him. Before that moment, he hadn't realized he'd selfishly been hoping that she had, so he wouldn't have to say the words himself.

"How dare you?" Abram spat, red creeping up his neck. "Do you know who I am?"

Damon sneered. "I don't need to know. All you pigs are the same."

"Do you lump my son in with the rest of us as well?" Abram demanded, growing angrier by the second. "Because I'm sure he'd be please to know what his supposedly loving boyfriend *really* thinks of him."

Damon's face twisted in annoyance. "Do you have dementia, old man? I don't know what the fuck you're talking about, but you need to back up out of Micah's space before you really start to piss me off."

Micah wasn't sure what hurt worse – the pounding in his head or the ache in his chest, where he assumed his heart was preparing itself for imminent despair. Either way, he knew he needed to step in before things escalated. After all, odds were both of the men in front of him were packing.

Micah dragged in a shaky breath. "It's fine, Damon. This... this is my father."

Damon froze in place.

Micah couldn't see his expression, not with his back turned, but when the man slowly spun to face him, Micah took note of how every one of his muscles had tensed. His expression, which had been so open with swirling, chaotic emotion a moment ago was now almost entirely shuttered. Only his eyes, blue and hyper-focused on Micah, remained burning with feeling. They demanded an explanation.

So Micah forced himself to give one. "Damon, this is Captain Abram Hart of the 105th precinct. He's my dad." He gestured vaguely at the others who surrounded them. "This is Detective Tessa

Gallagher and Detective Yusuf Jensen, also of the 105th precinct. They're my friends... and colleagues."

Damon stared uncomprehendingly. "Your name is Micah Gallagher," he said after a beat. "You're an ex-prostitute, who used to sell your body on the streets before I found you." (Before I *saved* you, is what he meant.) Damon's voice was like steel – hard and unyielding – daring Micah to deny it.

And Micah really, *really* didn't want to.

"My name is Micah Hart," he said anyway, voice soft, sorrowful, but ringing with truth – the opposite of Damon's, really. "And... and I'm a detective of the same precinct."

Micah could only watch as Damon's eyes emptied of emotion and became vacant, hollow things. A voice in Micah's head screamed at him to *fix it* as the wild creature who'd shown up on the scene mere minutes ago became something closer resembling a cold, emotionless machine.

Damon's expression – his voice – was completely unreadable as he turned to face Tracy, the medic, who Micah hadn't even realized had returned from the front of the ambulance. "Is he going to be okay?"

Micah wanted to believe it was a good sign he'd asked – the man must have still cared, at least a little. But how wooden and detached Damon sounded took away from any relief Micah might have felt.

"Micah has a minor concussion along with some scrapes and bruises, but with some rest and classic TLC, he should make a full recovery." She sounded entirely too sprightly considering the situation, somehow misreading the mood of her audience.

But what about my heart? Micah wanted to scream.

It was like a vice in his chest, constricting somehow further when Damon merely nodded at her before taking a pointed step backward. Micah wanted to shout for him to *come back* – wanted to somehow come up with the words to explain. But he didn't think he was capable of speech at the moment. His chest was too tight, and his throat felt inexplicably swollen – like the time he'd foolishly attempted to eat fried shrimp as a kid.

But then, without sparing Micah so much as another glance, Damon was walking away – and Micah found he *was* capable of words, after all.

"Damon, wait!" He sprang up from the stretcher, ignoring the immediate dizziness that followed. "I'm sorry! Let me explain, *please*. I didn't mean to-!"

Abram and Jensen each had an arm locked around an elbow before Micah could take more than a few wobbly steps forward. Tessa helped them corral him back onto the stretcher, all three of them attempting to calm him.

"You have a concussion, Micah."

"That's enough now. You need to rest."

"Let him go, son."

But Micah didn't want to let him go.

Whatever was happening to his heart must have transferred to his lungs, because before Micah knew it, he was hyperventilating like a child. The panic that he probably should have felt hours ago while being held at gun point hit him like a tidal wave.

He was vaguely aware of his father asking Tracy for something to help take the edge off.

Micah didn't fight it when she injected him with some kind of drug that slowed his breathing and made his eyelids heavy. He didn't fight it either, when unconsciousness beckoned. He welcomed the dark oblivion of sleep, where he didn't have to think or feel a thing.

CHAPTER TWENTY-ONE

"Sweet pea, you look like a coke addict who got hit by a car and decided to walk it off."

Micah stared blankly. "Yeah, well, I *feel* like a *homeless* coke addict who got mowed down by a *bus*, so it must not be as bad as I thought."

Tired, disheveled, and generally miserable as he was, Micah still must have pulled off sarcasm pretty well because Tessa at least had the decency to look apologetic. "Sorry. I brought ice cream." She pulled two quarts of the stuff from the reusable bag hanging off her arm – one mint chip, and one double-fudge brownie.

He waved her inside.

She'd been by his apartment every day since Damon had unceremoniously dropped his ass and triggered his panic attack in the back of the ambulance.

Micah's father hadn't wanted him to return to his apartment at all. At first citing his "episode" in the ambulance, and then his concussion. The real reason, however, had quickly become apparent on the way back from the hospital.

"Does Romano know where you live?" Abram demanded as they pulled up to Micah's apartment.

Micah didn't see the point in lying. "Yes."

Abram grimaced, his knuckles turning white where they gripped the steering wheel. "Perhaps you should consider moving back in with me for a while. Just until things blow over."

"What 'things'?" Micah asked listlessly. Surely his dad wasn't referring to his pseudo-relationship with Damon – because that was done. Finished. Over. The man had made that clear when he'd walked away. "Trust me, Damon has probably already wiped my existence from his memory, as indifferent and unconcerned with me as he would be a flobberworm."

Abram hadn't been convinced. (Also, confused over what a flobberworm was.)

Ultimately, though, Micah was an adult, and his father didn't have the authority nor the ability to keep him away from his own apartment. Abram had slept over that first night, however, and had insisted someone drop by once a day to check on him.

Tessa had eagerly volunteered.

It wasn't as if Micah's father was being unreasonable in his concern.

Although Micah didn't necessarily *fear* Damon, he had still half-expected his place to be ransacked when he'd walked through his front door with his dad. He imagined the clothes Damon had bought him torn to shreds, the mattress the man had gifted him gutted with its stuffing thrown about.

Reality was worse.

A careful pursual of his apartment revealed that nothing had been touched. Everything was exactly as Micah had left it. Which meant nearly everything in his apartment reminded him of Damon.

It was beginning to drive Micah insane.

He would open his closet to find something to wear, and there the perfectly pressed suits the man had bought him would be, draped innocently over wire hangers.

So Micah took to wearing the same stained sweats for days in a row.

He would manage to drag himself into the bathroom shower, only to be confronted with the expensive soaps and shampoos the man had got him when Micah demanded to know what sort of products Damon used that he always smelled like Christmas trees.

So Micah forwent showering, allowing his hair to become limp and greasy.

He would pry open his cabinets or the fridge to make himself something to eat, and see they were still filled with the expensive, organic snacks Damon had been constantly having delivered, and suddenly he'd lose his appetite.

Don't even get Micah started on the damn mattress.

The bed in his apartment – the one Damon had bought him – was the most comfortable one he'd ever owned. Yet, every time Micah tried to sleep on it, guilt or shame or anguish – *something* – made it feel like he was attempting to sleep on a sheet-covered slab. He always ended up migrating to his lumpy couch halfway through the night.

It had only been four days since Jason had lured Micah to his house and held him at gun point. Not even a week since Micah had utterly destroyed his relationship with Damon.

But not once in that time had Micah mustered up the willpower to shower or change his clothes, he was averaging probably three to four hours of sleep at night, and he'd probably managed to lose about five pounds.

Coke addict hit by a car probably wasn't too far off.

"How was work?" Micah asked, more out of habit than anything else as he pulled two spoons from his silverware drawer and gave one to Tessa.

He flopped down onto his couch, wasting no time digging into his ice cream as soon as Tessa handed it over. "Boring," she said, sitting beside him. "It was slow for a Saturday, and desk duty sucks." She looked for a second like she might say something more, but then she seemed to think twice about it, and returned her attention to her ice cream.

Micah frowned. "What?"

"Nothing."

Yeah, right. "Is it about Nico's case?" he asked. "Did something happen-?"

Being unable to work on Nico's case was about the only reason Micah regretted being stuck at home. Officially, he was on paid leave due to the concussion, but thanks to Jensen, everyone at the precinct knew the truth: that Micah had nearly been killed because he was dating Damon Romano, a well-known mafia don.

Micah suspected his father would make him pass a psyche eval before he even allowed him to return to his job – and not just because of the potential trauma at being held at gun point.

"No, no," Tessa hastily assured, "I would have told you if there were any new developments with that."

"Then what is it? It's not like my reputation could have gotten any worse than it already is."

Tessa had done her best to protect him from the rumors swirling at work, but Micah had nagged her until she'd told him the truth. It was how he knew that Jensen had told everyone about Damon.

Tessa scowled. "Stop that. Like I've told you again and again, most of our co-workers are sympathetic."

That was only because, apparently, most of his colleagues thought Micah was a naïve, little idiot. For the most part, they all assumed he'd had no idea he was involved with such a dangerous man until Damon's brother-in-law had attempted to kill him.

"Then what aren't you saying?"

Tessa bit her bottom lip. "It's just... we got a call from the liaison of the 9th precinct in Manhattan – the one that booked Vitali."

Micah felt himself tense at the sound of Jason's surname. "And? He didn't post bail, did he?" Wealthy as Jason was, all of his finances were tied up with Damon's, and there was no way the man would allow Jason to walk free. Even if he gave less thought to Micah than a pissant, Jason had hurt Caprice, and Damon wouldn't let him get away with that consequence-free.

"No, he didn't make bail." Tessa sighed. "It's the opposite, really. He was- he was found dead in his cell this morning."

Any relief Micah may have felt at the man not making bail was immediately washed away by the ice water suddenly rushing through his veins. Dread filled his stomach like a lead weight. "Was... was he murdered?"

"Officially, it's being investigated as a suicide. He was found hanging from the ceiling by his belt." Tessa grimaced. "But, of course, his belt was confiscated with the rest of his clothes when he was booked, so no one knows how he got a hold of it again. It doesn't help matters that he was being held in one of the only cells *not* under constant surveillance."

So, Jason had either been so fearful of prison life and what it held in store for him that he'd offed himself. Or Damon, who Micah imagined had connections everywhere – even on the police force – had ordered a hit.

Either way, it occurred to Micah that everything he'd done by making that 9-1-1 call – blowing up his life, risking his reputation at work, worrying his father, utterly *destroying* his relationship with Damon – had all been for nothing.

Feeling the beginnings of a panic attack brewing, Micah put down his ice cream and dug the heels of his palms into his eyes, telling himself to *just breathe.*

You'd probably be better off right now if you had just allowed Jason to kill you.

It was a horrible, selfish thought – and Micah didn't truly believe it – but he allowed himself to experience it fully, let the anguish and melancholy that powered it wash over him – before letting it go.

"I think you should stay with me for a while."

Micah stiffened. Consumed by his spiraling thoughts, he'd forgotten for a moment that Tessa was still there. Regardless, he didn't have to think about it long before giving her an answer. "No."

Tessa frowned, and recognizing the stubborn tilt to her chin, Micah braced himself for a fight. "But what if it was one of Damon's cronies that got to Vitali? What if-?"

"Even if it was," Micah interrupted, knowing exactly where she was going with this, "Damon would never hurt me."

It was something Micah clung to – something he knew to be true deep down in his gut even as he'd watched the man wipe himself of emotion and walk away from him four days ago.

"You can't possibly know that," Tessa argued. "And even if you're right, and Damon wouldn't lay a hand on you, it doesn't mean his associates would have the same qualms. You've told me how temperamental his sisters are, how his uncle threatened you at that gala. Are you really so sure *they* won't come for you?"

Micah allowed his gaze to flitter to the floor, knowing he didn't have a sufficient answer – because while he knew with his entire being that Damon would never hurt him, he wasn't sure if the man had enough residual fondness left in him to stop Joelle, or Caprice, or Marco from seeking revenge if they were so inclined.

His lack of answer was telling, but Micah must have been doing a passable impression of a kicked puppy, because Tessa sighed. "It's not just that," she said. "I'm worried about you. It's not healthy for you to be cooped up here alone all day, brooding and miserable."

"Your only spare room is the nursery. You can't dismantle that for me. The babies could be coming any day."

Tessa waved a hand. "It's no big deal. They'll sleep in a bassinet the first few months, anyway."

She was lying. It *was* a big deal. A couple months ago, when they'd first started converting their apartment's spare bedroom into a nursery, Jasper had apparently bought paint the wrong shade of white (Eggshell White instead of Oatmeal) for the walls, and Tessa had called Micah and *cried* about it for over an hour.

It was sweet of her to offer the room, but even if he wasn't putting them out by agreeing to move in…

Micah shook his head. "I can't leave."

Tessa threw her hands up in the air, exasperated. *"Why?"*

Because even though he knew Damon had washed his hands of him the moment he found out Micah was a cop, there was a tiny, hopeful part of him – just a speck of a speck, really – that thought *maybe* if he gave Damon time to think, he would forgive Micah for his treachery and come back.

And Micah had to be home if that happened.

It was pathetic, really, how tightly he hung on to that hope – so embarrassing that he couldn't even admit to it out loud. But his thoughts must have been written all over his face because Tessa's expression softened. "Oh, Micah."

And he found himself wrapped tightly in her arms, her massive baby bump flush against him.

Micah clung to her like a child. "It wouldn't be so bad if everything in this place didn't remind me of him."

When Tessa eventually pulled away, she had a thoughtful expression on her face. "Well, if you really won't come stay with me, maybe you should consider getting rid of some of this stuff." She fingered the diamond-encrusted Rolex wrapped around his wrist. "I mean, this watch alone is probably worth a year's rent.

Micah snatched his wrist – and the watch – away from her, an anxious pang shooting through him at the thought of getting rid of it. It was the last gift Damon had given him, and he hadn't taken it off since it had been recovered from the crime scene.

Micah hadn't told Tessa, but he'd tried calling Damon on the iPhone the man had given him at the beginning of their business arrangement the day after the debacle. He'd had a minor breakdown when the robotic voice of an operator answered, informing him the number he was trying to reach was no longer in service.

The watch – with its panic button – was truly his last way to get in contact with Damon. Late at night, he contemplated what would happen if he set it off – if the man would come if he thought Micah was in trouble.

So far, Micah had been too much of a coward to find out.

Realizing Tessa was waiting for an explanation for his behavior, Micah crossed his arms over his chest, conveniently hiding the timepiece from view. "Not the watch."

He probably should have been embarrassed over how possessive he sounded – especially when Tessa's brow furrowed in concern – but Micah couldn't muster up the energy.

Besides, it wasn't like he needed the money.

He had finally worked up the nerve to check his Venmo account – the one Damon had been sending his "pay checks" to the past month, and he'd had a miniature panic attack at the six figures that glared back at him.

Way more than what the contract Micah had signed stipulated.

After calming himself down, Micah had debated whether he ought to give the money to charity, or maybe to one of the homeless or domestic abuse shelters scattered throughout the city. But it felt even more wrong to touch the money now than while he'd technically been "working" for Damon, so there it sat – yet another reminder of how colossally he'd screwed up.

Realizing Tessa was waiting for an explanation for his behavior, Micah thought over the premise of her idea. Maybe it wasn't the worst idea in the world to get rid of some of the stuff Damon had given him. Maybe, if he got rid of it, he'd be able to move on, too. (He wasn't parting with the watch, though.)

So, taking in Tessa's worried expression, Micah took a deep breath in through his nose. "Maybe... maybe we can start with the clothes first?"

The way Tessa's worried expression melted with relief let him know he'd made the right call.

She stood from the couch. "I'll get the garbage bags."

* * *

The Uber driver who picked Micah up the following afternoon watched with wide eyes as he loaded the three huge, lumpy garbage bags into the back of his van.

"Um, it's not like a dismembered body or anything, I swear. Just old clothes. Well, one is mostly shoes, but... you know. I'm not committing a crime." Although folding the custom suits Bianchi had made him into plastic bags had felt particularly illicit.) "I'm actually a detective."

The driver held up his hands. "Hey, man, I didn't ask."

Micah loved New York City.

A half-hour later, the man helped him unload the bags at the nearest men's shelter. Micah had considered donating the clothes to Goodwill or a thrift shop, but seeing how many of the clothes still had price tags – showcasing how ridiculously expensive they were – he was afraid an unscrupulous shop owner or worker would turn around and try to sell them online for a profit, which defeated the purpose of donating the clothes in the first place.

Making sure to give his Uber driver a generous tip, Micah left the clothes with a young volunteer, whose eyes had nearly bulged out of his skull when he'd started digging into the first bag. He held up one of Bianchi's suits. "Are you sure you want to get rid of these?"

Micah had been sure – until that exact moment.

Seeing someone else, even a pockmarked volunteer, who was probably fresh out of high school, holding something Damon had given him... an unexpected bout of possessiveness twisted his insides, and Micah had to fight the urge to march up to the guy and snatch the suit away.

But that was silly. Micah had no need for such fancy clothes anymore. It's not like he'd be attending any more galas or other white-tie events now that Damon was through with him.

Still, the feeling persisted. Not trusting himself to say anything, Micah offered a quick, jerky nod before hurrying out the door.

Burying his hands in his sweatshirt pockets, he sped mindlessly down one block – and then another and another – before he could change his mind. Micah didn't know where his feet were taking him, and he didn't care either. He wasn't sure when he wound up in vaguely familiar territory, but when he finally looked up from the sidewalk, he hadn't expected his body to have subconsciously taken him to El Taco Rosa.

It was where Jason Vitali had picked him up nearly a week ago, but more importantly, it was where Micah and Damon had first met. (Not counting the decrepit alleyway, anyway.)

Micah went inside.

It was only 4:00 – too early for the dinner rush, so the place wasn't very full. The booth Damon had all but frog-marched him to all that time ago was empty, so Micah sat.

It wasn't until he spotted Adella enter from the kitchen – not donning a waitress's apron this time, rather a black-and-white pinstripe jumpsuit that hugged her curves in all the right places – that he realized how stupid it was.

He didn't know what had possessed him to come in here – only that he wanted to feel connected to Damon somehow after he'd done something so... so *wrong* in getting rid of the clothes the man had given him.

Despite the fact he was dressed in jeans and a simple Mets sweatshirt – and not full on hooker gear – Adella's brown eyes lit up in recognition, and Micah stiffened, trying to mentally prepare himself to face the consequences of his brainless actions.

After all, there was no way she hadn't heard about his betrayal. Even if Damon hadn't told her, Joelle – loudmouth that she was – certainly must have. He figured the woman would cuss him out, and maybe even slap him, before chasing him out of her restaurant, probably instilling a lifelong ban.

But none of that happened.

"Mi precioso!"

To Micah shock, Adella pulled him into an unprompted hug, nearly suffocating him with her breasts. He felt slightly oxygen-deprived when she finally released him. "I was hoping you would come in again! You didn't even try the food last time, *pequeño diablo!* You had poor Damon out of his mind with worry." She winked, abruptly dropping the light scolding quality of her voice. "Not that he couldn't use the excitement of a chase. I was so pleased when I heard he'd located you, even more so when he made you his sweetheart."

She frowned, seeming to realize for the first time that Damon was not there with Micah.

"Where is that rat bastard, anyway? He hasn't shown his ugly mug since that night."

Apparently, she *didn't* know what had happened between Micah and Damon.

Micah didn't know what to do with that information, but when she demanded to know where Damon was, he couldn't stop tears from springing into his eyes unbidden. "I-I don't know."

Adella's curious expression morphed into something pitying. "Oh, you poor boy. What did that man do?"

Micah couldn't take it. Because Damon hadn't done anything. Micah was the one who'd fucked up, who'd ruined whatever sense of trust they'd built between them.

Adella kept speaking, and Micah was vaguely aware of the fact that she was insulting the man, a mix of English and Spanish cuss words filtering in his ears through the sound of his heart trying to beat out of his chest.

He shouldn't have come in here.

Micah leapt up from his seat so abruptly, he clumsily bumped his elbow into the hard ledge of the table.

Adella frowned, clearly perplexed by his baffling behavior. "What-?"

The poor woman probably thought he was on drugs, but Micah couldn't care less what she thought.

(That was a lie. He cared about what everyone close to Damon thought.)

"I-I have to go."

Then, like a possessed person, he bolted.

Down more blocks he flew, first at a healthy jog and then a full on sprint, paying no mind to the shouts that followed after him as he shouldered pedestrians out of his way, the winter wind freezing the tears on his face before they had the chance to fall.

Eventually, when he felt far enough away from the place that reminded him so much of Damon – his lungs burning from inhaling frosty air – he stopped running. Resting against the brick exterior of a random building, Micah scrubbed his face with the overly long sleeves of his sweatshirt.

For the first time since the snow had started falling in late November, he wasn't wearing a coat. Perhaps it'd been a subconscious *fuck you* to Damon since he was always on his case about dressing appropriately for the weather, or maybe Micah just didn't care now that no one was there to care for him.

Either way, his extremities were red and felt numb from the cold as he tucked his hands up under his armpits. "Pull yourself together," he muttered to himself.

But how could he when he was missing so many important pieces?

It was a melodramatic thought, but that didn't make it any less true, so when Micah eventually pushed himself away from the brick building he found himself leaning against and looked up, only to see that he'd subconsciously settled in front of a bar – not a popular club, just some hole-in-the-wall called Artie's Pub – he thought, *why the hell not?*

A blast of heat hit him as soon as he entered the place.

Although he'd never been there before, it looked like any other dive bar he'd visited. There was a pool table and some dart boards in one corner and a decades-old jukebox in the other, currently playing some crooning country song he didn't recognize. The actual bar was stretched across the back wall, the rest of the pub filled with mismatched tables and chairs.

There were only a handful of customers milling about, and all of them were huddled on the side near the pool table, none of them paying a lick of attention to Micah as they laughed – the sound loud and boisterous – at some joke one of their companions had made.

Satisfied with their lack of interest in him – he was there to drown his sorrows in liquor, not make friends – Micah took a seat on the other side of the bar.

The lone bartender, a pretty girl with the top half of her hair tied up in a messy bun and the bottom half completely buzzed, greeted him with a smile. Micah noted that she had an intricate sleeve of tattoos crawling up one arm, disappearing where it hit the cuff of her t-shirt.

"Hey there, handsome, what can I get for you?" she asked.

Micah forced a smile on his face, but it felt like a brittle thing. "I'll take a vodka soda, please, and a shot of the strongest whiskey you have." He pulled out his wallet and handed over a card. "You can start a tab."

The woman's smile wilted a little, like she was concerned that a young man with wounded, red-rimmed eyes, sitting all alone, was opening a tab so early in the evening, but after a moment, she simply shrugged. (After all, it wasn't her job to interrogate every sad-faced customer coming in desperate to get shitfaced, just to help them accomplish the task.) "Sure thing, honey."

Micah didn't blame her.

In fact, he felt nothing but grateful for the woman when she returned a minute later with both drinks in hand. He wasted no time downing the whiskey, the alcohol a painful burn down his throat. He followed it up with a swallow of his vodka soda.

"Let me know if you need anything else."

Micah took his time nursing the rest of his drink – he was looking to get pleasantly plastered, not blackout drunk. (Mostly, he just wanted to be numb.)

Still, it wasn't much later, that he was ordering another vodka soda.

As Micah sipped his drink, he read the labels of the liquor bottles showcased behind the bar, counted the number of grooves in the wooden bar top by running over them with his fingers, made up stories for the bartender's tattoos – basically anything he could think of so he didn't actually have to think.

It was dark by the time he ordered his third vodka – the sunset was painfully early in the winter – and the bar was slowly filling with a surprisingly boisterous crowd for a Sunday night.

Micah didn't really want to be surrounded by people he didn't know (or even those he did know, to be honest, unless their name was Damon), but he didn't want to go home either, so he flagged the bartender down and ordered another drink.

Micah's lips were tingling pleasantly, and his smile felt a bit more genuine when the woman handed him his fourth vodka soda. "Here you go, sweetie."

Maybe it was the constant pet names or maybe it was the concern shining in her eyes, but for whatever reason – even though she looked absolutely nothing like her – the woman reminded Micah of Tessa.

That, combined with the amount of vodka he'd consumed, was what probably made him blurt, "My boyfriend hates me!" when she went to walk away.

The woman's eyebrows shot up in surprise before she realized what he'd said, and her brow crinkled in consternation. "Who could hate a sweet thing like you?"

And just like that, the whole story came spilling out. Well, not the *whole* story. Micah wasn't quite drunk enough to reveal the fact that Damon was a mafia don. He didn't feel like telling her he worked for the police either.

So he wound up spinning a tale about how his friends had dared him to dress up like a hooker for a night, and how Damon had beat up some pervert who'd tried to assault him. Micah even told her how he had ditched him by squeezing out the bathroom window of a restaurant Damon had brought him to afterwards.

Micah described how they kept running into each other, despite the fact that millions of people lived in the city. Then he explained the deal they had made – about Micah working as Damon's escort – and how the man lived in a huge penthouse and showered him with ridiculous gifts. He told her about Italy.

But then Damon had found out what an unconscionable *liar* Micah was – that he wasn't a prostitute who needed help getting off the streets – and he'd had to describe, in excruciating detail – how the man had unceremoniously dumped him.

Working in a bar, Micah was sure the woman had heard more than her fair share of break-up stories, but she was incredibly sweet as he told the sordid tale, making sympathetic noises at the appropriate places and not questioning the massive holes in the story – like how Damon made so much money, or what Micah's job was that the man would considerate it to be worse than a prostitute.

Micah resolved to leave her a huge tip. Hell, he might even be drunk enough to dig into the funds Damon left him to do it – even if he knew he would regret it in the morning.

(It was probably still cheaper than real therapy, sadly.)

Micah hadn't realized he'd finished his drink and that he'd been hogging the woman's attention until her co-worker, another bartender who'd showed up slightly before rush hour, called over, clearly annoyed. "You planning on taking any orders any time tonight, Zoe?"

The woman rolled her eyes, offering Micah an apologetic smile. "Sorry, doll. I have to get back to work." She eyed his empty glass. "Maybe take a little break before the next one, though, hm?"

Normally, Micah hated being babied, but she probably had a point considering how flushed he could feel his face was, so he merely nodded instead of arguing.

It really had gotten busy in the past hour, the relatively small pub nearly overflowing with people. Most of the seats at the bar, and all the tables, were occupied. Micah was surprised no one had taken either of the chairs by him, but he supposed the melancholy rolling off him in waves had put off anyone who may have considered approaching.

He must have jinxed himself with the thought because not a few minutes later, he heard the legs of the chair next to him scrape against the floor.

"Hi."

At some point, Micah had decided to lay his head against the countertop of the bar, the wood pleasantly cool against his warm cheek. He reluctantly lifted his head and turn to look at the newcomer.

Micah hadn't consumed enough liquor that his vision was blurry, but he still had to concentrate more than he should have to take in the man's features. Micah's first thought was that he was very average looking.

Probably in his thirties, and neither tall nor short, the man had plain brown hair and eyes. The most remarkable thing about him was the large, square-frame glasses perched on his nose and the crocheted sweater he wore – strange apparel for a bar.

Still, something about him niggled at Micah's brain, though he had no idea why. If he'd ever seen this man before, it hadn't been a noteworthy occasion.

Regardless, he tilted his head to the side and asked bluntly, "Do I know you?"

It was rude. He probably should have at least said "hi" back first – but the man didn't seem offended if the bright smile he flashed – he had straight, white teeth – was anything to go by. "I don't think so. My name's Ren, Ren McCormick."

Micah's thoughts were moving slowly, but not so slowly that he thought giving his full name to a stranger was a good idea. "I'm Micah," he offered simply in return.

His lack of enthusiasm didn't seem to disgruntle the man – this Ren person. "Hi, Micah." A pause. "I hope you don't mind me saying so, but you looked awfully sad from across the room. I thought I would come over and try to cheer you up – maybe lend an ear to whatever's troubling you."

Micah blushed, grateful his face was already pink from the alcohol. It was pretty embarrassing – being so pathetic that even strangers felt sorry for him. "I'm fine. Just going through a bad break-up."

Micah wasn't even sure if he and Damon were technically ever even together, but he didn't know how else to describe it.

"That's rough." Ren sounded sympathetic. "Did he not treat you well?"

Micah blinked. "How did you know it was a 'he'?"

It was Ren's turn to blush. "Oh, uh, I just assumed. Am I wrong?"

"No, you're not wrong," Micah admitted – though he had no idea how the man had guessed he was gay. "As for Damon, well… he wasn't exactly nice. I mean, he was!" he immediately backtracked at the man's concerned expression. "To me, Damon was *very* nice. It's just, he was kind of a dick to other people at times, you know."

Judging by his expression, Ren didn't. "Hm. Well, I'm a firm believer that everyone deserves to be treated with love. We're all children of God, after all, are we not?"

Micah blinked. That kind of came out of nowhere. "Er, right."

The man beamed. "You look like you deserve someone to treat you nicely – spoil you even." He pulled out his wallet. "Maybe I can start by getting you another drink?"

"Uh-"

"Micah's finished drinking, actually. I just closed his tab." The bartender – Zoe – appeared out of nowhere, sliding Micah's card across the countertop. "After all, getting too drunk when you look like Micah and you're out all by your lonesome is practically asking for *some creep* to take advantage."

Her voice couldn't have been more pointed.

Nevertheless, Ren merely nodded along, pretending like it wasn't a jab towards him at all. "Of course," he agreed. He turned to Micah. "Maybe a burger then, or something to eat. You're looking a little sickly."

Micah frowned. That was rude, even if the man wasn't exactly wrong. (He'd caught a glimpse of himself in the mirror after his shower this morning, and the bags under his eyes rivaled the size of some of the potholes on Queen's side streets.)

Anyway, Zoe – who'd once again been pulled away by her impatient co-worker – was probably right. It was time for him to head home. "I was just getting an Uber, actually," Micah said, pulling his phone out of his pocket and wincing when he saw he had three missed calls from Tessa. She must have dropped by his apartment and was probably wondering where he was.

"Let me drive you," Ren offered. "That way you don't have to worry about fare. Plus, the back seat of my van is really spacious."

Micah fought to mask his incredulity, but he didn't think he completely managed it. *Did that line actually work on people?*

"That's okay. I wouldn't want to put you out."

If Micah was looking, he probably would have seen the annoyance cross Ren's face before he schooled his expression, but he was too busy searching his pockets for whatever spare cash he had to leave as a tip. "You wouldn't put me out. It'd be my pleasure."

Micah put his money on the countertop before climbing down from his chair. "The Uber's only five minutes out, so… thanks, but no thanks." He turned to walk away, but-

"At least let me wait with you!"

Micah tensed when the man – Ren – grabbed his shoulder. Even with his thought process being fogged by too much vodka, he knew Ren was being weirdly persisted.

"Like the bartender said, there's a lot of creeps out there."

She was referring to you, Micah wanted to say. But the Uber was only five minutes away, and he doubted the guy would try anything on a public sidewalk, so after a moment, Micah just shrugged. "It's a free country."

He regretted his compliance almost immediately.

Ren didn't say anything while they waited outside for Micah's Uber – just stared at Micah out of the corner of his eye – like he was trying to be subtle, but failing miserably. The silence was painfully awkward, and Micah was debating the merits of canceling the Uber and just walking to the subway when-

"Did you hear that?"

Micah felt himself tense in reaction to Ren suddenly whipping his head around in the direction of a nearby alley.

Micah frowned. "No."

"It sounded like shouting, like someone was yelling for help."

Admittedly, Micah was pretty buzzed, but he didn't think he was so drunk that he'd miss a noise like that. Regardless he took a step closer to where Ren indicated and listened closely.

After a minute of nothing but silence – well, as silent as it got on a city street, anyway – Micah shrugged. "It was probably just a stray."

"But what if someone needs help? I'm going to check it out."

"What? Wait, no-"

But before Micah could stop him, Ren was hurrying down the sidewalk and disappearing into the mouth of the alley. Micah groaned, wondering if his vow to protect the public extended to circumstances like this, but he obediently followed after the man regardless. He knew he'd have a hard time forgiving himself if someone actually *did* need help and Ren got hurt trying to aid them.

The alleyway was dark, the overflowing dumpsters casting foreboding shadows against the walls of surrounding buildings – like every other alley in Queens at night time. Micah walked the entire length of it, examining the nooks and crannies, even as Ren stopped somewhere behind him.

It was empty.

"I don't see anything-"

Micah didn't even get the chance to finish his sentence before something coarse was being pressed roughly into his face, over his mouth and nose. He stiffened, immediately swinging back an elbow and connecting with something soft.

Someone's – Ren's? – gut, judging by the grunt whoever had grabbed him let out. But neither the hand holding the... towel?... to his face, nor the arm that had wrapped itself around his chest released.

Micah threw his head backward, a satisfying *crunch* reaching his ears. He knew he'd managed to nail the fucker in the nose even before he started cursing. "Stop fighting," Ren demanded, his voice pained, but angry – proving Micah's theory about who'd grabbed him correct.

The man pressed Micah against the wall, trapping him between porous brick that scratched at his skin where his sweatshirt had ridden up and his own solid form.

He was surprisingly strong beneath the old lady sweater he wore.

Micah had avoided breathing in as soon as he recognized the fact it was a damp rag being held to his mouth and nose, but eventually, black spots started dancing in the corners of his vision from oxygen-deprivation, and he had no choice.

It had no smell or taste, but Micah knew instinctually, as soon as he breathed it in, that it was chloroform.

He fought valiantly against the darkness encroaching on his vision, and the sluggishness invading his body that made his limbs feel like 100-pound weights, but it couldn't have been more than a couple of minutes – if even that – before he lost the battle.

The last thing – the last person – Micah thought of, before unconsciousness claimed him, was Damon.

CHAPTER TWENTY-TWO

Micah's head hurt.

It felt like someone had scooped out his brain and filled his skull with cotton, and the entire thing was sore – even his ear canals, even his eye sockets.

It seemed counterintuitive. Because how could his head be pounding so fiercely if it was only full of fluff? But that's how it was.

He was lying on something cold and uncomfortable – hard like cement – but his brain wasn't functioning well enough to realize it was cause for concern. In fact, it wasn't until Micah tried to move – to stretch his arms, to scratch a persistent itch on his nose – that he realized his shoulders were on fire.

Not literally.

They'd just been forced at such an uncomfortable angle that his muscles were all but screaming at him to move. But he couldn't. Because his arms were tied behind his back with something coarse – *a rope*, his brain dazedly suggested – that was also connected to his ankles. Much like his wrists, they were tied behind his back, his thigh muscles sore as he was forced to keep such an unnatural position.

It took him longer than it should have to comprehend the fact he'd been hogtied.

The realization was finally enough to power on his brain.

Micah felt his pulse increase immediately, tendrils of terror latching onto him and threatening to drag him down into a panic attack. But Micah forced the feeling away, along with the impulse to open his eyes.

There was no point in letting whoever had done this to him know he was awake.

Instead, Micah focused on keeping his breathing even as he fought to remember how he'd gotten here – wherever "here" was.

He remembered dropping Damon's clothes off at a men's shelter and wandering into El Taco Rosa in a pathetic attempt to feel closer to Damon, only to immediately regret it when he'd been accosted by Adella.

He'd run away like an idiot and ended up at a bar – Artie's Pub – and in yet another poor decision in a long line of them, he'd decided to get drunk. He hadn't gotten completely plastered – not like the time he'd attempted to suck Damon off through his pants – but enough that his senses had been dulled and that he'd grown careless. Leaving himself vulnerable to deranged kidnappers that enjoyed wearing old lady sweaters.

Micah remembered Ren – if that was even his real name – and how he'd tricked him into wandering into a dark alley, and felt like an absolute dunce.

Micah couldn't hear anything to give away the fact he wasn't alone over his carefully controlled breathing, and knowing he needed more information – like where he was, or a clue as to why he'd been taken – he opened his eyes.

He was right. The floor was cement.

The room he was in was dark – there were no windows – and Micah strained his neck as he tried to take in as much of his surroundings as he could from his awkward position on the floor. There wasn't much to see. There were some chairs and a piece of long wooden furniture pushed up against one side of the room (*a pew?*), and against the other side of the room, there was what looked like an old desk that had seen better days. On top of the desk sat a pile of clothes, neatly folded.

Micah's clothes, to be precise – the diamond-studded Rolex Damon had given him perched innocently on top.

He'd been doing his best to ignore the fact that he was naked except for his briefs before then – a tricky task considering how sharply the cold of the cement floor bit into his bare skin.

He wasn't mentally prepared to deal with the connotations of it – the least of which was that he'd been stripped down to his underwear while unconscious. He felt defenseless and exposed enough without that particularly fucked up detail flashing bright warning lights in his mind.

Ripping his gaze away from the clothes, Micah looked at the walls. They were bare except for the one directly in front of him, which featured a mass-produced painting of Jesus, all muddy browns and earth tones except the halo of light shining directly behind his head, and a small, metal crucifix.

That, combined with *the frickin' pew* on the other side of him, made Micah suspect he was in a church. Taking into consideration how musty and stale the air was – not to mention the lack of windows – probably a church basement.

But who would kidnap a person only to drag them to church?

Ren, apparently.

The man hadn't even bothered to tape Micah's mouth shut – which either lacked foresight on Ren's part, or was an ominous sign for Micah.

He was debating the merits of opening his mouth and shouting for help – on one hand, maybe someone who *wasn't* his kidnapper would hear him, on the other hand, it would *definitely* notify his kidnapper that he was awake.

He hadn't made a decision before the sound of the door creaking open behind him reached his ears. Judging by the lack of horrified gasp, it was his kidnapper. He could feel eyes roaming his form, and goosebumps broke out across his arms.

Micah cursed the fact that he was positioned so he couldn't see who had entered the room – no matter how he strained his neck. (Though he knew by the way his body had gone into full fight-or-flight mode, that it was Ren.)

"You're awake." The man finally walked around so that Micah could see him. He knelt near Micah's head. "I'm surprised. I thought you'd be out longer, but then, you're a fighter, aren't you?" He pointedly tapped his nose, which was noticeably swollen, the bruising extending to under his eyes. His glasses were nowhere in sight.

Micah didn't know until that moment how he was going to play this.

If he was going to take on the role of docile prisoner, play nice, and attempt to appeal to Ren's moral compass (assuming he had one) or the complete opposite – if he was going to snarl and spit at the man like a cornered animal, antagonize him until he snapped and maybe made a mistake.

"If you expect me to apologize for breaking your nose, you might want to consider the fact I'm currently tied up in some dank basement because you decided it would be a good idea to *fucking take me* like *a goddamn psychopath.*"

Option two, it was.

Ren frowned. "You're scared. I understand that, but that's no reason to take the Lord's name in vain."

Was this asshole serious right now?

Then Micah remembered the man's strange religious-fueled comments at the bar. "What happened to everyone being a child of God? Treating everyone with love and respect? Was that just some line to bait me?"

"Of course not," Ren denied, and Micah stiffened when he laid a hand on his hair, *petting* him. "You don't understand right now. You're too cloaked in sin to see. But I'm doing this to help you."

"Help me?" Micah repeated incredulously. "How is drugging me or kidnapping me or taking my motherfucking clothes supposed to help me?"

"Did you know that people saw no need to cover up before Adam and Eve committed the original sin in the garden? That they felt no shame in their naked forms? They were made in the image of God, after all."

Micah tried to lean away from the man's wandering hands, but he *couldn't. fucking. move.* "And yet you're still wearing that ugly grandma sweater," he muttered.

Ren pursed his lips. "It's symbolic," he said eventually. "I'm going to cleanse you of sin – make you pure like in the times before Satan's wickedness ran rampant."

"Really? Because I just think you like the view, you motherfucking pervert-" Micah cried out when the man suddenly grabbed him by the hair, tugging so hard that tears sprang into his eyes. His neck strained at the unnatural position. His shoulders screamed.

"That is exactly why you are here," the man scolded. "You're a sinner whose mind is overwrought with filth, infesting others with your vile urges. You have no shame, brazenly flaunting your abnormality and enticing others to sin. You don't care that your sick perversion is damning not only your own soul, but all those who come in contact with you."

Frankly, that was some of the most victim-blaming, gaslighting bullshit Micah had ever heard a single person spew in so short of time. Also: "What the fuck are you talking about?"

A muscle in Ren's cheek ticked as he clenched his jaw. "Fornicating with other men," he said very slowly, like he was talking to someone particularly slow – which, rude, "is a sin. Especially when you go out of your way to lure innocents into taking part in your depravity."

It figured the man saw himself as innocent in this situation when Micah was the one tied up in nothing but his underwear in some skeevy basement, and it hurt his heart in a way that was all too familiar that Ren was apparently doing this simply because Micah was gay.

Perhaps Micah shouldn't have been as surprised as he was – he still saw the results of the occasional hate crime working for the NYPD, after all – but that didn't change how aggrieved it made him feel.

Part of what he was feeling must have been playing out across his face because Ren suddenly released his hair, trailing the back of his fingers down Micah's cheek in a sick parody of a lover's touch. "Don't worry. I'm going to make you better. That's why I took you, to show you the error of your ways and help you repent. When I'm satisfied you've renounced your ways, I'll set you free."

"What? So I apologize for being gay, and you'll let me go? Just like that?" The thought of being forced to apologize for something out of his control, something that comprised so much of his identity, made Micah feel physically sick. But if it made the asshole let him go...

"Even better. I'll send you home into God's arms, never to be tempted by sin again."

Micah froze.

Ren was going to kill him, is what he meant. And Micah didn't know why it took so long to put the pieces together, but when he did, it was like they all clicked into place at once.

Micah had been dosed with chloroform and kidnapped.

His wrists and ankles were tied tightly together with rope.

He'd been taken because he was openly gay. Sure, Micah wasn't a prostitute or involved in the sex industry like any of the man's other victims, but...

"You're the Hooker Hunter."

Ren scowled, shooting to his feet so that Micah had to strain his neck to keep looking at him. "That's a foul name the media came up with for what I do. I don't hunt anyone; I *save* them."

"You *kill* them," Micah argued, the panic that he'd been doing such a good job fighting down making a valiant effort to tighten its grip on him. "You're a murderer."

"Our bodies are temporary. It's our souls that are everlasting, and I save them from eternal damnation. If anything, I'm an angel."

Micah felt sick. "No. What you do is kidnap people and torture them – make them apologize for something they can't help, for *who they are* – and then you kill them." Ren was the serial killer the NYPD had been after for months, the one Jensen was convinced he'd captured... the one who'd killed Nico. The realization had Micah swallowing down bile. "You're a fucking monster."

Ren scowled. "Stop that."

"No!" Micah was experiencing too many emotions to have a hope in hell of containing them all, the strongest one at the moment being *rage.* "You sit there preaching all this bullshit about people like me being a blight against God, but it's *you* who's the abomination. Or have you forgotten one of the church's most sacred rules? Thou shall not kill."

"Don't you go spouting scripture at me," the man snapped. "I'm a pastor. I've studied the Bible and all related works from front to back."

Yet another piece of the puzzle clicked into place.

Miriam Murphy, the owner of one of the IP addresses they'd been investigating, had been a secretary for some church – Ren's church, apparently. And Ren had been using her wi-fi connection to watch Nico's webcam shows and connect with him – to eventually lure him out under the pretense of a date.

"I'm sure you know all about hell then – the dark, fiery pit God created specifically for pieces of shit like you. I hope when you die – which if I have anything to say about it, will be sooner rather than later – that He makes you experience every bit of hurt you've inflicted upon your victims, all the fucking terror they felt. You're a disgusting, deplorable, vile piece of-!"

Micah cried out when a heeled boot came down hard on his shoulder as the man stomped him – apparently having had enough of Micah's vitriol. He heard a disconcerting *pop* and realized half a second later, when his shoulder screamed at him, that it had been dislocated.

Micah choked back the urge to vomit.

Ren took a deep breath in through his nose. "I can see you're in no state to listen. That's fine; I'll come back later. In the meantime, *please* do your best to calm yourself."

Micah didn't bother to respond to that, too busy trying to bite back pained whimpers. The sound of Ren's boots echoed as he crossed the room, and then the door clicked shut.

Time moved strangely after that.

Micah tried to wiggle his hands out of the rope, but one arm was completely useless, and whenever he so much as bumped it with the other one, a jolt of pain shot up the limb, all the way to where his misshapen lump of a shoulder sat.

That didn't stop him from trying to yank his good hand free from the rope, but when he felt a trickle of blood start dripping down his wrist, he knew he needed to quit.

Resting his cheek against the cold floor of the basement, Micah forced himself to push away the pain and *think*. He glanced around the room as much as his awkward position on the ground allowed, figuring maybe he'd missed something useful – like a piece of furniture or piece of stray debris that could be converted into a makeshift weapon.

The metal cross on the wall looked like it had sharp edges, but, of course, Micah had no way to get to it. Or wield it, for that matter.

Inevitably, his gaze was drawn back to the pile of clothes sitting on the desk – his watch and its hidden panic button. If only Micah could access it somehow.

Even if you do get your hands on that watch, there's no guarantee Damon will come for you.

Micah ignored the cynical voice in his head, having more important things to do than entertain such negative thoughts – like figure out how to escape. But his mind kept returning to that damn watch. It *was* perched awfully precariously on top of his sweatshirt. Maybe if Micah could somehow jostle the desk hard enough, it would fall to the floor.

It was better than any other plan he'd thought of so far, so mentally bracing himself for the pain he knew was about to encompass his arm, Micah attempted to shimmy in the direction of the desk.

Turns out, he'd vastly overestimated his pain tolerance because Micah nearly blacked out at the white-hot agony that shot up his arm. He cried out, immediately trying to muffle the sound by tucking his head into his good shoulder.

After taking a minute to recover, he continued on with the plan.

It had to have taken at least an hour, and his vision was fuzzy from pain, but eventually, Micah managed to wriggle his way over to the desk.

Now how to shake it?

Realizing quickly he didn't have much choice, Micah took a deep breath before walloping his head against one of the desk's wooden legs.

Thwack.

Fuck, it hurt – and the desk hardly moved. It was a sturdy thing, made of real wood – not the cardboard-like stuff they liked to make furniture with nowadays. But Micah forced himself to do it again.

Thwack.

And again.

Thwack.

Until his ears were ringing. But the watch *was* moving, inching closer and closer to the edge of the pile.

Thwack.

And then it was falling – but in the wrong direction – and Micah couldn't contain his anguished shout when it toppled over the *back* of the mass of clothing, out of Micah's sight, falling onto the middle of the desk instead of to the floor.

Micah cried.

He cursed the desk. "Fuck you, you goddamn miserable piece of furniture!" He cussed out Ren. "You fucking bitch! You psychotic asshole!" Eventually, he even turned his ire onto the painting of Jesus that hung on the wall. "What the fuck are you looking at? How can you claim to be this righteous, all-powerful being and still allow absolute bullshit like this to happen?"

He screamed until his voice was hoarse – until his throat was raw and ragged – and what small part of him wasn't enveloped in pain was weighted down by the exhaustion of it all.

Micah was tired – physically, mentally, emotionally. And despite the precariousness of his situation – despite the fact his injured shoulder felt like it was on fire – eventually the bone-deep fatigue made it difficult to keep his eyes open.

Still, he hadn't realized he'd begun to drift until the sound of the door creaking open startled him awake an indeterminable amount of time later.

"What's this?"

Ren sounded upset, which Micah found pretty ludicrous all things considered. "What are you doing all the way over there? And you've hurt yourself."

Micah heard more than saw the man leave the room, but not more than a few minutes later, he returned with a bucket that he set down near Micah's head. Micah hadn't realized the man had also grabbed a washcloth until he dipped it into the bucket before using it to carefully dab at Micah's temple.

The cloth came away pink.

Apparently, he'd banged his head good enough against the desk to make himself bleed. He'd been so distressed he hadn't even noticed.

Micah fought back a flinch when after cleaning the washcloth in the bucket, Ren used it to wipe tenderly at his cheeks. The man frowned. "You've been crying."

The dried tear tracks must have given it away.

Micah wasn't proud of the way his voice cracked when he opened his mouth. "Why me?"

Ren's brow furrowed. "We've been over this," he said, sounding disapproving.

"You took me because I'm gay, I know. But everyone else you kidnapped were prostitutes or strippers or camboys. *You* approached me at the bar."

It was the one thing Micah couldn't figure out, unless the man was simply escalating, which was certainly possible. Judging by the way the man *clucked* at him, however, that wasn't the case. "Don't act innocent. I saw you out on the streets, months ago, practically begging for attention from men, wearing women's clothes. You ended up getting in a fancy car with some man in a suit."

It didn't take a genius to put "fancy car" and "man in a suit" together and come up with Damon.

With a jolt, Micah realized Ren had to be talking about one of the times he'd gone undercover. Micah's mouth felt dry in his shock, but he forced himself to lick his lips and get past it because maybe, just *maybe*, he could use this.

"Listen, Ren, there's been a mistake. I'm not a hooker."

Ren scowled. "Did you not hear me? I *saw* you."

"I'm a cop!" Micah blurted, so loudly that Ren actually jumped back in surprise. "I work for the NYPD. The night you saw me, I was undercover, pretending to be a prostitute in an effort to..." Micah paused, dry swallowing, "...to bait the serial killer we were searching for, the Hooker Hunter... you."

"No," Ren snapped. "I don't believe you. You're lying."

"What day is it?" Micah asked.

Ren eyed him warily, like he was debating if Micah could use the information against him in anyway before reluctantly answering. "It's Monday night."

"So I've been missing for about 24 hours. I missed work this morning. I'm not like those other people you took. My dad is a police captain. Odds are, the whole precinct is already out looking for me, and they won't stop until they find me – find *you*."

Ren shook his head in denial, but there was a nervous glint in his eye that hadn't been there before.

"Look it up if you don't believe me. My name is Micah Hart. Please, you've made a mistake."

"No!" It was the first time Micah had heard the man raise his voice since he'd taken him, but instead of being scared, Micah was satisfied to have finally prompted a genuine reaction. (A reaction that didn't include him suffering bodily harm.) "No. Even if you *are* a cop, I saw the way you acted at that club-"

"*You* came onto *me!*"

"Not the bar," Ren snapped, "the club, that new one in Queens – Club Trinity. You were letting strangers buy you drinks and *lick* your neck-"

Micah felt himself stiffen at the mention of Club Trinity because suddenly he knew *exactly* where he had seen Ren before. He knew he'd looked familiar when he'd approached him at Artie's Pub. "You tried to buy me a drink."

Ren frowned at the interruption, but when he took stock of Micah's mumbled realization, he seemed pleased. "You remember."

"That- that was the day before Nico went missing."

"Yes." The way Micah was tied up afforded him very little movement, so he couldn't even twist away when Ren cupped his cheek and ran his thumb fondly over his brow. "That could have been you."

Ren sounded *regretful*, and Micah wanted nothing more than to beat him bloody, but he forced himself to school his expression, focusing on what Ren claimed to have seen at Club Trinity.

"What you saw in the club – that man licking the salt off my neck – that was my *boyfriend*. His name is Damon Romano. He's a dangerous man with the money and means to track the both of us down when he finds out I'm missing and that you took me. When he finds us, you'll be begging him to send you to hell by the time he's finished with you. But if you let me go *right now* and get a head start on running, you might be able to put enough distance between you and him to make a clean getaway."

"It's sweet of you to worry over my well-being," Ren said, words laced with sarcasm, "but even if you're telling the truth about your boyfriend being some thug, I'm not worried." Ren tilted his head to the side. "Or have you forgotten what you told me at the bar? You broke up."

Micah's stomach plummeted. Fuck, he *had* forgotten that he'd told Ren that.

"He doesn't care about you anymore, Micah, and he's certainly not coming for you. No one is. Even if the police are looking for you, there's no way they'll find you. Just like *you* couldn't find Nico."

"Fuck you," Micah spat, voice low and gritty, but full of meaning. "You're sick."

"That's where you're wrong. *You're* the sick one. But it's okay. God brought you to me to make you better."

"God has nothing to do with this – and if he does, then he's just as much of a sadistic fuck as you are!"

Ren's grip on his face grew uncomfortably tight – until Micah's teeth were scraping against the tender insides of his cheeks, until Micah was sure it'd leave bruises. He braced himself for another explosion of violence, like when Ren had stomped on his shoulder earlier, but after a moment, the man only sighed and released him. "Clearly, you need more time to yourself to reflect on your behavior. There's no sense in starting your lessons when you're still so worked up."

Ren stood, taking the bucket with him.

Micah's throat closed up in panic.

It wasn't that he longed for Ren's company, but the prospect of being stuck down here alone again, for who knows how long this time, with nothing to do but overthink and panic, seemed indefinitely worse in the moment.

Micah unstuck his throat. "No, Ren, wait-!"

But he was too late, and the door swung shut behind the man.

Micah groaned, allowing himself to rest his forehead against the cold cement. "Fuck."

Clearly, he was going to have to rethink his strategy, because being a brat and lashing out at Ren was *not* working. It made his stomach churn, but it seemed he was going to have to play along with the sick game Ren was playing.

It would be a tricky balancing act, because if Micah acted completely "cured", Ren might decide it was time to "free" him. In the end, Micah resolved to at least be polite the next time Ren came down into the basement, and act like whatever religious mumbo-jumbo he preached in an effort to disparage Micah's sexuality wasn't pure bullshit.

The only problem was, Micah had no idea when the man would be back.

Minutes ticked by in the dark, and then hours. Eventually, Micah tried to sleep, but he was unsuccessful.

At some point, what had been minor issues when he'd first woken up – a parched throat, an empty stomach, an uncomfortably *full* bladder – became more pressing concerns.

"Ren!" he called in a fit of desperation when he thought his bladder might burst from holding it in. "Ren, please, I have to pee!"

There was no response.

He'd hurled insults up at the ceiling then, spouting every blasphemous thing he could think of to get the man's attention – until he was convinced that the basement had been soundproofed, and that no one, not even Ren, could hear him shouting.

The realization only served to make Micah feel more alone, and it made the room feel smaller, nearly triggering a claustrophobia-induced panic attack.

At some point, Micah had been unable to hold his bladder anymore and had been forced to urinate on himself, soaking his underwear and the floor beneath him.

That was how Ren discovered him some time later, lying in a puddle of his own piss, his arms and legs numb from being tied together at an awkward angle for so long. (Barring Micah's shoulder, which still radiated fire.)

Micah snapped his eyes open when he heard the door open. Ren was behind him, so Micah couldn't see him, but he could *feel* the way his eyes roamed over him, seeming to stutter to a stop on his urine-soaked underwear. *Be polite,* Micah reminded himself, *not belligerent.*

It was a task made indefinitely harder when the man actually *tsked* at him. "My, my, what a mess you've made of yourself. You're positively repugnant."

Humiliation burned brightly in Micah's chest, outmatched only by his anger, but somehow Micah forced both emotions down. "I tried to call for you," Micah said as calmly as he could instead. "I couldn't hold it any longer."

Ren hummed, walking around Micah's prone form, examining him – likely trying to tell by his expression if his spirit was as beaten down as his body. "Sometimes we need to be reduced to filth to realize that's what we really are – a foul stain upon God's glorious design." Ren paused. "But you don't have to be. You can be pure again – *clean.* Would you like that, Micah?"

Micah took a deep breath in through his nose. "Yes."

"Yes… what?"

Just say it, Micah's brain urged him, but his mouth remained sealed stubbornly shut.

Ren raised an unimpressed eyebrow. "Do you want to wash up? Or would you rather stay another night on the piss-covered floor?"

"Yes, *please,*" he said, pushing out the last word through clenched teeth.

"Good boy." Micah barely withheld a flinch when the man patted him on the head. "I'm going to untie your ankles now." Ren leaned over Micah, where he began loosening the complicated series of knots that tied his limbs together. "There's a shower in the back corner of the room. I'm going to walk you there and help you wash up. If you try *anything,* you'll wind up right back on this piss-covered floor, except instead of having one useless arm, you'll have two. Do you understand?"

"I understand."

Having secured verbal confirmation from Micah, Ren finished freeing his ankles – though he left Micah's hands remained tied behind his back.

Micah wasn't prepared for the intense pins-and-needles sensation that crawled up his calves and then his thighs as blood returned to where it was supposed to be. Even if he'd been tempted to spring an attack on Ren and make a mad dash for the door – or even the watch – he quickly realized the futility of such a plan.

Even if his hands weren't tied behind his back and his right arm wasn't completely useless, Micah could barely walk, crying out involuntarily when Ren heaved him up by his good arm and he was forced to put pressure on his feet.

He'd been tied up for so long, it felt like he was walking on shards of glass with each shuffling step forward. Luckily, it was only about ten feet to the spout and floor drain that Ren had generously termed a "shower". Unsurprisingly, when Ren cranked the water on, the spray that burst from the spout was freezing cold.

Micah's muscles locked up at the sensation, but he stayed under the water as long as Ren allowed, swallowing as much of it as he could while he was under the spray, not sure when he'd get another chance to quench his thirst.

It couldn't have been more than a few minutes before Ren was shutting off the water. Micah didn't look forward to being tied up again, the dread in his belly growing heavier by the second as Ren hauled him back to the wet spot on the floor.

To Micah's relief, however, instead of forcing him back onto the cement ground, Ren grabbed one of the upholstered chairs from near the dusty pew and placed it in the middle of the room. He sat Micah on the chair, making sure he was facing the picture of Jesus.

After securing Micah's ankles to either leg of the chair, he untied Micah's wrists, binding them to the chair's arms. Micah's vision blurred, little black spots dancing at the edges of his vision when Ren handled his dislocated arm, but he would gladly endure the pain again and again if it meant being tied to a chair instead of hogtied on the floor like an animal.

Not only was the new position much more comfortable, it was much easier to escape from – at least in theory. Micah's mind was already brimming with ideas. He'd made sure to flex his muscles as much as possible when Ren had tied him, in an effort to create slack. Could he wriggle free a hand or foot when Ren left? Could he break the chair if he toppled it over?

"Thank you," Micah said, actually meaning it – to his own surprise – and Ren's, judging by the way the man's eyebrows shot up.

"Of course. See how you're rewarded when you behave?" A smile pulled at the corners of Ren's mouth. "I think you're ready for your first lesson."

And just like that, any sense of gratitude Micah may have felt bled away as apprehension crept up his spine. Micah had no idea what these "lessons" with Ren would entail. He tried to take comfort in the fact that, besides the severe rope burn on their wrists and ankles, minimal physical damage had been done to any of the Hooker Hunter's victims – not counting the bruising on Nico's torso.

Still, Micah's brain couldn't help but conjure up all sorts of terrible scenarios, conversion therapy horror stories flooding his mind. His thoughts leapt from torture as inhumane as electroshock therapy to ideas as outlandish as Ren making him sit and watch straight porn for hours on end.

It felt a bit anticlimactic when Ren merely walked to the desk, opened one of its drawers, and took out a weathered-looking Bible. After pulling up another chair, Ren sat, making sure he and Micah were facing each other. "Listen and reflect. When I'm finished, we'll say a prayer."

With that, Ren cleared his throat and began to read.

Micah tried to focus on the text the man was reciting – something about two cities overflowing with perverts and degenerates – for all of a couple minutes. But much like when Micah was a child and his mother was still around to drag him to church on Sundays, he found his mind wandering almost immediately.

Mostly, his thoughts centered on escape. He rotated his ankles and working wrist, covertly checking for slack in the rope. It would be tough, but if he created enough friction against the edges of the chair's legs, *maybe* he could fray some of the rope and get a foot free.

"Micah!" Ren barked, abruptly yanking him from his thoughts. "Are you listening?"

Crap.

"Yeah, yes, of course. You were reading about two Biblical cities and their... uh, sexually promiscuous citizens."

Ren narrowed his eyes. "And what were the names of the two cities?"

Dammit, Micah couldn't remember. He had a vague idea of what they had been called, but for some reason, he didn't think Ren would appreciate him blurting out "Semen" and "Gonorrhea".

"Sodom and Gomorrah," Ren snapped after a full minute had gone by and Micah had failed to answer. "They were cities full of prostitutes and homosexuals who committed all sorts of depraved acts. God destroyed both cities, and all who lived there, to stop their debauchery from spreading. God *is* merciful, but only to those who repent and atone for their sins. They refused. Will you refuse, Micah?"

Fuck, what should he say?

Micah didn't want Ren to think he'd broken him already, knowing what laid in store for him once the man deemed him "cured", but he didn't want to invite his wrath either.

"Micah," Ren said warningly when he didn't immediately answer.

"I'm cold!"

Ren frowned.

"I'm sorry! It's just- I'm cold. It makes it hard to c-concentrate on what you're saying." Micah didn't even have to fake the slight tremble in his voice. He'd been shivering since Ren had yanked him out of the shower. It was the middle of winter in New York, and he was in nothing but damp underwear in some drafty basement, water still dripping from his hair. He *was* cold.

Seeming to realize he was telling the truth, Ren's expression softened. "Hold on."

Like Micah had a choice in the matter.

Ren disappeared out the door, only to reappear a few minutes later with a bath towel. Micah tensed when he used it to tousle his hair before patting dry his arms and chest. His stomach churned when Ren moved the towel lower, but to Micah's relief, he bypassed his lap completely, focusing instead on rubbing dry his thighs, calves, and feet.

Still, it was an uncomfortably intimate process, and Ren was kneeling before him by the end of it, a slightly glazed look in his eyes as he peered up at Micah, gripping the towel in one hand, knuckles white, while the other mindlessly thumbed one of the scars on Micah's knee that he'd acquired playing baseball in his youth.

Ren's pupils were blown wide, and there was no mistaking the *want* in his gaze.

If Micah could have shoved the man's hand off him, he would have. As it was, all he could really do was nervously lick his lips – a move he immediately regretted when Ren's eyes latched onto the movement.

Sure, Micah had known logically that Ren most likely only hated gay people because he was gay himself, but couldn't accept it – and that part of the reason he'd chosen the victims he had was because they'd brought out those "unnatural" urges in him.

But knowing something and seeing it were two different things. And painstakingly aware of the fact he had no way to cover up – no way to defend himself from Ren's gaze *or* his hands – made Micah feel helpless in a way he hadn't ever in his life.

Then again... maybe Micah could *use* the man's obvious attraction against him. He took a deep breath in through his nose. "It's okay," he said, making sure to pitch his voice low, keep it as soft – as soothing – as possible.

Ren's fingers tightened almost painfully around his knee at the words, but he didn't otherwise respond.

So Micah pressed on. "I don't know who hurt you, or convinced you that being attracted to other men was some unforgivable sin, but it's not. I'm not an abomination." Micah waited until the man's gaze finally shifted from his lips to his eyes, and then… "*You're* not an abomination."

Micah was anticipating it, but he still tensed when Ren suddenly stood, practically catapulting to his feet as he stared Micah down, his eyes a dark, bottomless pit. He wasn't sure what he was expecting Ren to do in retaliation for calling him out. Yell? Smack him? Spew Bible verses? But Micah could safely say he did *not* expect the man looming over him to suddenly swoop down and press his mouth to Micah's own – no finesse involved in the action at all, teeth clacking violently against teeth.

Micah yelped in surprise, nearly choking on the tongue suddenly invading his mouth, desperately seeking out his own, *suffocating* Micah with it.

Shock made Micah slow to react, but when Ren moaned loudly into his mouth, he finally regained his bearings enough to respond to the unwanted kiss by biting down viciously on the other man's tongue.

Ren yowled, yanking himself away, but not before the coppery tang of blood flooded Micah's mouth. Micah spit it out onto the floor in disgust, but he couldn't deny the satisfaction that filled him when Ren bared his teeth at him in response and blood leaked between the cracks.

"What the fuck?" he demanded.

At the same time, Ren exploded, "You manipulative whore!"

Micah blinked in shock, knowing he shouldn't have been surprised, but still taken off guard by the pure venom in Ren's voice. "*You* kissed me."

"You *made* me," Ren hissed back, eyes wild. "*Looking* at me like that. *Talking* like that. Acting like a wanton slut even with the gaze of God himself bearing down upon you."

More victim blaming then. Lovely.

Micah forced himself to remain calm. "I'm sorry," he said evenly. "I wasn't trying to- to seduce you. I just wanted to let you know that you're not alone. We're the same, you and I, and it's okay."

"We're *not* the same," Ren snarled at him, face red. "I recognize these... these sick urges for what they are: the workings of the Antichrist. You *bask* in your sins, *flaunt* them, encouraging others to eat from the same poisoned fruit."

Ren was right; they *weren't* the same. Because Micah was a rational human being, and Ren was an unhinged zealot with the biggest case of internalized homophobia Micah had ever seen.

"God made me in his image," Micah argued reasonably, figuring he might as well try the religious route since that seemed to be the only language Ren spoke, "and He doesn't make mistakes. Isn't that what the church teaches? By that logic, it *is* okay to be gay – it's natural even."

Micah knew he was walking on thin ice, even before Ren began curling and uncurling his fingers at his sides and his already colored face took on a purple tinge. Still, he wasn't prepared for the sudden backhand to the face, the force of the blow causing the chair to topple sideways.

He landed on his bad shoulder, and a strange, aborted sound escaped his mouth as his breath caught in his throat, choking on the sudden onslaught of pain.

In addition to the agony radiating from his shoulder, Micah's cheek stung fiercely, and there was a slight ringing in his ears.

"How dare you twist God's words to validate your depraved lifestyle?" Ren spat, his voice cutting through the resonance. "'If a man lies with a man as one lies with a woman, both of them have done what is detestable. They must be put to death; their blood will be on their own heads.' *That's* what God has to say about homosexuals."

Micah didn't dare open his mouth to refute him. Despite Tessa's constant grumbling, he did have *some* sense of self-preservation. Besides, he was too dazed from the blow to formulate an intelligent response. (Not that it would have done much good.)

Seeming to realize Micah wasn't in any condition to argue, Ren ran an agitated hand through his hair before pinching the bridge of his nose – clearly trying to calm himself. "I thought we were making progress, but plainly I was mistaken. It appears you need yet more time to reflect on your poor life choices. *Do* try to act like less of a shameless slut when I return." With that last jibe, Ren turned on his heel and strut out of the room.

Micah felt nearly light-headed with relief when he heard the door latch shut behind him. (Well, it was either that or the blood rushing to his head from the awkward position Ren had left him in on the floor.)

In hindsight, Micah deeply regretted letting Ren know that he knew that he was gay – and that it was okay. He hadn't anticipated the man mouth-raping him in reaction to being shown a bit of compassion. But, apparently, Ren was so starved for affection that simply being told he wasn't an abomination was taken as an attempt at seduction.

Micah didn't want to think about whether or not Nico – and all the others before him – were forced to bear Ren's twisted attraction as well.

Regardless, Ren's behavior certainly hammered home how unpredictable the man was – how *dangerous*. He was as liable to calmly read passages from the Bible as he was to shove his tongue down Micah's throat as he was to pummel him.

Even if Micah kept fighting him – even if he *never* renounced his gayness – Ren seemed just as likely to kill him in a fit of rage as he was to "send him home to God's arms" after a successful rehabilitation. Micah needed to escape – and soon. That had never been so clear.

So he schemed. Micah scanned his surroundings, considered the position he'd been left in on the floor, tested the rope that secured his wrists and ankles to the chair (again), and he came up with a plan.

He forced himself to wait until what had to have been at least thirty minutes had passed – just to make sure Ren wasn't planning on coming back anytime soon – before putting said plan into motion.

The rope was loosest around his ankles. There wasn't a lot of slack, but there was enough that Micah could move his feet back and forth about half an inch in either direction. Crisscrossing beams connecting the legs of the chair made it impossible for Micah to simply slip his ankles free, rope and all, so he'd have to focus on creating more slack – maybe even fraying a bit of the rope against the legs of the chair – by simply causing friction.

Simple. *Ha.*

Micah's calves burned after what must have been hours of forcing his feet to move continuously back and forth in a seesawing motion. He'd long ago drawn blood, little rivulets of red running down his heels and speckling the floor.

He likened himself to a woodland animal that had been caught in a hunter's bear trap, and was gnawing his own leg off to survive. It was arduous work, and… unpleasant to say the least, but ironically, the pain radiating from his shoulder made it bearable. (After all, it didn't seem so bad in comparison.)

And it was worth it.

Because after what must have been hours of rubbing his own broken skin against the unforgiving wood of the chair legs, and dozens of failed attempts to free himself, the rope had loosened enough around his right ankle that Micah was able to wiggle it loose.

Micah stared in shock at his freed limb. It was a gnarly sight, a ring of destroyed skin encircling his entire ankle. He didn't let himself look too closely at the wound, however. There just wasn't time. He had no idea how much time had passed since Ren had left or when he might return, but he had a feeling the punishment if he was caught attempting to escape would be brutal.

So Micah moved onto stage two of his plan, which involved using his unrestrained leg to kick at the wall with enough force to make the metal crucifix tumble to the floor. It was the perfect size to wedge up under the rope around his wrists so that Micah could repeat the same process with them as he had his ankles.

But first he had to get closer to the wall. Trying his best to ignore the pain that flared every time his arm was jostled, Micah bucked in the chair, using the momentum it created to shift jerkily towards the wall until he was in prime position.

Then he pulled back his leg and kicked the wall as hard as he could.

Wham.

The wall trembled, but the cross didn't budge.

So Micah kicked it again.

Wham.

And again.

Wham.

And over and over until his foot was numb from the sting and tears of frustration were rapidly filling his eyes. "Goddammit!"

Wham.

"Come on, you motherfucker!"

Wham.

Micah didn't know if it was desperation or hysteria that found him refocusing his gaze from his target to the mass-produced painting of Jesus, but he took in the benevolent smile and the halo of light behind the glossy, brown hair and prayed. "*Please.* If you even exist, if you truly care, just... I need your help."

Micah kicked again. The wall quivered, but nothing.

"Fuck! What do you want? I'll go to church every frickin' Sunday!"

Wham. Nothing.

"I'll pray every day!"

Wham. Nothing.

Micah sniffled, on the cusp of balling like a fucking baby, and moved on from making hopeless promises to listing all the things he'd been looking forward to that wouldn't come to pass if he didn't somehow get out of this dank, dark basement.

"I won't get to meet Tessa's babies."

Wham.

"I'll never get to tell Damon I'm sorry and that I love him."

Wham.

Micah had all but resigned himself to the fact that his plan was doomed, so it took a moment for him to recover from the shock when the cross finally fell, clattering onto the cement floor. But disbelief quickly gave way to relief.

"Thank Christ," he muttered before stiffening, eyes immediately swiveling to the painting of Jesus. "Uh, thank *you*, I mean," he said, unsure if it'd truly been divine intervention that had caused the cross to fall or simple physics, but Micah was high on the feeling of relief, and he figured it couldn't hurt.

It took some awkward repositioning, but eventually Micah was able to grab onto the cross with his toes and bend his leg to bring it to his working hand. The rope was tight, and it was trickier than Micah thought it would be to force it between his wrist and the rope, but he managed.

Then, keeping a careful hold on the top of the cross with his fingers, Micah began sawing at the rope. It was strenuous work. His forearm burned and his wrist bled, but unlike with his ankles, Micah could actually *see* the rope fraying.

The edges of the crucifix were sharp, and it took much less time to free his hand than it had his ankle.

A whimper of jubilation escaped him as he flexed his liberated hand, but Micah didn't dare stop to celebrate. The closer he got to escape, the more afraid he grew of Ren barging into the room.

He turned his attention to the rope looped around his other wrist, picking frantically (*carelessly*) at the knots until his nails were chipped and bleeding, and the binding was loose enough that he could carefully maneuver his useless limb through the rope.

He repeated the same process with his bound ankle.

Carefully cradling his dislocated arm with his working one, Micah shakily got to his feet. He felt woozy – whether it was the adrenaline rushing through his system or the nerves or the fact that he hadn't had anything to eat for days, Micah wasn't sure – but he didn't let it stop him.

He staggered over to the desk – his clothes, his *watch*. Micah picked up the diamond-encrusted timepiece, fingers fumbling as he quickly found the panic button Damon had had installed.

All it would take was three jabs to have his exact coordinates sent to Damon.

But to Micah's own surprise, he found his thumb hovering uncertainly over the button. *What if he didn't come?*

On the other hand... *what if he did?*

There was no way to know whether or not Damon had any idea Micah was missing and in danger – being held by an unhinged madman who might *hurt* Damon if he showed up unexpectedly, or worse, *kill* him.

Then again, if even an iota of Damon still cared for Micah, he knew the man would want him to press the button – would be furious, actually, if he didn't. So trusting his instincts, Micah carefully pushed down the button three times.

Looking at the watch, there was no alarm or any other indication that the panic button had worked, but perhaps that was the point, so Micah would just have to trust that his coordinates had been sent.

Not that he was about to wait around for Damon – or anyone else for that matter – to come save him.

Setting down the watch, Micah went to the door, jiggling the knob and testing the thickness of the wooden slab. It was locked, and too sturdy to try to kick or bulldoze down – especially with a bum shoulder.

He briefly considered attempting to set his shoulder, but a single glance at the black and blue lump convinced him he would probably only make it worse.

Realizing he was stuck there until Ren (or with any luck, Damon or the police) let him out, Micah returned to his clothes to hastily dress himself before searching for a weapon.

(Well, he *tried* to dress himself. It was harder than he expected with a useless arm. He was able to pull his pants up with his good hand, but quickly gave up on zipping or buttoning his fly. He didn't even attempt the sweatshirt.)

Micah pocketed his watch then crossed the room to stash the cross he'd used to free himself as well. If it was sharp enough to fray rope, it was sharp enough to break skin. Then he turned his attention to the chair, stomping on one of the legs until it splintered from the seat. He picked it up with his good hand, intending to wield it like a club.

A quick search of the room revealed no other potential weapons, so Micah huddled near the door, intent on catching Ren by surprise the next time he came to check on him. The plan was simple: hit the man as hard as he could in the back of the head with the chair leg and hightail it out of there.

Of course, Micah hoped the next person to walk through the door *wouldn't* be Ren. More than anything, he wanted it to be Damon.

He couldn't have been crouched there long when his whole body suddenly tensed, every cell going on alert as he heard the faintest trace of footsteps approaching the door. The lock unclicked. The knob turned.

But, of course, Micah's luck was absolute shit, and God must have hit his daily quota for answered prayers, because it was Ren who stepped into the dank, dreary room.

"Micah?"

Ren's back was turned towards him so Micah didn't have the pleasure of seeing the shock seize him, quickly overtaken by panic – but he *did* see the way his shoulders stiffened in alarm. Micah didn't give the man time to discover him; he merely pulled the makeshift club back behind his head, and *swung.*

Ren staggered forward when the chair leg collided with his skull, but Micah didn't stick around to see if he went down.

It didn't matter. Micah ran. He shot out the open doorway, which revealed a steep set of stairs. He booked it up the steps, taking them two at a time as he braced his bad arm with his good one. It affected his balance, and Micah's toes caught on the top step. He tripped, but didn't fall – though steadying himself cost him precious seconds.

The stairs led to a kitchen.

Micah barely registered the fact that he wasn't in a church, after all, but a very normal-looking house – *parsonage*, his brain supplied, *the typical housing arrangement for a pastor* – when he was suddenly slammed into from behind.

He was tackled to the floor.

Micah tried to catch himself with his good arm, but his damaged one took the brunt of the fall. He screamed – the sound taking a turn towards guttural when Ren grabbed him by his dislocated shoulder and forcefully flipped him onto his back.

The man sat on top of him, looming over Micah as his knees caged him in on either side. Ren's eyes were like brown, molten lava, spitting fire at him, and blood dripped down from his hairline where Micah had struck him – though not hard enough, apparently. *Fuck.*

The man looked crazed.

"There's nowhere you can run, nowhere you can hide, that He does not see you, that *I* cannot find you."

Micah gripped the length of the metal cross in his pocket. "Choke on Satan's cock," he spat, pulling it out and jamming it as hard as he could into the man's side, right beneath his ribs.

Ren howled.

Micah took the opportunity to wiggle out from underneath him. Before he could get all the way to his feet, however, Ren had him by the ankle, fingers digging mercilessly into the exposed flesh of Micah's rope burn as he tugged him back down onto his knees.

Micah watched in fascinated horror as Ren pulled the bloody crucifix from his side. The wound was probably only about three inches deep, but red quickly began seeping through his white dress shirt.

But that didn't stop Ren from lunging at Micah.

They tussled on the floor. Micah kicked with his feet and threw punches and elbows with his good arm, but he was weak from lack of food and water and being tied up for so long, and not even Ren slowly bleeding out from a stab wound could make up for the fact that he only had one working arm.

He ended up right back where he started: pinned under Ren. Except this time the man had learned his lesson and had Micah's wrist restrained above his head. They were both breathing hard as Ren's eyes flitted over him. He wasn't sure what the other man was looking for, or if he was just categorizing all the new damage. (Micah was a bruised, bloody mess – his only consolation being that Ren was too.)

To Micah's surprise, the longer Ren looked at him, the more his eyes lost their frenzied edge. He almost seemed resigned by the time he finally addressed Micah. "You stabbed me."

If Ren was expecting an apology, he was about to be disappointed.

"You *kidnapped* me."

Ren nodded, his gaze finally meeting Micah's. "I'm sorry."

Micah blinked. "For holding me against my will?"

"No. I'm sorry that I cannot save you." He lifted his heavy gaze from Micah, staring somewhere out into the distance. "I thought I could, but the devil's claws are too deeply embedded in you. You're beyond my help. There will be no glory for you in heaven, only eternal suffering in hell."

It took less than a second for Micah to work through the flowery bullshit to realize Ren intended to kill him, but even that was too long. His eyes widened. "Ren, wait-!"

Ren didn't wait.

One second, Ren's hands were pressing his wrists into the ceramic tiles of the kitchen floor, and the next, they were wrapped around his neck, *squeezing*.

Micah fought.

He only had one hand, but he used it to punch at Ren and attempt to pry the man's fingers off from around his neck. When that didn't work, he savagely jammed his thumb into Ren's stab wound. But it was like Ren was powered by something beyond the physical realm because he didn't so much as flinch.

Micah's vision blurred.

His fingers went back to trying to pry Ren's hands from his throat.

He could see Ren's lips moving from where he hovered over him – probably reciting some sort of prayer, the fucking psycho – but Micah couldn't hear the words. It was like he was underwater.

It was violent, but also peaceful in a strange sort of way – almost serene.

Micah wondered if the others had felt this way, too.

Death seemed inevitable, and it'd be so, *so* easy to give into it. No more pain. No more suffering.

But also no more watching the Mets with his dad, no more solving crimes with Tessa, no more arguing with Jensen. No more Damon.

So as tempted as he was to give in, Micah refused. He fought against that false sense of calm with all he was worth – even as his grip on Ren's hands weakened, even as his face turned blue, even as his eyelids began fluttering incessantly.

He would not go quietly... *he. would. not. go.*

And then, right as he balanced on the edge of consciousness, something happened. A sound so stark, so loud and sharp and *familiar,* ripped through the air that Micah was able to hear it even through the metaphorical water in his ears.

A gun shot.

The hands around his neck suddenly loosened, and Micah sucked in a breath at the same time Ren collapsed on top of him, blood and brain matter leaking out the side of his head where a bullet had carved a perfectly round hole into his skull.

Micah was thrust back into awareness, shock shielding him from the horror of the fact a dead body was currently pinning him to the ground. Luckily, Ren was only atop him for a few seconds before being carelessly thrown to the side, and suddenly all Micah could see, hear, *smell* was Damon.

The man kneeled over him, eyes wild as they obsessively scanned his form over and over again. A muscle in Damon's jaw spasmed when he took in Micah's discolored lump of a shoulder, and a tiny, punched out sound of devastation escaped him when he saw the unzipped fly.

Large, calloused hands were everywhere, first smoothing back Micah's hair, and then stroking his good arm, and finally gingerly cupping his face. All the while, Damon spoke to him, voice uncharacteristically soft, his words a mix of English, Italian, and even Spanish.

"Ti ho adesso, tesoro. Ti ho adesso."

"No one will ever touch you again."

"Estas seguro ahora. You are safe now, my heart."

Damon's unique scent of Christmas trees, cedar wood, and something darker, spicier that was all man flooded his nose.

For the life of him, Micah couldn't comprehend it.

It was like a dream – so much so, Micah nearly convinced himself that he *had* died, and this was merely his idea of heaven. But he hurt too much to be dead.

More likely, he was in shock, or his brain had been deprived of oxygen for so long that it was having trouble powering back on – maybe a mix of the two.

"Please, *tesoro,* say something."

Damon seemed to be growing more frantic the longer Micah remained unresponsive, so he forced his throat to unstick. Remembering what he'd wished for – what he'd *prayed* for – in the basement, Micah reached up with his good hand and grasped the wrist of one of the hands holding his face. "I'm sorry," he croaked, the words like shards of glass against the tender insides of his throat, but a balm to his soul. "I love you."

Damon's face crumpled, and he said something back, but forcing out the words had taken the last of Micah's energy. Damon was here now, so he knew it was safe to finally succumb to the inviting lull of oblivion that still hovered over him, pulling at his eyelids and making him feel tired – like he hadn't slept in days.

(To be fair, he hadn't.)

There was the stormy blue of Damon's irises, and then nothing but black.

CHAPTER TWENTY-THREE

Beep. Beep. Beep.

Micah's thoughts were groggy and sluggish, almost like they were underwater – like *he* was underwater – desperately swimming against the tide that wanted to keep him firmly in the grips of unconsciousness.

Why was that thought so familiar?

Beep. Beep. Beep.

Really, if it wasn't for the incessant beeping, he would probably have been swallowed back under. Which would have been just fine with Micah. He felt like he'd slept too long and not nearly long enough all at once – and everyone knew the only cure for that was *more* sleep.

Beep. Beep. Beep.

Where the hell was it coming from? It wasn't his phone – unless Tessa had changed his settings without telling him *(again)*.

Beep. Beep. Beep.

Not loud enough to be the fire alarm. (Not that they were up to code in his apartment building, anyway.)

Beep. Beep. Beep.

Maybe the microwave? Had he fallen asleep with a tv dinner in there again?

Honestly, it took Micah far longer than it should have to finally muster up the energy to pry open his eyes and realize he was in a hospital. From there, it was easy enough to deduce that the annoying beeping was coming from the patient monitor set up near the head of his cot. There were tubes in his nose, and his right arm was in a sling.

His dad was sitting in an uncomfortable-looking chair on the other side of the bed. Abram was out of uniform with his arms folded across his front and his chin resting on his chest. Judging by the light snoring intermittently emerging from his direction, the man was asleep.

Micah took all of this in, but he didn't understand it.

What the fuck?

"What-?"

He'd only meant to repeat his confusion aloud, but as soon as that first scratchy word formed, it was as if his throat constricted painfully around it, and nothing else would come out – and just like that, everything came back to him.

Artie's Pub.

The basement.

Ren's hands squeezing unrelentingly around his neck until he had turned purple, and he could hardly see, and there was only silence-

The gunshot that cut through it, and then…

Damon.

Micah didn't know which one of the thoughts running through his head was causing his heart to race, but the machines surrounding him suddenly went berserk. The steady beeping that had roused him from sleep became a manic *beepbeepbeep* that sounded not unlike a screech, broadcasting his panic to anyone within earshot.

In a frenzied daze, Micah ripped the electrodes from his chest and the nasal cannula from his nose. His thoughts a disoriented, jumbled mess, he even yanked the IV out of his arm.

Of course, all of this only caused a bigger clamor as more alarms blared.

It was no surprise that the commotion woke his father.

The man sprang up from his chair, immediately attempting to hold Micah down onto the bed. "Stop it, son, you're going to hurt yourself."

Being restrained did *not* help the rising hysteria, and Micah's breath got caught somewhere in his swollen esophagus.

Thankfully, a few seconds later, a pair of nurses rushed in the door, having been alerted by the multitude of alarms.

The male nurse – a thirty-something with brown skin and even browner eyes – gently pried his dad off of him, while the female nurse – who was blonde and blue-eyed, and probably old enough to be Micah's grandma – coached him into getting his breathing back under control.

When the threat of a panic attack had dissipated, she offered him something that would take the edge off the anxiety he was feeling without interfering with the pain-managing meds he was on. After she assured him it wouldn't put him back to sleep, Micah agreed.

Her partner reattached the IV, and she injected something clear into the line – she'd told him the name, but his brain was too overstimulated to remember it. Shot straight into his blood stream, the drug took effect quickly. By the time the doctor – a pretty Indian woman in a pant suit and her hair pulled back into a no-nonsense bun – was fetched fifteen minutes later, Micah was able to listen to what she had to say with a clear mind.

After a quick check of his vitals, Dr. Talati described his injuries – starting with the most severe. Apparently, his shoulder had been so seriously dislocated that they'd had to put him under for surgery when he'd arrived. He would have to keep it in the sling for four weeks, and she recommended physical therapy to help strengthen the joint for another six weeks after that.

Then she moved on to the bruising around his neck, explaining how the damage was serious enough that the trauma had extended to the inside of his throat. He had a bruised, swollen windpipe, basically. While he could still breathe on his own, the passageway had narrowed enough that they'd inserted the nasal cannula in his nose while he'd been asleep to keep his oxygen levels up.

He seemed okay now that he was awake, however, so she agreed he could continue on without the tubes – unless he needed them again. Dr. Talati seemed confident there would be no permanent damage, but she warned him that talking would be painful – which he had already figured out on his own – until his throat was healed.

At that point, she'd sent the male nurse off to fetch a small whiteboard. She handed it to Micah, along with a marker, recommending he use it to communicate through writing for the remainder of his hospital stay.

She'd also prescribed him a diet of soft foods for at least a week to keep from aggravating the injury.

The rest of the damage Micah had sustained was relatively minor. He'd been dehydrated when he'd been brought in – hence the IV – and his wrists and ankles had been bandaged where he'd suffered rope burn.

Dr. Talati removed the gauze, showing him how to rub in a special balm that was supposed to enhance the healing process and help reduce scarring, before redressing the wounds.

Besides discussing treatment, Dr. Talati didn't mention anything about how Micah had gotten any of his injuries, for which he was grateful. She merely told him that they had a psychiatrist on staff if he felt the need to speak to one, authorized another dose of pain meds, and then was off to check on her next patient.

The nurses left soon after, which left Micah alone in the room with his father.

He'd been silent throughout Micah's entire "discussion" with the doctor, and Micah had no idea how he was feeling. He was a difficult man to read at the best of times, and this was certainly not one of them.

What did he know?

Even after the hospital staff left, he remained quiet, the heat of his gaze burning a hole into the side of Micah's head from where he stood by his bed.

After a while, he couldn't take the silence anymore. "What-?" he started to ask, but immediately regretted the attempt when his throat seized around the word, forcing out a painful cough.

"Use the whiteboard," his father urged.

Micah huffed, but obliged. **What happened?**

He left the question vague and open-ended on purpose – a common enough interrogation tactic, employed to worm as much information out of someone as possible, and gauge what they knew.

But, of course, Abram was the captain of a police force, and he sidestepped it easily. "What's the last thing you remember?"

Micah worried his bottom lip, deciding to be honest without giving much away.

Damon.

Abram scowled in reaction to the name. "Fucking Romano. That egotistical bastard – that goddamn *criminal* who thinks he's above the law, above justice-" Abram abruptly paused, his tone – which had started snide and angry, taking a turn towards incredulous, "...he found you. He *saved* you."

Micah nodded.

"Apparently, he had given you some sort of fancy watch for Christmas that you were able to send your coordinates from. He should have informed the police immediately – as soon as he got the alert. We'd already summoned him in for questioning *twice* since we found out you were missing. Instead, what does that bastard do? He marches into McCormick's place, guns blazing, and shoots the fucker in the head. Feds are on our asses, and paperwork has been a goddamn nightmare."

Micah tried not to feel hurt that his dad was apparently more concerned about paperwork than the fact his only son had almost died.

"But you know the worst part of it all?"

Micah forced himself to shake his head.

"I'm indebted to that fucker – *genuinely* fucking grateful for him. Because at the end of the day, he saved your life. Rest assured, Micah, I would have shot McCormick dead just the same as he did. I know I'm not always great at expressing it, but... I love you, son, and I'm so glad you're okay."

There definitely weren't tears in his eyes when his dad bent over and gingerly took him into his arms, careful not to jostle the sling as he hugged him. And even if there were, Micah would pretend it was the pain meds starting to wear off. (Not that his father was in any state to notice. The man was dabbing suspiciously at his own eyes.)

I love you, too, Dad.

Abram shook his head. "Don't think this means I approve of him. No one is good enough for my son, let alone some violent mafioso who's up to his eyeballs in organized crime. That doesn't even take into consideration how you two met. The man thought you were a prostitute, for Christ's sake, and he was *paying* you to spend time with him. An unorthodox arrangement to say the least."

Micah felt his face heat. Sure, his father had known that he and Damon were *involved* after the fiasco at Jason and Caprice's house, but he hadn't known the details.

How had he found out?

The question must have been written across his face because his father added, unprompted, "Tessa told me everything."

A little zip of betrayal shot through him at the revelation, and Micah was unable to stop a scowl from forming.

"None of that now," his father scolded. "She was worried as all hell when you disappeared, and considering the events of last week, she was convinced Damon had taken you and stashed you away somewhere, or hurt you, or *worse*. So was I. She was only trying to help by giving me a clearer picture of the situation."

Knowing his father was right, Micah reluctantly nodded.

Does everyone at the precinct know?

"About Damon, and how you two met? No. Just Tessa, Detective Jensen, and I." Abram winced. "Speaking of Tessa, the woman is going to kill me. I promised I would let her know as soon as you woke up. Just a second." His father pulled out his phone. He wasn't the most proficient texter, so it took him more than "just a second" to type up a message, but he eventually hit the "send" button. "There."

Micah gave him a thumbs up.

Abram cleared his throat, shifting on his feet from where he continued to hover near the bed. "Now, about McCormick... eventually, you're going to have to give a statement. Not to anyone at the precinct – conflict of interest, obviously. An agent from the bureau will probably conduct the interview, but if you want, I can go with you." Micah must have made a face at that because Abram immediately backtracked, "I mean, not if you don't want me to. It's just... I guess what I'm trying to say is, if you feel like talking, I'll listen – to anything you want to tell me."

Micah appreciated what his father was doing – really, he did. He knew how hard it was for the man to be open with his emotions, and offering to be a listening ear for his son to recount all the ways he'd been brutalized by a madman was no small thing.

But the offer was a reminder that Micah wasn't sure if his father knew that Ren hadn't hurt *just* him. There had been so many other victims, so when he went to write on his whiteboard, it wasn't to express his thanks, it was to make sure his dad knew the truth.

Ren = Hooker Hunter

Abram nodded gravely. "Yes, we know."

Micah blinked. **How?**

"He kept trophies from all his victims – clothing items, mostly – and there was a whole plethora of evidence in that basement. You were right that the missing persons case you were working on was connected. Nico Sanchez was one of the Hooker Hunter's victims. You should know that his parents were very concerned about you when they found out what happened, and very thankful."

Micah flushed at the praise.

"We're still not sure why Normandy falsely confessed to the crimes. Or why McCormick targeted you. Everyone else he kidnapped was involved in sex work somehow. We think it might have just been a mix of escalation and opportunity, considering your, uh… emotional state at the time-"

Micah could tell his father was trying to be sensitive, but he shook his head, cutting him off by quickly scribbling a message on the board and holding it up.

He saw me when I was undercover. Thought I was a prostitute.

"But that was over a month ago," Abram said in disbelief.

Micah shrugged.

Abram shook his head. "You're *never* allowed to go undercover again – especially not as a sex worker. Jesus Christ," he muttered, mostly to himself, "you encourage your son to wear a skirt *one* time, and suddenly all the creeps come crawling out of the woodwork."

Micah glowered. **Damon is not a creep.**

"I'm sorry, violent mobster with unlimited resources and unfiltered access to weapons manufacturers. Is that better?"

Micah winced.

Thankfully, he was saved from having to listen to his father disparage Damon further by the door to his room suddenly bursting open. Tessa marched in. Her eyes immediately found Micah's. "You absolute ass," she accused. Then she was practically leaping into his arms, her hug much less careful than Micah's father's had been, the whiteboard trapped between them and digging painfully into his sternum.

The woman was a force of nature, and it took Micah a moment to process the dramatic entrance before realizing she was dressed in a hospital gown – the same pale green, paper-thin garment he was donning. And her stomach was noticeably smaller.

"Babies-" he blurted, flinching immediately at the mistake.

"Don't speak, you imbecile," Tessa snapped, finally releasing him from her embrace. She took a step back, but kept her hands on his face, squeezing his cheeks. Her eyes were red-rimmed and watery, but instead of seeming sad, she just looked pissed – like she wanted to slap him, and she was only holding herself back due to his pathetic physical state. "The babies are fine. Jasper's rolling them in behind me."

Sure enough, Jasper was plodding through the door next, pushing an infant cart in front of him. There were two babies inside, both swaddled in blue blankets with matching caps on their heads. They were *tiny*.

"I knew it was only a matter of time until your shenanigans would send me into early labor, and sure enough, what do you do? You go and manage to get yourself *kidnapped*. And less than 24 hours later, my water is breaking all over the interrogation room floor."

"Hey, Micah," Jasper said, ignoring Tessa's tirade and offering him a tired smile. "You'll have to excuse my wife. She hasn't slept in four days and pushed the equivalent of two six-pound bowling balls out of her vagina less than 48 hours ago." He touched his lips to the side of her head, and to Micah's surprise, pressed a kiss into his hair as well. "What she *means* to say is that she was really worried, and she's so glad you're okay. We both are. After all, she knows you didn't get kidnapped on purpose, *right?*" He eyed his wife pointedly at this.

Tessa glared at her husband, but when she turned her gaze back onto Micah, it had noticeably softened. "Want to meet my babies?"

Micah was nervous to hold something – some*one* – so small, especially with only one arm, but there was no universe in which he would ever deny her, so he nodded and watched as Tessa picked up one of the infants and cradled him to her chest before placing him in Micah's arms.

He'd seemed tiny in the cart, but somehow, the baby was even smaller up close. He was wrinkly, with an egg-shaped head, even with the cap on – probably from being squished through the birth canal. He was also the most perfect thing Micah had ever seen. He could count his little baby eyelashes, and his button nose scrunched adorably as he yawned before turning his face into Micah's nonexistent cleavage and resettling back into sleep.

Micah was struck by the fact this experience had almost been ripped away from him – his *life* had nearly been ripped away from him – and suddenly, without his permission, tears were streaming down his face.

With both hands occupied, there was no way to hide the fact he was crying, and Tessa – who had picked up the other twin – burst into her own tears at the sight. Soon enough, they were both sobbing, being careful not to crush the babies wedged between them as they huddled together.

Abram coughed awkwardly into his hand, clearly alarmed at the sudden onslaught of waterworks. "Er-"

"Don't worry," Jasper assured, carefully taking one baby from Tessa and then the other from Micah before relocating them back into the cart. "It's mostly the hormones, I reckon. Want to see if we can find a vending machine? I'm not sure about Micah, but chocolate tends to perk Tessa up."

Latching onto any excuse to leave the room, Abram nodded. "Yes, *please*."

Micah wasn't sure how long they sat there, crying into each other's arms – a sweet release of their pent-up emotions – but by the time their tears ran dry, Tessa had managed to squeeze herself into the bed with him – possible only because of her recently shrunken stomach – and was stroking his hair.

When he felt calm enough to do so, Micah picked up the whiteboard.

Names?

"Jackson Henry and Maddox James," Tessa answered promptly. "Jackson's middle name is after Jasper's late father, and Maddox is named after my grandfather who died last year." She sniffled. "Jasper, he… he suggested using Micah for Maddox's middle name, and I lost it. We named our children in honor of people who are dead. *You* weren't dead. I knew you weren't."

She clung to his relatively uninjured side.

I'm sorry.

"Stop that," she scolded, pushing the board away. "It's not your fault. I'm sorry for yelling earlier. I'm not mad at you, obviously – just McCormick." She paused here, hesitating for a moment before asking, "What did he do to you, Micah?"

It was a loaded question.

Clearly, Tessa could see the results of what Ren had done to him. The man had tied him up, he'd broken his shoulder, he'd *choked* Micah until he was on the brink of a blackout. But what Tessa was asking had nothing to do with his physical injuries, and Micah didn't know how to answer. He didn't know if he *wanted* to answer. After a moment, he picked up the marker.

Ren was gay. He hated himself and wanted to punish anyone who brought out those so-called "unnatural" urges in him.

It was brief, and vague, but an accurate enough description.

Tessa's face fell, and she looked on the verge of tears – again. "Oh Micah, I'm so sorry." She took a deep breath in through her nose and managed to compose herself. "I'm just so glad that the bastard is dead. Your gun-toting, mafioso boyfriend turned out to be good for something at least."

Micah wasn't entirely sure what to say to that.

"You know I thought it was him at first, who took you," she admitted after a moment.

Micah huffed, rolling his eyes.

I know. My dad told me you spilled everything.

"Can you blame me? I was scared! It was less than a week before you were taken that Damon found out you were a cop!" She shook her head, letting out a breath. "But it became obvious after we interrogated him that he had no idea you were even missing until we told him." She shot Micah a mischievous look. "He didn't *have* to come in for the interview, you know; it's not like we could subpoena him with no evidence. Personally, I think he only agreed to come in because he thought *you* were going to be there, and he was going through Micah-withdrawals and wanted to catch a glimpse of you."

Micah snorted, letting her know what he thought of *that* idea. (After all, Micah was pretty sure that the man had still been pissed at him at the time.)

"No, really, Micah," Tessa said, voice taking on an uncharacteristically somber tone. "He *freaked* when he found out you were missing. He *punched* Jensen in the face. I thought he might trash the interview room. The captain – your dad – tried to have him arrested for assaulting an officer, but Damon convinced him he was more good to you on the outside than locked up – even if we probably would have only been able to hold him for a couple hours." She shook her head. "I think Damon thought one of his enemies or maybe a rival snatched you. It was sweet, actually, how worried he was. Not that I've forgiven him for breaking your heart!" she quickly added when she took in Micah's dumbfounded expression. "I'm still furious with him for how he reacted to finding out you were a cop. He may have saved your life, but rest assured, that doesn't change the fact that if he hurts you again, I'll kill him."

If he hurt Micah *again?* But that implied Damon would allow Micah to get close enough to be hurt.

Sure, Micah had come to terms with the fact that he loved the man, and he missed Damon so much it was like a physical ache. But that didn't mean Damon felt the same way, even if he *did* forgive Micah for lying to him for so long.

After all, if Damon cared about Micah half as much as Micah cared about him, wouldn't he be there?

Micah loved his dad, and Tessa, and Jasper, and he appreciated their presence in the hospital more than he could say, but that didn't mean he hadn't noticed that someone else was conspicuously absent.

He'd been desperately trying to ignore the fact that Damon wasn't there, but he couldn't avoid it any longer.

Where is he?

Tessa frowned at the question. "Honey, where do you *think* he is?"

Micah shrugged, only expounding when Tessa pointedly raised her eyebrows.

I don't know. Work? His penthouse?

"Micah, sweetie," Tessa said, sounding exasperated, "he's been here since they brought you in. He even rode in the ambulance with you. He hasn't left the hospital – not even after he got into it with your father and Abram threatened to arrest him. He's been skulking outside your room this whole time. Honestly, the only reason your dad hasn't tried to drag him out in cuffs – besides the fact he saved your life – is that he brought a couple of goons with him to watch your door, bodyguards or something. One has a particularly interesting mermaid tattoo on his neck.

Micah numbly wrote on the board.

That's Geoffrey.

"Geoffrey?" Tessa snorted. "That figures."

But Micah had more important things to focus on. *Damon was here.*

But that didn't explain why he hadn't come in to see him. He had to know Micah was awake between all the alarms he'd set off in his panic earlier and the sudden barrage of visitors.

Why hasn't he come in to see me?

Tessa sighed. "Has it occurred to you he might be scared to face you after everything? That he's not sure how his presence will be received?"

Micah shook his head.

Damon doesn't get scared. He underlined the words.

"You didn't see him at the station when he found out you were missing," Tessa immediately disagreed. "That man *definitely* gets scared, at least when it comes to matters concerning you." She paused, and then carefully asked, "Do you want me to send him in?"

Micah almost forgot himself and opened his mouth to blurt out *"yes!"*

But then he remembered the last time he'd seen Damon – not counting when the man had rescued him – and his stomach came alive with nerves. He'd been *so* angry at Micah.

Ultimately, Micah's desire to see the man outweighed any doubts he had, so after sucking in a grounding breath, he nodded.

Tessa smiled, pulling him into one last suffocating hug before rolling out of bed. "I'll be back later," she promised before crossing the room and shutting the door behind herself.

Micah stared at it – waiting for it to open and for Damon to come striding in. Except a minute passed, and then another, with the door remaining perfectly still, and he began to think that maybe Tessa was wrong.

Maybe Damon *didn't* want to see him.

Then the handle twisted, and the man stepped into the room, carefully closing the door behind himself. Damon kept his back to Micah, facing the door for a long, drawn-out moment before finally turning to meet his gaze.

Micah wasn't sure how he pictured his reunion with Damon after everything that had happened, but it certainly wasn't *this*.

Micah knew he had no room to talk, but Damon looked awful. He was in joggers and a t-shirt, a blotted reddish-brown stain along the bottom hem. Blood, Micah realized – Ren's, most likely. Damon hadn't even changed since blowing the man's brains out. In addition to his slovenly appearance, Damon's hair was messier than Micah had ever seen it, and the dark circles under his eyes probably rivaled Micah's own.

More than all that, though, Damon's shoulders were ramrod straight with tension, and he looked inexplicably nervous.

Tessa was right – he *was* scared.

As soon as the realization struck him, Micah was lifting his good arm, stretching it out towards the man and beckoning him, not unlike a child begging to be picked up and held.

Damon abided immediately, crossing the room in two rushed strides before sweeping him into his arms. Micah buried his nose into the crook of the man's neck, inhaling Damon's comforting musk like a drug.

"I was so worried," Damon murmured into his hair.

Damon's hold around him was frustratingly loose – he was obviously trying to be considerate of his sling – but Micah didn't want Damon to be careful, he just wanted him closer – so he squeezed the man with his good arm for all he was worth.

Micah didn't want to ever let go, but he knew he and Damon needed to "talk", so, eventually, he forced himself to release the man and pick up the board and write.

Damon sunk to his knees by the side of Micah's bed, foregoing the nearby chair completely.

Micah hesitated for only a second before showing the man what he'd written.

I thought you hated me.

"I could never hate you," Damon immediately disputed, his hand a grounding force on Micah's knee. "When I found out you were a cop, I was... upset."

Pissed is what he meant, judging by the brief hesitation.

"I was confused – shocked even – and it's very hard to catch me off guard. I immediately assumed the worst. That you'd been assigned as... well, bait, essentially – specially tailored for me. I figured you had been spying, gathering evidence to build a case against me-"

Micah couldn't take it anymore.

"Never," he pushed out through his swollen windpipe. "I swear-"

"Hush," Damon immediately scolded him. "Don't hurt yourself. Tessa explained. You *were* undercover when we met, and you *were* bait – but not for me, for... for McCormick." Damon's face twisted. "And it fucking worked. That lowlife *took* you. He *hurt* you."

Micah would do anything to take away the pain that contorted the man's face, the anguish that filled his voice.

I'm okay.

Damon scowled. "You're in a hospital, fresh out of surgery. There's a ring of purple bruises around your neck in the shape of handprints. You're missing damn near an inch of skin around your wrists and ankles. What part of that is okay?"

Micah had trouble holding eye contact with Damon with his injuries being thrown in his face so boldly, and he tried to look away, but Damon wouldn't allow it. He took him by the chin. "I need to know. You were half naked when I found you. Your pants weren't done up properly. Did McCormick – did that swine touch you?"

Micah could feel himself blanch, and his first instinct was to immediately deny it, because Ren hadn't touched him – not in the way Damon thought. But then he remembered the way the man's eyes had trailed over his exposed skin, and the way their teeth had clacked during that forced kiss, and he couldn't suppress an involuntary shutter.

Damon exploded into a rage, shooting to his feet – cuss words and threats flying out of his mouth. Something about bringing the bastard back to life and making him eat his own cock.

Micah needed him to *stop* – before the hospital staff came running and kicked him out.

It was just a kiss.

Micah nearly had to smack the man with the board to get him to notice the words, but Damon's anger didn't dissipate even after he'd read them.

"*Just* a kiss?" he hissed, momentarily stopping his pacing. "I ought to go to *l'obitorio* and rip *la sua lingua sporca* from his mouth."

"Stop."

"Don't speak," Damon snapped.

"Then d-don't-" Micah squeezed the words out past his rapidly contracting throat.

Damon covered his mouth with a large, warm hand before he could push out any more. "Enough. You've made your point. I... I'm sorry." Damon took a deep breath in through his nose before allowing his hand to drop – and suddenly, it was Damon avoiding eye contact. "It's my fault – everything. If I had been watching out for you like I should have been, none of this would have happened."

No.

Micah underlined the word twice, shaking his head emphatically.

"I never should have walked away from you."

It was ridiculous.

What Ren had done wasn't any more Damon's fault than it was Micah's. Even if Damon had never broken off their agreement – their relationship – who's to say Ren wouldn't have still taken him? It's not like he and Damon were together every second of the day. Damon had a life outside of Micah, and Micah... well, he had his job, anyway.

But there wasn't room on the whiteboard for Micah to write all that out, so...

You came for me. You saved me. Micah hesitated. **I wasn't sure you would.**

"I'll always come for you. It kills me that I made you think, for even a second, that I might not. I'm so sorry, *tesoro*."

I'm sorry for lying about being a detective.

Damon nodded. "I understand why you did, considering my... familial duties." (That was *one* way of admitting you were a mafia boss.) "It's also why the arrangement we came to before I found out your real job – and the contract we both signed – is officially null and void."

Micah nodded robotically. He had known it was coming. He'd had plenty of time to think it over the past week, and he'd come to the same conclusion. Even if the man forgave him – which it appeared that he did – it wasn't fair to ask Damon to trust him again.

Not when Micah was a proven liar. Not when Micah still worked for the police.

It left his whole operation entirely too vulnerable to potential espionage.

"It's not safe for you. And it's not fair for me to ask you to choose between me and your career." A pause. "I know you took an oath, and that asking you to resume what we had before would put you at odds with it."

It was true.

Micah had felt torn in two different directions since he'd met Damon. Damon was so good at keeping the more... *felonious* aspects of his work out of Micah's sight (and mind) that he forgot at times just how dangerous the man was. But it had all come to a head after the fiasco with Jason Vitali.

"Only married people are immune to testifying against each other."

Everything Damon said made sense. Micah didn't blame him at all for wanting to break it off – for good this time. But that didn't mean he was just going to let him go.

So when Damon opened his mouth again, he quickly interrupted.

You're right.

Damon raised his eyebrows, a strange, almost... hopeful glint in his eyes. "I... am?"

Micah nodded, quickly scribbling more.

That's why I'm quitting.

"I... what?"

If Micah was forced to choose between Damon and helping people, he honestly didn't know which one he'd pick. But choosing between Damon and working for the NYPD? Easy.

I'm going to use the money you gave me to open my own detective agency. I already have the credentials. But I can't lose you again. I just can't.

"Please," Micah whispered.

"I thought I told you to hush," Damon said, but there was no heat in it. He looked flabbergasted, like he actually thought Micah would let him go without a fight again.

Don't leave me. Please.

Micah didn't care how pathetic it was, he would beg on his hands and knees if he had to.

Thankfully, those words were enough to finally prompt a reaction out of Damon. "I'm *never* leaving you again," he said, looming over Micah, drilling into him with his blue, blue eyes. "Make no mistake about that. I just thought..." he trailed off, shaking his head. "Never mind what I thought."

Micah blinked. But he thought... Damon had made it sound like...

I thought you were through with me.

Utterly vulnerable, Micah held up the sign.

Damon's jaw tightened at the sight of the words, but then, a beat later, the man was on him. Hands grasping either side of Micah's face, the man kissed him.

Kissed was too bland a word.

Damon utterly ravished his mouth with his tongue and teeth and lips, until Micah was reduced to a breathless, brainless, puddly mess – unable to *think* or comprehend anything beyond the smell of Damon in his nose, the taste of the man on his tongue, the feel of him all around him.

He moaned in protest when the man eventually pulled away. "Can't you tell how much I utterly adore you? Can't you *feel* it?"

Micah *did* feel it, but he couldn't leave anything open to interpretation – he needed to be sure – so he picked up the whiteboard with shaky hands.

I need it to be real this time. No money deposited into my account. No pretending for your family. REAL.

"Oh, Micah, to me it's always been real."

Tears sprang into Micah's eyes, and he worked quickly to blink them away. The confession was easy to make after Damon's own admission.

Me too.

There *may* have been some more hasty, impassioned kisses after that. At least until Micah accidentally jostled his own shoulder and Damon made them stop. Damon was too big to fit into the hospital bed with him, so they had to settle for holding hands, Damon using his free hand to alternatively rub soothing patterns into Micah's thigh and squeeze his knee.

There was nothing sexual about it, but it was undeniably intimate as Micah listened with half an ear to Damon reluctantly describe his family's various reactions to finding out Micah was a cop – at Micah's insistence.

According to Damon, Sophie had merely accepted the news at face value, and Caprice was being surprisingly tight-lipped about her opinion on the matter – having hardly said a word about Micah since the Jason incident.

Unsurprisingly, Joelle had been loud in her disapproval, but apparently, she liked Micah enough that she'd offered to assist him in a career change. (Ostensibly, she was on the lookout for new "performers" to work at Lust. Damon's answer to that suggestion had been an unequivocal "no".)

As for Uncle Marco, he'd been more angry at Damon than he was Micah, not understanding how his nephew could have fallen for such a ruse. (Although Damon didn't explicitly say, Micah also suspected that Marco had offered to put a hit out on him.)

But Micah didn't care if he had. He would gladly put up with Damon's manipulative and (likely) murderous uncle, and his trio of borderline crazy sisters (sans Sophie), if it meant he got to "put up" with Damon, too.

Micah was the happiest he'd felt in weeks – maybe ever, honestly – just basking in the man's attention, like a cat in the sun, happy to let the loll of Damon's husky voice wash over him, the man's hand on his knee.

Unfortunately, the peace was rudely interrupted by the sound of Micah's stomach growling loudly. (Though, to be fair, his last meal had been days ago, and it had consisted mostly of vodka.)

"Are you hungry?" Damon asked worriedly, doing a fair impression of a mother hen.

Micah reluctantly dislodged his hand from Damon's to write on the whiteboard.

Crepes?

A smile pulled at the corner of Damon's mouth, but he shook his head. "When we go home, I'll make you a hundred crepes if you want. Hell, I'll even bake you a cake. But until your throat is healed, soft foods only. I'm sure the hospital has some mashed potatoes or pudding in the kitchen."

Micah pouted – not even bothering to wonder how the man had known he'd been ordered on a soft foods diet.

Chocolate shake?

Damon snorted. "I'll see what I can do."

With visible reluctance, he stood. "I'll be right back," he assured. A pause. "Stay here."

Micah shot him an incredulous look as if to ask, *where would I go?*

Then Damon was walking through the door, out of sight – but definitely not out of mind. (Or Micah's heart. Micah had a feeling he'd be there always – for better or worse.)

* * *

The hospital doors were made of heavy metal, to help enforce privacy, so Micah didn't see Geoffrey – Damon's driver and one of the bodyguards stationed outside of his hospital room – perk to attention when the man reentered the hallway.

"How'd it go, boss?"

Geoffrey wasn't one to initiate conversation with his superiors. He knew Damon preferred silence over small talk, and he *especially* didn't appreciate unsolicited questions or suffer the fools who asked them. (Unless the fool's name was Micah.)

But judging by the slight spring in Damon's step, and the fact that the pale visage the man had been sporting the past week and a half was all but gone, his boss was in the best mood Geoffrey had seen the man in since the incident with Jason Vitali.

It gave him enough confidence to press. "Did he say yes?"

Geoffrey hoped he did.

In his opinion, Micah was the best thing to have ever happened to Damon Romano. Micah softened some of Damon's more ragged edges; he made him *human*. Some small-minded individuals might think anything – any*one* – who softened a mafia don was a liability. But clearly they'd never worked for a savage like Damon Romano.

The day after Damon's... *tiff* with Micah, Geoffrey had witnessed the man play amateur dentist on the uncooperative grunt of a rival cartel who'd been selling fentanyl-laced drugs under the Romano name. Damon had reduced the man to a bloody, blubbering mess with a rusty pair of pliers before deeming the information he'd spilled to be inconsequential and ordering his body to be dumped back out onto the streets – as a message.

Two days after that, Geoffrey had watched Damon shatter a man's kneecaps for offering him a fuck with his high school-aged daughter when he was unable to repay a debt on time. Damon had impassively watched him howl on the floor in agony for an entire half-hour before shooting him square between the eyes, expression blank.

That was nothing compared to some of the more brutal scenes he'd witnessed over the years. Geoffrey had seen Damon crush men's fingers with hammers, pry toenails out of their beds with pliers, and he'd seen all sorts of hardware store contents stuck into eyeballs.

Geoffrey shuddered at the vivid memories.

Yes, he'd take a Damon tempered by Micah over a Damon bereaved of him any day.

"Micah's last name remains Hart... for now," the man revealed after a moment. Damon eyed Geoffrey pointedly before transferring his glacial gaze to Ricky, the other man standing guard outside Micah's door. "I trust you know better than to bring up any future arrangements with Micah – or anyone, for that matter."

That was the thing about Damon. He didn't even have to threaten you for you to know you were being threatened. The dried blood stains on his shirt only added to the dangerous aura surrounding him.

Ricky swallowed, immediately bobbing his head up and down.

"Of course," Geoffrey agreed gruffly.

Damon offered them both one last hard look before nodding and walking away, but Geoffrey didn't fully relax until he'd turned the corner.

While it was true that Micah brought out a hidden gentle side to Damon – and by "hidden", Geoffrey meant so deeply repressed, it was damn near nonexistent – there was no denying no one was safe from his boss's ire once it was provoked – no one except, perhaps, the man in the room behind him.

END

ABOUT THE AUTHOR

Fifer Rose is a happily married mother of four human children and two very spoiled cats.

When she is not wiping snotty noses or being bullied into feeding her cats (*again?!*), she can be found obsessing over M/M romance. She loves all the tropes, some of her favorite being enemies to lovers, hurt/comfort, sugar daddy, and mistaken identity. She also has a penchant for A/B/O dynamics.

While Fifer is a sucker for angst, a happily-ever-after is a MUST in all she reads and writes.

Unrelated hobbies include baking, *attempting* to golf (for her husband's sake), and daydreaming about traveling. (No actual traveling because did you see the part about *four* kids?)

Made in the USA
Columbia, SC
10 December 2022

73220083R00215